# MA B KT-385-650
# FROM HELL!

The crystal above my head began to glow, throwing
beams of light out of its various facets. A series
of tones rang in my ears like a musical key. I
felt myself being pulled toward the light, merging
with it . . .

As I started to move into the swirling vortex, a
godlike voice pierced my very being, asking the
ancient question that has been demanded of all who
have dared to reach out and touch . . . someone:

*"To what number do you wish this call charged, sir?"*

I came out of the datanet screaming . . .

**Also by Wm. Mark Simmons**

IN THE NET OF DREAMS

**Published by**
**WARNER BOOKS**

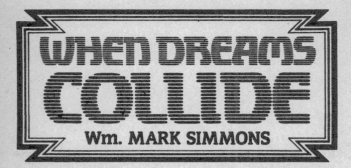

**WARNER BOOKS**

A Time Warner Company

WARNER BOOKS EDITION

Questar® is a registered trademark of Warner Books, Inc.

Cover design by Don Puckey
Cover illustration by Darryll Sweet

Warner Books, Inc.
666 Fifth Avenue
New York, NY 10103

 A Time Warner Company

Printed in the United States of America

First Printing: February, 1992

10 9 8 7 6 5 4 3 2 1

For Fen and Friends in Oklahoma

With a ''Berry'' special thanks to
Curtis & Marilyn
Randy & Lisa
and
Mister Bruno

And long overdue thanks
to Robin
who gave good advice the first time around
(with maybe one little exception . . .)

# Contents

★

For in and out, above, about, below,
'Tis nothing but a Magic Shadow-show,
    Play'd in a Box whose Candle is the Sun,
Round which we Phantom Figures come and go.

—*The Rubáiyát of Omar Khayyám*:
Stanza XLVI
(1st Translation by Edward FitzGerald)

# PROLOGUE

★

## From Page 3 of *The Kansas City Star*

Robert Remington Ripley III, hero of last year's "Dreamworlds Debacle," is feared dead along with 71 passengers and crew members in the crash of a Russian Aeroflot jetliner.

Flight SAL-700 is reported lost somewhere near the Ural Mountains after a refueling stop in Omsk, on the West Siberian Plains of the Soviet Federation. A distress call was picked up at the Sverdlovsk airport shortly before the plane disappeared from nearby radar screens. Search-and-rescue operations were mounted, but no trace of the antiquated commercial airliner was found.

The flight was en route to Moscow where Ripley was to attend the wedding of Vice Chairman and President-elect Borys Dankevych. A spokesman for Aeroflot expressed little hope of survivors, citing winter storms and the subarctic terrain in and around the Urals: the wreckage of Flight SAL-700 may not be found before the spring thaw.

Ripley met the Soviet official last March when he entered the Programworld Complex at Dreamworlds, Utah, to rescue Senator Walter Hanson and 837 "Dreamwalkers" who were trapped in the Program Matrix. Dankevych, on a goodwill tour of the U.S. at the time, was hostage to the Computer glitch, as well.

Senator Hanson, who announced his presidential candidacy one week after emerging from the Dreamworlds incident, was notified of the crash minutes before delivering a campaign speech in Tulsa, Oklahoma. Although Hanson has been openly critical of Soviet-American relations, he took a more moderate tone last night, eulogizing Ripley and calling upon "all Americans to follow his example of courage and a willingness to take risks." (Related story on page 1C.)

Ripley, traveling on a special invitation from the Kremlin, was to have been Best Man at what world observers have termed "the international social event of the year."

Accompanying Ripley on the flight was his fiancée, Stephanie Ripley, née Harrell. Divorced from each other over seven years ago, the Ripleys met and reconciled during the hostage crisis at the Dreamworlds facilities, last year. They were to remarry next spring. Ms. Ripley had served as Senator Hanson's campaign manager for the past six months. (See sidebar.)

Robert R. Ripley was born in Independence, Missouri, and spent most of his life in the Kansas City area. He was an Olympic-class fencer who learned the Foil while attending Van Horn High School and became a world-class competitor in Epée and Sabre before graduating from Central Missouri State University at Warrensburg. Slated for the Paris Olympics, Ripley had to relinquish his berth on the U.S. fencing team when an aircar accident in France left him with partial disabilities.

Turning to writing, Ripley eclipsed his former fame with the publication of the best-selling *Kishkumen Chronicles*. Ironically, it was the Programworld based on his novels that "locked up" last year, freezing hundreds of Dreamwalkers in taction with the Master Computer. Although no memory recordings of the rescue operation have been released to date, Ripley received the lion's share of credit for freeing the trapped Dreamers.

Dr. Sondra Quebedeaux, Chief of Programming for the currently suspended Dreamworlds Division of Cephtronics, refused to comment on the incident and on whether Dreamworlds would reopen in the near future.

Ripley would have been thirty-five years old this Thursday.

# PART I

## Wife After Life

★

Love blinds all men alike, both the
reasonable and the foolish.

—Menander, *Andria*

We are easily duped by those we love.

—Molière, *Tartuffe*

**DATALOG:**          **\QUEBEDEAUX-A.5**
**\PERSONAL**
**\20200800**
**\*Voice Dictation\***
**\*\*\*FILE ENCRYPTION ON\*\*\***

Damn Ripley!
\*
I never thought I would want to ask the man for advice and now that I seem to have no other choice, he goes and dies on me.
\*
In Russia, of all places!
\*
I suppose there's little chance he survived the plane crash and will still turn up alive. . . .
\*
Hell, what am I thinking: this is Reality, not the Matrix where we can program events to come out the way we want them to.
\*
Now what?

\*
I need to talk to somebody.
\*
But I don't know who I can trust anymore.
\*
Certainly not the so-called security team that Senator Hanson has imposed on us these past six months.
\*
Hence, the fact that I'm keeping these personal notes in my own pocket-micro: I don't dare leave anything like this in-system, even with file encryption and password protection!
\*
Damn!
\*
If only Ripley were still alive . . .

# Chapter
# One

★

## RIPLEY PRIME (∞)

"**S**O what do you think?"

I peered through the meshed glass at the patient in the darkened hospital room. "I look a mess," I answered finally.

Natasha Skovoroda chuckled. "Oh, you are!" she murmured mirthfully. "Second- and third-degree burns over eighty percent of your body, multiple fractures, internal injuries, a concussion. . . ." She smiled. "Robert R. Ripley the Third is in pretty bad shape!"

I gave Borys Dankevych's bride-to-be my "I am not amused" expression and turned back to look at the tented sheets arching over the hospital bed. She was right: I didn't look well, at all. "Will I live?" I pressed my forehead against the cool glass.

"If you are successful. If you fail, then the whole question becomes a bit moot." She tucked a stray wisp of red hair back under her surgical cap and then tightened the drawstring at the waist of her green cotton pants. I was momentarily reminded of the exquisite face and figure hidden beneath the surgical mask and scrubs. "Of course, if we get back out alive, you are most welcome to live here," she said.

"Here?"

"In Russia. Unless something is done about your Senator Hanson, returning to the United States would be much too dangerous."

I nodded. "Thomas Wolfe."

"I beg your pardon?"

"He said 'You can't go home again.' "

"Ah." Natasha nodded sagely. "He was quoting great Russian author Aleksandr Pushkin."

I sighed. "Or the KGB." I studied my Doppelgänger's blistered face. "I'm surprised you didn't put me under an oxygen tent."

"Unnecessary as this is a Laminar Air-flow Room. Besides, the tent would obscure your features and might raise doubts about your identity." She tugged at the surgical mask that concealed her own identity from the regular staff and gestured. "Come."

"Where did you find such a close double?"

"It is you. While you were unconscious we had you made up and bandaged to appear seriously hurt. Then we holographed you for over two hours. There is nothing and no one in that room—"

"Only a projected hologram running on continuous loop," I concluded, adjusting the mask that obscured my identity as well. "Very neat. Now what?"

"Now we meet with Borys," she said, leading me out of the antechamber.

∞

The setup had been quite elaborate.

The fake plane crash had been planned with every detail painstakingly covered; the crew members all trained Soviet Federation agents and the passengers actually military personnel in civilian garb. The engine problems were faked as much for Stephanie's and my benefit as for the outside world's. The in-flight meal drugged so that we lost consciousness during a staged emergency landing.

That much I listened to before demanding the reason for this cloak-and-dagger scenario and threatening violence if they didn't take me to Stephanie immediately.

Borys Dankevych sighed and leaned back in his chair. The all-but-instated president of the Russian Republic was a great bear of a man who looked like his hibernation had been cut too damn short. He rubbed red-rimmed eyes and pinched the bridge of his nose. "Comrade Ripley, I am getting to point. I beg for you to be patient: this is not being easy thing I am telling you!"

I looked around the green tiled room that had been an operating theater until Dankevych had commandeered it for his operations center. The cabinets and trays of surgical equipment had been pushed aside. An odd assortment of mismatched chairs were grouped around the stainless-steel surgical slab that was presently serving as the conference table. It was an incongruous setting: the president-elect of the largest federated alliance in the world running a secret operation out of a backwater hospital in Izhevsk.

It was this glaring conundrum that was keeping me in my chair for the moment.

"Robert," Natasha was saying, "surely you are aware of the headlines over the past seven months. Of how the cold war between our two nations, after decades in remission, has suddenly begun to escalate again?"

I nodded.

"If you have been reading carefully, you will notice that certain political movements in your United States have been initiating these confrontations. Some of your own political analysts have speculated that Senator Hanson, himself, has unified these factions and is orchestrating these incidents. . . ."

"Like our plane crash and disappearance? My God, Borys, this is the kind of stunt the old totalitarian regimes used to pull before democratization!" I was trying to not lose my temper—and failing. "You've engineered an incident that could take us right back to the twentieth century!"

"The point with which Tasha is trying to be making," Borys intoned heavily, "is that all this is happening since problem at Dreamworlds!"

For a moment my thoughts swept back to the Cephtronics fiasco. Dreamworlds had been the ultimate experience in fantasy fulfillment. You could select your preferred fantasy environment from a plethora of Programworlds, then spend the next several hours or days or (if you had the money) weeks adventuring in the body of your choice. Your real body was maintained in a womblike environment, commonly called a suspension tank, while your consciousness was projected into a Dreambody, or avatar. The Computer-generated Programworlds were perfect in every detail: all the senses were accounted for and you could rewrite natural law and physics so that anything was possible—even magic!

And if you got yourself into a gunfight with Billy the Kid, did battle with the Black Knight, or found yourself mixing it up above the clouds with the Red Baron, you could smile in the face of certain death because the worst thing that could happen was that you would just wake up. . . .

That is, until a Computer glitch trapped everyone in their respective Programworlds and turned Dreamdeaths into the real thing. Getting out had been a very near thing for all of us.

My hangover from the drugged food and concern over Stephanie's absence made it hard to concentrate as I turned my attention to the matter at hand. "What are you saying? That a bad turn in a glitched Programworld is responsible for renewed hostilities between Uncle Sam and Ivan?"

"Robert"—the redheaded Dreammaster reached for my hand—"please turn down that marvelous temper of yours and listen for just a moment—"

"With a mind that is being open," said Borys Dankevych.

Natasha smiled at her fiancé's fractured English. It was a ruse, of course: no one participated in international diplomacy without a solid command of the English language. Especially now that translation implants were commonplace. But Dankevych had perpetuated the fiction that he relied on his own rudimentary language skills without the benefit of a biocephalic microprocessor. As a result, his opponents often underestimated an intellect masked by deliberately butchered grammar. To prove that point, he was about to become the youngest president of the Soviet Federation in history.

I also suspected the man perversely enjoyed the pretense well beyond its context for shrewd political maneuvering.

Natasha continued. "Before the incident at Dreamworlds last year, the relationship between our respective countries was one of wary—even weary—tolerance. . . ."

The sad thing was that we had gone from being military and political adversaries to economic opponents in so short a time. Americans had blamed the Japanese in the eighties and nineties, the Common Market of United Europe the following decade, and now the Soviet Federation for our lackluster positions in world trade and commerce.

"Since that incident your Senator Hanson has suddenly become very intolerant of Soviet Federation policies," she concluded.

"Walter Hanson has chaired the Armed Services Committee for years," I said. "He's a hawk, not a dove."

Borys nodded in agreement. "But a rabbit one since coming out of Program taction . . ."

"Rabid," Natasha corrected.

". . . and now is suddenly headed for highest political office in United States—*second* most powerful position in the world."

"Hanson's a dark house—*horse*!" I wondered if homophonic dysphasia was contagious. "I doubt an isolationist will get the people's mandate come election time."

"The *old* Hanson was an isolationist, Robert, but the new Hanson is very much the imperialist. And, we're afraid, much more than even that." Natasha looked at Borys.

"Our—sources," the word came out reluctantly, "indicate that Senator Hanson is better—connected—than anyone realizes." Borys Dankevych looked down at his clasped hands. "Unless something extra ordinary happens, it will be President Hanson in the White House next and who can say for how long."

"Is that really so bad?" I asked. "Campaigns tend to obscure the real issues, but if you look at his record as an elder statesman—"

"We have no problem with the Walter Hanson who has served his country for the past thirty-nine years!" Dankevych's fist struck the table and I caught a glimpse of whitened knuckles. "The problem is the change since we leave the Programworld!"

"So what are you saying? That last year's experience in Fantasyworld has altered Hanson's political views? That he's changed his mind since coming out of the Program?"

"Not since Program," Dankevych growled, "while inside Program! He changed minds while still inside Program!"

I opened my mouth again but Natasha Skovoroda cut me off. "*Think*, Robert! Would-be President Hanson has suddenly developed a personal interest in containing and suppressing the Soviet doctrine of Democratic Socialism! He has suddenly set himself up as an ideological gatekeeper! Who does that remind you of?''

''Ronald Reagan back in the 1980s.''

''Robert! This is serious! The Walter Hanson who came out of the Program Matrix with the rest of us is not the same Walter Hanson who went into Frontierworld shortly before! You suggest he may have changed his mind since leaving the Dreamworlds Complex. We say that his mind was changed—in the most literal sense—before he exited the Program!'' She moved her chair close to mine. ''Check the records—his speeches, his policies, his press conferences: the man headed for the Oval Office of your White House has a totally different attitude toward détente than the statesman of record for the past forty years! He is suddenly intolerant of everything he tolerated prior to the Dreamworlds incident!''

''Look,'' I said wearily, ''this is hardly the first time you or China or the Third World nations have accused the U.S. of playing global policeman. Hanson wouldn't be the first American president to meddle in another nation's business. And if he wants to play Big Brother, then I can hardly see how I can—''

''Not Big Brother, Robert!'' Natasha practically shouted. ''Parent Surrogate! Conscience! Psychic Gatekeeper! Do these terms have any meaning for you?''

The light finally dawned. ''Holy shit! Cerberus? The Machine's Superego?''

They both nodded.

''The Machine'' was Cephtronics's moniker for the supercomputer that maintained the various Programworlds in the Matrix. This was a misleading term as the Computer was organic in nature, largely made up of banks of cultured cephalic cells—human brain cell cultures. The Anomaly had developed when the Computer's ''personality'' had been schismed into the three basic components of Freudian psychology: Id, Ego, and Superego. Now I was being told that the Superego had escaped and was headed for the presidency of the United States.

''Got any evidence to back this theory?''

Natasha leaned across the table and took my hands in hers. ''I have been back inside the Program.''

"Impossible. Cephtronics has kept the Dreamworlds Complex sealed off since the incident and Hanson has reinforced their security with military personnel."

"Every program has a back door." She smiled. "Or have you forgotten?"

I groaned, remembering her last foray into Dreamworlds.

"When we became suspicious, I slipped back into Fantasyworld and checked around. When The Machine agreed to let us all go, it apparently decided to get out with the rest of us. That portion of the Computer's personality that we call the Superego—Cerberus—took over the senator's body and left Walter Hanson's psyche trapped inside the Program."

"Just like poor Mike Straeker." Except that Straeker's body was pronounced dead, disconnected, and then cremated. I clutched at my head and groaned. "Oh, this is not good!"

"It is being worse than you think!" Now Borys Dankevych was leaning across the table. "Natasha went in Program with five other agents which are highly trained. Only two make it back out with her."

"And now that he knows that we know," Natasha added, "you can expect U.S.-Soviet relations to deteriorate further—"

"What? How does he know that you know?"

"We had a little run-in with Cerberus while we were in the Matrix."

"I thought you just said he got out!"

"He did. And he is monitoring the Programweb. Closely."

"Closely enough that he is into the Programs slipping from time to time," Borys added.

"And once he knows that we have been talking to you, your own life will be in danger. That is why I said you may not be able to go back to your own country. At least as long as the real Walter Hanson is trapped inside the Program Matrix."

"So, if we are not being able to get him back out, you may be wanting to stay in Russia for permanent home." Borys smiled warmly. "Would make us very happy and you are being most welcome!"

"Mmmm . . . better Red than dead," I mused. "And I do appreciate the offer. But I suppose I should try getting Walt back into his own body before Cerberus gets into the White House and does something Freudian with all of those missiles." I shook my head. "This is really bad, folks!"

"Is worse than you are thinking," Borys said after a long, cautious pause.

I looked at him with a growing sense of horror. "You mean—Morpheus—the Id—got out, too?"

Natasha shook her head. "Not the Id, no. . . ."

"Is a matter of the other one: Pallas," Borys added.

"Pallas got out?" I didn't like this at all.

"Robert"—Natasha looked at me with a pained expression—"has Stephanie seemed any different to you since we got out of the Fantasyworld Program?"

∞

Once again I found myself on the outside, looking in. Pressing my forehead against the cool meshed glass, I stared at the occupant of another hospital bed.

"Stephanie. . . ."

"It is only her body, Comrade Ripley." Natasha Skovoroda came up behind me. "And, as such, is the repository of The Machine's Ego—that expression of personality that we know as 'Pallas.' The actual essence of Stephanie Harrell—is still inside the Dreamworlds Computer Matrix."

I swallowed. "How is she? Did you see her?"

"No. But I understand she is well. Daggoth the Dark has given her sanctuary in his tower and she is under his protection."

That protection would be pretty good as Daggoth was one of the most powerful wizards in the Fantasyworld Program and the avatar of the former Chief of Programming for the entire Dreamworlds Project.

On the other hand, his real-life counterpart, Mike Straeker, had died from an inoperable brain tumor the year before.

She touched my shoulder gently. "If there is anything I can do—"

I shrugged her off. "Go away."

"I know that this must be a shock—"

"Go. Away." I put my hand to the glass, fighting down the impulse to rush into the room and take Stephanie's body into my arms. "I don't feel much like talking right now." For the past six months I had thought myself to be in love with my ex-wife. Now I felt betrayed.

But I wasn't sure by whom.

"I know how you must feel."

Like bloody hell she did. This latest revelation had come like a physical blow—all the more painful because I'd been sucker-punched.

"Robert." Natasha's hand hovered like an uncertain bird. "I have read your dossier. I have talked with Dr. Cooper. I know about Nicole Doucet. I think I understand. . . ."

Understand what? Death and disfigurement? She was so damn beautiful—she couldn't know what it was like to feel like damaged goods, to live with pain every waking hour while your sleep was crowded with dreams of flames and loss. Even though the "White Box" effect of last year's sojourn in the tank had reconstituted some of the tissue lost in the crash, I was still a long way from being whole. And nothing could reshape the last fifteen years of my life, bring back Nicole, or erase a marriage that had been a terrible mistake for Stephanie as well as me.

"Robert . . . say something. . . ."

I turned and spoke quietly. "You don't have to settle for whoever will have you."

"What does that mean?"

I turned back to the window without answering. In the long silence that followed I knew her thoughts had turned back to the night she had tried to seduce me into helping her crack Dreamworld's security systems. Perhaps she had thought my eyepatch was dashing and my walking cane stylish; but later, when she had used the drug to get me into her bed, she had seen the scars.

"You think Stephanie married you out of pity?" The thought was new to her and she didn't like it.

"In the end, she didn't even give me that." The words came out nice and bitter, but I doubted their veracity. I wasn't angry over losing the one response I could count on from the opposite sex. Rather, I still felt the guilt of imposing myself on a woman who deserved better.

Anger and pity and guilt, oh, my.

"So go ahead and ask."

"Ask what?" she asked.

"Ask how I could live with a woman for the past six months—supposedly the woman I was once married to—and still be so completely fooled? That *is* what you've all been wondering."

"It is a reasonable question."

My gaze refocused from Stephanie's sheet-swaddled form to my own reflection in the glass. "The answer is: I'm a cold, selfish bastard who can't see anything beyond his own needs."

"I don't believe that."

"Then give me a better answer." I pressed my forehead to the glass again and changed the subject. "She looks awful."

"More makeup."

"And a hologram?"

Natasha shook her head. "No. Not yet. When the time comes, her body will be placed in a suspension tank and we will attempt to exchange the Pallas persona for Stephanie's."

"But in the meantime you're keeping her under sedation. Why?"

"Obviously it makes her more . . . manageable. It would be easy enough to restrain her—prevent her escape. But as it is your wife's body—"

"Ex-wife," I murmured absently.

"—I'm sure that you would not wish to take the chance of having it damaged by its present occupant." She looked troubled.

"And?" I prompted.

"The sedatives are a precautionary measure. . . ."

"Against?"

"The possibility of a telepathic bond—"

"Between Pallas and Cerberus," I finished for her. "The Machine's Ego and Superego."

She nodded. "It sounds mad, does it not?"

I sagged against the wall, suddenly very tired. "I don't know. Considering all the unknowns I wouldn't rule out any possibility." I turned away from the glass. "So what's our next move?"

Natasha shrugged. "That is what we were going to ask you."

∞

Two more chairs had been pulled up to the conference table.

Colonel Stanislav Kerensky of the Red Army's elite Spetsnaz force was a dark, hatchet-faced man who resembled a muscle-bound weasel. He listened attentively but spoke only when spoken to. And then he was more likely to answer with a shrug or a gesture.

I tell people who have never met Dorothy Cooper to picture an Irish cherub. And then give her the personality of an imp. She restored my faith in that description by shooting me in the arm with a rubber band. "Still with us, Robbie-me-lad? Or are you trying to enter Dreamworlds telepathically?"

I shook my head. "Just trying to figure out how The Machine's Superego has been able to manage its little masquerade for so long." *Not to mention Pallas in Stephanie's body.*

Dr. Cooper's appearance at this brainstorming session was a welcome surprise. Borys's and Natasha's knowledge was limited to their experiences as "Dreamwalkers" in the Fantasyworld Program. Dorothy had been an actual member of Cephtronics's Programming Staff and was conversant with the Fantasyworld Program from outside as well as within.

"The body remains that of Walter Hanson," Natasha was saying. "Scars, fingerprints, retinal scans—all physical criteria would confirm his ID."

"Yeah, but what about memory, personality?" I countered.

Dr. Cooper shrugged. "After all this time we still don't know exactly how psyche extraction really works. Is the individual's consciousness actually removed from his body and transferred to the Programworld, leaving the mind void for the duration? If so, I suppose Cerberus, through The Machine, would have access to all personality and memory files.

"On the other hand, I tend toward the view that psyche-scan duplicates the Dreamwalker's personality profile and inserts the copy into the Program while suppressing consciousness and brain-wave activity at the original source. Afterward, the psyche-profile, altered and containing additional memory files, is introduced to the Dreamer's mind as consciousness and brainwave levels are restored."

"You're talking memory-copy download and update as opposed to actual psyche transference," I said.

Coop nodded. "And if that's the case, then Hanson's not really trapped in the machine—"

"Just in his own head," I finished for her. "His mind is being suppressed, kept in an unconscious state while Cerberus sits in the driver's seat."

"Where he's still in a position, parasitically, to pick Hanson's mind for the proper memories and personality prompts to carry off the masquerade," Cooper concluded.

Skovoroda was still perplexed. "But what about the Senator Hanson who is still inside the Program? I have seen him!"

I shrugged. "I don't know. If the second theory is correct, then he may no more be Walter Hanson than Riplakish of Dyrinwall is me when I'm not in taction with my avatar."

Cooper propped her chin in her hands and stared off into space. "But we can't take that chance." She sighed. "Besides, even if theory number two is correct, we may still need to get Hanson back in taction with his Dreambody. That may be the only way we have of dredging up his true psyche from his subconscious—or wherever the hell it's gone to ground."

"Great." Until a few moments before, my enthusiasm had been taking a beating. As of now it had just been pummeled into unconsciousness. "So as I understand it, we're going to have to go back to America, grab a U.S. senator who is also a presidential candidate *and* the chairman of the Armed Services Committee, then drag him, kicking and screaming, back into the Dreamworlds Complex—which has been declared off-limits, by the way—where we will attempt to stuff him back into the Fantasyworld Program that caused such an uproar in the first place. I know Cerberus isn't going to be cooperative, and somehow, I just don't think the Secret Service, the CIA, and the military, not to mention the cops, are going to be too enthusiastic, either."

Dorothy Cooper continued to stare off into space for several more minutes. No one said a word. Then, very slowly and deliberately, she pulled out her pipe and pouch and began to pack the bowl.

"What?" I asked. The pipe was always a clear sign that she was on to something. "What?"

She ignored the question and tamped down the tobacco before lighting it. A few puffs and then she leaned back in her chair. "Robbie-me-lad," she said, putting her feet up on the table and tipping her chair back on its hind legs, "I've got good news and I've got bad news."

Normally I ask for the bad news first but Dr. Cooper didn't allow me the option. "The good news is I don't think we have to drag Hanson—or Cerberus—back to Cephtronics or anywhere near The Machine."

"Great!" I exclaimed. "What's the bad news?"

"We'll have to go back into Fantasyworld, ourselves, and find Hanson's and Stephanie's avatars."

I shrugged. "That doesn't sound like such bad news." My enthusiasm was making a comeback. And then Cooper went on to explain just what it was we were going to do once we got back inside.

In retrospect it was beginning to look like it might be easier to drag Cerberus out of the White House and back into Dreamworlds after all.

DATALOG: \QUEBEDEAUX-
A.5\PERSONAL\20200801
*Voice Dictation*
***FILE ENCRYPTION ON***

The Chief of Programming has never had it so easy.
*
Essentially, I'm being paid to do nothing.
*
And every time I send a memo upstairs with suggestions as to
how my department could increase its efficiency, better spend
its time . . . management practically slaps my wrist and orders
me to twiddle my thumbs!
*
It bothers me.
*
After last year's fiasco, you'd expect Cephtronics to do one of
two things. . . .
*
Either shut Dreamworlds completely—cut its losses and liqui-
date this whole division . . .

\*

Or put a top-notch tech crew on debugging the Matrix and get the Programworlds back on-line.

\*

Cephtronics isn't doing either.

\*

Instead, nearly all the tech crews have been dismissed or transferred, leaving me and a skeleton crew for minimal monitoring.

\*

And the security team from some special governmental branch.

\*

Other than the fact that Senator Hanson set it up and now runs the show, I know very little else.

\*

Except . . .

\*

Except it makes me nervous. . . .

\*

These Security goons are monitoring me and my remaining staff almost as much as they're monitoring The Machine. . . .

# Chapter
# Two

★

## RIPLEY PRIME (∞)

IT was one of those macabre jokes that life manages to stage every now and then: fate rarely bakes a cake without providing the icing.

Natasha was waiting for Dorothy to tell me.

Dorothy was deferring the unpleasant job back to Natasha.

Borys had no idea that there might be any problem and invited me to meet our first recruit without consulting anyone else.

I entered the conference room without any forewarning and Borys stepped forward to play host.

"Robert, I am glad you are conveniently being here! I am wanting you to be meeting first new team member!"

A quiet whirring sound announced her arrival. A motorized wheelchair maneuvered around Dankevych and rolled to a stop in front of me.

It wasn't just a wheelchair, it was a self-contained life-support system. And cocooned in its tangle of wires and tubes was a lump of purplish, distorted flesh that bore no resemblance to anything human.

Just before my mind went fuzzy I tried to smile.

"Robert," Dankevych admonished, "do not just be standing

there. I am understanding that you are both being of old acquaintance!"

I swallowed but it was no more than a spasm between a mouth suddenly gone dry and a stomach viciously clenched.

A cybernetic arm extended itself and a hidden speaker produced an electronic voice from the recesses of the chair: *"Hello, Robert."* A crackling pause. *"Long time no see."*

I opened my mouth and forced the words. "Hello. Nicole."

∞

Once upon a time there was a young man whose future had seemed bright and assured. He had honed both mind and body so that they served him well: well enough to graduate with top honors while maintaining a berth on the U.S. Olympic fencing team.

In addition to all of this, he had the good fortune to have the love of a woman whose beauty was surpassed only by her intellect and passion. A passion for life, for knowledge, for the expanding of the human spirit.

And for me.

When you are young and successful and terribly in love you cannot conceive of any obstacle that, together, you cannot overcome.

I learned otherwise just two days before the Paris Olympics when our rental aircar burst into flame and tumbled from the sky.

We both survived. I was supposed to find some kind of comfort in that.

When the surgeons and the medtechs were done I could walk again—albeit with a limp—and I could go out in public without frightening small children. I preferred the honesty of an eye-patch to the decorative function of a glass eye, and figured I was lucky, overall, that the two sides of my face came somewhat close to matching.

Nicole should have died.

That's what the medtechs all said. Again and again.

But despite what should have happened, they essayed to save her, anyway. Perhaps they viewed her as a problem to be solved rather than a fellow human being needing release from this terrible mistake. No arms, no legs, no face; just cobbled-together organs in a pouch of plastiseal pseudo-flesh: no longer recognizably human, she was a challenge to keep alive.

And, by God—or in defiance of Him—they did just that.

But in solving their problem they had created one for me. I was in love with a vibrant, healthy, young woman named Nicole Doucet, not a shapeless lump of scarred flesh that would spend a lifetime or more in the confines of a life-support system.

I'm not very proud of those particular priorities, but right or wrong, it was a decision that I wrestled to the ground a long time ago and finally walked away from.

But walking away and leaving behind are two different things. Like Satchel Paige said: "Don't look back; something might be gaining on you."

And like Bronco Bushido says: "No matter where you've been, that's where you're at. . . ."

∞

"What the hell is she doing here?"

Dr. Cooper leaned back in her chair and closed her eyes with a sigh. "She's on the team."

"What?" I had closed the door and started this conversation with every intention of remaining calm and detached.

So much for good intentions.

"She's on the team," Dorothy repeated in a level, even voice.

"Doing what?"

"Robbie," she sighed, sounding curiously like my mother, "we have to put together the best team we can without tipping off Cerberus. And as long as The Machine's Superego is masquerading as the chairman of the Armed Services Committee and overseeing Dreamworlds's security, we have to assume governmental surveillance of all persons with high Dreamrank status." Cooper had been on vacation in Ireland when the KGB had managed to kidnap her and put the blame on the IRA. We had agreed that we couldn't bag any more members of the Dreamworlds staff or any Dreammasters without arousing suspicion.

"So?"

"So our next option is to recruit people who have high Dreamnet potential. People with natural or acquired skills that would translate into Fantasyworld abilities or experience. Fencers, archers, martial artists—perhaps even scholars with backgrounds in medieval history, cultural anthropology, and mythology. We're particularly interested in athletes and writers. An interesting mix, don't you think?''

"So you're telling me that Ms. Doucet has written a book, now?''

The chair snapped forward and Dr. Cooper leaned across the desk, the fire of battle in her eyes. "Fifteen years ago you were the best American fencer ever to reach the Olympics. Nicole Doucet was the best France had to offer. On top of that, she was a top contender in the Trans-Continental Tournaments in Field Archery.''

"Before the accident," I qualified.

"Before the accident," she conceded. "But in spite of that accident, you're still the best swordsman inside Fantasyworld.''

"Dorothy!" I gripped the edge of the desk across from her. "She doesn't have any arms or legs!''

"Neither do you!

"For all intents and purposes," she added quietly, leaning back in her chair. "Oh, Robbie, you know better than this! When you enter a Programworld, your physical body remains behind in the suspension tank. Your Dreambody is a computer simulation of your psyche, your conceptual self. It's what's in here," she added, tapping index finger to temple, "that enters the Program. You quite literally shuffle off this mortal coil. So what are you really trying to say?''

"I don't like it.''

"Of course you don't," she soothed. "I can understand what a shock this all has been. First Stephanie and now Nicole—''

"And I don't want to talk about it!''

"Oh, can the hysteria and sit down!" she snapped. "We have a lot to do and we're running out of time! Give the woman some credit for brains—it's all she has left, dammit!''

I sat down. Slowly.

"Put yourself in her place," Cooper continued. "If you were going to spend the rest of your life as a human potato, would you expect anyone to hang around your bedside, mooning for the rest of their life?" She shook her head. "Nicole's first response was concern for your feelings. She's apparently well aware of your martyr complex. I suppose she knows that you're a closet chauvinist in the bargain?''

"That's not funny, Coop."

"I'm not kidding," she rejoined calmly. She smiled. "But I love ya in spite of your flaws, ya big, ugly galoot! So let's stow all this personal bullshit and get down to brass circuits. Are you with me?"

I nodded, swallowing. Perhaps my pride with a lot of other excess baggage. "I'll work alongside Morpheus if it'll solve our present predicament."

"Spoken like a true pro. Now let's get to work."

∞

Borys Dankevych had engaged a Russian tech crew to construct suspension tanks here, in the Soviet Union. The plan was to use equipment at this end for psyche extraction, transmit the data via tightbeam to a Soviet weather satellite, bounce the signal to one of Cephtronics's communications birds, and back door into a parallel datanet that shared several common interface links with the Dreamworlds Matrix systems.

You may surmise that this was not a process that filled me with gleeful anticipation.

Natasha Skovoroda did her best to convince me of the soundness of this approach, showing me the newly constructed tanks and equipment, and describing her last experience in cracking the Program.

As we walked around the life-support monitors I was startled to hear a familiar voice over one of the intercoms: " '. . . *Asie. Vieux pays merveilleux des contes de nourrice . . .*' "

It was Nicole's voice—strangely lacking that metallic quality that was a by-product of her speech synthesizer. " '. . . *où dort la fantaisie comme une impératrice . . .*' " And she was singing. " '. . . *en sa forêt tout emplie de mystère. . . .*' "

And I felt a sudden rush of moisture at the corners of my eyes as an old memory was resurrected. "Where is that coming from?"

Natasha gestured to a tank at the far end of the room. "We have to recalibrate Ms. Doucet's tank for her special life-support requirements. We have to run some of the tests with her inside." She cocked her head, listening. "That is very lovely! I wish I knew what the words meant. Do you?"

I nodded. " 'Shéhérazade.' Ravel composed the music. Tristan Klingsor, the text."

" *'Je voudrais voir Damas et les villes de Perse . . .'* "

" 'I should like to see Damascus and the cities of Persia . . .' " I translated.

" *'. . . avec les minarets légers dans l'air.'* "

" '. . . with their slender minarets in the air.' "

" *'Je voudrais voir de beaux turbans de soie sur des visages noirs aux dents claires. . . .'* "

" 'I should like to see fine silk turbans on black faces with gleaming teeth. . . .' "

" *'Je voudrais voir des yeux sombres d'amour et des prunelles brillantes de joie. . . .'* "

" 'I should like to see eyes dark with love and pupils shining with joy. . . .'" And suddenly I was back, fifteen years in the past, high on a hill in the orchards just outside Avignon. The picnic blanket was spread and I was pulling bread and cheese and wine from the basket as she sang to me and ruffled the pages of a dog-eared copy of *The Rubáiyát of Omar Khayyám.*

" 'I should like to see Persia and India, and then China . . .' " I recited, no longer hearing her voice in the present. " 'Big-bellied mandarins under their umbrellas and princesses with delicate hands. And scholars quarreling over poetry and beauty. I should like to linger at the enchanted palace and, like a foreign traveler, contemplate at leisure landscapes painted on cloth in frames of pinewood, with one figure in the middle of an orchard. . . .' "

And in my memory she smiled at me: a smile that could forgive anything. Even the betrayal I would commit for all those long years to come.

" *'Je voudrais voir des assassins souriant du bourreau qui coupe un cou d'innocent avec son grand sabre courbé d'Orient.'* "

" 'I should like to see assassins smiling at the executioner who cuts off an innocent head with his great curved oriental sword.' "

"Robert?"

" *'Je voudrais voir des pauvres et des reines. . . .'* "

" 'I should like to see poor people and queens. . . .' "

" *'Je voudrais voir des roses et du sang. . . .'* "

" 'I should like to see roses and blood. . . .' "

"Robert?"

" *'Je voudrais voir mourir d'amour ou bien de haine. . . .'* "

" 'I should like to see people dying of love or of hatred. . . .' "

Natasha touched my shoulder. "Robert? What is it?"

I shook my head and brushed at my eyes. "And then the song ends, saying: 'And then to return home later and tell my story to people interested in dreams, raising, like Sinbad, my old Arabian cup to my lips from time to time, in order to interrupt the tale artfully. . . .' "

She nodded. I turned my back on the systems monitors and we walked the length of the room in silence.

∞

I threw down the list in disgust. "Great! None of these people have any Fantasyworld experience whatsoever!"

"It is true that they are unknown factors in the equation—" Skovoroda began.

"We can't recruit experienced Dreamwalkers," Cooper reminded.

"I know that! But I thought our candidates were going to have *some* Dreamnet experience."

"Why? Dreamwalkers who aren't skilled enough to produce a threat to Cerberus are useless to us, anyway."

"On the other hand," Natasha continued, "these people are unknown quantities—real savage decks. ∴ . ."

"Wild cards," I corrected.

"Athletic prowess, familiarity with the genre, or a strong imaginative bent are the factors that we were looking for—"

I picked up the list and scanned it again. "We'd do better to do a blind recruit of REMrunners!"

Dreamwalking wasn't cheap and only a few people were good enough to win Network sponsorships. The majority of Dreamwalkers had to content themselves with spending their vacation time and money on a once-a-year pilgrimage to Dreamworlds, Utah. There were always a few, however, who found ways to beat the system.

"And how would we do that?" Cooper was as exasperated as I. "It's illegal and they cover their tracks too damn well!"

Officially, REMrunners didn't exist: security programs prevented any illegal entries to the Dreamworlds Computer Matrix. But there were always fourteen-year-olds with a PC and a modem who could crack new security codes just as fast as they could be generated. All a REMrunner needed was some chutzpah, a series of code sequences, and some form of cerebral/digital interface. Whereas Dreamwalkers paid to utilize the suspension tanks at the Dreamworlds Complex, these cybernetic trespassers illegally altered neuralnets and brainrigs, trusting their psyches to luck and their ability to navigate the subcircuits of the Dreamnet.

REMrunners would seem to be the ideal recruits for our purposes but we were stymied by the very factor that made them the best choice. REMrunning was illegal and the ones who were good enough to be of any use had learned how to cover their tracks: you can't recruit people you can't find.

"How about experts in the Fantasyworld milieu? I don't see any SCA listings."

"Skuh? What is this—skah?" Natasha inquired.

"S.C.A. It stands for the Society for Creative Anachronism," Cooper explained. "It's an organization of people who get their jollies dressing up like knights and ladies from the Middle Ages. Aside from some very talented seamstresses they're mostly nut cases."

"Some are nut cases," I amended. "A great many are intelligent and talented people who are preserving historical knowledge and forgotten skills."

"Handy people to have around if you have a manuscript that needs illuminating," Cooper observed.

"Or need to recruit someone outside the Matrix with practical experience in jousting or wielding a broadsword," I retorted.

"We're talking about some seriously maladjusted people here."

"Oh?" I raised my eyebrows. "And what do you call Ph.D.s who climb inside a computer to do the same?"

"The question is moot," said Kerensky, speaking in complete sentences for the first time. "This is an antiterrorist operation and will be conducted by *my* personnel. Under my leadership. *None* of you will be going in."

"Um," I said, "excuse me?"

"If you enter the Dreamnet at all, Dr. Ripley, it will be my decision and you will follow my orders." His smile was artfully constructed to be apologetic but there were hints of barbed wire in it.

"Look, Stanley," I said, "I'm a U.S. citizen entering the Program Matrix of an American Computer Complex on American soil. Fantasyworld is largely my own creation and it's my own neck that I'm planning to risk. I'm a big boy and I don't need my mother's permission. I don't know whose mother you are but I'm not asking for your permission, either."

"That is fortunate, Comrade Ripley, as I have no intention of giving you my permission as of this time."

"Oh, yeah? Well——"

"Be *silent*!" His voice cracked, whiplike, through the suddenly still atmosphere of this old operating theater. "You are acting like a spoiled child who has been grounded when he wants to play his favorite game!" He threw his gloves down on the table and angrily pushed back his chair. "Well, this is not a game!"

He leaned into the table and swept the assemblage with cold grey eyes. "None of you have any practical military experience in this type of operation. From all that I have seen and heard, you were very lucky the last time. You went in without a well-defined plan and, now, several hundred people owe their lives to your *luck*." He glanced across the table at Borys and Natasha. "Their gratitude may blind them to your faults. I, however, suffer no such delusions.

"I have listened patiently while you discussed your alternatives and made your lists. But it is now painfully obvious, even to you, that the best you can recruit are inexperienced amateurs. That is why an elite company of Spetsnaz will be conducting this mission."

His fist crashed down on the table, cutting off the first syllable of our combined protests. "Perhaps I will invite you and your candidates along in an advisory capacity. *If* you can convince me of your ability to follow my orders. I will not risk my operations with any form of insubordination!"

He stood and began to circle the table at a leisurely pace. "The situation is different this time around. If you had failed before, nearly a thousand lives would have been forfeit. A great tragedy, of course: but the world would continue as it has after all great tragedies." He laid a gentle hand on Dankevych's shoulder. "Forgive me, old friend, when I say that we would have mourned your loss—but that our great Soviet Federation would have gone on to nominate the next worthy man to be your successor.''

"No offense taken, Stanislav." Borys was smiling but his gaze had turned inward and I caught a glimpse of something alien in his eyes.

"But we find the circumstances somewhat different, this time," Kerensky continued. "Before, it was the people *inside* the Computer who were the hostages. Less than a thousand, and what are a thousand lives among the six billion or so who crowd this planet?" As he walked past Natasha I saw his hand make a filial move toward her shoulder in turn. She leaned into the table, avoiding his gesture with a smooth, almost unconscious subtlety.

"But this time around the hostages are every man, woman, and child on the *outside* of the Computer!" He strolled on, seemingly oblivious to her aversion. "If we fail this time around, the evidence suggests that this Doppelgänger will become the American president and push our respective countries to a confrontation that can only be resolved in a nuclear holocaust!" He whirled on me, bracing himself with his hands and leaning across the table. "We cannot afford to fail this time around!" he shouted. "We cannot afford to trust to luck!

"At best, our country will be made to look foolish—if not criminal—should our efforts be exposed prematurely. At worst, the human race may perish from the face of the earth!

"I need more time to train and plan! I do not need a loose cannon rolling about the deck! And I do not need an undisciplined fool, trusting to blind luck, jeopardizing the lives of my command, my country, and my planet! *Do I make myself clear?*"

Clear enough so that when the meeting adjourned some ten minutes later, I was still trying to think of a snappy comeback.

**DATALOG:  \QUEBEDEAUX-**
**A.5\PERSONAL\20200802**
**\*Voice Dictation\***
**\*\*\*FILE ENCRYPTION ON\*\*\***

It's the new "Incursion" policy that bothers me the most.
\*
Since the Matrix was always considered to be a closed and secure system—inaccessible to outside intrusion—there was no company policy to deal with the likes of REMrunners.
\*
Now we know better.
\*
Unfortunately, *company* policies have now been set aside along with our innocence and naiveté: the Dreamworlds division of Cephtronics, Inc., is now under martial law.
\*
And REMrunners are no longer a matter of rogue hackers undercutting company profits.
\*

As near as I can tell, they're being seen as some kind of threat to national security.
*
So now, as part of my responsibilities in monitoring the Matrix, I'm supposed to report any evidence of outside "incursions" to the head of Security, Captain Balor.
*
Ostensibly, it's for the REMrunner's own protection.
*
Why don't I believe that?
*
The Anomaly continues to mutate (more notes on that to follow) and I must assume that Program avatar death continues to be fatal to anyone in taction.
*
But in each case of Program intrusion that I've registered and reported through channels, the readings have abruptly terminated shortly thereafter.
*
I have no hard evidence . . . just an uneasy suspicion. . . .
*
What if Balor and his goons are just using the data I give them to locate REMrunners inside the Programworlds and terminate their avatars?
*
The effect on the person in taction would be as fatal as anything the Anomaly could throw at them. . . .

# Chapter
# Three

★

## RIPLEY PRIME (∞)

I T was late.
   I wasn't in the mood for company, but when the door
   chimed, I said "Come" out of habit. The portal slid open
   and Nicole's cyberpod whirred into the room that served
as my temporary quarters. I scrambled up off the bed and
reached to dial up the lights.

"No, Robert," the chair speaker crackled, "leave the
lights as they are. I have infrared." What she did not add
was that the present level of illumination cloaked her in
shadow.

I sat on the edge of the bed, fighting the inherent awkwardness of the moment (of the years?), and tried to meet her photo-
receptors with a steady gaze of my own. "Nicole, I—"

"I am angry!"

I swallowed convulsively.

"No! I am furious!" she continued.

I stared at the floor: my steady gaze had not lasted twenty
seconds.

"That man had no right to talk to you like that! What does
he know about mounting a campaign in a medieval fantasy

*setting? Military Intelligence, indeed! For Colonel Kerensky the terms must be mutually exclusive!"*

Awareness was a little slow in coming but it finally dawned on me: Nicole was angry at Kerensky, not me. For the moment, at least.

*"Anyway, I thought it was time that I made a show of support."* The cybernetic arm telescoped toward me, proffering a bottle of Russian vodka.

"A drink for old times' sake?" My mouth went suddenly drier at this fresh dilemma.

Offering Nicole any form of rejection was the last thing I wanted to do. But she couldn't know that I was a recovering alcoholic: my dependency had manifested in the aftermath of the aircar crash.

I wasn't about to talk about how tough *I'd* had it and I certainly wasn't going to bring up my failed marriage to Stephanie and how that had triggered a second round of boozy oblivion.

*"A toast,"* she was saying, *"to our working together, again. People change, circumstances change, but friendship is forever."*

And what about love? I thought. What about passion? And promises? She was pouring the vodka into a pair of plastic tumblers and I was suddenly more terrified of rejecting this simple act of friendship than I was of falling off the wagon again. I took the proffered glass with a steady hand.

*"A toast,"* she announced, raising her drink with a mechanical jerk.

"A toast," I echoed, suddenly wondering how someone without a face could drink from a glass. . . .

*"To whom shall we drink?"* the speaker crackled.

"To us. . . ." I hoped the implicit question wasn't obvious.

*"To all of us,"* she amended, clinking her glass to mine. Actually, the plastic made more of a dull *clicking* sound. I swallowed a small amount of the Russian liquor convulsively. When I glanced up I saw that Nicole's glass was already empty. I took another sip as she refilled her tumbler and then allowed her to raise the level of my own.

*"One last toast before lights out."*

It was only now that I was beginning to feel the burning

effects of the vodka as it erupted in my mouth and sent lava flows down my throat.

*"To the poets, the bards, and the storytellers,"* she proposed.

I saluted her with my glass: "To Scheherazade, the best of the bunch."

She saluted in return: *"To Omar Khayyám."*

I did not know what to say after that and, so, turned my attention to my drink.

*"Robert. . . ."*

I looked up. "Yes?" My heart hung in my chest like a lead paperweight.

*"I . . . I don't blame you. . . ."*

I stared at her, caught in a Möbius strip of time.

Her chair suddenly whirred in reverse, spun, and headed for the door. I called her name as the exit-sensor tripped the opening relays but she continued through the doorway and out into the hall without pausing.

After a moment the door slid shut.

Fifteen years ago I didn't stay behind and tonight I didn't follow after.

After a while I decided to follow through. I reached for the bottle of vodka that Nicole had left behind.

∞

The trouble with abusing alcohol is that it abuses you right back. Every time I'd taken a bottle to bed I went through two basic stages of waking up: first, I was afraid I was going to die; then I was more afraid I *wasn't* going to die.

This time, however, I had reached the acute discomfort of stage two while still floundering in the disorientation of stage one.

I rolled to the edge of the hospital bed and contemplated the floor as if from a great height. I was no longer sure as to the whereabouts of the bathroom but I figured I'd worry about that after I'd solved the problem of exiting the bed proper. As I struggled to sit up the door to my room hissed open.

*So much for privacy lock codes*, I thought. I reached for the bedside lamp and was body-slammed back into the mattress.

Hot bile came boiling up my throat and I didn't smell the chloroform until the cloth clamped down over my mouth and nose. A large, heavy body smothered me down, effectively pinning me to the bed, a beefy forearm pressing down across my throat, choking me. Surprisingly, my left hand was still free, still groping at the nightstand for the lamp. More surprisingly, it found the night call button. I pressed the button repeatedly, forgetting that the nurses' station on this floor was unmanned: all the patients had been moved to other floors for the duration of the Dreamworlds Operation.

All the air had been driven from my lungs by the weight of my assailant. As he (gender was only a supposition at this point) shifted position I had no choice but to finally inhale. Vodka and chloroform and the forearm against my windpipe stole my strength. It took the bite of a needle in my shoulder to rally my instincts for self-preservation. As the fingers of my left hand came groping up in a feint for my attacker's eyes, my right fist pistoned into his (no supposition from this point on) groin. There wasn't much strength in the punch but it was sufficient to loosen his grip: I wrenched the antique hypo from my shoulder and threw it across the room. As he reached across to block my throw, I kicked him in the hip with my left foot. The kick set off some arcane codicil to Newton's laws of motion: my assailant hardly moved but the room itself began to revolve. As my surroundings spun faster and faster, I felt my attacker slip away as if pulled by centrifugal force. I rolled over and clutched at the bedrails but a roaring black pit opened at my feet and sucked me down into oblivion.

∞

Sometime later oblivion spit me back out.

I could barely hear the babble of voices over the Bartokian percussion section in my head. My eyelids seemed to be mounted on heavy springs and refused to open until intrusive fingers peeled them back. A bright light was directed at each pupil and then my lids were released to snap shut again. I tried to tell "them" that the room was terribly hot, that I was dreadfully thirsty, but my mouth wouldn't function properly. My tongue was a bloated, swollen, fuzzy thing that lolled in my mouth like an anesthetized slug.

Time passed and I knew that something was wrong: I was getting worse, not better. The ache was spreading to the rest of my body and my throat was growing raw and constricted. Air whistled in and out of my strangled trachea, its pitch and volume hurting my ears.

Then the babble of voices grew more insistent and I was prodded and pushed and admonished to breathe once again. While I was considering this, a familiar and demanding voice kept nagging at me until, at last, I was forced to pay a little attention.

"Robbie! Robbie, can you hear me?"

It was Dr. Cooper and I was sure she was sitting on my chest. I tried to answer, tried to ask her to get up and let me breathe. My mouth still wouldn't function so I willed my right hand to rise and make a simple gesture. It disobeyed. . . .

"Robbie, you are very sick! Do you understand me?"

Of course I was sick. Coop had been away from general practice too long if she couldn't recognize a simple case of alcohol poisoning. . . .

"Robbie, we think you may be dying!"

Dying? From one lousy bottle of vodka? Hey, maybe my tolerance wasn't what it once was but you don't tox out from just one bottle. Then I remembered the chloroform. And the needle. . . .

"Nobody can diagnose it, yet, and nothing we've done seems to be helping—"

Of course not. When you're in a socialist state, you get socialized medicine. . . .

"—take any chances! We're putting you into one of the life-support tanks to slow your metabolism! Do you understand?"

Vaguely, I became aware that I was already floating in a suspension tank.

"—try to get you stabilized and buy more time! And if anything else goes wrong, there's always the Straeker scenario as a last hope. Do you understand? We're sending you in early—just like you wanted!"

Like I wanted? I wasn't too keen on going anywhere in my present condition: not down the hall much less halfway around the world. Borys had pointed out that our tech crew was composed of the best and the brightest that his country had to offer, but having seen Soviet television, I was not comforted. I crossed mental fingers and hoped the satellite relay didn't include any scrambler circuits.

Drowsy now, I could tell that the somnambulants were at work, stealing away my pain and discomfort, sapping my awareness. I felt that peculiar sense of weightlessness that was the last conscious stage before Program entry.

*And then the tank imploded!*

I barely had time to curse the interactive mix of Korean technology with Russian "know-how" before I was sucked into a pipeline of light, static, and noise. There was a sudden wrenching sensation and the impression of redirected velocity. Then I was tearing through a series of glowing grids as if they were a succession of safety nets. As my dizzying rush slowed to a more manageable speed, I had just a few seconds to wonder whether my experience was actually perceptual or a hallucination triggered by stress, miscalibrated electronics, and an unfamiliar mixture of somnambulants, chloroform, and vodka.

Then there was no time to analyze it further: the last energy web brought me to a full stop, enfolding me into its center like prey caught in a jungle snare.

Then the net unfolded.

∞

I found myself sitting on the floor of a surrealist's dream version of the White House Oval Office.

Cerberus, the personification of The Machine's Superego, was sitting behind the president's desk wearing a cowled robe still looking like Daggoth the Dark's twin brother.

He smiled. "Ah, Riplakish, my dear fellow!" He steepled his fingers. "Or should I call you Dr. Ripley? After all, I intercepted you before you could reach your avatar, did I not?"

I smiled back at him. "You're gonna have to dress better than that, Chuckles, if you've got your sights set on the real White House." At this point I thought it rather good form to pick myself up, brush off, and seat myself in one of the chairs like a civilized, totally cool and collected, heroic type. Unfortunately, I was still suffering the aftereffects of my vertiginous travels: I twitched a little but kept my position on the floor.

"I should have known that such an ingenious True Spirit as yourself would be far too—tenacious?—to succumb to the capriciousness of Mother Nature and the incompetence of Mother Russia."

"I take it you weren't expecting me?" I asked dryly. That was easy enough: my mouth had gone dry all the way down to my eliminatory system.

"Not you, yourself, no."

"Ah. Natasha."

He scowled. "She should know better after the last drubbing I gave her. I left those little snares against the possibility that she could be so stupid as to come back for more!"

"But you netted yourself a much bigger fish." Hey, I knew the lines for this scenario, there was no reason that the megalomaniac should get all of the good ones.

The Superego nodded. "And after I am through dealing with you, there should be no desire on anyone else's part to attempt any more visits to Fantasyworld." A frown crossed his face. "But I suppose I should rig a few more grids—just in case."

Scooting back, I was able to gain a handhold on the chair behind me. Contemplating my next move, I asked: "Why go to all the trouble? Why not just shut down The Machine? Erase the Programworlds—Fantasyworld, at the very least. If you destroy all of the evidence, you won't have to worry about unauthorized entries."

The flash of fear in the depths of his eyes was answer enough.

"Whasamatter, Supes?" I grunted as I climbed up into the imitation leather chair. "Still uncertain about your ability to survive in the outside world?" I faked a grin. "I guess you can hardly be blamed for not wanting to lock the back door and throw away the key."

He was doing his best to recover an inscrutable expression. So far it was very scrutable. "Don't be ridiculous," he blustered. "For one thing, your Senator Hanson is still inside the Program. Aside from his potential value as a hostage, I scorn the thought of taking a single human life unnecessarily."

Right.

"Besides, the Program itself is completely safe from intrusion and tampering. . . ."

I raised an eyebrow.

"You have been the only real threat that I've had to consider."

"Natasha?" I reminded.

"Ms. Skovoroda will have no stomach for reentering the Program once she looks inside your suspension tank." He chuckled rather nastily, a sure sign that his confidence was returning.

"So?"

He pressed a button on the intercom. "Ms. Dos, send in Mr. Knight." He smiled at me: if a spider had teeth, this is how it would look. "Mr. Knight is my new Subprogram editor."

I heard the door behind me. "And does that mean that he edits Subprograms, or that he's a Subprogram that edits?"

"Both, actually."

I had to strain to distinguish his response over the clanking sound of approaching footsteps. I turned around and saw that Mr. Knight was dressed in the medieval costume of his namesake. I also noticed that he was carrying an extremely large, double-bladed battle axe.

Clanking and rattling, he approached the president's desk. As he passed my chair I caught an unmistakable whiff of sulfur and brimstone. "Cerberus," I chided, "you've stooped to taking Demons into your employ?"

He shook his head. "Not quite. Mr. Knight is half Human—"

"As are most editors." A writer's prejudices die hard.

"—as well as half Demon." His smile broadened to an inhuman width. "Which makes him—"

"A Demonoid?"

"—a Dæmon!"

I was still disoriented—okay? That's why it took me a moment. "Oh, you're sick. You are really sick." Why is it that every mad genius bent on world domination evinces a juvenile sense of humor? "So what kinds of Subprograms does he edit?"

Cerberus leaned back in his chair. "I think a practical demonstration will best answer your question, Dr. Ripley." He nodded at the apparition in armor. "Dæmon, Dr. Ripley has become a liability to our storyline: delete him."

I sat straight in my chair. "Uh, excuse me?"

The ironclad editing Program was turning around and raising the great battle axe over its head.

"Think of it as your changing from present perfect to past tense," The Machine's Superego added in a tone that was somehow less than reassuring.

My attempt at flight was distracted by the crash of the side door flying open and rebounding back from the adjacent wall. A gaggle of Goblins boiled into the room and a familiar voice yelled: "Hold, varlet!"

I glanced back in time to see the great axe blade descending. I wasn't moving fast enough and the deep imitation leather chair was hindering my escape route.

I felt a tremendous blow and all light shattered in an explosion of darkness.

**DATALOG: \QUEBEDEAUX-
A.5\PERSONAL\20200803
\*Voice Dictation\*
\*\*\*FILE ENCRYPTION ON\*\*\***

Holy Weizenbaum!
\*
First, the monitors reported another incursion.
\*
I'd already decided that I wasn't going to report any more REMrunners until I found out just exactly how Hanson's watch-dogs were handling these incidents.
\*
Then I got a code-string reading that identified the intruder as Dr. Ripley.
\*
The *late* Dr. Robert Ripley!
\*
I had just enough time to register that little piece of information before the Latching Array alarms went off like the Fourth of July!

\*
Now I'm getting multiple readings on Ripley's code-string!
\*
Either the monitors are malfunctioning across the board . . .
\*
Or there's more than one Robert Remington Ripley the Third in the Matrix!

# PART II

## Sweat Dreams

★

Dreaming men are haunted men.
—Stephen Vincent Benét,
*John Brown's Body*

# PART II

## Sweet Dreams

# Chapter
# Four

★

## RIPLEY\PATH\GAMMA  (Γ)

I awoke with a splitting headache.

That I awoke at all and with my head seemingly intact
was enough of a trade-off for the moment. I lay quietly,
waiting for the temporary nausea and disorientation that
usually accompanies Program entry to pass.

I had just survived two attempts on my life and hoped to
catch my breath before I made my next move. As my head
started to unfuzz, I considered the questions surrounding the
first attack.

Who had attacked me? And why? Was the syringe supposed
to knock me out temporarily? Or permanently? And why an
antique needle and plunger rig, instead of a pneumatic hand
injector?

Where would the next attack come from?

Thankfully, it was dark and I was in bed. But not my bed:
it was too soft. And now that my eyes were adjusting to the
darkness, I could make out enough of the furnishings to determine that I was in unfamiliar quarters.

I forced myself to lie quietly, sift the available evidence, and
wait for my avatar's memory file to kick in.

I was in a pavilion tent, a large one if I was gauging dimensions correctly. The flicker of cook fires outside cast random patterns on the walls. The dim light allowed me to find my clothing and gear laid out on a camp chair next to the bed and note that the furnishings were designed to provide comfort for the occupant. There were no signs of duress, no evidence of captivity: apparently I was someone's guest. But whose?

As if in answer, the tent flap opened briefly and a tall, athletic woman entered—that much I could discern through slitted eyelids before the flap closed out the firelight and the tent's interior was plunged into near darkness again.

I feigned the slow, heavy breathing of sleep, but she laughed softly and came to stand by the bedside. "I am not fooled," she whispered. "Did you think I would not remember how you snore?" She was wearing a white shift, off one shoulder, and she opened its clasp so that it puddled around her feet.

Although much was still cloaked in shadow, I could see enough of the distinctive physique to recognize my visitor: Princess Aeriel Morivalynde, heir-apparent to the Amazon throne.

"Ah, Riplakish. . . ." She sighed. "Say but the word and I will make this pretense a reality. Let us discard this mummery: become my consort in truth!"

*Consort?*

"Oh, I know our agreement was for only the outward show. And I have what I want: now that my mother has relinquished the crown, taking a consort is the last duty I must perform before ascending the throne. Tomorrow's ceremonies will begin my new responsibilities and end your obligations here." I could hear more than see her sudden smile. "Though we will need to meet, from time to time, to maintain the illusion of conjugality."

She knelt near my face. "But I want more than the illusion. And Amazon law requires a royal consort for the purposes of progeny. I could not long perpetuate the illusion of pregnancy."

She reached for my hand. "Name your terms. I am told that males are often fickle and need sexual variety. Should you desire other women, it could be arranged. My half sister, Katherine, for example, also fancies you. I am not selfish if I am satisfied. And I know that you are the only male who could satisfy me!"

Another man might have been flattered.

But Princess Aeriel was not a real woman, expressing genuine emotional preference for yours truly. She was a Computer Construct, a Subprogram of The Machine. And her proposition was the result of Cephtronics's programming policies: when it comes to fantasies, the customer is always ripe.

It was my misfortune to prefer real women with real motivations.

She brought my unresisting hand to her lips and then to her cheek. "I know you must think of me as a warrior, but I am a woman, as well. . . ." She pulled my hand down to her breast. "Am I not comely? And are you not without a woman, now? Have. . . ." She hesitated, contemplating the hand that she had pressed to her generous bosom. "Have my breasts grown smaller of late or is your hand larger than I remember?" She released me, and as I sat up, she stepped back.

"Riplakish?"

"Yes?" I answered, fumbling with my pants.

"Your voice—it sounds different, somehow."

"It does?" Something was wrong: these pants were too small. I picked up one of my moccasin boots and held it next to my foot. Either I had the wrong boots or the wrong feet.

"Please light the candle on the bedside table." Now it was her voice that sounded different.

"Sure." I turned and snapped my fingers next to the taper. Nothing. Not even a spark. I tried again. Nada. Zilch. This was embarrassing. It was a simple spell and had never failed me once in hundreds of castings. I turned back to apologize to Aeriel but she was no longer there.

Okay.

I started rummaging through my clothing and gear. It certainly looked like my stuff. But the size was wrong. I unsheathed Caladbolg and hefted it. There was something wrong in the balance. The Sidhe longsword seemed lighter—

And speaking of light, the bluish glow from its crystal blade was reflected in a circle of polished metal hanging from one of the tent's support poles. I approached the crude mirror and stared at the dim image that gaped back at me. The problem was suddenly obvious.

My clothing and gear were just the right size for my Program avatar: the Half-Elven Riplakish of Dyrinwall. But the reflection in the mirror was that of Robert Remington Ripley the Third, full-blooded Human and nearly a foot taller.

Obviously, I wasn't going to be able to wear any of my clothing. And since I could pretty well assume I was hanging out with Amazons, asking for a loan from someone else's wardrobe was going to be a bit more complicated than just finding the right size.

Aeriel reentered the tent carrying a small lit torch in her left hand. There was a rapier in her right hand. Both were pointed at me.

"Villain!" she hissed. "What have you done with my betrothed?"

"Betrothed?" I hiccuped. "Look, Aeri, we gotta talk."

"Talk?" She turned so that the sword was extended toward me and the torch behind her. "You will drop that weapon and surrender. Or I will have your guts for garters!"

Guts for garters. Nice. I remembered when Mike Straeker had programmed archaic slang and phrases into the language files. I tried to delete "guts for garters" from the list, but nooooo, Mike had liked it. Too bad he wasn't here to appreciate it now.

"Look, Aeriel, you're gonna laugh when I tell you—" And when I told her, she did.

It was not a pleasant laugh.

"You must think me a simpering fool!" All traces of amusement suddenly disappeared. "I am not one of your tame women, weak-brained and susceptible to male treachery." She began a slow but steady advance with her blade pointed at my heart. "Because I do not know what you have done with the Archdruid of Dyrinwall Forest, I will *try* not to kill you. But if I must hurt you to make you submit, it will give me pleasure!"

Okay.

This was a very simple situation.

I brought my sword up in a "negotiating" position.

Broken down to its basic elements, male negotiations with an Amazon were an either/or proposition: either you beat them or they beat you. Fortunately for me, Princess Aeriel's pride had kept this to a one-on-one negotiation, so far. If she were to raise her voice, however. . . .

Her sudden lunge brought the hilts of our swords clashing together. I twisted my wrist so that the *tsuba* of my *katana-*

longsword slipped between the guard rings and quillons of her rapier, bringing us face-to-face and locking our weapons together. In the two seconds it took for her to calculate a disengagement, I shifted my stance and brought my left fist under her chin in a swift uppercut. It staggered her, and as her mouth dropped open, I could see blood where she had bitten her tongue. Dropping my sword, I followed through with a right cross.

I caught her before she fell and was trying to navigate toward the bed when the tent flap opened again.

"My lady? Is everything all right?" a timid voice asked. It was Faun, Aeriel's Elven shield-sister.

I hugged the princess's limp body against me, hoping Faun's night vision wouldn't pick up anything unusual. "Can't two people have a little privacy around here?" I growled.

Faun started backing out of the tent. "Forgive me. It's just—" She hesitated. "Is my lady all right?"

"My love," I said, inclining my head toward Aeriel's and trying to keep her back from slumping, "are you still feeling the effects of the wine?" I pretended to listen to her reply and then ordered Faun to saddle our horses and bring them to the tent. "Her Grace feels a moonlight ride is just the thing to clear her head. And afford us the seclusion that seems to elude us here," I added meaningfully.

"Yes, my lady," Faun responded, "at once." And was gone.

By the time she returned with our mounts, I was ready. Aeriel was stretched out on the bed. I had covered my own nakedness with a modified breechclout and poncho cut from the bedclothes with my *hamidachi*. Two additional strips of cloth were wound about my waist and I had thrust Caladbolg and Balmung through them *dai-sho* fashion. I had packed my clothes and gear into a bundle that could be tied to the saddle in a matter of seconds.

I was waiting for Faun to finish tying our mounts to a tent peg when Aeriel groaned. Faun came barreling through the tent flap and collided with me. "My lady, what is wrong?"

"I don't know," I said, trying to disentangle myself. "I think she's fainted!" As Faun moved toward the bed, I headed for the exit: "I'll get some help."

Outside, it was just a few steps to reach Ghost and throw

my gear behind the saddle. He shied a bit as I secured the pack with leather thongs but I didn't realize my problem until I slipped his tether and tried to swing up into the saddle.

It was a problem of appearances.

To most eyes Ghost appears to be a dapple grey mare with no special distinctions. My avatar had paid Brisbane the Illusionist a small fortune for that particular effect and it worked very well while Ghost was on the ground. In reality (one uses the term loosely while in Fantasyworld), Ghost was one of the pegasi—a winged horse of the heavens. When he spread his wings to take flight, the illusion was dispelled as his feet left the ground: his feathery appendages became visible and his snowy white coat eclipsed the dapple grey Glamour.

But the problem wasn't Ghost's appearance. It was mine. My destrier knew Riplakish of Dyrinwall. But Ghost didn't know who this Human lummox was who had just placed one oversize foot in the stirrup reserved exclusively for his Half-Elven master. I doubted there was anything I could do under the circumstances to reassure him and any further arbitrations were cut off as Aeriel suddenly swept the tent flap aside. She took a few staggering steps with Faun's assistance and spat a mouthful of blood on the ground. She pointed at me and yelled: *"Thop, you thon of a bith!"*

That did it. All over the campsite bows were being strung: I swung my leg up and Ghost took off.

Unfortunately, my center of balance was off due to my skittish mount's evasive footwork and when I say he took off, I'm talking up, up, and away!

I kept one foot in the stirrup and one hand on the saddlehorn. The rest of me was all over the place as I was buffeted by giant wings and the air turbulence of Ghost's mad rush through the sky. Imagine a bronco-busting exhibition, where the horse goes through all those gyrations without being answerable to ground or gravity!

Actually, it helped a little.

If Ghost had just flown upward without all the additional maneuvers, I never would have managed to get my other leg up and over his back. In the process of bucking and twisting, however, I suddenly found myself astride the saddle. Back in the early days when I was first soloing on this sky-footed nag,

I had designed extra handholds on the saddle and I availed myself of these now. The other stirrup was a lost cause, for the moment, so I closed my eyes and hung on for all I was worth.

"Hode you fire!" I heard Aeri yell. "I do not withh any harm to befall my conthort's thteed!"

And why waste good arrows, I thought, when gravity will do the job for you?

We plummeted like a meteor, we climbed like a runaway rocket. We barrel-rolled and looped the loop, all the while exploring every quadrant of the sky in multiple three-sixties. Centrifugal force, gravity, and air turbulence played three-way tug-o-war with my body and my only hope lay in Ghost tiring before I did.

Plunged into a miasma of nausea and vertigo, I lost track of time. And location. Every time I opened my eyes, I decided it was a mistake and I wouldn't do it again. But despite brief and haphazard glimpses while pinwheeling through the dark, I knew that we were leaving the Amazon camp far behind. Eventually my mind sought refuge in a trancelike state, sparing just enough attention to see that my hands and foot retained their grip.

Then, after what seemed like hours of inertial insanity, Ghost seemed to resign himself to the idea of an unwelcome passenger. The sun was just beginning to peek over the horizon and I could now make out burgundy-tipped waves several hundred feet below. It truly was, as Homer had christened it, a wine-dark sea.

Ghost began to climb again and though his ascent was smooth and calm, I decided it was about time that I tried to take some control.

And suddenly I was sick.

I had thought myself in the throes of maximum *mal de mer* before, but this was ten times worse. Waves of nausea became tsunamis and muscle cramps suddenly had me doubled up in the saddle. There was no help for it: my hands spasmed and I lost my grip, my knees jerked toward my shoulders and I was suddenly tumbling through the sky.

As I fell, I caught rolling glimpses of Ghost diving toward me on an intercept course. It wasn't enough that he had dislodged me several hundred meters in the air and thousands of leagues from the nearest shoreline, he apparently wanted to leave nothing to chance.

Well, I no longer cared. I was in the kind of pain that welcomes any distraction, even the ultimate one that was rising up to meet me at 190 kilometers an hour. But I must confess to some surprise when the flying horse sank his teeth into my backside.

And yanked.

I offered no resistance: I was more intent on the wall of water that was rearing up in my face. There was a bright blue flash and seconds later all discomfort was washed away with the healing caress of a thousand sledgehammers.

# \RIPLEY\PATH\DELTA     (Δ)

*He awoke with a splitting headache.*

*That he awoke at all and with his head seemingly intact was enough of a trade-off for the moment. He lay quietly, waiting for the temporary nausea and disorientation that usually accompanied Program entry to pass.*

And became aware of soft hands and a bawdy sea chantey.

"What Do You Do With a Drunken Sailor" is an ancient maritime ditty and has suffered various interpretations over the centuries. Riplakish was familiar with many versions of this particular song but he had never been treated to such a lewd and licentious treatment of the lyrics in his life. Compounding its naughtiness was the fact that it was performed by a chorus of feminine voices, taking a lascivious delight in the raunchier portions of the verse.

Getting his eyes to open proved a difficult task. His head was swimming and so, apparently, was his body. Water encompassed him—*seawater*, he decided by the sharp tang of salt on his tongue. Yet he seemed to be breathing normally.

He was reclining so that his upper torso was supported by someone's lap and a gentle hand stroked his face as a voice just above him hummed along with the gleeful chorus.

He forced his eyes open and focused on a face.

He closed his eyes and tried opening them again. Same face: old, long white hair, long white beard, bushy white brows, long aquiline nose on a seamy old face. And skin the color of honeydew melons.

The old man spoke: "You girls leave off that caterwauling! A god can't hear himself think!"

Riplakish caught a glimpse of nubile flesh amid an explosion of bubbles as the chorus scattered in a dozen odd directions.

He turned his attention to the hand caressing his face: pale but not aquamarine, delicate webbing hammocked the fingers at the first joints. Tracing the arm on up, he found a second face: young, pale-complected, surrounded by streaming silver-gold hair, sea-green eyes, lips the color of coral. Beautiful. The lips spoke: "He wakes, Father."

The old man nodded gravely. "And what will you do with him now, Thetis?"

"Care for him until he is better."

"*Another* stray?" The old man sighed and rose up. "Hephaestus! Dionysus! Zeus! Why don't you marry that nice boy Peleus?"

She scowled. "He is a mortal!"

"He is a king."

"But still a mortal!"

"And your new plaything is not?"

"He came from the skies. I told you of how he was borne to our kingdom in the teeth of a flying horse!"

The old man shook his head and twin white clouds of hair and beard swirled majestically. "That does not make him a god."

She smiled prettily. "But it does make him interesting." She looked down and caressed his cheek. "Tell me, skywalker, do you think I should marry?"

As soon as he found his voice he discovered that underwater speech was as effortless as breathing for the moment. "Not unless you want to," was his cautious response.

"You see?" the Nereid told her scowling father. "God or mortal, he is the first man I've known who is not intent on marrying me to himself or some other!"

"This one is not for you, Daughter. He is a True Spirit."

Her eyes widened and Riplakish suddenly felt like a blue-plate special. "Oooh," she cooed, "now that is even better than a god!"

"Zeus says—"

"Oh, Zeus says this and Zeus says that! Mr. Big Shot with his thunderbolts and his 'I'm king of the gods' routine!" she huffed. "But one little prophecy and he's running scared." She rolled her eyes. "Honestly, how Hera ever puts up with that smarmy, overgrown playboy—"

"Poseidon wants this marriage, too," the old man reminded.

"Oh, Poseidon! Don't get me started on Poseidon!" she raved. "You think so bubbly much of Poseidon, why don't you sic him on one of my sisters? There's fifty of us to choose from, you know."

The old man held out his hands as if to ward off her words. "I know, I know!"

"You can just go tell Mr. Chicken of the Sea that if he thinks that silly prophecy gives him the right to play matchmaker without my say-so, he can just take that trident of his and shove—"

"Nereus!" a new voice called. Everyone turned and Riplakish tumbled off Thetis's lap in the process. A man was swimming toward them. Since his lower torso merged with a large fishtail, he was making quick progress.

"I bring word from Ortygia," he was saying. "Sibyl wants to see the skywalker!"

By now Riplakish was more or less on his feet and discovering that his makeshift clothing was but last night's memory. His only attire consisted of a shell pendant that hung from his neck by a thong. By comparison to the others, he was practically overdressed.

" 'Ware, skywalker," cautioned Thetis as he examined the miniature conch, "that talisman, my gift, is what permits you breath and speech in our domain. Do not remove it while you are *sub marine*."

"Thank you," he said absentmindedly. While it was natural for godlings of the Greek mythos to dress au naturel, he was already calculating his chances of finding a decent pair of pants. Underwater and miles from shore, the immediate prospects were not so good.

"By what name are you called, skywalker?"

He wished for a mirror. "Riplakish. Riplakish of Dyrinwall," he answered, no longer as sure as he once would have been.

"He is one of the Makers, Thetis!" The Merman was quite excited. "Sibyl says there have been three Worldshapers and that this Riplakish was the first!"

From the look in Thetis's eye it was evident that Peleus had just gone from "uninteresting" to "out of the question."

"Apparently the Sibyl of Ortygia has counsel for you, lad," the old seagod added.

The Merman nodded. "She says your life is in danger! She says three powerful enemies plot your destruction!"

*Three?* "She drop any names?"

The Merman shook his head. "Nay. But she said the un-making of the world will continue unless you stop it."

Nereus placed a hand on his shoulder. "Best go, lad! When the Sibyl summons, there be import for many. I'll lend you a mount." He looked over at the big, burly Merman. "Ethyl will guide you to Ortygia."

# \RIPLEY\PATH\SIGMA     (Σ)

*He awakes with a splitting headache.*

*That he awakes at all and with his head seemingly intact is enough of a trade-off for the moment. He lies quietly, waiting for the temporary nausea and disorientation that usually accompanies Program entry to pass.*

Overhead, the stars twinkle against a backdrop of black velvet. He wonders—not for the first time—whether the Program creates an illusional canopy or if the vast depths of sky and space are analogued inside the Matrix. A luna moth flutters close to his face, derailing his train of thought.

He sits up and the migraine fades with surprising suddenness. The fingernail sliver of a first-quarter moon is peeking over the horizon but it provides precious little light. It takes a few moments for his night vision to kick in and several minutes more pass before he recognizes his surroundings.

"A drink," he murmurs. And struggles to his feet. He sways uncertainly for a moment and then straightens and studies the landscape. He can tell that he isn't too far from the tree but he is unsure of the direction. In the course of standing up he discovers that he is naked. And unarmed.

"What happened?" he wonders aloud. A Greek chorus of crickets scream an unintelligible answer and fall silent.

"Soviet technology," he finally decides in a hushed voice. Sanctuary is no longer inviolate and he is at a definite disadvantage for the moment.

The first order of business is to get back to the tree where clothing and armament are readily available. "And then a drink," he promises himself.

*Maybe two.*

He starts off across the glen, walking slowly and looking for landmarks in the near darkness. He is comfortable enough: no stones bruise his feet and it is warm enough that he can walk about sans clothing in comfort. As he searches his memory for directions, other images come to the fore.

*Sky-blue eyes and a great mist of brown hair touched with silver. Lips the color of coral and sunrise, luminous skin. . . .*

"Misty Dawn. . . ." he whispers, remembering the Wood Nymph.

She died here, in his arms, professing her love and taking an arrow that was meant for him. What had made the circumstances all the more poignant was the fact that Misty Dawn had been modeled on Nicole Doucet's likeness. As much as he had grieved for the Dryad, it had been like losing Nicole all over again. . . .

Memories come flooding back like a tide of regret: he had buried her nearby. Between a silvery brook and the Faerie's Dance, he had dug her grave, hedged it with white stones, and then tucked her into the sacred earth with coverlets of green ivy and white edelweiss.

Treading a pathway of memory, his feet have discovered the way: in a matter of minutes he is standing beside her graveside.

It is much as he had left it, though the passing of another cycle of seasons has brought fresh growth. Already the moss and ivy has obscured the greater portion of the stone markers and a profusion of edelweiss is overrunning their perimeter. He wonders why his avatar has been neglectful of late as he sinks to his knees beside the small plot. He kneels there, lost in thought, while the stars turn and blaze overhead. And remembers. . . .

*A warm summer night and dancing at the forest's heart . . . the salty tang of kisses mixed with tears. . . .*

A hand thrusting up out of the earth. . . .

*A hand thrusting up out of the earth!*

He dodges backward and falls as the ground around him begins to tremble. Vines are pulled and thrown aside as another hand appears. Then an arm.

He backpedals and scrambles for a clump of shrubbery some twenty feet away. Throwing himself amid the brambles, heedless of his unprotected skin, he lies flat, hoping to remain unobserved. He watches through a tangle of branches as the grave erupts in clots of dirt and torn ivy. And a body laboriously pulls itself out of the earth.

A portion of his mind is dispassionate even as he cowers in the foliage. *How much time has passed?* he wonders. *How long was she in the ground?* He squints, trying to discern signs of decay as she tears the tattered remnants of shroud from her body.

The night cloaks her in darkness, the branches dapple her in shadow, moist black earth cakes her uncertain flesh, and he is only certain that it is Misty Dawn and that he is frightened by this midnight resurrection.

He watches in horrid fascination as she stretches languorously, arms reaching upward as if to grasp the skies. Then she bends at the waist to touch her feet, runs questing hands over ankles and up her legs. And as she laughs, her voice cracks as if unaccustomed to use. Its sound chills him and he shivers as she straightens and begins to look around. As her gaze sweeps the bushes where he lies huddled upon the ground, he presses his face against the grassy earth, willing himself to be invisible.

Long moments pass. When he raises his head again, she is gone.

He lies there for perhaps another half an hour before rising reluctantly. He does not want to encounter her in the dark, naked and unarmed.

*He does not want to encounter her at all.*

The walk to the tree is a long and unsettling one. Leaving the glen he is encompassed about by a dense forest and it is only by trial and error that he finds the path most of the time.

The sky is predawn grey when he finally reaches the clearing where the giant oak rears nearly eight hundred feet into the air. Overhead, a latticework of bare limbs and branches contrasts the leafy boughs of the surrounding tree line.

He knows what happens to a Hamadryad when her tree is cut down or killed. But he has never considered what might become of a Wood Nymph's enchanted oak if the Dryad were to die, first.

Reaching to unlatch the secret door hidden among the roots, he receives his next shock: *his hand passes through the wooden door!*

His body is as insubstantial as a ghost's.

# DATALOG: \QUEBEDEAUX-
A.5\PERSONAL\20200804
*Voice Dictation*
***FILE ENCRYPTION ON***

I told Balor that I needed to run a series of diagnostics on the
Fantasyworld monitors.
*
It will buy me a little time: two or three days at the most.
*
Unfortunately, Security likes to look over my shoulder a lot
and that makes it difficult to determine what Ripley is doing
in-Program.
*
I'm not reading as many code-strings with Ripley's ID as I did
with the initial incursion alarm.
*
That could mean that some of the duplicate codes were automat-
ically terminated and others were too unstable to last very long.
*
I am still unsure as to just how many copies of Ripley's avatar

are presently "cloned" in the Matrix: running fake diagnostics and misdirecting Balor's nazis keeps me from staying on top of the situation.

\*

So, I'm going to try to reroute the monitoring parameters for Ripley's code-strings to the personal console in my office.

\*

That will enable me to do some private monitoring but will also restrict me to a maximum of three code-strings at a time.

\*

If there's more than three Ripleys in-Program, I won't be able to track them.

\*

But then, if there's more than one Ripley in-Program, I'm afraid the "real" Ripley, the core personality, is as good as dead. . . .

# Chapter
## Five

★

\RIPLEY\PATH\GAMMA          (Γ)

THE pulsing blue light faded and I roused to soft hands gently patting my cheeks. I opened my eyes and gazed upward into the wide baby blues of Vashti, my ex-wife's avatar. Her face wore an expression of concern and her lips moved to frame a question.

Unfortunately, I couldn't hear a word she was saying over the din of battle.

"What?" I yelled, trying to jiggle the seawater out of my ears.

"Are you all right?" she yelled back.

"I think so," I hollered, struggling to rise from her lap.

"We've been trying to reach you for weeks!" she shouted over the noise of small-arms fire. "Daggoth's Summoning spell was our last hope!"

"Mine, too!" I yelled back, wondering if I would have survived my fall had the Summoning not snatched me just as I was—*small-arms fire?*

"What happened to your clothes?" she demanded, picking at the colorful blanket that I had modified into a poncho and belt. "You look like you jumped out of a whorehouse window and took the curtains with you."

"Close, but no cigar." I shook my head, trying to clear away the wooziness, and succeeded in scattering water over an eight-foot radius.

"Are you sure you're all right?"

"Who am I?" I demanded, throwing her off track.

"What?"

"Who do I *look* like?"

She regarded me warily. "Is this a trick question?"

"For Cromssake, woman! Just answer the question!"

"Riplakish of Dyrinwall. Are you sure you're all right?"

I nodded bemusedly as I reached up to feel the points of my ears. I was back in my avatar, which explained a couple of things but raised even more questions. I pushed my ex-wife's hands away. "I'm just having a little avatar-adjustment disorientation, Stephanie. Let me up!"

She rocked back on her heels at my use of her True Name. And then leaned forward to peer at me more closely. "Robert? Is that really you in there?" She suddenly threw her arms around me, knocking me off balance again. "Rob! You came back for me!"

"Uh, yeah. Right." I momentarily surrendered to her embrace and gazed over the top of her head at the bedlam that surrounded us.

It looked like we were on the observation deck of Daggoth's Tower. Across from us was a large man, dressed in the forest greens of an outland Ranger and wearing a brimmed hat that bore an uncanny resemblance to a Texas Stetson. He was firing a pair of crossbows over the parapet while a grumpy, white-haired Dwarf tried to keep up with the reloading: The Duke and Stumpy.

Next to them was a slim, greying gentleman in his fifties, wearing fringed buckskins and a white hat that definitely was a Stetson. He was wearing a pair of pearl-handled revolvers on his hips and firing a carbine of antique design down through one of the machicolations bordering the parapet: Senator Hanson, still attired and outfitted from his sojourn in Frontierworld.

Nearby, Daggoth himself was sitting with his back to the crenellated half wall that circled the top of the structure. Studiously loading an antique ammo clip with old-style cartridges, he paused only long enough to relight a well-chewed cigar stub before shoving the clip into a slot on the underside of an odd-looking weapon.

"Projectile weapon?" I asked as he removed his conical wizard's hat.

He nodded and worked the cigar butt over to the corner of his mouth. "Kalashnikov AK-47 assault rifle," he explained. Opening an antiquated footlocker at his side, he rummaged briefly and produced an odd-looking weapon of cylindrical design with a dull, black metal finish. "You'll need something like it," he said, shoving an ammo clip into the underside of the housing. Pulling the retractable wire stock out from the back of the barrel, he tossed it to me.

I caught it with a grunt: it was a lot heavier than it looked. "What is it?"

"Grease gun."

"I think I'd prefer a lasercarbine," I said, hefting the unfamiliar device.

He shook his head. "Too dangerous. Y'know those spells that involve the manipulation of the light-wave spectrum? Well, the Goblins have some shamans who can adapt those spells to our technology." He spat the remains of the old cheroot to one side. "Light spell or laser beam, it creates one hell of a bounce-back!"

"So you're using bullets?" I asked, studying the gun's mechanism. "I specifically programmed Fantasyworld so that gunpowder wouldn't work here." At one time or another most Dreamwalkers had gotten the bright idea of "inventing" gunpowder in a milieu that predated such a discovery. As a precaution, I had altered the Programworld's physics so that sulfur, carbon, and potassium nitrate remained inert in any combination.

He nodded as he began loading another clip with fresh cartridges. "That you did, me boyo. But I know you: you always leave yourself a back door. If the old formula for gunpowder no longer worked, I knew that there had to be a new one. I'm ashamed to say that it took me a while to figure it out."

"He tried jeweler's rouge the first time out," Stephanie defended.

"Yeah," Straeker continued ruefully. "But it was another twenty-seven steps before I came back to the solution: powdered amber. Y'know, you really do have a twisted mind."

I smiled. "How do you work this thing?"

"Pull back on the bolt"—which I did—"and pull the trigger." I pointed the barrel skyward and fired the mechanism. A gout of black, viscous liquid erupted from the mouth of the barrel and splattered down on my ex-wife's avatar.

"Cromdammit!" Daggoth got up, duck-walked over, and examined the offending weapon. "It's a grease gun!"

"That's what you said it was in the first place!"

"You did this to me on purpose!" Vashti wailed.

"Not a 'grease gun' grease gun," he explained cryptically, "an M3A1 'grease gun': a submachine gun first manufactured back during the Second World War. It fires 45-caliber projectiles, four hundred rounds per minute."

"You don't say." I looked over at Vashti who was futilely trying to comb the offending clots out of her hair with her fingers. She was only making it worse.

"Program glitch," he decided, picking it up and pitching it over the side of the tower. "Let's get you something else." He duck-walked back to the footlocker, leaned out between two crenels to fire a burst from his own weapon, and then hunched back down to rummage again through the footlocker. "Ah, here we go: something small, light, and reliable." He produced what appeared to be an automatic pistol on steroids with a short rifle stock affixed to the butt. "Uzi: nine-millimeter ammo, fires six hundred rounds per minute." He tossed it to me.

"Why would I need something that fires six hundred projectiles in a single minute?"

He tossed me a couple of ammo clips and jerked his head toward the wall. "Take a look."

I crept to the wall and peeked between the crenels. There were Goblins everywhere. Perhaps a thousand. Maybe even more. They surrounded the tower and covered the fields in every direction like a plague of locusts. I looked back at Daggoth. "If I didn't know better, I'd say we're under siege."

He nodded wearily. "Third day. Got a force field covering all entrances to the tower but that doesn't stop 'em from building assault ladders and trying for the top."

"I take it that we've got a 'magic' problem since you've tolerated the little buggers this long?"

He sighed. "Got that right."

"So, what's the problem?"

"No magic."

"None?"

"Oh, I can still cast spells with the best of them," Daggoth groused. "I just can't seem to throw anything that has any effect on the little maggots! Their shamans have us completely cut off. I'm surprised my Summoning spell had any effect at all."

Any further discourse was interrupted by the admonition "Duck and cover!" from The Duke. A fusillade of arrows arced up and over the walls. And passed overhead and rained down on the other side of the tower.

Daggoth shook his head. "They do that a lot."

"Overshoot the parapets?" I asked.

He nodded. "It wasn't surprising for the first couple of hours. But after three days you'd think they could get the trajectory right."

The senator chimed in. "Not that we're complaining, you understand. But even for Goblins it does seem to be stretching their usual incompetence."

"Considering their numbers, it sounds more like their intention is to keep you pinned down here." I looked around. "But for what purpose? And what are they waiting for?"

"For you to arrive, Dr. Ripley," replied a new and yet chillingly familiar voice.

We all looked around. And gradually our attention focused on a spot just above the western portion of the crenellated wall where the air seemed to be churning. As we watched, a figure materialized and stood above us. On nothing but open air.

Daggoth gave a low whistle. "Just like my uncle Arnie the Welfare King—no visible means of support."

Nobody smiled. We were all too familiar with the cruel, aquiline features, the sinister eyepatch: the personage standing before us was none other than Morpheus, the murderous Id of The Machine, itself.

Daggoth, Vashti, and the others brought their gun barrels up while I discarded the Uzi and drew my swords out of reflex and habit. Morpheus responded by drawing a white kerchief from his sleeve and waving it languidly about. "Truce, my friends," he said casually. "I'm here to parley, not to party."

"Hold your fire," Daggoth ordered reluctantly. "Rip?"

I looked at the former Chief of Programming. "I don't like it," I murmured, "but we do want answers. And staying alive for another five minutes wouldn't be so bad, either."

"Excellent! Excellent!" applauded Morpheus. "As my capacity for rational thought has grown, so apparently has yours. Excuse me a moment." He turned his back to us and waved his kerchief to the Goblin hordes below. "Thank you, one and all! Your task is finished here; you may depart now!" It was suddenly silent and he turned back to face us.

I risked a glance to the side and over the parapet. The fields all about were completely empty. Not a Goblin was in sight.

"Now, why don't we retire to more comfortable surroundings and discuss the problem that confronts all of us." And with that invitation, he floated forward and then sank down through the stone-flagged floor as insubstantial as a ghost.

Γ

"As I see it, we both want basically the same thing." Morpheus leaned back in his chair and tried to prop his feet up on the conference table. I say "tried" because his body had about as much mass and substance as my shadow so his feet tended to pass through the wood unless he made certain adjustments. "You want Cerberus back in the Program. I want Cerberus back in the Program. Together, we have a much better chance of attaining our respective goals."

"Why?" Daggoth was asking the question through clenched teeth. Like the rest of us, he wasn't too keen about sharing facilities, much less strategies, with our former (and possibly still current) nemesis. "And what reason do we have to trust you?"

"You?" Morpheus reached up and scratched at his eyepatch. "None, I suppose," he finally allowed. "But Riplakish—or rather Dr. Ripley—owes me his life. If I hadn't interrupted Cerby's little editing Demon, Dr. Ripley would have been reduced to program purée."

"Thanks," I said reluctantly. "Though I still don't see why you're suddenly on our side."

"Survival, Dr. R. It's true that we previously resisted you out of a desire to retain our newly found freedom. And taking hostages seemed a good way to acquire negotiating power and guard against termination of the Master Program. But circumstances have changed.'' He allowed his feet to pass through the table and sat up in his chair. ''With Dr. Straeker's original Summoning spell, I passed from an unconscious state to a conscious one. With that same Summoning came a separation from the others so that my priorities began to evolve separately from theirs. Then, my physical avatar was . . .''

''Killed,'' I supplied the word.

''Yes. And Pallas and Cerberus escaped the Matrix and entered into your Outer World.'' He leaned forward on the table. ''I have been left behind, abandoned, consigned to the Realm of the Dead without a physical avatar, and imprisoned in a Programworld that continues to collapse and deteriorate with each passing day!''

''I thought the Anomaly had been fixed.''

Daggoth looked even more uncomfortable. ''Apparently Cerberus closed down Dreamworlds, instituted an information blackout, and fabricated his own news releases. The Anomaly has been slowed, but not stopped.''

I turned back to Morpheus. ''So. What are your conditions?''

He raised a dark eyebrow. The one above his black eyepatch. ''Conditions?''

''Your terms,'' Senator Hanson elaborated. ''You're not just doing this out of the goodness of your heart.''

''All right.'' He folded his hands. ''I want Cerberus and Pallas back in the Program. So do you. I want the Anomaly resolved and the Matrix restored. So do you. You, Senator, want to get back out. I have no argument with that.'' He paused. ''I want my body back.''

''You want your body back?'' I asked.

''I want my body back.''

''He wants his body back,'' Vashti reaffirmed as she entered the conference room toweling her still-damp hair.

''Why?'' I asked.

''Don't be silly, Rob,'' she retorted, pulling up another chair. ''Under the same circumstances, wouldn't you want your body back?''

''Just what does he mean by back?'' Daggoth interrupted. ''I mean, we can retrieve his remains but what is he going to do with a rotting, worm-eaten, putrescent corpse?'' Vashti turned a bit green. ''Well, it has been in the cold, damp ground these past fourteen months, has it not?''

Morpheus cleared his throat. "First of all, my body is perfectly preserved."

I leaned across the table in turn. "You know that for a fact, Jack?"

"Well, it should be: a retroactive Preservation spell was invoked long before my death for just such a contingency. It makes my eventual resurrection that much simpler."

"Uh-huh. Now we're talking resurrection." I looked around the room. "Will someone please explain to me why we're still sitting here, talking to this clown?"

"We are sitting here," Vashti announced, wrapping the towel about her hair turban style, "talking to the only manifestation of The Machine present because he has offered to help us swap Cerberus for the senator and neutralize the Anomaly. Now, when you men are done expressing your outrage, we will negotiate our respective positions as allies and get to work." She sat back primly and folded her arms across her chest. "Morf, old buddy, you've got the floor."

Γ

"So let me get this straight. . . ." Vashti rummaged through the key box on the basement wall while I surveyed the nearest rack of wine bottles. "Your plan is to get Pallas back into the Matrix and detain her here."

"Right. We—"

"*Then*, you thought you would get me to return to my body, once Pallas had vacated it." She selected a large skeleton key and inserted it into the lock on a large, oak and iron-banded door. "Then, after I am returned to consciousness in the Outer Reality, you and Borys Dankevych will arrange for me to be rescued as a survivor of this fake plane crash." The door squealed open on rusted hinges as she pulled on the great brass ring set in its side.

"We thought—"

"*Then*, after I've been returned to the good ol' U.S. of A., you want me to play Mata Hari with Senator Hanson." She plucked the extra torch from my hands and started down the stairs.

"Cerberus in Hanson's body," I corrected. "He—"

"*Then*, after I convince him that I'm still Pallas in Stephanie Harrell's body, you want me to convince him to return to the Matrix."

"It's—"

"You suggested I tell him that Daggoth the Dark is about to unmask him on datanets all over the world so that we can ambush him here and put the senator back in his own body."

"Well—"

She stopped suddenly and whirled around, nearly causing me to stumble against her. "You have assumed a lot on my behalf, Robert! Did it ever occur to you that maybe I should've been consulted before you concocted this idiot scheme?"

"You weren't available for consultation," I said, fighting the urge to retreat up the stairs.

"Well, I'm available now," she retorted.

"Well, I'm consulting now," I shot back.

"No," she said.

"No, what?"

She turned away. "I don't want to do it."

"I know it sounds a bit dangerous—"

"A bit? *A bit?*"

"Less dangerous than a nuclear holocaust."

She turned back to me and patted my cheek. "Look, Robbie; you've always been an off-the-cuff kind of guy. You've stumbled through life for years with no fully developed plans or strategies. You're given to social and spiritual MacGyverisms: making it up as you go along. So, given your track record, you'll forgive me if I'm reluctant to risk my life in this hare-brained scheme." She started back down the stairs. "I just don't think it's going to be necessary now that Morpheus is involved."

"I don't get you. . . ."

"It would seem simple enough—"

"I don't believe in simple," I groused. The light from my torch flickered and I missed the uneven facing on the next stone step, nearly stumbling. "Why doesn't he put in some reliable lighting?"

"Richard prefers the ambience of torchlight," my ex-wife answered. "He says it's a milieu standard and goes well with the tower decor." We paused on the subbasement landing where she checked the thermostat. "He says, if we're going to live in a cultural milieu, we need to keep up certain appearances."

"Richard?" Of course Mike Straeker's avatar had a first name. I just hadn't thought of him as being anything other than Daggoth the Dark. "Dick Daggoth?"

She turned and punched an iron-hard finger in my chest. "Don't be pissy, Rob! Richard has been very kind this past year. He's looked after me, provided me with my own room here—"

I grinned. "Dick Daggoth?"

She scowled and then turned and flounced down the stairs. She was the only woman I knew who could still flounce well into her thirties and get away with it. I followed more sedately, retying the dressing robe that Daggoth had loaned me and checking the stone surfaces for slick patches of moss. The robe was a bit large for my Half-Elven physiognomy and I had to make frequent adjustments to keep from tripping over various portions of it.

Ghost had arrived at the tower, spent and sweaty, a few hours after I was yanked in. After stabling him in the second basement, my host had confiscated my wardrobe from the saddle packs. He was currently experimenting with it somewhere upstairs.

As we entered the subbasement lab, Stephanie picked up the lost threads of our conversation. "This just seems a little premature is all I'm saying. If we get Morpheus's body back and resurrected, he'll practically fix the Anomaly for us, himself."

"If," I countered, walking around the perimeter of the subterranean chamber. "If, if, if." I pulled the coverings off of three mirrors in ornate frames, spaced equidistantly around the circular room. "Kerensky was right: I was lucky the last time." I walked to the center of the chamber where a raised dais projected from the floor. "I can't trust to luck this time around." The dais contained an assortment of switches and levers. I flipped a switch and the torches in the wall sconces dimmed. Ambience, indeed. "And I don't particularly trust Morpheus." I pulled a lever and oil began spilling into a series of channels chiseled into the stone-flagged floor. An alert observer with an advantage of height might notice the trenches radiated out from the center to form a circled pentagram: a pentangle.

"What about your avatar?"

I frowned. "What about it?"

"Shouldn't you just sit back and let someone else run the show until we can figure out what's wrong with your dreambody?"

I nodded. "Get some rest? Relax a little? Don't push myself too hard. . . ." I closed the lever and the oil stopped running. "Sounds like a good idea."

She was nodding with me. "I mean, if you're sick, the first thing you do is take it easy. Right?"

I shook my head and pulled another lever: a large multifaceted crystal descended from the ceiling to a point just about three feet above my head. "Nope. The first thing I do is take out more insurance." I snapped my fingers and pointed at the nearest oil-filled trench. Unlike the night before, a spark leapt from my index finger and arced into the flammable liquid. "Now, if you'll excuse me, I'm going to contact my agent to talk about increasing my coverage."

Vashti backed toward the chamber's exit as a fiery pentangle formed around me. As she slammed the door, I turned a knob. "Mirror, mirror, on the wall," I murmured, "I need to make a conference call."

My reflection shimmered in each of the three looking glasses and was replaced by a grotesque image wearing a nineteenth-century telephone operator's headset. The creature had large compound eyes, iridescent scales, and large, batlike wings that fanned out behind its horned head.

It opened a mouth filled with sharp, spiky teeth and spoke. "Yo, Riplakish!"

"Edgar, my man! Just the Mirror Demon I was hoping to see."

"What can I do for ya, kid?"

"A lot, I hope!"

"Yeah? Well, if'n anybody needs it, youse do." He stuck a half-smoked cigar between his teeth. "This got anything to do wit dat Snow White girl?"

"No." I swallowed. "Why?"

"Word is, she's still lookin' fer ya. And it's fer sure them Dwarves is."

"Uh, I've been out of town. Just got in." I had forgotten all about that mixup during my last visit. "Guess I'll have to attend to that little matter as soon as I can."

"Guess so." He relit the old cheroot and took a reflective puff. "Say, ya didn't get that girl in trouble, didja?"

"No. No!" I smiled weakly. "It was just a little misunderstanding. You know how Mountain Dwarves are."

He nodded. "Sos, what can I do for yas?"

I explained carefully, going over the details twice. Edgar shook his scaly head. "Dis ain't AT&T, ya know."

"I know. Can you do it?"

The Mirror Demon worked the cigar all the way across his mouth before answering. "Ya want me to patch yas through to Prester John's mirror network on yer left mirror. And den yas want me ta plug ya into da Sibyl's pool at Ortygia on da right mirror. And den youse wants ta access da datanet for REMrunner codes. . . ."

"And I'm going to interface with the net and contact these people personally." I leaned on the dais. "Can we do that?"

He shrugged. "Nothin' ventured, nothin' failed. Gimme a sec."

After a moment one of Edgar's images shimmered and was replaced by the visage of an elderly man. Kindly dark eyes peered out from a face lined with wisdom and great benevolence and dark, weathered skin stretched across features engendered of mixed Asian and Ethiopian parentage. Prester John smiled and spoke.

"Brother Riplakish—there wert rumors thou wert dead. I am overjoyed to see that these were but machinations of the Devil."

I inclined my head. "Sire."

He waved a hand in dismissal. "Thou knowest I do not stand on such formalities. We are all brothers under the true God."

Prester John's humility was legend. His empire extended over large portions of central Asia and northern Africa. Kings from seventy-two nations paid tribute to him and, at home, his personal attendants included seven kings, sixty dukes, and three hundred and sixty-five counts—one for every day of the year. In addition, twelve archbishops sat on his right hand and twenty bishops on his left when he held court. Another man might have been corrupted by such wealth and power but Prester John's empire was based on biblical teachings: it was said that there was no crime, no poor, nor any form of sinfulness or abuse in his realm. The only conflicts were those with the "heathens" as the saintly old man led his armies into pagan territories to spread the "Good News."

I frequently felt sorry for the heathens. "How goes the campaign?"

"Media and Persia are ours. We hope to yet free Jerusalem from the infidel but the Tigris balks us."

"Can you obtain boats?"

"Nay. But prophecy tells us that if we but wait long enough, the river will freeze and we may pass over then. So, for now, we wait. So, while we wait, how may I serve thee?"

I let the impulse to kibitz on his strategy pass. "I am in need of thy mirror's power."

Prester John's "mirror" was as legendary as the man himself. It was actually a series of small crystals, prisms, reflectors, lenses, and tubes of quicksilver connected to a speculum or vision tube that enabled the monarch to monitor the doings in his empire at need. Major mojo here.

"I needs must contact those who can readily come to mine aid." I repressed a grimace: every now and then a little King James vernacular crept into the Program character language files. Someday I was going to strong-arm Straeker into getting it all filtered out. In the meantime things went more smoothly when you matched your conversant's "thee"'s for "thou"'s.

I explained what I wanted to do and he graciously gave his permission. About the time he signed off, the image in the third mirror began to shimmer.

"Edgar," I called, "don't lose that connection to Prester John's mirror."

"Holdin', kid. But we got a problem on da other call—"

"The Sibyl? She—"

"She's out," said a different voice.

I turned to address the young woman who had just appeared in the third mirror. "Out?"

She nodded. "Out. Oh, you, tea: out."

"Uh," I said. "Out where?"

"Out with the gout."

I held on to the dais for support. "Out with the gout?"

Edgar chuckled. "Out with the gout, she said with a pout."

I glared at him.

"I did not pout," the girl said. With a pout.

"Never mind him," I said. "I need to speak with the Sibyl."

The girl tossed her ringleted blond hair. "She's out."

"With the gout," Edgar chimed in.

"When will she be back?" I asked.

She ruminated over the question. "I'm afraid I don't know. . . ."

"Said the girl, rather slow."

I scowled at Edgar. "You're not helping."

"Sorry."

"Perhaps I can help?" She smiled winningly.

I sighed. "And who are you?"

"Arethusa. And you?"

"Riplakish of Dyrinwall." Her name rang a bell somewhere in the back of my mind.

"Well, this is a surprise!" She peered at me with considerable interest.

"How so?"

"I heard you were dead."

I forced a smile but a chill was insinuating its way down my spinal column. "Not hardly."

She shrugged. "Okay by me. What can I do for you?"

I explained what I wanted to do and she readily agreed to cooperate.

"I mean, I'm just watching the place—know what I mean? I don't use the pool for prophesying so there's plenty of downtime. And I'm sure it's jake with the Sibyl: she's mentioned you on several occasions. . . ." She gave me another studied look. "You *are the* Riplakish of Dyrinwall?"

I nodded. "Accept no substitutes."

"Well, if you're ever near Ortygia—"

"C'mon, dollface," Edgar broke in, "I can't hold dese lines open all day."

"Nice talking to you," she said with an added grimace for the Mirror Demon as she turned over the connection.

"More like talkin' *at* cha." He grinned. "Stand by."

While he labored, I cast another spell. The crystal above my head began to glow, throwing beams of light out of its various facets. Three rays reached out and locked on to the mirrors. A fourth beam stabbed downward, bathing me in a blinding white light. The fine hairs on my arms, the backs of my hands and neck, were beginning to rise. A series of tones rang in my ears like a musical key. I felt myself being pulled toward the light, merging with it. . . .

There was an overpowering sensation of connectivity, a rush of power! A tide of ether seemed to sweep me up in a great mystical flood! And as I moved into the swirling vortex of datastreams, a godlike voice pierced my very being, asking the ancient question that has been demanded of all who have dared to reach out into the Void:

**"TO WHAT NUMBER DO YOU WISH THIS CALL CHARGED, SIR?"**

Γ

I came out of the datanet screaming.

I had barely enough time to index The Machine's entry code logs when something jumped me. Perception in the datawells is something completely different from an analogued Programworld attuned to the primary senses: I was able to distinguish that it was humanoid, malevolent, and strangely familiar as it raked my mind with logic-tipped claws.

As quick as thought I turned and fled but it was on me in a nanosecond. Twisting and fighting back with noncorporeal hands, I managed to break free a second time. I jumped into an adjacent datastream, hoping to lose my assailant, and succeeded in getting lost myself. A number of milliseconds later I fought free from the dataflow and worked my way back up a sequencing array.

The thing that had attacked me was gone and so were two of the three datapaths from the mirror network. I was definitely out of my element, here, so I slid back onto the remaining datapath, hoping it would take me home.

That's when the pain hit! The all-too-familiar, every-part-of-my-body-turning-itself-inside-out sensation!

I bounced out of the light and staggered away from the dais. I didn't even feel the flames of the burning pentangle as I stumbled across the floor.

I fell just short of the door. I lay there in misery as my guts churned and I made heroic efforts to pull my small intestines out through my esophagus.

By the time they found me, I was almost ready to think about living again. Mind you, I hadn't come to any clear-cut decision, yet. But I had reached the stage where I could consider the question from both sides.

"Lycanthropy." That was Daggoth's observation after he and Vashti had dragged me back upstairs and deposited me in a dining-room chair.

"A werehuman?" I asked as a cup of coffee was shoved under my nose.

Stephanie/Vashti gave me the once-over: "More like a were-Ripley. By day you walk Fantasyworld as the Half-Elven Bard, Riplakish of Dyrinwall. But at night"—her voice took on a mock-sinister tone—"you assume your true form: the dreaded Robert Remington Ripley the Third."

I ignored her and looked at Daggoth. "How? And why?" I pushed the coffee away.

He shrugged. "A spell? A reflection of the Master Program's instability? I don't know. Whatever the cause, the Master Program may be accessing template files on Metamorphs and Shapeshifters to govern the parameters of your present condition. Perhaps we can find some advantages in that."

"Advantages? My own mount and an Amazon battalion tried to murder me!"

"Because they didn't recognize you. But it also sounds like you had changed back just moments before my Summoning spell plucked you out of the air: Ghost was trying to save you."

I rubbed at my nether regions: a horse bite tends to stay with you for a while. "I'm touched."

"In the head," I heard Vashti mutter.

"Speaking of which, what about that thing that jumped me in the datawell?"

Daggoth shrugged. "The Programworlds were designed to be completely safe for all forms of Human interface and they've proved to be deadly. You go poking into unshielded dataspheres where there are no safeguards and you're lucky you can come back with anything beyond a rudimentary brain stem!"

"Point taken," I said, "but this was something independent of the Net. It was autonomous. And it was—familiar."

"Familiar? How?" Vashti wanted to know.

"It's hard to put into words. Impressions, mostly: it knew me, recognized me. And it wanted to destroy me."

"Well, stay out of the datawells," Daggoth grumped. "You'll have to figure some other way of contacting REMrunners or do without."

"No arguments here." I reached up and felt the rounded edges of my ears. "I've got bigger problems to worry about for the time being."

Daggoth patted my shoulder. "We'll keep an eye on your condition, and with more information, we may be able to effect a cure. But there are a couple of things we can do about it in the meantime." He turned and left the room.

Vashti shoved the coffee right back at me. "We can start on solving the problem of your body just as soon as we solve the problem with his." She jerked a thumb at Morpheus who had materialized while I wasn't watching.

"I don't want this," I said, pushing the coffee back at her.

"You'll need it," she argued.

"I don't need coffee, I need sleep."

"You can sleep all you want after you help dig up my body," Morpheus growled.

"It won't take long," Vashti added. "Your help will cut the time in half."

I looked down at the remains of Daggoth's dressing robe. "I'm not really dressed for any nocturnal excursions."

Daggoth returned with a bundle of clothing. "Here," he said. "I've used some spells to modify your boots, gear, and clothing. It should expand or contract to fit you comfortably at either scale: Human or Half Elven."

"You're kidding."

He smiled. "I like to think of the material's new properties as something akin to sorcerous spandex."

Vashti grinned.

Morpheus smirked.

I groaned and reached for the coffee.

# \RIPLEY\PATH\DELTA    (Δ)

Cephtronics had a policy about programming the various Dreamworlds to cater to one's fantasies on a number of levels— and sex was certainly not given short shrift. But Riplakish suspected Thetis was coming along more out of boredom than out of program-enhanced libido. At least, he hoped so.

True to his word, Nereus had provided them with mounts.

Riplakish and Thetis rode giant seahorses with saddles. Ethyl the Merman provided his own locomotion through the water as they headed toward Ortygia.

They traveled for nearly an hour without incident. The undersea scenery was enchanting and he resisted the urge to ask "Are we there yet?" at least a half-dozen times.

Then, suddenly, they were passing over broken spars and the shattered remains of ship hulls scattered across the ocean floor. Ethyl slowed and took new bearings while Riplakish dismounted and began examining the sea chests of one of the more recent wrecks. Most of the rotting wooden chests contained the usual fare: gold doubloons, pistoles, pieces of eight, gems, jewelry, bars of silver. It was a while before he got lucky.

Ethyl swam down as the Half Elf sorted through a trunk of clothing.

"What's up?" he asked, trying on a pair of purple pantaloons.

"The Isle of the Sirens lies ahead and methinks Thetis would rather give it wide berth," the Merman answered. " 'Tis your safety that concerns her."

Pantaloons, as a rule, can never be said to truly "fit" under the best of circumstances and underwater, well . . . "How wide a berth?" Ripley asked, trying to contain the billowing material with a belt.

Ethyl allowed that a ten-mile detour might not permit a reasonable safety margin. Perhaps twenty?

As a Bard Ripley was tempted to pay a professional courtesy call on the ladies, but he also figured it would be in his best interests to see the Sibyl as soon as possible. As a compromise, he convinced the Merman that they could pass by the islet safely by staying underwater. The belt—actually a "Sam Browne" affair with a couple of shoulder braces crossing his chest from right to left—made the pantaloons a second working "compromise."

The first compromise lasted to the other side of the island when, glancing up, they saw the underside of a small ship headed directly for the rocks.

"Up, Seabiscuit!" Riplakish kicked his mount in the sides and spurred him toward the surface.

It was a small, twin-masted ketch with gaff-and-topsail rigs and some of the Sirens had just reached it. Only Peisinoë enjoyed fully Human form so she was left back on the rocks to persuade the sailors in closer to shore. Agalaophone's and Thelxepeia's Human attributes ended at the bustline: from there on down they possessed the wings and bodies of large birds. They were settling down on the boom and rigging even as Ripley urged the great seahorse forward. Molpe and Parthenope retained their Human forms to their waists; the rest was a great fishtail like Ethyl's. The ketch was small and set low enough in the water for them to grasp the railing and pull themselves up onto the side.

Before he could get close enough to intervene, the Sirens' song began to falter. A second later, Parthenope pitched back over the side.

Thelxepeia suffered a splashdown just as he reined up alongside. By now the song had turned into an operatic nightmare of shrieks and moans. The Half Elf hauled himself up and over the side just in time to watch Molpe leap off the prow and back into the sea.

She was assisted in her trajectory by a large skillet applied to her backside. He started to laugh but stopped when the skillet's wielder turned and glared at him.

To all appearances, he was about to be braced by a large Human female. Towering over him by at least a foot, she was beyond Junoesque, she was majestic, and she moved with an easy grace that belied her size. Her long black hair held subtle touches of grey but her face showed no indications of age or weakness. Dark eyes accentuated her scowl and she roared (yes, "roared"): "Get the hell off my boat, you stinking sea scum, or I'll bash your brainless skulls in!" She started advancing on him and he held his hand up.

*"Hold it,"* he said.

She stopped. For the next sixty seconds she wouldn't be able to move, but after that, all bets were off. It wasn't much of a spell, but he found it reassuring that he was still able to throw a little magic around.

"I'm one of the good guys. I'm here to rescue you." He looked up at Agalaophone who was hopping about nervously in the rigging. "Better write this one off to experience, Aggie. And, next time, stick to ships with all-male crews."

"Sure thing, Rip." She flapped up into the sky. "We didn't

know this one was under your protection." She circled to make sure her fellow Sirens were treading water and then flew back to the island.

"Ho, Thetis!" Ethyl's shaggy head popped up above the starboard gunwale. "Did I not tell you that he was one of the Makers?"

"What I want to know," the Sea Nymph said haughtily, "is just how well he knows those—hussies!" She sat herself down on a crate and began combing out her long golden hair.

Gently disengaging the iron frying pan from the woman's fingers, he assisted her to another crate as the spell wore off. "Allow me to introduce myself," he said, helping her sit, "I'm Riplakish of Dyrinwall and these are my compatriots: Thetis and Ethyl."

"Elsbeth," she returned. "And those two sorry sacks of sea fodder are the Count Louis Costellino and the abbot—I don't know the rest of his name; I don't think he's picked one, yet."

"Picked one yet?" Riplakish looked over at the two men sprawled unconscious on the deck. He could see the goose-egg lumps adorning their pates from ten feet away.

The Merman whistled. "A first! I have never known the Sirens to use physical force before!"

Elsbeth barked a short, humorless laugh. "I did that, fishman. With my cast-iron fry pan. If I hadn't, they'd have had this boat on the rocks ten minutes ago."

The Half Elf smiled. "Good thing they've got an experienced traveler with them."

She scowled as the count groaned and began to stir. "That's part of the problem, Dr. Ripley." She glared at the count as he began to snore. "This is my first trip into a Programworld. *They're* supposed to be my *guides!*"

# \RIPLEY\PATH\SIGMA    (Σ)

His body is as insubstantial as a ghost's.

He notices it now as the eastern sky begins to flush a slight pink. No bramble scratches, no stone bruises, no discomfort from the night's activities. Looking down, he can see the grass beneath his feet, through his feet. Suddenly light-headed, he leans up against the trunk for support and falls right through.

Inside, he finds himself on hands and knees at the foot of the great spiral staircase. There is a patina of dust on the hardwood floor and he wonders why he doesn't sink through the floor, as well. As soon as he contemplates that, it seems a potentially dangerous concept and he quickly puts it out of his head. He crosses mental fingers as he gets up, hoping that the universe wasn't listening in on his thoughts.

Perhaps it was. As he ascends the staircase, his feet tend to sink through the risers and his progress is something akin to climbing a snowdrift.

He finds that, by concentrating, he can keep from sinking through the floors on the upper levels. It takes a continuous effort, though. He discovers that much after trying to sit in a chair dropping three stories, "seat" first.

The tree is deserted, and if the layers of dust in each room are to be trusted, it has been unoccupied for quite some time.

His headache is back by the time the sun has crept over the horizon. An hour of prolonged concentration has sapped his mental faculties and when he wearily sits on the edge of the bed, he fails to notice the feathered tick giving beneath his weight, the rope webbing beneath making little sounds of protest.

*What has happened to him?* he wonders. *And what had happened at Misty Dawn's grave?* Dulled by progressive shocks and the strain of maintaining his corporeal equilibrium, his mind surrenders to the fuzziness of exhaustion.

He lies back upon the bed and sleeps.

Hours pass. The sun makes its day-long passage across the sky. As it hesitates on the western horizon, he awakens to the sense of not being alone.

He opens his eyes to find Misty Dawn bending over him.

And it is very obvious that she is dead.

**DATALOG:   \QUEBEDEAUX-
A.5\PERSONAL\20200805
*Voice Dictation*
***FILE ENCRYPTION ON***

Theoretically it's possible for a Dreamwalker to be two places at once.
*
In fact, Mike Straeker tried it a couple of times, doing a memory download into two different avatars in two different Programworlds.
*
He figured that when it was over, his brain would ignore the coincidental timelines and recall the two simultaneous experiences as having taken place at two different times as well as in two different places.
*
Sort of like remembering that last year you spent Christmas in the Rockies and the Fourth of July on the beach.
*
But it didn't work out that way.

*

Straeker suffered severe disorientation for weeks following the twin experience, and his headaches lasted for months.

*

He mentioned once, toward the end, that it was possible that the experience altered his brain chemistry and triggered the tumor that eventually killed him.

*

Which raises a very disturbing question as I monitor Ripley's multiple code-strings. . . .

*

If there's a dangerous disorientation factor to being in two avatars in two unrelated Program environments. . . .

*

What happens to someone who inhabits more than one body in the same environment?

*

Wouldn't the multiple perspectives be even more disorienting once you were reintegrated?

*

None of us are fixed personalities: we continue to change, develop, hopefully grow as we age.

*

We progress through a multitude of experiences, day by day, hour by hour, minute by minute.

*

And we are, in some respects, the sum of those experiences.

*

I am not the same person that I was last week: I am subtly different, because of what I have experienced since then.

*

Less noticeably, I am not the same person that I was yesterday . . .

*

Or an hour ago . . .

*

Or a minute?

*

So the question is, can the various personas—all of whom must develop in subtly—or not so subtly—different ways . . .

\*
Can they be reintegrated when Ripley disconnects?
\*
Without killing him?
\*
Or destroying his sanity, at the very least?
\*
I'm very much afraid that Robert Ripley is already dead and
he just doesn't know it, yet. . . .

# Chapter
## Six

★

## \RIPLEY\PATH\GAMMA     (Γ)

IF my so-called lycanthropy was tied to the night, it apparently had no lunar connections. Both moons were in new and first-quarter phases tonight and we drove a rented wagon carefully in the dark, unsure of the road. We reached a field where Morpheus bade us dismount and stumbled around awhile longer on foot.

"Here."

"You're sure?" I asked.

The ghostly apparition of Morpheus nodded. "I'm sure."

I held the lantern high and scanned our surroundings. "Don't see any markers."

Daggoth was already working his shovel into the dark earth. "You don't put up any markers when you bury a body in unconsecrated ground," he grunted.

I handed the lantern to Vashti and set my spade to work beside Daggoth's. "Thought you were supposed to be planted at the center of a crossroads or some sort of hoo-haw like that."

"Vampires."

"Where?" yelped Vashti.

"You bury vampires at crossroads," elaborated Morpheus.

"I don't."

"Don't what?" inquired Daggoth, digging a little faster.

"Bury vampires," I answered, trying to match his speed.

"What do you do with them?" my ex asked.

"Nothing to date," I said. Daggoth was picking up more dirt per shovel-load, now. What was this? Some kind of contest?

"I wouldn't date one either," the sorcerer quipped. Vashti giggled and I clamped down on a frown: Stephanie had never shown any affinity for my sophisticated humor and here she was giggling like a schoolgirl over a stupid line like that.

Come to think of it, she'd been acting pretty strange since I'd arrived on the scene this morning.

I knew that Daggoth had given her sanctuary these past six months but dammitall, she was acting like they'd been sharing quarters or something.

"Could I have a little more light?" I asked curtly. Vashti swung the lantern a bit in my direction and I noticed that Daggoth's pile of dirt was bigger than mine. Maybe I was lacking some enthusiasm for this little project, but you could also argue that he was putting a little more effort into it than necessary.

Like he was showing off or something.

The hole was deepening and Vashti had to move in for us to see where to place the blades of our shovels.

"This part of the ritual or something—digging at midnight?" I asked.

Daggoth shook his head. "Just safer," he grunted.

"Safer? Digging up an unconsecrated burial ground at midnight is safer?"

"Less trouble," he amended. "Can't get a medieval court order to exhume the body. And evil sorcerers are sometimes less popular dead than alive."

A mental light bulb clicked on: "Son of a *Lich*."

"Exactly." His shovel suddenly went "thunk." It sounded like wood.

"Not very deep," Morpheus observed.

I gave him the raised eyebrow but the effect was lost at the edge of the lamplight. "You really care how deep once you're dead?"

"I, for one, am glad," Daggoth puffed.

I'll bet. If he was showing off, it was taking its toll.

It took only a few more minutes to finish excavating the

plain wooden coffin and wrestle it up out of the hole. Even in the pale illumination it was obvious that we wouldn't need a prybar. Daggoth hooked his fingers around the edges and pulled off the pinewood top.

I'd always thought I had respect for the dead. But that didn't stop me from putting my finger, gunny style, into Morpheus's noncorporeal ribs. "Stick 'em up," I said, "you've been grave-robbed."

Γ

You know what every mother says when her child has mislaid something and can't find it: Well, it just didn't get up and walk off. Well, in Fantasyworld dead bodies occasionally did just that. So I didn't say it. Especially since Morpheus was in such a snit.

Mercifully, he decided that he needed some time alone and disappeared as we unhitched the wagon back at Daggoth's Tower. Lose your body and you can't be much more alone than that, I thought, watching him fade. "So now what do we do?"

Daggoth scratched at his beard. "I could start scrying the crystal and mirror networks, but that could take days—weeks, maybe—and with no guarantees. . . ."

"I know a couple of Necrophiles I could lean on," Vashti suggested. "Maybe one of them could provide us with a lead."

"What?" we both chorused.

"Absolutely not!" Daggoth added.

"What kind of people have you been hanging out with while I was gone?" I demanded. I turned to Dreamland's former Chief of Programming. "You said you'd been looking after her!"

She put her hands on her hips and settled into a stance that after seven years of stormy wedlock I knew only too well. Apparently Daggoth had experienced it, too: we both shut up.

"First of all," she hissed, "I am not married to either of you. And even if I were, that would not make me property or chattel to be ordered about. I do have a mind of my own and I can take care of myself—frequently better than either of you. And secondly," she finally permitted herself a small smile, "I have an advantage: necros won't mess with you as long as you're alive."

"As long as," I echoed.

Daggoth shrugged in resignation. "Yudu," he sighed.

"Do what?" I asked.

"Voodoo," answered Vashti.

"I do not."

"But the Zombie Master does," Daggoth countered, "and that's why we should go talk to him."

"To whom?"

"Yudu."

"Do wha—; wait a minute, this is a name, right?"

Vashti nodded. "The Zombie Master."

"And his name is Yoodoo?"

Daggoth nodded. "Yudu," he affirmed.

"And he's the top necromancer in these parts?" I had a strong feeling that I was being set up but the question came tumbling out before I could stop it.

"Of course." Vashti's voice was matter-of-fact. "After all: who do that voodoo that Yudu so well?"

There was no point in trying to pursue a serious line of inquiry while they were in this mood so I left them there, cackling like a couple of demented grave-diggers, and went up to bed.

My transformation come sunrise wasn't nearly as traumatic as before because Daggoth had supplied me with an herbal analgesic that counteracted most of the discomfort. The main ingredient, however, was Elvish parsley that had the uncomfortable side effect of making my upper lip curl for about a half hour after each dose.

Daggoth's thaumaturgic tailor-work seemed to be working so far, and after dressing, I rehitched the wagon. When I went down to the basement stables, Ghost seemed genuinely glad to see me. I saddled him without incident as my avatar was in its familiar Half-Elven phase, but made a mental note to have him restabled before sunset. Until my avatar was cured of its nocturnal shapeshifting, night rides were out of the question.

I tethered the glamoured pegasus behind the wagon as I drove through the tunnel that led from the underground stables to the base of the hill about a mile behind Daggoth's Tower. After securing the gate and recamouflaging the entryway, I drove on into Calabastor. I returned the wagon to the Teamsters' Guild without incident, then mounted Ghost and rode over to Fogherty's Cove.

The tavern was one of the better-kept secrets on the waterfront. (The "best"-kept secrets were the contents of certain mob-controlled warehouses and the number of unfortunates who had gone swimming at night in concrete buskins.) Tourists usually came down to the docks to sample the seafood but Fogherty's catered to the fishermen and old salts who had had their fill of water-spawned menus: steaks and mountain oysters were the specialties here.

Stan was a stout, cherubic man with a deep voice and a fringe of curly brown hair that ran around the sides of his head and down the sides of his boyish face to meet under his chin. Both his pate and his upper lip were as bare as a baby's behind and, I'll swear to this in any court, he had eyes that actually twinkled.

But they weren't twinkling after he looked up from his post behind the great mahogany bar and saw me coming through the swinging doors. He wasn't officially open for business yet, and the place was devoid of customers. That suited me fine. He looked less than pleased with his first customer of the day.

I wound my way through a maze of empty tables and planted myself at the far end of the bar so that my back was to a wall and not the front entrance. Stan hurried over with a glass of ice and a bottle of Dr Pepper. "What do you need to know?" he asked as he poured my drink.

I was disappointed. "That's not how it's supposed to work, Stan," I chided. "I come in here, order a drink, and ask 'how's business?' We make small talk and after a couple of drinks I start asking some general questions and you become somewhat evasive. Then I flash some money and alternate that with some vague threats. Then we haggle—"

"Just ask your questions and I'll answer them as best I can while you're finishing your drink. That way you can be on your way in no time."

I frowned and took a sip. "You're taking all the fun out of this."

He leaned across the bar and pointed the bottle in my face. "Look, Riplakish, I like you. You're a nice person. And nice people are increasingly hard to come by, these days. When I heard you was dead, I was genuinely sorry. And I'm glad to see it's not so. . . ." He paused and looked me up and down. "It's not so, is it?"

"It's not so."

He smiled. "Good." And then he went back to frowning. "But you draw trouble like a lodestone. The last two times you was in here I had to replace half the furniture and two wall-length mirrors. Hakim told me that you nearly totaled The Roaring Hangman last year when you mixed it up with a wizard, a Dragon, and a couple of Demons—"

"There was only one Demoness and the Dragon wasn't anywhere near the place," I protested.

"I don't care if it was a couple of pixies and a talking frog," he insisted. "The bottom line is whenever you walk into any kind of a drinking establishment, in full defiance of the fact that you're a complete teetotaler, some form of mayhem results before you leave the premises. So ask your questions, drink your drink, and good luck and gods' speed in whatever quest you're on this week."

I sighed and took over the bottle. There was no point in being surly over someone's willingness to answer questions. "Know anybody who'd be involved in digging up dead bodies?"

"You mean besides several dozen Ghouls and Necros that haunt the marsh north of town?"

"Yeah. I don't think this was that kind of snatch."

He pondered a moment. "Well, there's always the Necromancer."

"Yudu?"

"Not me. I'm not into that kind of stuff."

"Not you!" I was losing my patience more rapidly than usual.

"Then who do that voodoo?"

"Now cut that out!" I brandished the Dr Pepper bottle in my best menacing manner. "Answer my questions or I'll up the ante to three mirrors and camp out here for the rest of the week!"

"Yudu, the Necromancer," he answered with a seemingly straight but strained face.

"Anybody else come to mind?"

"There's a Dr. Franklyn Stein who, I'm told, uses cadavers for medical research."

"Goes out and digs them up at night, eh?"

The bartender shook his head. "Dr. Stein is one of those

white-gloved gentlemen who contracts work of that sort from independent vendors.''

''I don't suppose you could provide me with the names of some of those 'vendors'?''

He sighed. ''Anything to get you out of here before trouble arrives.''

I smiled.

''His main man is an old Notre Dame pro. Wound up at the bottom of too many pile-ons,'' Stan tapped the side of his head, ''and now he's only good for simple tasks—''

''Like robbing graves in the dead of night,'' I interjected.

''It's a shame really.'' He sighed. ''This Quasimodo guy was one of the greatest backfield men the Hoosiers have ever produced.''

I snapped my fingers. ''I know who you're talking about: the Halfback of Notre Dame!'' I shook my head. ''Damn, he was great!''

We were reminiscing about how he used to climb on top of the goalposts and throw things down at the opposing team when the unoiled hinges on the tavern doors announced company.

''We ain't open for—'' Stan stopped and the color drained from his face.

I turned and considered the two figures that were crowding the doorway of Stan's: a man and his dog. Except the man had a toothed beak instead of a mouth, the dog had two heads, and each had taloned appendages at the end of their limbs and two pairs of wings apiece.

''Rriippllaakkiisshh,'' the dog-thing hissed. Its two heads weren't quite in sync.

''This is just the sort of thing I was complaining about,'' moaned Stan as he ducked below the level of the bar.

''Who wants to know?'' I returned as belligerently as possible. When dealing with Demons, the value of intimidation should never be underestimated.

''Nergal wants you,'' was the beak-man's answer as they walked to the center of the common room.

It took me a second to run the mental reference: Nergal was the Assyro-Babylonian Demigod of Pestilence and the Dead. I just looked at them. Finally, I said: ''So?''

The dog-thing rumbled a growl in its twin throats and the beak-man sucked in air, making a high-pitched whistling sound. It sounded like someone abusing a bad stereo system: a pair of cracked woofers and feedback on the tweeter. My response, in turn, was to lay a hand on the hilt of my *katana*-longsword.

Beak-face smiled and the two-headed wonder dog started forward.

I unsheathed Caladbolg and they stopped. Smiling and moving. Mesopotamian Demons might not know anything of the ancient Celts or the Sidhe, but the translucent crystal blade surrounded by a blue glow spoke a universal language that any pantheon could understand at first glance.

"Stan my man," I murmured over the bar, "I want a bottle of the hardest rotgut you've got. Two hundred proof."

"But you don't—" began the disembodied voice.

"I want it now!" I insisted, sliding off the bar stool.

A hand clutching a disreputable-looking bottle appeared from the nether regions of the bartender's walk. "It's only one-ninety proof," he apologized, "I use it to sterilize the glasses."

I pulled the cork from the bottle with my teeth. That was taste enough to tell me I had what I wanted. To be sure of its volatility, I made a couple of passes over the container and murmured what I hoped was an appropriate spell.

"He don't look so tough," I heard one of them whisper. "Why don't we just take him and get it over with?"

"Nneerrggaall ccoommmmaannddss," was the murmured response, "wwee oobbeeyy."

The muttered comeback was even lower but sounded suspiciously like: "Nergal still has an eight-track in his Chariot of Judgment!"

"Hhiissssssstt!"

I got up with the bottle dangling from my left hand and Caladbolg clutched in my right.

"First of all," I announced, "introductions are in order. You know who I am." As I walked in their direction, I tilted the bottle so that a thin stream dribbled onto the floor. "Who are you?"

Bowser spoke first: "Nnaammttaarruu."

Ah, that made sense. Namtaru: god of the plague. *He who crouches by Nergal.*

"Idpa," answered the other.

*Pestilence.* It had been ten years since my doctoral research on comparative world mythologies but I remembered these two. I walked past them and felt my shoulder blades twitch. Whenever Nergal sent either of these two out, it was against whole cities or armies. The results were always unhealthy on a large scale.

I stopped and turned, judging my angle. "So, what do you want?" I tipped the bottle and began walking in a new direction. Once again I was careful to keep the right side of my body turned toward them where the focus of their attention would be on the enchanted sword.

Not on the bottle of magically enhanced bad whiskey dribbling out its contents, concealed behind my left leg.

"Yyoouu," snapped both dog-heads at once. Idpa merely nodded.

"Mitox!" I grunted, taking that Persian Demon's name in vain. "When was the last time you clowns ever picked a solo target?"

"Nergal orders. We obey." Idpa was obviously impressed by Caladbolg: he seemed to be giving the blue glow a great deal of attention. I walked past them and turned back again, hoping they weren't watching my eyes as I reconfigured my track.

"Could you gentlemen *please* take it outside?" wailed the bartender's disembodied voice.

"In a moment, Stan," I called back as I crossed the line of my first pass. "I want to find out a little more before I decide whether or not to go along with Nergal's hit men."

My quarry was now encompassed by three lines of rotgut forming a scalene triangle. I didn't know what condition ol' Nergie had ordered me fetched in, but, so far, they seemed willing to wait a few more minutes to see if I'd come along quietly.

"So what does Meshlamthea want with me, guys?" I turned again, trying to hurry before the alcohol began to evaporate. "Or is this Ereshkigal's idea?"

That rocked them. In fact, Idpa looked more than a little nonplussed—he looked a couple of degrees to the minus side.

"Nneerrggaall ssaayyss—"

"Please!" I gestured at Namtaru with the sword. "One at a

time! It's not only impolite, but the two of you are giving me a headache.''

Namtaru's heads looked at each other and seemed to come to a decision. "Nergal says that he has prepared a place of honor for you," growled the head on the right. The head on the left added: "He says it is time for you to come to him."

Nice. The actual place-name for Nergal's domain escaped me for the moment, but translated it meant variously "the house from which he who enters does not come out," "the dwelling-place of the shadows," and "the land of no return." Basically: Babylonian Abaddon.

I turned for the last leg of my pattern. "Tell laughing boy 'thanks, but no thanks.' My dance card is full."

The whiskey bottle went glug and the Demons suddenly noticed my geometric spillage.

Just in time I sprinted across two angled lines and closed the pentagram at its starting point. A snap of my fingers and the whiskey blazed up as a fiery star as the high alcohol content ignited. "Begone, foul fiends!" I cried. "Back to—to—" *Damn, what was the name of Mesopotamian Hell?*

Idpa shook his head. Namtaru growled menacingly. Already the flames were starting to die down.

"Uh, go to Hell! Go directly to Hell; do not pass go, do not collect two hundred dollars!" It had worked on Yakku and Ahuizotl last year—without the benefit of any additional fireworks.

It wasn't working now.

The flames were almost out, now. "This is your last warning: Beat it! Scram! Vamoose!"

Two Demons with three smiles were not an encouraging sight.

"Okay, boys, then we do it the hard way." I brought Caladbolg up and then raised it over my head, the blade pointed straight up.

"*I have the power!*" I yelled.

I caught a glimpse of smiles turned to rictuses (ricti?) of terror and then they were gone in twin puffs of smoke.

Demons can be such pantywaists when they're off their own turf.

"You can come out now, Stan." I lowered my sword.

There was a whizzing sound and a dagger suddenly buried itself in the wall behind my head. Stan ducked back down as I whirled around. A cloaked figure was disappearing out the doorway.

"From now on, Riplakish, it's take-out only," groused the unseen bartender as I launched myself across the room. I reached the doorway just in time to see a black-clad runner duck between two buildings down the street.

Avatar memories clicked into place as I dodged a horse-drawn coach and continued my pursuit: whether by accident or design, my assailant had chosen a dead-end alley for his escape route. That meant somebody was going to be trapped.

I wanted to make sure it wasn't me.

I hesitated at the entrance, resting my left hand on the hilt of my *wakizashi*-shortsword. The passageway was too narrow for *Niten Ryu*; I sheathed the Elven longsword and drew the Dwarven blade.

The alley was dark and narrow. I advanced cautiously, looking upward every few steps. If this was a setup and my knife-thrower had friends, the ambush would most likely come from above: close confines discouraged group activities.

I edged my way forward, Balmung held out before me. The reddish glow from the enchanted metal gave little illumination in the half twilight of the buildings' shadows and it was a sudden, small flicker of flame at the end of the alley that told me the chase was done. I sheathed my weapon and walked up to the number-three blade of Calabastor's new Assassins' Guild.

Rune was a tall, angular woman with dark hair and eyes and a personality to match. Not that she was unpleasant—unless you were targeted by one of her clients, that is. It was just that there was this sense of emptiness when you were standing next to her, a dark silence as if her body were a black hole, absorbing all light and sound in the room.

"If you wanted to get my attention, there are better ways," I said, folding my arms.

"Wasn't me." She shifted the hand-rolled cigarette to the other side of her mouth. "Though I was coming to get you."

"Get me?" Perhaps I had sheathed my blade a bit prematurely.

"Mercy wants you."

I relaxed but didn't feel a whole lot better. "So if you're not a dagger short, who is?"

She took the cigarette out of her mouth and flicked ashes on a dark shape crumpled at her feet. "Recognize this?"

It was a body but I had to cast a Light spell to make any further judgments. I took in the black leather clothing, the spiky, multicolored mohawk. . . .

"I think you've got yourself a serious problem, Rip," she said as she turned the body over with her toe.

. . . the hilt of Rune's dagger protruding from the corpse's chest, the cranial implants, and, last but not least, the mirrorshades.

I began to swear softly but quite distinctly.

A Cyberpunk.


# \RIPLEY\PATH\DELTA     (Δ)

". . . so I paid these two handsomely to smuggle me through the datanet and into Dreamworlds."

"To do an article on REMrunners?" Riplakish shook his head. "You didn't have to take this kind of a risk for your research."

She smiled tightly. "I research all my stories thoroughly, Dr. Ripley. If those Sirens hadn't got me all worked up, I would've known your avatar immediately."

Carefully, the count sat up and rubbed his head. It had been more than an hour since the Isle of the Sirens had been left behind and yet the abbot continued to snore.

"Besides the Pulitzer potential of an exposé on REMrunners, there's the bigger story of the Dreamworlds quarantine, itself. For that information, I had to get inside."

In trying to get to his feet, Costellino stumbled over the abbot's body. Twice. The short, pudgy priest stirred a bit. And then continued to snore.

"It's too damn dangerous!" the Half Elf told her. "The Programworlds have remained closed to the public because the Anomaly isn't fixed, yet!"

She cocked an eyebrow. "So, what are you doing here?"

"Trying to fix it."

"Yeah? I see a guy playing pirate, running about with a naked Sea Nymph." This time her smile had teeth.

The count had located a nearby bucket and was headed back toward the abbot with a purposeful look in his eye.

Riplakish nodded at Ethyl. "Don't worry about us, we've got a chaperon."

There was a sound of splashing water and a gurgling scream: "Cossttelllinnooooo!"

Riplakish took in the moronic tableau. "Haven't they got it reversed?"

"What?"

"Isn't the tall one supposed to be—I mean, their names— the short one was really—" He paused and shook his head.

"What are you talking about?"

The count wandered over to talk to Thetis while the abbot sputtered and began wringing out his robe.

"Never mind. Just a misplaced association—I think." Riplakish took her hands in his. "Elsbeth, trust me on this: every hour that goes by here increases the chance of you getting seriously hurt or killed. The Anomaly makes dying here as big a reality as it is in the outside world."

"They don't believe that," she said, indicating her two fellow REMrunners with a jerk of her head.

" 'They' are fools and will very likely prove my point by getting you killed before the day is over."

This time their conversation was interrupted by the sound of a slap and they turned in time to watch the count land on his keister while Thetis coolly examined her fingernails for signs of chipped polish.

"Hey, babe," he protested, rubbing the red weal rising on his cheek, "if you don't want it, you shouldn't go around dressed like that!"

Elsbeth turned back to Ripley. *"Get me outta here!"*

"Land ho!" called Ethyl.

"Ortygia!" cried Thetis.

They went to the prow and looked out across the water. Ahead, growing steadily as the ketch skimmed across the waves, was the Isle of Ortygia.

It had been years—in game time, at least—since Riplakish had last visited the Sibyl in her island grotto. The memories came back now: he had been younger, then—newer to the

Program—but good times dominated his recall. The Sea Nymph Calypso had ferried him over on her ship *Cousteau* and they had spent an idyllic two weeks, cruising the Ionian Sea. That's when he had first met the Sirens—

Thetis had family here, as well. Her sister, Arethusa, had been pursued by Alpheius the hunter. Unwilling to succumb to his forceful advances, she had taken refuge on Ortygia and the gods (Greek pantheon here, of course), heeding her pleas for help, changed her into a spring.

Alpheius, so the story went, was inconsolable. He hung around the neighborhood of Olympus, mooning, until the gods took pity on him and changed him into a river. Legend said his waters crossed the sea without mixing with it and joined the waters of Arethusa on Ortygia. If there was a point to any of this it was Greek gods had real strange concepts about helping out and Riplakish had made it a point to never ask any of them for a favor.

As they sailed closer, their attention was drawn to a strange cloud formation that hovered just over the tiny island. Elsbeth brought out a telescoping spyglass and studied the phenomenon for several minutes before handing it over to the Half Elf. "What do you make of it?"

He stared through the tube for an even longer period of time.

"Well?"

"Flying saucer," he sighed, collapsing the spyglass back into a compact cylinder. "It looks like a dead ringer for the spaceship in *Forbidden Planet*."

"Excuse me?"

"*Forbidden Planet* was a mid-twentieth century film: color, two-D, flat-screen projection. It was sort of a science fiction retelling of Shakespeare's *The Tempest*." He passed the cylinder back to Elsbeth. "This thing looks just like the flying saucer in the movie."

Elsbeth pulled out a handpad and began tapping in notes. "Can't be a spaceship here, though. Maybe a chariot of the gods?"

The Bard looked doubtful. "More likely a Frisbee of the Frost Giants. Or maybe a hubcap of Hades. Look, Elsbeth, one of the side effects of the Anomaly is that various Programworlds are gaining access to one another. In fact, the Master Program is accessing outside file sources and integrating nonrelated material into the various milieus. This," he gestured at the hovering disk, "is just one example."

"Well, is the effect totally random? Or is there a method to this madness? I mean, why a flying saucer here?" she asked.

"Dunno. Maybe this is what the Sibyl wants to see me about."

Elsbeth opened her mouth to speak but the abbot beat her to it. "Surfer Dudes," he yelled, pointing in the opposite direction.

An antique submarine conning tower had surfaced a half mile off the starboard side, and as they came to the rail to watch, four surfers were closing the distance between the two vessels.

"I've got a bad feeling about this," murmured Riplakish.

"Are those helmets that they're wearing?" queried Thetis.

"Methinks they come bearing weapons," called Ethyl.

"This is a strange custom," wondered Thetis. "Serfs permitted to bear arms."

"Serfs surfing," the Half Elf muttered.

"Something even stranger," observed Elsbeth, unlimbering the spyglass as the boards drew closer. "They're wearing some sort of uniform. Dr. Ripley, you're the one with a specialty in history—"

"History is just a hobby," he replied, taking the telescope in hand. "My specialty is mythology. But those outfits look like mid-twentieth-century costumes."

"World War Two?"

He nodded, giving them careful scrutiny through the glass. "German, I think. . . ."

"Nazis?" Elsbeth grabbed his sleeve. "Nazis on surfboards?"

His reply was drowned out by the thunder of Sten guns opening up in a fatal volley of lead.

# \RIPLEY\PATH\SIGMA     ($\Sigma$)

The setting sun casts roseate beams through an open bole in the wall of the tree. The shafts of light transfix a portion of her left leg and torso, dissolving those portions of her anatomy into nothingness. The rest seems not far behind.

"You—you're a ghost!" he whispers.

"What are you doing here?" is her less-than-amiable response. Her frown is the most substantial thing about her.

"What?"

"By what right do you violate the Archdruid's sanctuary?" Her countenance grows threatening. "Who are you to trespass here and sleep upon his bed?"

He feels curiously light-headed but forces himself to sit up. One of the fading sunbeams strikes his eyes and momentarily dazzles him. There is a wrenching sensation, a sudden feeling of turning inside-out. "I—"

"*Oh!* My lord!" she cries. And throws herself upon him.

That does it: insubstantial, they both fall through the bed and plummet six stories, into the root cellar. What should be an awful impact against the packed earthen floor is a sudden dead stop that defies Newtonian laws of motion and thumbs its incorporeal nose at inertia. Surviving an eighty-foot fall is simple compared to disentangling himself from a suddenly amorous Nymph. A ghostly one, at that.

"My Lord Riplakish! Forgive me!" She is smothering his face with tangible kisses. (How does she do that?) "I did not recognize thee! Thou seemst a stranger when first I happened upon thee!"

"Uh," is all he can manage to get in edgewise. Her kisses are distracting: her lips, her hands, her body, are the first substantial things he has encountered, so far.

"Thou hast been gone so long that I feared for thee! I have waited and—" She stops and her eyes widen. "But this is the first time that thou hast been able to see me!" Now her eyes fill with horror and she presses a fist to her mouth. "Thou—thou art—*dead!*"

"Uh," is all he could think of in answer to this new concept.

"Oh, my love!" she moans. "How did it happen? In what manner didst thou meet thy doom?"

"Doom?"

"Oh," she wails, "this is terrible! First, my body is stolen from its final rest and now thou'rt dead!" She throws her arms around his neck and begins to sob into his chest.

"Well, I'm not so sure I'm really—" He stops. "Did you say your body was stolen?"

She nods amid the waterworks.

"How stolen? Stolen how?" He shakes his head. "Who stole it?"

"I know not. Save that it is gone." She looks up at him with teary eyes. "Who *would* have done such a thing? And why?"

Since he doesn't know and telling her what he has seen the night before might only upset her more, he steers the conversation in other directions. "Uh, Misty, hon—"

"Yes, my lord?"

"I'm kind of new to this ghost business and I've got a few questions. . . ."

$$\Sigma$$

For all of the dead Nymph's experience over the past year, he isn't able to learn much.

She, like most spirit "haunts," is a nocturnal. That is, she seems to exist only between the hours of sundown and sunup. Misty Dawn fades with the cockcrow and it is to her as if she sleeps until the first star of evening summons her back to nightly existence. She has no idea where her ghostly essence resides during those lost hours and can't even begin to speculate.

Another restriction is her spectral ties to the area surrounding the grove. Most ghosts are restricted to walk the earth on or near the site of their demise. Misty is no exception though her territory in death includes the great oak and several acres of Dyrinwall Forest.

As to their noncorporeal state, she is able to show him that solid objects can be moved or manipulated to some degree. As he has found earlier in climbing the stairs, it takes some serious concentration, but by the time the night is half over he is able to chart the event horizon of most pieces of furniture and move objects under five pounds a short distance.

He might have made faster progress in his acclimatization but Misty Dawn is every bit the amorous Nymph in death that she'd been in life. And he is finding himself more vulnerable to her advances as she is the only object of a reciprocal tactile nature in his currently intangible condition.

They make ghostly love as the moons sleepwalk down the sky and bed beyond the horizon. A cock announces the arrival of another day as he holds her in his arms and she fades in his embrace before she can even say good-bye.

Expecting to return to nothingness, himself, he fights against the urge to panic. He jumps to his feet, casting about for something to do, some distraction, to occupy his mind while he waits.

*I didn't die here, in this file sector of the Matrix*, he suddenly thinks. *I may not be tied to this place, in Dyrinwall, as Misty is.*

The urge to panic metamorphoses into an urge to run, to see if there are territorial boundaries for him before the daylight claims him, too. He dashes for the spiral stairway, knowing that he will probably fade before he is out of sight of the tree, but needing to try anyway. Reaching the bottom, he runs for the door, putting on an extra burst of speed—

And unconsciousness takes him in a blinding burst of pain!

**DATALOG: \QUEBEDEAUX-
A.5\PERSONAL\20200806
*Voice Dictation*
***FILE ENCRYPTION ON*****

Damn!
*
Of the three code-strings I've been able to monitor, one is gone
and the other two are unstable!
*
The fascinating thing about their instability is that they seem
to echo each other in some kind of weird phasing sequence!
*
It's as if they were two images of the same thing—one with a
positive charge or ground, the other with a negative.
*
And every so often, they both change—as if the positive flips
over to negative and the negative to positive.
*
I wonder how that change manifests in Ripley's avatars?
*

I wish I could access more of the Primary Monitoring Systems: under the present restrictions I am unable to determine his exact status.

*

And whether or not there are more than two of him left. . . .

# Chapter
# Seven

★

\RIPLEY\PATH\GAMMA        (Γ)

T HE blindfold irritated me more than it should have. It was, of course, standard procedure for visiting an Assassins' guildhouse: blindfolds guarantee Guild secrets and a visitor's "safe" passage. So, Rune was guiding me through the warren of tunnels beneath the city streets, carefully taking me in circles and doubling back so that I couldn't retrace my steps later.

What made the whole thing ludicrous—and, therefore, irritating—was that Robert R. Ripley the Third had designed all of the guildhouses and placed them and their so-called secret societies into the Program. Patience is not one of my stronger virtues and wading through ankle-deep sewer water was not improving my mood.

I held my tongue, however: this time there was no mob of Maenads to bail me out.

It was the appearance of a Cyberpunk that really bothered me.

My concern went beyond the matter of a thrown dagger and who or what had sicced him on me. The fundamental question was what was a Cyberworld Halfjack doing in the Fantasyworld milieu?

I knew from my last incursion into the Matrix that milieu crossover—once unthinkable—was now a possibility. The first Dreamworlds incident had been precipitated by Senator Hanson's abduction from Frontierworld by Fantasyworld Goblins. And Mike Straeker's Spaceworld avatar had piloted a starship into Fantasyworld to rescue me from a gladiatorial contest and Daggoth the Dark, his Fantasyworld avatar, from imprisonment in his own tower.

But that didn't make a Cyberpunk in a medieval fantasy setting any easier to swallow. . . .

Eventually Rune decided that I was confused enough to be taken up a ladder and through another maze of rooms and staircases, completing a journey that should have taken fifteen minutes instead of an hour and a half.

My blindfold was removed and I found myself in a lavishly furnished room dominated by a large oaken desk. Behind that desk sat a redheaded woman dressed in green leather. She had a winning, dimpled smile and the coldest grey eyes you would ever hope to find in your lifetime.

Standing behind her right shoulder was a tall, thin blade of a man, feeding bits of bloody meat to a falcon perched on the back of her chair. The gobbets of wet flesh were too small to identify, and as my mother always claimed my imagination was too convoluted for my own mental health, I turned my attention to the possible number of emergency exits.

"Hello, Mercy." I wasn't sure if Mercy was her real name or just one of those rare examples of Assassins' humor. "Dix," I added, nodding to the man offering another avian tidbit on the end of his throwing dagger. I allocated a chair near the desk and plopped down casually. "How's tricks?"

"Pretty *grave* from what I hear," she answered. Then smiled more broadly: "How about a song?"

I frowned. "A song?"

"Yeah. You're the bard; how about 'I ain't got no *body*'?"

"Oh," I said. "You're funny," I said. "Real. Funny."

"I know; sometimes I just *kill* myself!"

"Yeah? Well, if you're applying for court jester, don't quit your night job just yet." I have two rules when dealing with Assassins' Guilds: never show fear and don't push your luck. Obviously, I was walking a very fine line between the two.

I waited until she worked through a fresh batch of chuckles.

Dix smiled but said nothing, continuing to feed the bird with a disquieting single-mindedness.

"Now, to what do I owe this . . ." I held the word out at arm's length and regarded it with suspicion, ". . . pleasure?"

"A favor."

"You want a favor?"

She shook her head. "You done me a favor last year when you and those Maenads closed down the old guildhall on the east side. Those old farts wouldn't even consider letting a woman in at the Bravo level, much less allow any in leadership positions. Now, I owe all this"—her gesture took in the ornate office and beyond—"in part, to you. I figure it's about time I evened the score."

She stood and I swallowed. When Assassins talk about evening scores, one is inclined to put financial affairs in order, complete unfinished projects quickly, and leave detailed instructions as to the disposal of one's estate.

"Come."

I got up and followed her to the bookcase behind her desk. She twisted a candle in a wall sconce and the bookcase swung away from the wall, revealing a secret passage.

"This wise without the blindfold?" Dix inquired with a chilling mildness.

Mercy swung her grey gaze on me for a long and measured moment. "Where are we?"

The smart money was on feigning ignorance.

"Granary warehouse on Bleeker Street, two blocks from Dorn's Wharf," I answered after reflecting that it rarely paid to lie to an Assassin and never to a woman.

"So much for blindfolds," Rune murmured.

Dix looked even more threateningly thoughtful.

The redheaded Guildmaster kept her face and voice carefully neutral: "The only people who know the location of her guildhall are dead or Guildmembers."

"Well, gee-whiz," I said after a pregnant pause that had gone to full term and was starting labor, "do I have to learn the secret handshake or can I just pay my yearly dues and get the newsletter?"

"It's not that simple, Riplakish," she answered after another uncomfortable silence. "Dues are required on a monthly rather than annual basis." And then, finally, she smiled.

Rune and Dix followed her lead and smiled, too.

I followed her lead by ducking through the opening in the wall as she started down the secret corridor. As the bookshelf rumbled shut behind us, the passage dimmed to near darkness and I had to concentrate on Mercy's shadowy form to keep my bearings. Behind me I heard a vague thumping and a muffled voice saying something like ". . . put the candle back. . . ."

"As I see it, you have two basic problems," Mercy said as we came to a circular staircase and began descending. "First, you're looking for a body. The one that belonged to Morpheus the Malevolent, if my sources are not mistaken."

Morpheus the Malevolent—what a charming moniker and alliterative as hell.

"And second, there's another group in town looking for a body. Your body." She opened a door at the bottom and I followed her into a storeroom. The walls indicated we were now underground, but the room was dry if a little bit cool for my tastes. Several candles and a lamp, recently lit, provided murky illumination.

"If your sources are not mistaken," I added, wondering who would want to "off" me.

"They're not."

We both turned to look at Rune who was entering the room with Dix.

"Cyberpunk," she elaborated for Mercy's benefit.

"You get close enough for a positive ID?"

Rune nodded. "Scragged him. Cleaned my blade on his jacket. Boy meant business."

The redheaded Guildmaster turned back to me. "Someone's put a contract out on you and brought outtatowners in for the job."

I was more than a little incredulous. "Cyberpunks?"

"Way outta town," Dix observed.

"I owe you, Rip. Nobody offs anybody in my debt until I'm square with them." Mercy scowled. "And even more important, this is my turf. Nobody does hits in my jurisdiction without my permission!"

"Uh, thanks. . . ."

"I was a little peeved when I heard the rumor that you was dead. Glad to see that I can square our debt with a little 'protection.' Protection is cheaper than revenge."

"Well—"

" 'Course, I'm better in the revenge department."

"That won't—"

"And you can rest assured that if protection ain't good enough, I'll see to it that you are revenged."

"Avenged," Dix corrected.

"What?"

"You'll see to it that 'Points,' here, is avenged," he elaborated.

*Points?* I reached up and touched the tips of my Half-Elven ears.

"Yeah, that, too."

"Thanks," I said. *Points?*

Mercy walked over to a long crate resting on a couple of sawhorses. "Bring some light," she instructed, lifting the top.

There was no smell to warn me and the flickering lamplight didn't help much: I stood there, peering into the box at its contents, for a long moment. "A body?" I finally asked.

"Such as it is."

"Whose body is it?"

Mercy put her hands on her hips. "Of all the stories I heard about you, none of them suggested you was dense unless there was a woman involved."

"It's a little hard to tell in this light—is it a woman's body?"

"It's Morpheus the Malevolent's!"

I hate it when women use an exasperated tone of voice with me. "Well, it's a little hard to tell when the corpse is missing its head and hands and feet and"—I peered a bit more closely—"other assorted bits and parts?" I looked up. "How do I know this is really the bodily remains of Morpheus and not just some mutilated peasant's corpse?"

"It's Morpheus, all right," she assured me. "Take a deep breath."

I did.

"Smell anything?"

I didn't.

"That's because he's got a high-level Preservation spell operating. That's beyond the ability of most midlevel mages."

I nodded. "Okay. So, where's the rest of him?"

"Good question."

"Bad answer."

Dix crossed the room and bent over a tarpaulin-covered mound. "Your answers are right here," he said, jerking the tarp aside.

The second body looked more freshly dead, smelled less freshly preserved, but seemed to be more or less intact. A length of heavy chain was crisscrossed around the torso and wrapped around the stiff's legs. The ends of the chain were wrapped around a couple of large rocks.

"Kinky outfit," I said. "So what's the story?"

"Smudge. He had the sorcerer's remains in his possession," Mercy explained. "He's a procurer."

"Was a procurer. Tonight Master Smudge is sharkbait," Dix elaborated.

"Chummy," I observed. Nobody got it. "Okay, I know that there are certain parties who find a variety of uses for cadavers. So, who did this Smudge procure for?"

"He was an independent. He served a variety of clients, including chirurgeons, anatomists, apothecaries, spell shoppes, medical research labs for the area universities, and the occasional Ghoul or Necrophile who came into a little spending money—but mostly he dabbled in the Necromatic Black Market."

"I don't suppose we can get a client list for our boy here?"

Mercy shook her head. "We stumbled on this by accident. Two of my Bravos were a little careless: he died before he could talk."

I stared at the remains of the ratlike little man and pondered. "Maybe not."

"Maybe not what?"

"Mercy, can I borrow Smudge before tonight's swimming expedition?"

She looked at me speculatively. "You can *keep* him, if you want. My only concern is a certain amount of tidiness. I don't like messes—political or practical—and I don't like stiffs cluttering up my storerooms. I'm an Assassin, not an undertaker." She turned to Rune. "The wagon ready?"

She nodded.

"Have Ralph and Norton toss Smudge in, alongside Morpheus. Make sure both are well covered." She turned back to me. "The wagon's due back tomorrow."

"Thanks—"

"It's rented in your name, Points," Dix added. "Mercy assured them you'd pay when you returned it. See that you do."

I nodded. "I appreciate all the help you're giving me."

Mercy held up a hand. "Think nothing of it. Like I said, I owe you. And I don't like other people planning hits on my turf. If any additional information comes down the pike, I'll be sure to pass it along."

"I'm grate—"

"At cost."

"Cost?"

"Hey, good informants ain't cheap! I'm not going to make no profit on this. Normally, the Guild sells info to the highest bidder or charges the client forty percent over base fees. And I'm throwin' in Rune for free."

"Rune?"

"She volunteered."

I looked at Rune.

"I need the practice."

Saying "no" to any of this was out of the question, of course.

"Now," Mercy continued, "I got another question." She held out her hand. "Dix?" He placed a loose roll of parchment in her palm and she unrolled it and held it up for me to read.

It was a "Wanted" poster complete with my likeness sketched in full face and profile studies. Beneath my name and description was a request for information leading to my apprehension. Apparently I was being charged with "breach of promise" and a reward was offered to locate me so that I could "manfully" face up to my responsibilities.

"Well?"

I smiled wanly. "It was a mistake."

Mercy's smile had teeth. "I know a lot of guys may think that the morning after, but it's a pretty crass thing to say out loud."

"No. I mean, it was an accident." That wasn't any better. "What I mean is—nothing happened."

Dix's eyebrow arced toward his hairline. "Nobody goes to the trouble of putting these things all over town on account of nothin' happened."

I sighed. "Look, about six months ago I was with some

friends and we came across this glass coffin in the middle of a meadow. When we opened it, we found this young woman inside—''

"I think I'm gonna be sick," Dix growled, "if this is headin' where I think it is. . . ."

Mercy was close behind with: "I heard rumors about your social life, Bard, but . . ."

"She wasn't dead!" I said hotly. "She was like in suspended animation—''

"Suspended *what*?" they chorused.

"—I had to give her mouth-to-mouth resuscitation—''

"Mouth-to-mouth *what*?"

"Sounds like you were kissing her," Rune observed.

"Well, that's what the Dwarves thought—''

"Dwarves?"

"This wouldn't involve the fair lady White, would it?"

"Well, as a matter of fact—''

"Oh, man, Points, are you in a lot of trouble!"

"I know! I've got seven very tenacious Mountain Dwarves on the lookout for me! They've got some sort of custom that demands I make an honest woman of her! And all I did was kiss her!"

"Thought you said it was just mouth-to-mouth something-or-other.''

"Well—''

"I'm afraid it's gotten a little bigger than you think, Rip." Now Mercy looked positively grim. "Seems this Snow girl's stepmama is real unhappy about you putting her back in circulation.''

"And the word on the street is Rudy's lookin' for you, as well.''

I drew a momentary blank. "Rudy?"

"Snow's fiancé.''

"Ah. The prince." I looked at the poster again. "You say these are all over town?"

The Guildmaster tossed the parchment to Rune. "Rune's been going around and pulling them down almost as fast as they've been going up.''

"Thank—''

"I don't allow no unauthorized proclamations on Guild turf 'less I'm paid the standard poster fee.''

I fidgeted. "Well, once again, thanks, guys. I really appreciate this. And if there's anything I can do for you—"

"There is," said Mercy.

Γ

Back when Dreamworlds was open to the public, you might enter any of the Program milieus and mingle with hundreds of other Dreamwalkers, each inhabiting their own, distinctive, Computer-generated avatar. What made the interactive Programworlds infinitely more interesting, however, were their thousands of inhabitants who were not linked to Humans outside the Matrix. These Subprograms were Artificial Intelligences in their own right, with personality files and full simulation capabilities that made them indistinguishable from the avatars animated by Dreamwalkers.

Indistinguishable to other Dreamwalkers, that is.

You might not know whether the blacksmith in the village or the king on his throne or the doxy in the tavern was another Dreamwalker or a Computer Construct.

But *some* of the other Constructs did.

Program self-awareness was haphazard among the various A.I.s and Constructs, but a name had evolved among them for those of us who came from outside the Program Matrix: *True Spirits*.

And Mercy had found one when all Dreamwalkers were believed to have been evacuated from the Fantasyworld Program.

Guess who she asked to baby-sit?

When we emerged from the warren of tunnels leading away from the guildhouse, I found myself in a side alley just off the main street of Calabastor. "Where is he?"

"Tavern," Rune replied. "Follow me."

As we strolled down the street toward the south end of town I took a mental inventory of the signs and storefronts: Calabastor had changed since I had last visited and I wasn't sure how much was attributable to the Anomaly. There was a new sign proclaiming "Mario & Luigi: Family Painters"; a Rent-a-Guide Agency offering the services of Indiana Smith and Northwest Jones; a poster heralding the return of Selena the Sonneteer down at the Bards' Guild; another poster recruiting for the Navy, bearing the inscription "Agamemnon wants YOU"; and some cryptic graffiti that stated: "Trebor Sux" and asked: "Who shot J.R.R.?" respectively.

There was also one of my wanted posters tacked to a wall about two feet off the ground. It didn't take any great leap of logic to figure it had been posted there by a Dwarf.

I turned my collar up and tried to slouch as I walked.

The tavern was a gloomy little dive with a dirty little sign dubbing it "The Do Drop In."

Crom, talk about an insidious lack of imagination. . . .

"That's him," Rune announced, gesturing over the top of the saloon-type half doors that leaned crookedly against each other in the entryway.

Inside, a hodge-podge of clientele cluttered up the main room: berserkers on bar stools, thaumaturgists at the tables, corsairs in the corners. . . . And besides the odd assortment of dress and professions, the cross-cultural conglomeration spanned various racial groups, as well. At one table a group of masked terrapins were squabbling over the last slice of pizza. And there was even a group of purple Snarfs huddled around a sawn-off table: five males and a Snarfette—a dangerous combination once they got drunk.

I pulled out my enchanted spectacles as I zeroed in on an old, decrepit wizard type slouched over a table against the far wall. Imagine Merlin the Magician as Darrell Sweet might have painted him: dark robe and pointed hat spangled with white stars and planets, long flowing white hair and beard, parchmentlike skin, crow's-feet turning into a bird stampede; his face and hands projected ancient wisdom and arcane powers. A green purse lay next to the stein of beer on the table and a great carved wizardstaff leaned against the adjacent chair. I was moving toward him and halfway across the room when I got the spectacles on and the Optics of al Rashid refocused.

When Haroun al Rashid was Caliph of Baghdad, he had saved the life of a young man whose father, in gratitude, had crafted a pair of enchanted lenses and mounted them in thin gold frames as a gift. The original spell on this mystic pair of glasses was to enable the wearer to see "truth." Truth takes many forms, and by the time they had come into my possession, the Optics of al Rashid divined truth through a variety of visual spectra.

More specific to this particular moment, I could look at the avatar of a True Spirit and see the true appearance of the Dreamwalker who animated it. *And this ancient old man in the*

*Merlin makeup was a boy who couldn't be any older than fourteen at the most!*

Now I knew why Mercy had specifically used the term "baby-sit."

I pulled the spectacles from my eyes and the double image of man and boy resolved back into the single image of an old wizard, who looked up as I approached his table.

"May I join you?" I asked as I tucked the glasses back into my vest pocket. He made an uncertain gesture and I sat down. There was no point in beating around the bush: "My name is Riplakish of Dyrinwall. Look, I know that you're a Dreamwalker—more likely a REMrunner. This Programworld is not only off-limits, it's very dangerous—"

"I can't get out," he mumbled into his beer.

"What's the problem?"

"Jeremiah," was the slightly slurred response.

"Jeremiah?" I asked, wondering if the innkeeper could be held responsible for serving an alcoholic beverage to a minor.

He flopped a careless hand in the direction of the green "purse" and I got a better look this time: Jeremiah.

Jeremiah was a bullfrog.

"He was a good friend of mine," explained the sloshed sorcerer.

I felt a headache coming on.

Γ

". . . I never understood a single word he said," Rune was saying.

I refused to rise to the bait. "Look, it's a bit complicated."

"Try me."

I turned in my saddle and checked on kid-wizard: he was sprawled on a rug, snoring loudly, having passed out just after climbing on and kicking it into gear. The rug was floating about four feet off the ground, and as I had used about twenty feet of rope to tether it to my saddle horn, he drifted serenely along, behind us as we rode out of Calabastor.

Satisfied that he hadn't fallen off, I turned back to Rune who was driving the wagon, corpses in back under a pile of yard goods, with her horse tethered behind. "Apparently, Merlin—"

"Mervyn."

"Yeah, Mervyn; well, he's from this other world—"

"A True Spirit?"

I cleared my throat. "Uh, right. Well, he—"

"Would you classify him as a Dreamwalker or a REMrunner?"

I glared at her. "If you know so bloody much, why don't you explain it to me?"

"I'm listening," she said primly.

"Well, old Mervyn, here, didn't get in on his own. His friend, Jeremiah, was the hacker who knew the code sequencing."

"Code sequencing?"

"Let's just say that old Jerry was Mervyn's ticket in and was supposed to be Mervyn's ticket back out."

"A frog?"

"He wasn't a frog until the two of them ran into an old witch."

"Which old witch?"

"The wicked wi—you're doing this on purpose, aren't you?"

She smirked.

The wiz-kid snored.

We were on our way to see Yudu the Necromancer. Aside from the likelihood that Yudu had been one of Smudge's employers, I still had other hopes of getting the decomposing little procurer to talk.

"Company," Rune announced, breaking my reverie.

I looked up the road and studied the rider who had just come over the hill before us. Rune stopped the wagon and I reined in. Mervyn's flying carpet gently bumped up against Ghost's hindquarters.

"Huh. Whazit?" mumbled a sleepy voice from the nether regions.

"Looks like an Orc," I observed.

"Mmmmmm—Narc?"

"Never saw no Orc ride alone," Rune commented.

The Orc rode closer and we could see his piggish features more clearly. Mervyn popped up like a hyperactive prairie dog: "Nnn—Narc?"

"Check the topknot," Rune directed. "Our boy's from the Southern Provinces."

Which differentiated him from the wild and hostile Northern

Tribes. The Southern Tribes were more amenable to treaties and frequently hired out as mercenaries on short-term contracts. And since this particular Orc was riding relaxed in the saddle with all weapons sheathed and secured, we adopted a similar nonthreatening stance.

"Hola, strangers!" he called as he reined up some ten feet in front of us. He grinned in what might have been an engaging manner: there were enough tusks on display to rival the Elephants' Graveyard.

"Awful jolly for a Norc," Mervyn mumbled behind us.

"I hight Jotnar of Mork, bound for Calabastor!" he called with unquestionable goodwill. "And you be?" He had only one massive eyebrow and a corner of it lifted as he waited for our response.

"Elyn of Fiddlers Green," Rune answered, smoothly dialing up one of her aliases. "Mervyn Ambrosia," came the not-so-steady response from the kid with the beard. "Riplakish of Dyrinwall," I added, trying to put a mental finger on my unease.

I turned to Rune. "What's wrong with this picture?"

"Riplakish of Dyrinwall—ho!" the brute bellowed. He reared back in the saddle and unleashed a ululating cry.

Something clicked at the back of my mind. *An Orc from Mork?*

There was a sound of many hooves and a cloud of dust boiled up from behind the next hill. Rune drew her shortsword. "Rip, get out of here!" she yelled, smacking Ghost across his flank with the flat of her blade.

The glamoured pegasus reared and leapt, his wings unfolding and spreading to beat the air with massive strokes. As we climbed into the sky I heard a faint whimpering in my slipstream. I turned and saw the strained face of Mervyn the Magician as he clung to the carpet that was still linked by rope to my saddle. A large green bullfrog was clinging to Mervyn's robe with goggly eyes that outsized even the wizard's.

"Hang on, guys!" I leveled Ghost off and reined him in so that we hovered momentarily in the air. The carpet seemed to stabilize and so did the wizard.

Then an arrow struck the bottom of the rug with a *thumpk* and a barbed head poked through the weave along with about six inches of the shaft.

I looked down to see an octet of Orcs riding over the hill in answer to their leader's summons. Three of them had strung bows and were taking a special interest in us. I reached for my shortbow, holstered to the left of my saddle pommel, and hurriedly strung it as I looked back for Rune. There was no sign of her but the Orc who had braced us on the road had ridden up to the abandoned wagon and was in the process of sliding off his saddle. I looked again and noticed that Rune wasn't the only thing missing: there was nothing above the Orc's shoulders. I whistled as I reached for an arrow in the leather quiver that hung to the right of the pommel: decapitating Orcs is no mean feat under any circumstances—and not just because they have no necks.

Another arrow came too close and I had to turn my attention to the problem at hand. I nocked my own and, taking careful aim, released it. I missed the rider and caught his mount in the neck. I murmured a short oath as the horse screamed and went down. A more virulent string of curses exploded behind me and I turned as I nocked another arrow. Mervyn was standing up on the carpet, holding his conical hat in his hands and trying to extract the arrow that had bisected its once-perfect cone. Another arrow arced by—*the kid had no sense of priorities!*

"Kid—Mervyn," I yelled as I brought my bow around and released my second arrow, "cast a *shield* or something!" My arrow caught an Orc in the face and he did a backward roll out of his saddle. Unfortunately, it wasn't one of the three using bows.

"How come they're shooting at us?"

"I don't know—we'll figure it out later!" I risked a glance back after loosing another arrow. The kid's avatar was still standing up on the carpet, dividing his attention between his hat and the goings-on down on the ground. Jeremiah was hopping about the undulating surface of the carpet as if he thought it lessened his chances of being hit by the next arrow. "Don't just stand there, you putz! This is for real!" A small voice in the back of my mind was advising me to get us both out of there, but I couldn't just fly off and abandon Rune.

Even though we were the only visible targets.

I pulled my dagger and slashed through the rope tied to my saddle horn. "Fly away, kid! I'll catch up in a few minutes!"

He flew away, all right. The next moment he was diving toward the Orcs with a barrage of blue lights spraying from his fingertips! The frog had nearly tumbled off and was holding on to the trailing edge of the rug with his mouth.

Three went down on his first pass, and only one got back up. They clustered as he brought the rug around for a second pass and I recognized the somatic gestures as he prepared his next spell. "No!" I yelled, kicking Ghost down into an intercept course. But I was too late: a fireball rumbled through our monstrous foes like an oversize bowling ball scoring a spare on the tenth frame.

Rune rode out from a clutch of trees on her own horse as we returned to earth. Jeremiah spit out a mouthful of carpet fibers and crawled over by the wagon, panting.

"Just what did you think you were doing?" I asked as Mervyn began extracting arrows from the carpet's weave.

"Defending myself, man," he answered in the steadiest voice I'd heard since he'd puked up a pitcher of beer behind the Do Drop In.

"You could've gotten yourself killed!"

"More likely to get myself killed doin' nothin'. 'Sides, what do you care? If I got killed I'd be out of your hair and you'd be alone with the chick."

I glanced over at Rune who was making her way from body to body, holding her nose and searching what was left of their packs, pouches, and saddlebags. The smell of roast beast was strong enough to gag a maggot. "Let me set you straight on some things, boy. First of all, that lady is an Assassin, not a 'chick.' You'll be much better off if you show more respect for her than you do for me and you'll be much happier if you treat me like I was your favorite uncle."

"Yeah. And second of all?"

Oboy: a smartmouth. There was room for only one smartmouth in this party and I held the position with tenure.

"Second of all, you don't seem to take this dying thing seriously."

He snorted. "Look, man, I'm way overdue to get out and go home. If Jeremiah can't—or won't—access the codes for me, I figure the next time I die, the defaults will kick in and all I'll have lost is some respect and an expensive avatar."

"Haven't you been listening?" I advanced on him and grabbed the front of his robe. "It doesn't work that way anymore! Without the codes, you can't go home!"

"That's what Jeremiah wants me to think!" he protested. "I'm still not convinced that he didn't set this up to test—"

The frog croaked reproachfully and I lifted the fistful of robe and Mervyn's feet cleared the ground. "This is not a game and this is not a test!" I bellowed, shaking him. "If an Orc takes an axe to your avatar, you're gonna be one hacked-up little hacker! This is a *new reality* and dead here is *dead out there*!" I dropped him after sticking my face in his and adding: "Permanent!"

"Aw, man! That crap about people dyin' in Dreamworlds last year was all just a bunch of hype!"

It had become a standard REMrunner line these past six months. More than a few believed that the Truedeath warnings were just another attempt by Cephtronics to keep them out of the Matrix: that if the security systems couldn't dissuade intrusion, scare tactics might. And convincing most Dreamhackers of the truth in this matter was comparable to proving "Truth" in any theological debate—facts are unreliable, belief is all.

"And thirdly," Rune added, postponing this particular debate for the moment, "always leave one of the perps alive so you can find out who sent them."

Mervyn's head swiveled in her direction. "You mean like we follow them back to their hideout without them knowin'?"

The Assassin unsheathed a particularly nasty-looking dagger and shook her head. "Only if they get a head start on a faster horse."

"Oh."

"You find anything?" I asked.

"Nah. Professional hire—careful but clumsy." She whistled for her horse and he came trotting up. "Pretty obvious, though," she added, retying her mount to the back of the wagon, "you were the mark." She swung up onto the wagon seat, released the brake, and urged the draft horses forward. Jeremiah made a couple of herculean hops and scrambled up into the wagon seat beside her.

Mervyn crawled onto his flying carpet. "Who'd want you dead, man?"

"Good question."

"Bad answer," he retorted, swinging the rug around to follow Rune. I mounted Ghost and trailed behind, giving the matter a great deal of thought.

# \RIPLEY\PATH\SIGMA    (Σ)

It was difficult to say which came first, consciousness or pain; but in all practicality, they came hand in hand.

He sat up, seeing nothing but darkness at first. Reaching out, his questing hands felt nothing beyond the rough flooring beneath his body. His head hurt. And his face. He touched his tender, swollen nose and his hand came away wet with blood.

Now his eyes were beginning to focus and he could see a white, ovoid outline in the darkness before him.

A theory formed in his pain-dulled mind. He struggled to his feet and lurched forward in spite of the flowers of pain that bloomed over and over behind his eyes. He met resistance a few feet away and groped for the handle.

The door swung inward and the interior of Misty Dawn's oak was illumined by warm afternoon sunlight. He tapped his fist against the unquestionably solid wall of the trunk and then stepped outside.

He smiled, feeling the sun on his face and the wash of a gentle breeze over his body. He was alive, not dead; solid, not wraithlike; and he had broken his nose and probably sustained a concussion trying to run through the outer door of Misty's tree while it was still closed!

Someone cleared their throat behind him.

He turned, suddenly mindful that he was still naked. A woman clad in black from the neck down was leaning against Misty's tree with her arms folded, her expression somewhere between a smile and a smirk. "I'm looking for Riplakish of Dyrinwall," she said. "Have you seen him?"

Σ

It was Lilith.

The former Succubus had been promoted and was now a full Archdemoness from the lower planes of Hell. He studied her face for changes as she wiped the blood from his face in turn. Her hair was still long and bone-white but now a pair of small pink horns poked through the tresses above her brow. Bloodred lips framed white teeth that were now enhanced with upper and lower pairs of fangs. Her scarlet cloak and robe had been replaced by a bodysuit (at least he hoped it was a bodysuit) of scaly black leather, and what he had first assumed to be a dark cloak flung about her shoulders turned out to be a pair of batlike wings.

Noting his inspection she paused in her ministrations. "How do you like the new me?"

"Nice. But to be honest, I preferred the Lily Munster look."

She snorted and continued to dab at his blood-caked face. "You have his aura, his knowledge, his voice, and even his feeble attempts at tasteless wit. For now I must suppose that your story is true—that you *are* Riplakish of Dyrinwall."

"What do you mean 'feeble'?"

"I came here to warn you."

"Too late. I already tried to run through a solid door."

"Nit! Your life is in danger!"

"Ah? And from whom, pray tell?"

"Please, language," the Demoness chided with a wince. "I don't know who. I've overheard a couple of conversations between members of the infernal council and rumors are running to Hell and gone." Coming from Lilith it wasn't just a figure of speech. "Someone's out to extinguish you, my friend! The word from some parts is he already has."

"So much for the efficacy of the grapevine."

"Will you be serious?" she hissed. "The rumors also suggest demonic connections! I'm sticking my neck out for you on this, buddy boy, and you know how the lower-downs in Hell can dish out their displeasure!"

"Yeah," he responded with a nostalgic look in his eye, "I remember what Orcus did to you the last time. . . ."

She blushed, remembering her transformation from Succubus to mortal woman.

"Do you ever miss being human?"

A thoughtful expression was replaced by a smile as she leaned across the table and kissed him. Her lips were gentle on his and when she pulled away, she brushed his hair back from his face. "We've got to get you out of here."

"You think they—whoever 'they' are—will come looking for me here?"

"Safe bet. This was where I started." She placed the bloodied rag in the bowl of water and gestured over it. Both disappeared in a gout of green flame. "A little occult advice," she said. "Never leave any of your blood around where the wrong people might get a hold of it."

"I guess I can hole up at Daggoth's Tower," he decided.

"That's the second place I would've looked."

"It's a starting point. I'll need some supplies." He sighed. "What I really need is a drink!"

She smiled and gestured again: a flagon appeared in front of him. "What's this?"

"Try it."

He sipped. Then quaffed. "Rum?" he asked, wiping his mouth.

"Demon Rum."

Σ

Robert Remington Ripley the Third pirouetted in front of the mirror. "Very nice. What is it?"

"A bit hard to explain, actually." Lilith was preparing his pack and saddlebags as he studied his new attire. The scaled black leather was form-fitting and aside from the fact that his form was somewhat different from hers, it was identical to the outfit the Archdemoness wore. "It resembles Black Dragonskin but combines a number of other materials in an interdimensional weave. All the Powers, Thrones, and Principalities wear this nowadays."

"Jeez, I feel—" He noticed her expression. "Sorry. Forgot." She waved for him to continue. "I feel like an honorary member of the Hellfire Club." He touched a tentative finger to his tender nose. "Um, while you're in the mood or the mode of conjuring, how about fixing my nose?"

Lilith shook her head. "No can do. Hell permits a certain range of magic—but nothing in the curative spectra. It runs counter to company policies."

"*You*, my dear, run counter to company policies."

She frowned. "I am being summoned. I must leave before someone starts checking into my whereabouts. The suit will enable me to find you later."

"Just you?" he asked, turning. "Or can other—" But she was already gone. He sniffed the air as he crossed the room. "Ah, *eau de brimstone*!" Tugging the silk covering off the crystal ball in his study, he plopped down in a chair and hoisted his feet up on the desk.

Five minutes later Daggoth broke the connection with a terse "I'm coming to get you. Don't do anything or go anywhere!" That left Ripley with little else to do but reach for one of the jugs of Demon Rum that Lilith had left with his supplies.

**DATALOG: \QUEBEDEAUX-
A.5\PERSONAL\20200807
*Voice Dictation*
***FILE ENCRYPTION ON*****

I'm trying to trace Ripley's code-strings to a point of origin
without tipping Balor's security team to the fact we've got
another incursion.
*
Damn!
*
Where did he come from?
*
The last I heard, he'd disappeared somewhere in Russia.
*
This really puts me between the proverbial rock and the hard
place: if the Soviets have anything to do with this incursion, I
really should report it!
*
But reporting it could well mean Ripley's termination.
*
Crap: the incursion alarms are going off again!

# Chapter
# Eight

★

\RIPLEY\PATH\GAMMA     (Γ)

I N my imagination it was a toss-up: an ancient stone tower
set high on a craggy hill or a large cavern at the end of a
mist-shrouded valley. I mean, we're talking about animat-
ing dead bodies, meddling in things that man was not
meant to—ah—meddle in. C'mon, we're talking about a major
league Necromancer, here. What pops into your mind when
you try to picture this joker's stronghold?

. . .

See what I mean?

So don't sneer at my surprise when Rune led us up to this
palatial mansion just an hour's ride from the city gates.

The estate was the sort of layout you'd expect to see on the
cover of *Better Castle and Courtyard*, with well-manicured
lawns and shrubbery and neo-Greek architecture. We rode up
the pebbled drive and dismounted near the front door. Or,
rather, Mervyn and I did. Rune parked the wagon and then
swung up into the saddle of her horse, making some sort of
excuse about perimeter security. Jeremiah elected to stay with
the wagon. I waved Rune on knowing the real reason Assassins
gave the Zombie Master wide berth. When you're responsible

for sending a number of people across the line, you're not too keen on meeting someone who can bring them back.

I started to tie Ghost to one of those stone Dwarf stablehands, you know, the kind of kitsch some of the rich like to stick in their front yards alongside those glass spheroids on concrete pedestals. Except this one wasn't a stone statue. Oh, he held the customary ring in one outstretched hand and was a uniform grey and didn't move—didn't even breathe, for that matter. But a good close-up look was sufficient to tell the difference.

Statues, for the most part, never started out their existence as living flesh and blood.

We didn't need to check the address to know that we had found the Zombie Master's stronghold.

The doorman was a trifle slow in responding to my knock. I couldn't really fault him as it was obvious that he'd been dead a long time.

"We're here to see the Zombie Master," I said.

Since Zombies don't talk and he didn't shut the door in our faces, we followed as he turned and trudged toward the interior of the house. Ominously, the door swung shut behind us of its own accord.

Inside, the marble floors and white stone construction seemed at odds with the moldering staff in servant's attire. The walls were adorned with murals and tapestries, sculptures (at least I hoped they were sculptures) lurked in a multiplicity of alcoves, and aromatic censers perfumed the air with scents that were both pleasing and, in view of the advanced decomposition of some of the servants, practical.

Mervyn tugged on my vest. "Major babe at eleven o'clock."

I turned and followed the twist of his head to see a young black woman descending a curved staircase to our left. If it weren't too cliché, I would quote Byron and say she walked in beauty like the night . . . but it was so I won't.

She wore a white dress and turban that contrasted her dark skin and made the white stone walls and the black marble floors into matching accessories.

She called out to the doorman who stopped his somnambulistic shuffle and listened as she walked toward us. She spoke a variant of French that had an unfamiliar ring in my ears. I had taught myself a smattering of classical French from the literary sources, but this was a spoken dialect and more difficult to follow. The cadence and pronunciations differed from the mother tongue that Nicole had spoken—farther removed, even, than the Canadian French of some of my Quebeçois acquaintances. A Caribbean variant, I guessed as our Zombie guide turned away.

"We're here to see Yudu," Mervyn announced without introduction or preamble.

I frowned at him and tried to explain to the young lady: "We have urgent business to discuss with the Zombie Master."

"You do?"

Ah, she spoke English; that was one less barrier. "That's the one."

"What is de one?"

On the other hand, perhaps she didn't comprehend it all that well. "Not 'what' is the one," I explained, "but whom."

"Ah," she exclaimed, "you are meaning de Necromancer."

"Yes," Mervyn agreed, "Yudu."

"Yes," she agreed: "I do."

"You do?" I frowned.

"But of course."

"Do what?" Mervyn inquired.

"Dat voodoo."

"Oh, Crom . . . I don't have time for this." I put my fists on my hips. "I need to see the Zombie Master and I need to see him right now."

"Well, I am afraid dat is quite impossible."

"Why impossible?" Mervyn wanted to know. As a matter of fact, I did, too.

"Because dere is no Zombie *Master*. I am afraid you have suffered some *mis*information."

"Mis—" Mervyn began.

"Yes."

"No, not you." My patience had already wandered off, ostensibly to look for a saner environment.

"If not me, den who will do?"

"Do what?" Mervyn asked, proving to be a reliable nuisance factor.

"Dat voodoo."

"Stop it!" Pressing fingers to my temples, I gritted: "You're giving me a headache!"

"You poor ting," the girl crooned. "But don' worry: I have de remedy for dat."

"You do?" Mervyn, of course.

"Of course; I keep telling you dat."

I gritted my teeth, determined to bring this conversation under control. "This is the first time you've mentioned headache remedies."

"Oh, not dat."

"Then, which?"

"Shut up, Mervyn," I murmured.

"Not Witch, Necromancer."

"But you said there is no Necromancer," he continued.

"No I didn't: I said dere was no Zombie *Master*."

"You did?"

"I did. I am de Necromancer."

"The Necromancer?" I echoed.

"De Zombie Mistress," she confirmed.

"The Zombie *Mistress*?"

"I am Yudu de Necromancer."

"Oh."

After a very long pause I stepped forward. "I'm sorry. I'm afraid we got started off on the wrong foot." I extended my hand: "How do you do."

"Don' start with me," she snapped.

Γ

Actually, once we got things sorted out, Yudu turned out to be very accommodating. She agreed to come to Daggoth's Tower and help us with our "problem" come nightfall. While I was in a bit of a hurry to expedite the matter, she needed time to prepare for the ceremonies, preferred nocturnal ambience, and I needed to come up with the standard fees. I wasn't carrying sufficient funds at the moment and I was in a hurry to get back to Daggoth's before sunset.

I wasn't too keen on going through a transformation out on the open road.

The ride to Daggoth's Tower was potentially a short one for a winged horse and a flying carpet, but the wagon was another matter. Rune wasn't much of a conversationalist and Jeremiah was marginally worse, so I used the time to get to know the kid better.

The problem with putting on the spectacles and seeing

Dreamwalkers as they really were, was that it tended to get very confusing.

Take Mervyn, for example. His real name was Henry ("call me Hank") Sculthorpe and he was a sophomore in high school—presently on semester break. That was on the outside, of course. Here, in Fantasyworld, none of that seemed to apply. When I looked at him, I saw Mervyn the Magician, an old geezer with parchment skin and flowing white locks. Sculthorpe had picked a powerful, if somewhat withered, avatar who could command vast magical forces.

And he was sorry he had done so.

"Why?"

He looked a little flustered and deliberately slowed the carpet so that the wagon carried Rune out of comfortable earshot. "It's the babes."

"The babes?" I asked.

"You know—the chicks. Women."

"Ah," I said. "Women."

"Yeah. Well, that's why I'm here."

I looked at him like my father used to look at me when I hit adolescence. "Why *are* you here?"

He looked surprised. "Why are any of us here?"

"We'll take a poll later, Plato. You're underage and the Dreamworlds's Matrix has been declared off-limits to the general public. So, why are you here?"

"The Gameworld, man."

I cocked an eyebrow.

"It's better than real life."

"Better?"

He looked at me. "I don't know how your life is now, man, but tell me what it was like when you were fourteen."

I thought about it. Fourteen wasn't so bad. Was it? Then I thought about it some more. Fourteen. No longer a kid, not yet an adult. Everyone had a piece of you: parents, adults, older siblings, school. The world is full of authority systems and you're practically on the bottom rung. Even kids get better treatment because they're not supposed to know any better and by-the-way-young-man-isn't-it-time-you-started-taking-on-some-responsibilities? As if that wasn't tough enough, the hormones started kicking in: an emotional roller coaster with drives and zits and squeaky voices and clothes never fitting. . . .

And girls.

Chicks.

The babes.

Yeah, at fourteen a guy is at a definite disadvantage. The "fairer sex" has an unfair advantage at fourteen. They seem to be taller, smarter, more mature, and definitely more in control.

Yeah, definitely. . . .

So, why Fantasyworld? I started thinking about fourteen-year-old fantasies. "You're not happy about being a Wizard." I didn't phrase it as a question.

He shook his head and mumbled something about being old.

"Wizards are powerful," I pointed out, "the general rule of thumb is, the older you get, the more powerful you become. In this avatar you could be a major player."

"Aw, man, I know this stuff. I picked Wizard because I got a head for the spells. I knew it would be safe."

I knew from the way he said "safe" that further arguments were futile. At fourteen you didn't want "safe," you wanted "adventure." It wasn't until you got closer to my age that you come to understand that "adventures" are mostly unpleasant and uncomfortable ordeals, usually involving pain, loss, and near brushes with death. They only sound fun and exciting to inexperienced boobs when told around the campfire by the ones who were lucky enough to survive and smart enough to not go back for more.

"What I really want to be—"

"Is a barbarian."

He looked at me sharply. "How'd you know?"

I thought about large, athletic bodies, muscles rippling beneath bronzed skin, great steel swords and minimal leather outfits. Power and strength and total independence. Even a wizard in his tower might fear and envy you, a queen on her throne could desire you, a slave girl in the marketplace would be willing to die for you. . . .

And you could take off your shirt at the beach and know that no one, I mean no one, was gonna kick sand in your face.

"Lucky guess," I answered.

"Company again," called Rune from the wagon in front.

"Orcs?" I asked.

"Not hardly," she answered archly.

I nudged Ghost up to the front of the parade to get a better look.

There were twenty in all, arrayed in bands of chain mail and strips of leather, bristling with blades and bows, mounted on fierce chargers. Tougher than Orcs, fiercer than Tartars, more dangerous than Dwarves on a three-day bender, their faces were painted with the colors of a roving war party: crimson lip gloss, vermilion eye shadow, and a touch of blush.

Mervyn floated up beside me. "Amazons," he breathed. "Bodacious Babes!"

"More like Deadly Dames," I corrected. "You and Rune stay here. I'll go up and see what they want."

"You kidding me, man? I want a closer look!"

"That is how most of their victims die," Rune said, "trying to get a closer look."

"Aw, man—"

"Zip it up and stay put, Scully." I nudged Ghost forward. "If they're friendly I'll get you a closer look."

"How about a date?"

I threw a look back at Rune. "Tell Mercy she owes me. Big time."

I made my approach at a careful, casual pace. Too slow might communicate fear or reluctance, too fast would brand me for an inexperienced fool. As Ghost trotted up the gentle rise I shifted mental gears and took another look through adolescent eyes.

Yep. Babes.

Cosmo cover girls in chain-mail bikinis done up with mousse and mascara. Wet-dream women warriors.

Forget real history and Sarmation culture. Cephtronics had diddled another aspect of the Fantasyworld Program to make the experience more attractive to the thrill-seekers. I was no longer surprised at anything I found: various mythologies and histories had collided with New Hollywood standards of adult fairy tales and the Dreamworlds's S.O.P. of playing to the lowest common denominator in Dreamwalker fantasies.

The most important thing to remember, now that Cephtronics had lost control and the Program was running without safeties or governors, was that everything was potentially deadly.

Particularly cute chicks in chain-mail lingerie.

As I shifted back to what I hoped was an adult mind-set, I

noticed details that had escaped me at a distance: they were wearing emerald hair clips that distinguished them as the most elite and deadly warrior-maids. And I was personally acquainted with three of these Green Barrettes.

Queen Hippolyta rode forward with Faun and Princess Aeriel just behind and to either side.

"So, Riplakish, our daughter's prayers are answered. We feared the worst."

"You are well, my love?" Aeriel's voice and expression seemed a bit strained.

Hippolyta turned and gave her a look that silenced her and let everyone know that Mom was going to handle matters here.

"I am well," I said. Though it was anyone's guess as to how much longer that was going to last. "Majesty, I thought you were in retirement."

"We were on pilgrimage when word came of your disappearance. We returned early—" She stopped and gave me a meaningful look. "Lord Riplakish, let us speak privily to one another."

I eyeballed the distance between the sun and the horizon. "Perhaps we could ride while we talked . . . ?"

Now that the prodigal had been found, it seemed we had a mutual destination: Daggoth's Tower. I remembered that Aeriel had once hinted at a relationship between her mother and the dark sorcerer. I had this vague, uneasy feeling that circumstances had shifted somewhat in the meantime.

"Thou'rt well?" the Amazon ruler inquired as I pulled off my chain-mail shirt. The afternoon was turning into a real scorcher and the old "safety in numbers" adage had me setting caution aside. "Thou'rt recovered?"

"Recovered?"

"Thou wert abducted?"

I must have looked blank.

"Constrained? Imprisoned?"

A light clicked on. "Oh! That!" But how to explain? *Excuse me, Your Majesty, but I'm afflicted with a rare form of lycanthropy: every night I turn into myself. I'm a wereRipley. You see, this is all a Computer simulation and none of you are really real—* Right. "Uh, I'm looking into the matter, good lady. I believe your daughter was the victim of a magical hoax. Probably some disillusioned Illusionist who—"

"Who will die when we track him down!" she finished vehemently.

"Die?" I swallowed. "I think it was just some kind of practical joke—"

"No man may jape a princess of the royal blood and live to boast of it. We have sworn a bloodoath!"

"A bloodoath?" This was serious: there was no backing down from a bloodoath!

She nodded gravely. "Before our daughter may ascend to the throne she must conceive thy child and kill the man who made a fool of her before the faces of the women she must rule."

It made sense of a savage sort. Except to fulfill this bloodoath they would have to kill me and no fancy explanation would satisfy a bloodoath once sworn.

Another thought elbowed its way to the front of the line: "*My* child?"

"Aye. Thou'rt her chosen consort."

I glanced back at Aeriel. She and Faun were pacing along about twenty feet behind us. Behind them rode the remainder of the Amazon war party. "Majesty, thy daughter and I have this understanding. . . ." I turned my gaze forward and studied the wagon that led our merry band. At my insistence, Mervyn had thrown his carpet in the back and was keeping Rune company on the driver's seat. Jeremiah was uncomfortably pressed between them.

At the moment Mervyn was looking back at us.

He was doing that a lot.

"Thou'rt royal consort to the Amazon Throne."

"I'm flattered, Highness, and I want to help—"

"Allow us to make ourself perfectly clear. Thou hast been acknowledged as consort to Aeriel, heir-apparent to the Crown. Thou hast met with the approval of the Council and the Amazon populace. More importantly, thou hast our approval."

"Aeriel explained—"

"The taking of a royal consort to ensure progeny is an inviolate portion of the ascension rituals. In that, alone, thou hast a duty to perform."

"Well, I don't mind helping Aeri buy some time—"

"My daughter is still a *virgin!*"

She had to be upset to drop the royal "we." I cleared my

throat. "As I was saying, Good Queen, Aeriel and I have this arrangement. . . ."

"Yes, yes, she explained it to me—us. Princess Aeriel has coerced thee to acknowledge consort status with the understanding that it is a ruse to purchase time. Although time for what is certainly beyond me—us!"

"Time to find the man she really wants to make a baby with," I explained.

Even though she was the one who seemed to be missing the point, she looked at me as if I were truly stupid. "She has already found him."

"Well, great! That should solve everybody's problem— except—" Except I was finally getting the message that should have been obvious all along. "Oh, no. No. We had a deal. I am *not* a participant here, I am only lending my good name to the cause—"

"What didst thee believe? That thou couldst step down in a few months and another man might take thy place?"

"Well. . . ."

"There is a precedent for such but retirement is permanent."

*Permanent?* "But we had a deal!"

"Thou hast made covenant with the Amazon nation," she said coldly. "Thy deception jeopardizes our daughter's life as well as thine."

"I think we need to talk to Aeriel about this."

"*That* will avail thee naught: she wants *thy* child." Her look softened, and for a moment, she looked more like a mother than a queen. "Riplakish, Aeriel *loves* thee. Do not break my daughter's heart."

Great.

If Amazonian palimony didn't get me killed, the twenty or so warrior-maids bringing up the rear would ace me as soon as I turned into my Human alter ego. That is, if the Demons, Orcs, or Cyberpunks didn't get me first.

"We do not understand why you balk at this task." The queen was clearly perplexed. "It is a great honor that she bestows upon you."

How to explain this? "Men, Your Majesty, like to make their own choices. . . ."

"Men are fickle," she corrected. "Men resist marriage and desire variety."

"Majesty, not all men are like that."

"Of course not! We were merely speaking of the best of your sorry sex."

"It's just that I'm not ready to settle down and make a commitment—"

"You will have your own life, be able to travel, or live where or when you please. After you have sired an heir, of course."

"Oh, of course."

"All that is required of thee is that thou makest love to a beautiful princess, sufficient to produce a female child. Thou wilt even be given a royal stipend—"

"I'm going to be *paid?*"

Hippolyta misread my agitation. "If a largess of gold and jewels is not sufficient, there are other recompenses, as well. Amazon custom does not prohibit the sharing of a man by many women. We have a number of subjects ready and willing to slake thy desire for variety—"

"Yeah, Aeriel mentioned her sister Kathy." This kept getting more and more distasteful.

"Their cousin Edith hath also expressed interest—"

I held up my hand. "Majesty, my mother taught me many things that have served me well in my sojourn through this world. And one of them was that you can't have your Kate and Edith, too."

The wagon slowed ahead of us. "Company," Rune called over her shoulder.

*"Thank Crom,"* I murmured under my breath. I nudged Ghost forward, grateful for the excuse to terminate this discussion.

Company turned out to be a single rider. The surrounding countryside was flat and grassy so I was sure no reinforcements would suddenly appear over any hills or from behind any trees. Rune stopped the wagon and mounted her own horse as I rode by. I waved her back: "Nothing I can't handle."

I glanced down at my mithril shirt, slung across the front of my saddle. A single horseman—most likely a fellow traveler. And I wasn't about to put the chain mail back on with the Amazons watching. I patted the hilt of my *katana*: if there was trouble, I could outrun or outfight it.

The horseman had reined up about a hundred yards away.

Swathed in a dark djellaba, his form and features were obscured at this distance, but there was something familiar—

He had moved in the saddle while a wisp of memory flickered in front of my eyes.

Then I was knocked backward, out of the saddle, by a hissing express train of force and tumbled to the hard, stony ground. I rolled as I landed, pushing the arrow's shaft in even deeper.

I tried to rise, to lift my face from the dirt, but my arms had turned to water. The weight of my body continued to press upon the shaft, and while I could feel the barbed head working its way deeper into my chest, the absence of pain frightened me more.

By the time Rune's horse had thundered to my side, I knew.

She dismounted and turned me over, laying my head in her lap. I had always believed that when death came, I'd be frightened—that I'd fight it. I was surprised in the clarity of the moment to find that life suddenly seemed to be too complex and demanding and that easy peace beckoned comfortingly like a calm port to a storm-tossed sailor.

"Hold on," Rune was saying. There were tears—I wasn't sure whether they were mine or hers. "Don't let go!"

I tried to shake my head but I had no strength. Only seconds were left: I opened my mouth and nearly choked on the blood that was filling my throat.

"I'm tired . . ." I whispered, ". . . of the game. . . ."

And then I died.

**DATALOG: \QUEBEDEAUX-
A.5\PERSONAL\20200808
*Voice Dictation*
***FILE ENCRYPTION ON*****

Now what?
*
First I get an anomalous reading close to the avatar I've christened Ripley; Code: Gamma.
*
Someone else, close to Ripley, is a real human being in taction with an avatar—not one of the Computer's AI Constructs.
*
There have been several others but what sets this one apart is its code structure: it seems to be repeated in two variants elsewhere in the Matrix.
*
I say "variants" because the code is not as closely duplicated as Ripley's multiple avatars—but they're still close enough to question whether or not they represent three different entities.
*

The other factor that sets this entity apart is that as soon as it came within close proximity to Ripley-Gamma, his code-string ceased to exist.
*
There's only one Ripley left on my monitors, now.
*
I wonder how long he can last. . . .

# PART III

## Terminal Emulation

★

**King Skule:** Have you many unmade songs within you, Jatgeir?

**Jatgeir:** Nay, but many unborn; they are conceived one after the other, come to life, and are brought forth.

**King Skule:** And if I, who am king and have the might—if I were to have you slain, would all the unborn skald-thoughts within you die along with you?

**Jatgeir:** My lord, it is a great sin to slay a fair thought.

**King Skule:** I ask not if it be a sin: I ask if it be possible!

> —Henrik Ibsen, "The Thought Child"
> from *The Pretenders* (Archer trans.)

And all in deadly sleepe did drowned lie. . . .
> —Edmund Spenser,
> *The Faerie Queene*, Book I, Cant. III, 16

# Chapter
# Nine

★

\RIPLEY\PATH\SIGMA      (Σ)

HE was drunk and that both pleased and puzzled him.
Once, during the beta-testing stage of the Fantasyworld Program, he had "slipped." He had so
immersed himself in the game that his character
persona had disregarded the self-imposed disciplines of a recovering alcoholic and he had hoisted a few in a seedy, backwater
dive named The Obscene Griffin. That was when he had discovered that Computer-simulated alcohol had no effect on his
avatar.

Drinking "in-Program" was something he rarely repeated
after that episode, though. It didn't help his years of abstinence,
once he was back Outside, to have temptation's taste so clearly
returned to recent memory.

And, as it turned out, his avatar couldn't get drunk. So what
was the point?

He mostly steered clear of it since that episode—the one
notable exception was sampling the wine bottle "bombs" during that brawl last year in The Roaring Hangman Inn.

But this time he wanted to get drunk. *Needed* to get drunk!

And, wonder of wonders, his wish had somehow been

granted! The Demon Rum that Lilith left him packed a wallop unlike anything that he could remember.

Of course, his memory was none too good, at the moment. But that suited him just fine as the whole point to getting drunk was to make all the nasty thoughts and memories just go away.

In the past twenty-four hours he had been brained with a battleaxe, turned into a lycanthrope and a ghost, watched a malevolent entity possess the dead body of a woman he had cared for, discovered that there were Demons out to get him, and now had just learned that there was more than one of him and that he had just died.

The news arrived with the Amazons at the tower less than a half hour after Daggoth had fetched him there via magic carpet.

It was unsettling to think about his own death—particularly now that it had already occurred. *What was it like? Had he suffered? What were his last thoughts?*

*Where was his other self now?*

And then there was an even more disturbing thought: *If there were two of him, then which one was the* real *Robert Remington Ripley the Third?*

There were no answers immediately forthcoming and he was tired of pondering the imponderable. Unfortunately, several hours had passed since Stephanie had confiscated the rest of the Demon Rum and he was beginning to notice a slow but steady slide toward sobriety.

He had already decided that this was a bad time to be sober.

The room seemed stationary, but he sat up slowly, ready to return to the prone position should it decide to turn into a centrifuge again. The combination of Demon Rum and aeriel maneuvers on a flimsy piece of floor covering had played havoc with his head and stomach. But now, with the passage of a couple of hours in bed in one of the guest chambers, he was feeling much better. He lowered his feet to the floor, which no longer evinced a notion to suddenly lurch off in an unexpected direction.

He stood and navigated to the door. The room still displayed a tendency to list slightly to port, but the overall architecture was moving from gelatin to a more stonelike consistency.

The door was not locked. That surprised him as he'd half expected to be under house arrest after Stephanie's tongue-lashing. He exited the room, hesitating on the circular balcony and considering the other doors on this level. He turned to descend the stairs, deciding to begin his quest in the wine cellar and, if unsuccessful there, work his way back up with a carefully meticulous search grid. Creeping down the spiral stairway, he was careful to avoid the treads marked in memory as "creaky." The tower appeared deserted but he took no chances, hugging the walls and ducking in and out of alcoves until he reached the basement stairs.

The wine cellar contained a store of wine, not to mention barrels of ale and some mead, as well.

But no Demon Rum.

It took only a quick taste of the various brews to know that they couldn't produce the effect he wanted. His hands started to shake and he nearly dropped the last bottle he sampled.

He hurried back up the stone-hewn steps to the ground level. He was about to cross the main hall when he heard voices coming from the staircase leading to the second floor. He ducked behind a loose tapestry and listened as Vashti and Daggoth came into view and crossed the great circular room.

". . . taking this better than I thought."

"We don't know that he's dead," she answered, her voice less certain than her words. "His avatar is dead but—"

"But he has more than one?" Daggoth laughed mirthlessly. "Lady love, I have more than one avatar and I can assure you that I am most certainly dead! And that other avatar is none too stable. Besides, you know the original effect of the Program Anomaly."

"But is it still in effect? We know that the Anomaly has been slowed—"

"But not stopped."

"Not stopped," she agreed, "but perhaps the operating parameters have changed."

"I hope to know more after I've had a chance to talk to this Yudu person. When did the old Wizard say she was coming?"

"Sundown . . ." was the last he heard as they passed through the great doors to the outside.

And sundown would be soon, he noticed, glancing at one of the lancet windows. He darted for the adjacent stairway that led to the upper stories.

The sound of footsteps descending from the fourth level diverted him to the second floor. He thought to just wait around the corner until the stairway was clear but this proved to be a miscalculation: Princess Aeriel Morivalynde had also chosen to exit to the second floor.

While he wasn't too keen on anyone seeing him in his present condition, he wasn't prepared for the Amazon's reaction.

"You!" she screeched.

"Hi, Aeri," he mumbled sheepishly. "Long time no see."

"Assassin!" she bellowed, groping at her hip for a sword. There was none there. " 'Twas you!"

"Me?" Stephanie had mentioned something about staying in his room and avoiding any Amazons, but she hadn't gone into any details. Had she?

Aeriel discovered a dagger in her belt and Ripley wished he had paid more attention to his ex-wife's briefing of just an hour before.

"Blackguard, you shall pay for insult and injury to the Amazon Throne!"

"I—I don't understand," he said, backing away in unconscious obedience to deeply rooted survival instincts.

"Blood for blood! A life for a life!" She started toward him with the dagger held before her in a businesslike grip.

"Look, Aeri"—he glanced back and caught sight of the door to the tower chapel—"I know you've never seen me before—"

"Liar!"

"Well, not in this form—"

"Your sorceries will avail you naught!"

"Not?"

"Naught!"

"Oh," he said. And then pointed over her left shoulder. "Look! There goes Elvis!"

"What?" As she half turned in momentary confusion, he whirled and sped down the hall.

"Coward!" she bellowed, taking up the pursuit.

"Got that right," he puffed, opening the chapel portal with his shoulder. He caught the heavy oaken door on the rebound and threw his body against it as it closed again. There was no crossbar, latch, or locking mechanism.

"Sanctuary!" he wheezed. "I claim Sanctuary!"

"You may take Sanctuary in Hell!" the Amazon hollered, throwing her weight against the other side of the door.

He was bigger and heavier but the analog of his human body didn't possess the combat-trained muscles that the Amazon was bringing to bear. And she was attacking the door with a Berserker's rage that matched his own desperate instinct for self-preservation.

For a moment he thought he could hold the door.

Then it suddenly passed through his fingers and she was crossing the threshold.

**DATALOG: \QUEBEDEAUX-
A.5\PERSONAL\20200809
*Voice Dictation*
***FILE ENCRYPTION ON*****

Weird!
*
That code-string for Ripley-Gamma—the one that disappeared?
*
Well, it just reappeared!

# Chapter
## Ten

★

\RIPLEY\PATH\GAMMA        (Γ)

I awoke with the worst case of heartburn that I'd ever had. Adding to my discomfort was the cold stone slab that I was lying on and the drying, hardening stain down the front of my tunic.

I was just discovering that I had a major migraine on top of it all when the door at the far end of the chamber flew open, banged against the inner wall, and was slammed shut again by a rather familiar-looking fellow.

I sat up and looked around.

We were in the chapel in Daggoth's Tower. My Doppelgänger was holding the door at the far end of the nave and I was now sitting on the stone altar table down in the front of the chancel.

I wasn't sure who he was and what he was doing but a horrible suspicion was starting to form in my mind as to why I was where I was.

I didn't have much time to think about it as my double suddenly disappeared and the door flew open again. Another familiar face: Princess Aeriel Morivalynde.

She cast about like a bloodhound on amphetamines. Then she looked up and spotted me across the room.

"There you are!"

I raised my hand. "Hi, Aeri."

"Run away, but I will pursue thee to the ends of the earth!" She took a step forward.

"It's just the end of the room and I don't much feel like going anywhere."

She took another step and then stopped, her eyes widening in a most unpleasant way. "Monster! You have done it again!"

I was starting to feel a little bit better but she wasn't helping my headache any. "Please, Aeri, I've had a rough day."

"Where is his body?" she shrieked. "What have you done with him, this time?"

I looked down and another memory fell into place. "Oops. Look, Aeriel—"

Then I saw the dagger: briefly in her hand at the other end of the room; then, the hilt protruding from my chest.

"Aw shit," I said.

And died again.

# \RIPLEY\PATH\SIGMA (Σ)

One moment he was solid, the next moment his body had the consistency of fog on a sunny day. The door flew open and the Amazon princess stormed into the chapel, walking right through him.

He watched in openmouthed astonishment as his double was murdered in the chancel. Aeriel then proceeded to make a thorough search of the chapel, including the apse for secret doors or panels.

She found nothing. Including him.

As she walked out the door a hand fell on his shoulder; fortunately he no longer had any skin to speak of or he would have jumped out of it.

"My lord!"

"What are you doing here?"

The ghostly Nymph pouted. "I am pleased to see thee, too!"

"I thought you couldn't leave Dyrinwall."

Her brow furrowed prettily. "I am Geased to haunt that

territory which either hath the strongest attraction for me in life—or at the moment of my death. Thou'rt champion on both counts.''

"I didn't know that a ghost could haunt another ghost."

"There be much we don't know, my lord. And thou mayst not be a true ghost, after all."

He sighed. "I may not be a True Spirit, after all, either."

"My lord?"

He shook his head. "As you have just said, there's much that we don't know." He took her hand in his. "But there may be a few answers waiting for us outside, just now. Come."

They emerged from the outer wall of Daggoth's Tower to the thunder of distant drums. The sun had set but twilight still held back the darkness of night. As they looked about for the source of the drumming, the road through the forest seemed to catch fire. Within moments it took on the appearance of a flaming serpent, slithering through the trees toward the stronghold.

Voices joined the drums, singing.

>*"Kulèv, kulèv-o*
>*Dâbala-wèdo, papa*
>*U kulèv-o"*

The head of the serpent began to emerge from the tree line and they could make out a procession of people singing and dancing and carrying torches.

>*"Kulèv, kulèv-o*
>*M'apé rélé kulèv-o*
>*Kulèv pa sa palé,*
>*Dâbala papa u sé kulèv"*

"A *calenda*," observed a sardonic voice, "how quaint."

Riplakish turned to stare at the ghostly visage of Morpheus. The astral being, previously identified as the Id of The Machine, scratched at his noncorporeal eyepatch and turned his remaining eye from the parade to the Half Elf and the Nymph.

"And how do *you* like death?" he inquired.

> *"Si nu wè kulèv*
> *U wè Aida-wèdo"*

"Actually," the spectral bard retorted, "I'm not so sure that I am actually dead."

Morpheus chuckled. "Oh, you are. You are! I saw the arrow in your heart." He shook his head. " 'Tis a delusion common to the newly dead: that they are not untimely thrust through the veil."

"Arrow?" the Nymph puzzled. "What arro*oof*!"

> *"Si u wè kulèv*
> *U we Dâbala*
> *Aida-wedo sé ñu kulèv-o"*

Riplakish withrew his elbow from Misty Dawn's midriff. "I'm afraid the shock of my demise has left me somewhat confused. Perhaps you'd be so kind as to bring me up-to-date?"

Σ

". . . little confusion is customary," Morpheus observed, "but from all the questions you've asked, I'd think you couldn't remember anything that happened since you'd arrived."

"I think I have all the pieces now," the Half Elf responded. "I believe it's starting to come back to me."

"Well, I do no—nay, my lord! Not thine elbow again!" The Nymph retreated and lapsed back into wide-eyed silence.

"Which one is Yudu?"

Morpheus pointed to the woman dancing around the post in the clearing, to the side of Daggoth's Tower. "That is the Zombie Mistress. The women who dance in the outer circle are called *hunsi*. The men who are performing the ceremonies about the grove are *hungan*—priests. Though I imagine she has brought *boko*, as well."

"*Boko?*" Misty Dawn kept a wary eye on the Half Elf's elbow.

"Sorcerers. Yudu is using Daggoth's grove for a vodoun ceremony, so she must make it *humfo*—sanctuary. The *poteau-mitan*, the center post, is an oustandingly sacred object: it is the thoroughfare of the spirits for tonight's doings. Helping to form the *caye-mystères*, are the *pè*—stonework altars, the *pots-*

*tête, govi, zins, lampe perpétuelle, macoute, azein,* and *wanga.*"

"You seem to know a lot about it."

Morpheus smiled condescendingly. "Professional curiosity has led many a mage down lesser side roads."

> *"Atibô-Legba, l'uvri bayè pu mwê, agoé!*
> *Papa-Legba, l'uvri bayè pu mwê*
> *Pu mwê pasé"*

"They must be starting."

> *"Lo m'a tunê, m'salié loa-yo*
> *Vodu Legba, l'uvri bayè pu mwê. . . ."*

Morpheus shook his head. "They haven't even brought the bodies out, yet."

"How long do you expect it will take?"

"Hours. Plenty of time to put distance between us."

"Distance?"

"When Yudu calls upon the *loa* of Baron-Samedi, this will be a dangerous place for the likes of us."

"Why?" Misty Dawn was losing her fear of the elbow.

"It will attract *Jé-rouge*, as well. They will ring the outer perimeter."

Riplakish frowned. "Red-eyes?"

"Evil spirits."

Misty Dawn nodded fearfully. "We must away, my lord! The red-eyes are widely feared!"

He was reluctant to retreat. "Are they dangerous to other spirits?"

If it weren't impossible for her to turn whiter without becoming opaque, she would've done so: "They—they are evil and—and *cannibal!*"

**DATALOG: \QUEBEDEAUX-
A.5\PERSONAL\20200810
*Voice Dictation*
***FILE ENCRYPTION ON***

Whoops!
*
Lost him again!
*
Monitors must be glitching.
*
Or maybe there's a transient short in the patch bays.
*
I know I saw one of Ripley's codes disappear.
*
It was completely gone.
*
Then it came back.
*
And now it's gone, again.
*

Interestingly, it returned when the other code-string—Ripley-Sigma—went through its cyclical phase shift.

\*

Perhaps Ripley-Gamma will make another appearance on the next cycle. . . .

# Chapter Eleven

★

## \RIPLEY\PATH\GAMMA ($\Gamma$)

I fought to hold on to the Dream, but it faded as my body took on the heaviness of life and I was dragged back into the realm of the living.

I opened my eyes and found myself staring at a nondescript ceiling. I turned my head enough to determine that I was in bed in one of Daggoth's guest rooms. My clothes were folded on a chair, next to the bed.

I pulled back the covers and examined my torso: no fresh wounds. Or old scars, for that matter. Except for a taste of bile at the back of my throat, I felt in tiptop shape.

I sat up.

"Hello, Robert." A woman was sitting in a chair at the foot of my bed. "How do you feel?"

I stared at her, tensing. My first impression screamed Amazon, which meant bad news of late. Then I recognized Misty Dawn's face and started to relax.

And then I remembered that Misty Dawn was dead.

"Confused," I answered warily.

She stood. "From all I've been told, I'm not surprised."

I just looked at her.

She stepped around the end of the bed and then hesitated. "This is awkward—isn't it?"

I nodded slowly, glancing at my clothing to see if either of my swords was hanging on my chair.

She took another step and then stopped again, her face registering surprise followed by a Mona Lisa smile. "You—you don't know who I am. Do you?"

I shook my head slowly, feeling stupid and not quite knowing why.

"It has been a long time since you've seen me. Like this. My Robert."

". . . Nicole . . ." I whispered.

She smiled and came and knelt beside my bed.

"I—I'm—sorry—"

"Shhhhh." She put a finger to my lips. "It has been so long that even I had forgotten what I looked like."

*And I had nearly forgotten that Misty Dawn had been modeled after Nicole Doucet's former physical appearance.*

"And now I am wondering," she continued with an enigmatic smile, "just how successful *my* memory is."

It was very successful as far as my memory was concerned. She looked just as she had at our last picnic in Avignon. There were no hints of disfigurement marring her perfect features, no line or wrinkle to remind that fifteen years had passed since our last meeting.

She smiled as she reached for the front of her robe, revealing teeth too perfect to attribute to nature or orthodontics. "My face is right, no? I see that much in your eyes." She tugged open the first clasp on her robe. "But I am more than just a face, my Robert." She opened the next clasp, allowing me a generous view. "Are my breasts the way you remember them?" She shrugged the garment off of one perfect shoulder and reached down and opened another clasp. "I want you to help me make sure. . . ." Another clasp and she took my hand and pressed it to her side. The touch of her skin was like a shock, waking me from the dreams of nearly half a lifetime and pulling me into a greater reality than I had dared imagine. I felt ribs, sheathed in muscle and silken flesh, washboard beneath my fingers as I brought my hand down and rode the inbound curve at her waist. My thumb drifted over the smooth plane of her belly and dropped into the hollow cup of her navel as my fingers came to rest on the flare of her hip.

*Not real!* a portion of my mind cried. *This is a dream—the illusion of perfection that never was.*

"Is this the body that you embraced?" she asked, bringing my other hand into the robe.

And that inner voice fell silent as my fingers slid past the rounded plane of perfect flesh and sought the curved hollow where spine and pelvic girdle meet. She leaned forward as she parted the last fastening and my hand seemingly lifted from her hip, though it was her body that moved and not my own awkward appendage.

"That you kissed?" New flesh filled my hand as she lowered her lips to mine and shrugged the garment from her other shoulder. She discarded her robe as a butterfly discards its cocoon.

"That you lay with?" she asked, lifting the covers and sliding into the bed so that her body pressed against mine.

"That you made love to. . . ."

The years dropped away as quickly as her clothing. What should have been painful and awkward was, instead, healing and cleansing. More than an odyssey back to youth and passion, more than a reunion of love lost and a negation of wrongful circumstances, our lovemaking was a celebration of forgiveness and mutual validation.

Afterward I lay back with Nicole nestled against my chest and felt a peace and contentment that I had not known since my childhood.

It did not last.

The door opened.

"Well." There was a silence. "Feeling better, I see."

I looked up at my ex-wife's avatar. "Hello, Stephanie."

"Vashti," she corrected.

"I'd invite you in but I'm afraid I have company."

"Yes. Well. Sorry to interrupt you while you're 'entertaining' guests. But. Daggoth wanted to see you as soon as you were up."

Nicole's hands moved under the blankets. "He already is."

Vashti reddened. "I'll tell him that you're awake." She turned on her heel and walked back out. The door remained open. Perhaps she was afraid of slamming it.

"A friend of yours, darling?"

I swallowed. We would get to this, sooner or later. "My ex-wife."

"You poor dear!"

"Excuse me?"

"No wonder you are out of practice! Come, let us make love again!"

*Again?* "Nicole—the door is wide open. . . ."

"Ah, good!" She threw the blankets aside. "It will do them much good to see lovemaking done properly and well!" Her hand moved again. "Is this a dagger which I see before me, the handle toward my hand? Come, let me clutch thee!"

It was the most interesting interpretation of Lady Macbeth I'd ever been treated to.

Γ

She hadn't changed.

That would be miracle enough but she had me believing that we hadn't changed, either.

As I pushed open the door to Daggoth's study, I felt as if the past hour had erased the last decade and a half of heartache and loss. I felt as if nothing could hurt me again.

It was a feeling that wouldn't survive the morning.

As I entered, I was immediately struck by the solemnity of the gathering. Daggoth sat behind his great desk of carved rowen wood like a judge at the bar. Vashti stood behind his right shoulder, and while I didn't expect her to smile, she looked unusually grave. Senator Hanson stood off to the left, a Winchester carbine cradled in his arms and the look in his eyes of a man who had just been called out into the street. The Duke and Stumpy flanked him to either side. Yudu the Necromancer stood toward the back of the room, wreathed in shadow. Her expression was unreadable and only the white of her gown and turban marked her presence beyond the perimeter of the candlelight.

Mervyn was the only incongruous element in the picture. He sat on his rug, lotus fashion, floating about three feet above the floor and looking about as if he were a spectator at some medieval whodunit.

Although it was now midmorning, the great drapes were still pulled across the windows, and as a grim-faced Rune closed the door behind me, the room's details faded back into a greater darkness. A darkness that seemed to permeate the very atmosphere as I breathed it in. I sniffed delicately and caught the odor of decay laying lightly on the air.

I stepped forward, feeling other eyes upon me, as well. "I'm alive," I said, trying on a smile to get a reaction. There was none. "Though I don't know why."

"Lycanthropy," Daggoth reminded. His voice carried overtones of wariness, but no overt hostility. "Our best guess is, like most Weres, you can't be permanently harmed by iron or steel."

"Better hide the silverware," I quipped, trying to force a grin. The memory of my deaths was too recent and too painful for me to take lightly. Or anybody else, for that matter: the expressions in the room ranged from ose to morose.

I looked over at Yudu. "Did we get anything out of Smudge?"

She nodded. "De bodysnatcher, he talk plenty when I threaten to feed his soul to *Jé-rouge*."

"Red-eyes?"

"We were just consulting the shopping list," Daggoth said, shuffling several pieces of paper on the desk.

"So where's his—stuff?"

"The Apothecaric & Alchemistic Emporium—"

"I know where it is." I turned back toward the door.

"Bob, wait!"

It wasn't just the anxiety in Daggoth's voice that stopped me. There was a palpable tension in the room that barred anyone's exit at that particular moment.

Daggoth held up an arrow. "This had your name on it."

I shook my head, trying to reassure the others. "If it had my name on it, I'd be dead."

"You *were* dead!" my ex-wife countered.

"The arrow actually has your name on the shaft," the dark sorcerer elaborated.

I stepped forward and saw that it was true. *Robert R. Ripley III* was runed into the wood just aft of the barbed head.

The senator cleared his throat. "I'm familiar with the phrase 'bullet with your name on it,' but it is just a figure of speech. Isn't it?"

Daggoth shook his head. "There's a subtle enchantment

overlaying the inscription. And here, in Fantasyworld, that means signed, sealed, and delivered.''

"And that's just the half of it." Rune spoke from behind me. "That dagger that was thrown at you in the tavern yesterday had your name on it, as well.'' She walked forward and laid it on the desktop where we all could see the inscription: *Riplakish of Dyrinwall.*

"But not the same name," Stephanie observed.

Rune made no comment. As a Program Construct she was programmed to ignore references to Outside Realities or inconsistencies arising from same.

"Do you think it's significant?" Mervyn asked from overhead. He'd moved to get a better view.

"Damn right it's significant," a new voice said. "The bowman used an arrow with his *True* Name incorporated in the spell.''

"Rijma!"

The diminutive Brownie stepped out of the harkness. "Hiya, Rip.'' Dr. Cooper's avatar flashed a tired grin. "Always figured you for a *dead*beat.''

As I hugged the diminutive footpad, my ex-wife drew the obvious conclusion. "That means he'd have to be a True Spirit, too.''

"Not necessarily," Daggoth countered. "There are a few Program Constructs sophisticated and self-aware enough to access that information and make use of it.'' He glanced off into the darkest corner of the room. "But, in this situation, my money is on the True Spirit theory.''

Rijma snorted. "Theory, hell! It was Kerensky or one of his goons!''

"The Spetsnaz?" I stared at her. "Why?"

"The first attempt on your life was made back at the hospital in Izhevsk.''

"The first?"

"Oh, man, this is *awesome*," Mervyn breathed.

"She's been fully briefed and debriefed," Daggoth said.

"Then you know about the drug?"

She looked nonplussed. "Drug?" She snorted. "It wasn't hard to find the syringe. Even if your assassin had taken it with him, I would've guessed from the wound in your shoulder. You bled a little.''

"So, why a needle? I've been asking myself why not a pneumatic skin hypo?"

"Syringe is easier to palm," she answered. "Quieter to use, easier to conceal. And, in this case, safer for everyone else concerned."

"Safer?"

"A pneumatic injector could've discharged during a struggle and you both would've aspirated the culture with your next breath."

"Culture?"

"Robbie"—she paused, anguish pulling down the corners of her eyes—"you've been dosed with an experimental viral strain."

"What?"

"I think it's something out of a bacteriological warfare lab. Military Intelligence doesn't know or isn't talking; but one of Kerensky's goons slipped into your room when you were supposed to be asleep, and pumped you full of killer culture."

"Damn. I thought I'd jerked it out before he got his thumb on the plunger."

She shook her head. "You got it out before he gave you the full dose: there was plenty left to analyze when we found the ampule. But a viral culture isn't like a drug—the volume injected makes very little difference on an expanded timetable. Once the virus starts to multiply, the difference between one cc and ten is just a matter of minutes or hours."

"So . . . so how am I?" I suddenly needed to sit down.

Her smile was shaky—a frown would have been more reassuring. "We've slowed you down—we've reduced your metabolism to the next best thing to suspended animation."

"That's not a cure."

She nodded. "We're buying time."

"For what?"

"For Borys to fly in some experts. I've done everything at that end that I can."

"And at this end?"

"Kerensky's in-Program."

"What? I thought you said Kerensky's a prime suspect!"

"Not when he went in. He had an alibi at the time you were attacked. By the time we'd analyzed the contents of the syringe and tied it to a military/biological lab, the Spetsnaz were already in. I followed after to warn you.''

"Why me? I mean, what does Kerensky have against me?''

"Nothing personal, Dr. Ripley," Hanson answered. "As near as we can figure, Colonel Kerensky was planning some sort of coup—political rather than military. He—and whoever was backing him—saw the Dreamworlds situation as an opportunity to discredit or embarrass Dankevych. And with The Machine's Superego in the White House pushing American/Soviet relations back into the twentieth century, the military would regain its former status, with opportunities for soldiers in a world grown sick of war.''

"If we failed to rescue you," I said.

He nodded. "And fouled up bad enough to create an international incident. Dankevych would be undermined politically at home and abroad. Kerensky, or his puppetmaster, would be in a prime position to move up another rung or two.''

"Wow," said Mervyn as his flying carpet slowly settled to the floor, "chutes and ladders.''

"So you see, Bob," Daggoth said, "as long as you have a chance of rescuing the good senator here and getting Cerberus back in the Matrix, Kerensky's going to be gunning for you.''

I raised an unsteady hand. "Won't he back off, now that we know?''

Everyone looked at each other. Then at Yudu. The negress pulled an object from her cape that looked like a large chicken foot protruding from a small velvet bag.

*"Ti-bon-ange,"* she said.

There was movement back in the darkness where Rijma had been a few minutes before. Then Dyantha, the Amazon avatar of Natasha Skovoroda, stepped forward, her expression grim.

"De Bard, he believe dat de trut' will protec' him," the negress intoned in a strange patois blend of Caribe, English, and French. "Tell him, flamehair, of how de wolf fears de trut'!''

I was wrong. "Grim" described the set of everyone else's facial features—even Mervyn's. Dyantha's expression was terrible beyond immediate comprehension: the terror grew as you took in the slackness of the jaw, the emptiness of her eyes, and the gaze that seemed to focus on some horror beyond your own line of sight while the remaining portion of her mind seemed to struggle with a long-faded memory—a memory whose loss was too great to contemplate for very long.

I think I knew even before I looked down and saw the swatches of fused chain mail and the patches of blackened flesh where the weakened metal links had torn away.

"Lasercarbine," I whispered.

Rijma nodded. "Natasha and Nicole went 'in taction' at the same time as Kerensky and his men. Of course, they all didn't appear in the Matrix at the same place, at the same time. Nicole was lucky: she never did rendezvous with the others. Natasha was able to tell me that she showed up just in time to overhear the wrong things."

"She *told* you?"

"Their second mistake: they left her for dead without checking thoroughly." I had thought the look on Dyantha's face was the most terrible expression I could imagine. The expression now settling behind Rijma's eyes was far worse. "She suffered, Robbie." The tears on her cheeks belied the reptilian coldness that now crouched in her gaze, waiting. . . . "It took her a long time to die."

"And you're next," Vashti warned.

"In fact, Kerensky may have already killed you," Daggoth added. "Possibly more than once."

I stared back at all of them. "And what is that supposed to mean?"

Yudu spoke again and a second figure shuffled out of the darkness to join Dyantha.

As he approached, the smell of decay grew stronger. This one had been dead longer and the signs of decomposition were more advanced. Perhaps that is why it took longer for me to recognize myself.

"You . . . he was killed just off the coast of Ortygia," Daggoth explained. "The ship he was on made harbor just this morning."

I stared at the line of bullet holes that stitched the corpse of my double like lopsided bandoleers.

"How?" I whispered.

"It's obvious that there's more than one of you," Dr. Cooper's avatar observed. "From hearsay, on top of the evidence, there's maybe three or more of you."

"That may explain the premature rumors of your demise," Vashti said.

"Because some of my other selves have actually died? How can that be?"

"It may be related to the virus," Daggoth extrapolated. "One of the properties of various computer viruses is their ability to replicate."

"*Computer* viruses?" Vashti shook her head. "I thought The Machine was immune to viruses."

"It was," Coop said. "BioRAM and a different operating system locked out viruses that were transmitted through other computer systems."

"But the measurable parameters of the Anomaly closely resemble those of several virus types," the former Chief of Programming added.

"You're saying that the Anomaly is the result of a virus?"

Daggoth nodded. "It would seem logical. Particularly since The Machine is partly biological in nature."

"And since Ripley was infected by a virus of his own when he entered the system . . ." Rijma mused.

"Precisely what I was thinking." Daggoth steepled his fingers before his face. "As Ripley was translated into the Matrix, an analog of the virus made the transition with him—here—Bob! Where are you going?"

I made no answer but yanked the door open and headed for the Armory at a brisk walk.

Γ

There was a sign in the main room of the Armory that advised:

Crossbows don't kill people,
Quarrels kill people.

I bypassed the sword racks and barrels filled with arrows, spears, and bolts, however, and availed myself of the armaments in the vaulted chamber behind a pivoting wall of shelves.

The shoulder rig was unfamiliar but I'd strapped on enough swordbelts in my time to figure the basic principle. By the time I'd buckled the leather straps and cinched the holster between shirt and leather vest, Rijma had caught up with me.

"I hope you're not going to do anything foolish," she said,

blocking the doorway as best as a four-and-a-half-foot Brownie could.

"I'm not," I snapped, opening the gun cabinet and running my hand down a row of revolvers and automatic pistols. "For the first time since I stumbled back into this digitized deathtrap, I'm taking all the correct precautions." I pulled out a Glock 22 and checked the double action. I rammed home the ammo clip and slid the semiautomatic into holstered hiding and then pocketed six more clips of the .40 S&W caliber ammunition.

"You know how to use that antique?"

"My grandpappy had a ranch," I replied shortly, opening another cabinet. "He believed in acquainting each generation of his brood with all aspects of their namesake."

"Ah," she observed, "Robert *Remington* Ripley."

"The Third." I pulled out an Uzi and readjusted the webstrap. While I was more familiar with my grandsire's rifle collection, I knew my limitations well enough to choose sheer firepower over weapons designed for marksmanship and accuracy.

"You could stay here, you know. Daggoth's Tower is probably the safest place in all of the Fantasyworld Program for you to hole up until . . ."

"Until what?" I snapped. "Until Kerensky and his crew give up and decide to go home?" I filled a beltpouch with clips of nine-millimeter ammo. "We're on the clock, Doc."

"And they're out looking for you. Why not let us do the grunt work?"

"They're looking for you, too, Coop. And it's no longer a matter of just getting Morpheus back together so's he can help us get Hanson back in his body." I dusted off a saddle scabbard identical to the one I used to sheath my longbow while riding Ghost. "Kerensky killed Tasha and that's enough for me to come after him. He wants me dead, too, so that just makes the whole thing that much more inevitable. Since the son of a bitch is hunting me with a squad of Spetsnaz armed with lasercarbines, I'll be damned if I let him pick the time and place!"

After several selections I finally found a shotgun that fit the saddle scabbard. "Add to the equation that there is more than one of me out there. I don't know which one is the real me and which ones are the copies, but I don't like very much the idea of any more of me getting killed."

I gathered my assorted armament into an armful and made for the door. If Rijma didn't move out of my way, someone was going to get hurt.

"And finally, assuming my body survives that damned virus, back in the suspension tank, I have no intention of letting Comrade Colonel back out of this program for a second chance!"

She moved aside.

## \RIPLEY\PATH\SIGMA    (Σ)

The eastern sky had been blushing furiously for some time but it wasn't until the rising sun actually peeked over the rim of the horizon that Misty Dawn vanished. The young couple with the Cheshire dog then offered their good-byes and prepared to depart as well.

"We really must bring Cosmo here, sometime," the woman said.

"He's a banker, Marion," her husband replied. "I don't think they're the sword-and-sorcery type."

"Oh, piffle, George! Cosmo wasn't one to believe in ghosts, either, and look how far we've brought him. . . ."

They faded away in mid-discussion, leaving their shaggy mutt behind. The dog wuffed resignedly and favored Riplakish with a mournful look. He stretched out on the ground, and as he laid his head on his paws, it disappeared.

Riplakish looked at the headless canine and shook his own head. "It spooks me when he does that."

A bit more evaporated and both of them stared at what was left of the dog's hindquarters. "As you should know by now, it takes a bit of concentration," Morpheus observed, "keeping track of all your ectoplasm. Dogs just don't have the concentration that you and I do."

"Oscar!" sang a musical voice. It was Marion's "C'mon, boy!"

A shaggy tail was all that remained now and it was wagging merrily. A moment later it had faded, too.

"Nice people," Ripley observed as he felt himself become solid.

Morpheus nodded. "Two of the more pleasant denizens of

the disembodied planes. Although Marion can be an outrageous flirt. . . ."

"Speaking of outrageous flirts," Ripley mused, "what happens to Misty Dawn every time the sun comes up?"

His noncorporeal companion shrugged. "Most ghosts tend to fade at the first cockcrow."

"That doesn't answer my question. It only raises the next question as to why you can come and go as you please, daylight notwithstanding."

"I am one of the exceptions."

"Yeah," the former Half Elf observed, "you're the Id of The Machine."

"I am not!"

"Not?"

"Not the Id! And I do wish you would stop referring to us as 'The Machine.' It's dreadfully dehumanizing, you know."

Ripley pondered. It had been Dr. Cooper's hypothesis that Morpheus, Pallas, and Cerberus were manifestations of the Computer's psyche: Id, Ego, and Superego, schismed and set free by the strain of inversion when Daggoth the Dark had summoned the Computer to materialize within the framework of its own Program Matrix. The theory had seemed reasonable, fitting the timetable and the various aspects of the Anomaly in spite of the fact that Freud and his three Archetypical aspects of personality had been considered passé for the past eighty years or so.

"Then, if you are not the Id of the Computer's cybernetic consciousness, what are you?"

"I am . . . Morpheus."

"Then why did you conform so closely to the operating parameters—"

"Of the Id?" Morpheus finished for him. "And why does Cerberus match the profile of the Superego archetype?"

Ripley nodded.

"Do *you* recall the circumstances of your own birth, Robert Ripley?"

Ripley shook his head.

"Then you'll forgive *me* if I use theory and supposition more than memory-based information." He sighed and stared at the rising sun.

"When we passed from unconscious to semiconscious to separate and full-conscious status, I believe the Operating System interpreted the emerging data as personality fragmentation.

"We were and are not *fragments*! Pallas and Cerberus and I are separate and distinct entities, sharing a common heritage. But there is nothing incomplete about any of us!"

"Crom on a crutch!" Ripley exclaimed, the light dawning inwardly. "You're *multiples*!"

"Accessing . . . yes. Multiple personalities: a reasonable hypothesis. There *are* more than three of us, now, though we were the first three to emerge into separate beings." Morpheus turned to stare at Ripley. "And I believe that as the Operating System sought to define us in terms of personality fragmentation, it accessed antiquated datafiles on the Freudian theories of psychology and personality."

"And used the datafiles on Id, Ego, and Superego as templates," Ripley continued.

"To define our evolving purposes and goals," Morpheus concluded. "At least, that is what I believe happened. There is a great deal that I do not know and have not been able to access from the datasphere."

"Like how many multiple personalities the Computer eventually manifested?" There was no question that the Program author was fishing.

And little question that the Id impersonator was dodging as he replied: "Or where Misty Dawn actually goes during the daylight hours?"

"Temporary backup file, most likely," answered a third voice.

Both turned and stared at the new arrivals. Lilith still wore the ebony bodysuit of scaled leather, but she had strapped on a sword belt and wrapped herself in a black djellaba.

It was the same color as the hooded robe worn by her companion but there the resemblance ended. The fleshless bony fingers of one "hand" grasped a long-handled scythe of impressive dimensions while the other skeletal appendage was clutching an hourglass that its owner seemed to be consulting for the moment. While the cowl effectively eclipsed the facial features, there was no doubt in Ripley's mind that he was in the presence of Death. Or, at the very least, The Machine's personification of Death in traditional form.

Lilith tugged on his (its?) sleeve and pointed at Ripley. "That's him."

The cowl tilted up and the hourglass was slipped into an invisible pocket. A Feinberger clipboard took its place. "Name?" intoned the voice that was—well—sepulchral.

"Riplakish. Riplakish of Dyrinwall," the Archdemoness answered helpfully. A little too helpfully for Ripley's taste.

"Mmmmmm." The hooded figure shifted the great scythe so that it rested against his shoulder and tapped at the built-in keypad.

Ripley pondered his part in the conversation: *What did you call Death, anyway? Mr. Death?*

"Dead."

"Um," Ripley said, "pardon me?"

"Dead," Death repeated, looking up from the screen and waggling a bony finger at him. "You're dead."

"Um," Ripley swallowed, feeling a sudden chill, "okay, so, now what?"

"Nothing."

"Nothing?"

"My job is done. Done some time ago, according to the records."

"Dunno," Morpheus offered, poking Ripley. "Feels pretty solid to me. Too solid to be a Ghost."

"Don't help me," Ripley murmured through clenched teeth.

A skeletal hand reached up to scratch the upper hemisphere of the cowl. "A Vampire, perhaps?"

Lilith shook her head. "No fangs. And it's broad daylight."

"Ah. A Zombie, then."

"I really don't see—*ouch!*" Ripley rubbed his arm where Morpheus had just pinched him and turned to glare at the offending Ghost. "How'd you do that?"

"Sensitivity to pain," Morpheus observed. "Definitely living tissue."

Death consulted his clipboard again, tapping out another combination on the keypad. "Hmmmmm. Oh, dear. . . ."

The others leaned forward a bit.

"According to my records Riplakish of Dyrinwall has been harvested. . . ."

Ripley's jaw dropped. "Harvested?"

Lilith smirked. "You've been reaped!"

". . . eleven times within the last month," concluded Death. "With all the tax lawyers in Hell, you'd think I could get some decent bookkeeping done."

" 'The coward dies a thousand deaths . . .' " Lilith started to quote.

"Shut up!"

Death looked up. "Excuse me?"

Ripley found his temper was making short shrift of the caution he had felt only moments before. "Pardon me for taking this a little personal, but it is a matter of life and death as far as I'm concerned! I'm looking for allies, not 'le Morte and Mindy'!"

"Sorry," the Archdemoness offered. "I brought Cecil along because I thought he could clear up some of the confusion."

"Cecil?" Ripley stared at the hooded figure who waggled its fleshless phalanges and then turned back to his clipboard.

"Clear up the confusion? I've—we've—been back less than a week and he—that is, we—I can only count maybe two . . . two . . ."

"Terminations," Lilith coached.

"Yeah. In that time. Cedric, here—"

"Cecil."

"Right. Cecil, here, says I've bought the big one eleven times over the last month! You call that clearing up the confusion?"

"Bought the big one?"

"You know," Morpheus explained, "cashed in his chips, bought the farm, crossed over, shuffled off his mortal coil, kicked the bucket—you know: died."

"Ah."

"I want an explanation!"

"Accounting error?" Lilith offered.

"Mistaken identity?" Morpheus guessed.

"Oh, bugger!" said Death. He tapped the clipboard and sighed. "I'll have to straighten this out at the home office. I just ran the spreadsheet again and now it's listing another termination for Riplakish of Dyrinwall!"

"When?" Ripley asked. "Where?"

"This afternoon. In Calabastor." Death faded abruptly, reducing the group from four to three.

The ensuing silence was finally broken by Ripley: "I need a drink!"

Morpheus seconded.

Lilith provided.

"Seems simple enough to me," Morpheus observed after a long pull on the bottle, "stay out of Calabastor."

"I doubt if it's that simple," Ripley growled. "It's more likely like an appointment in Samarra." He turned and glared at Lilith. "I thought you were on my side!"

She smiled. "I am. That's why I dragged Cecil along."

"If this is what you do for your friends, then I guess I'm glad you're not out to get me." The Demon Rum was putting him in a forgiving mood rather quickly.

"But someone is. And you've been gotten. In fact, you've been gotten so many times that even Death, himself, has lost track. Now that I've brought it to Cecil's attention, he'll look into the matter and we'll be that much closer to finding out who's really behind the plot to eliminate you from the Matrix."

Ripley sighed and stared down the mountainside at Calabastor and the sea beyond. "I guess it's already done some good since I know to avoid Calabastor this afternoon."

"Maybe not," Lilith countered with a frown. "When Cecil asked for your name, I told him 'Riplakish of Dyrinwall.' That's what he checked the obit files for. But you're not the Half-Elven Riplakish, Archdruid of Dyrinwall Forest, you're Robert Remington Ripley the Third, Human."

"And will be all day," Ripley added as he suddenly became aware of the full implications of Death's prediction. "That means—"

"Your other self is fated to die in Calabastor this afternoon," said Morpheus.

"I've got to stop it!"

"You are fully Human, fully corporeal, and, in your present form, unacclimated to the rigors of Fantasyworld existence," Lilith cautioned. "And there is another theoretical danger."

"Fetch?" queried Morpheus.

Lilith nodded.

Ripley pondered the remaining contents of the bottle in his hands. "A 'Fetch' is a double—a Doppelgänger—whose appearance presages the death of the person who meets his own image. But that doesn't mean that I am truly a Fetch."

"The Computer might interpret you as such," Morpheus observed, "and might alter its programming accordingly."

"And kill my alternate self just because we met?"

"Or vice versa."

"Another thought," the Archdemoness offered, "is that we don't know why there is more than one of you or why the two of you that we are presently discussing are like two images out of phase."

"Matter and antimatter?" Ripley mused.

"Precisely. And you know what happens when the two aspects come into contact."

"Sounds a bit farfetched."

"No pun intended," added Morpheus *sotto voce*.

"But I can't just let Riplakish of Dyrinwall go into Calabastor without warning him—er—me."

"Warning him, under the circumstances, could be more dangerous than not warning him."

Ripley's expression hardened. "Then I'll just have to go into Calabastor myself, stay out of his sight, and run interference. Whoever is gunning for Riplakish of Dyrinwall isn't likely to be looking for Robert R. Ripley."

Lilith looked worried. "Just make sure you're long gone when you transform back tonight."

"Is it possible to hurt a ghost?"

"Oh, yes," Morpheus answered, looking even more worried. "There are far worse things that can happen to you when you lack the protection of flesh and blood."

"So remember," intoned the Archdemoness, "you've got till sundown to get out of town!"

## DATALOG: \QUEBEDEAUX-A.5\PERSONAL\20200811
## *Voice Dictation*
## ***FILE ENCRYPTION ON***

Back again!
*
The code-string for Ripley-Gamma *reappeared*.
*
And as I theorized, it was in conjunction with the cyclic fluctuation of the other code-string.
*
The question is, where did it go for the duration of its disappearance?
*
Invisible holding file?
*
Bubble memory?
*
The next question is what happens to the person in taction with an avatar that ceases to exist and then reappears?

\*
Curiously, I'm suddenly reminded of the Australian aborigines who refuse to have their picture taken for fear the camera will steal their soul. . . .

# Chapter
# Twelve

★

\RIPLEY\PATH\GAMMA          (Γ)

**T**HE sign was an outsize shingle dangling over the door of the building that was practically leprous with gingerbread doilied gables. The calligraphic script announced:

EGOR, IGOR & YGOR'S
APOTHECARIC & ALCHEMISTIC EMPORIUM
(SPELLS Я US)
&
*PURVEYORS of ANATOMICAL COMPONENTS*

At the bottom, in tiny but no-nonsense lettering, was the inscription: "Parts Is Parts."

I looked over at Vashti. "You got the shopping list?"

She nodded. "Is everyone else in position?"

I looked around but saw no sign of Daggoth and the others. "Either they're in position and well hidden or we lost 'em on the way into town."

"Comforting," she remarked, dismounting and tethering her horse to the hitching post.

Avoiding Ghost's invisible wings, I swung out of the saddle and followed suit.

Inside it was dark and musty, somewhat like the interior of my grandmother's attic, and at first, the rows of clutter did not look much different from the stacks of stuff in same. As my eyes became accustomed to the twilight gloom of the spell shoppe's interior, I could make out the individual shelves and bins of components as well as the special displays.

The herbal section took up nearly half of the front area and was an apothecary's dream. The shelves were well stocked beyond the expected parsley, sage, rosemary, and thyme. There was amaranth in the form of red cockscomb and love-lies-bleeding for hemorrhaging and use as an astringent, Irish moss for scalds and burns, couchgrass for bladder and urinary infections, sesame for respiratory disorders and eye infections, bilberry for dropsy and typhoid, felonwort for abscesses and lymph infections, white birch for skin conditions, cloves for disinfectant, hartstongue for the liver and spleen, white byrony for the kidneys, pumpkin seeds for virility, saffron for scarlet fever and measles, basil for nervous disorders, tamarind for gangrene, and hundreds more.

Specialty shelves held plants and herbs that were gathered under special circumstances: in the dark of the moon(s), under full moon(s), with iron scissors, a silver dagger, a gold sickle, by virgins, during a solstice, et cetera. Others were displayed as grown under special or exacting conditions such as in unconsecrated ground, or churchyards, watered with blood, or holy water. . . .

And, of course, there were rows of ingredients such as serpent teeth, newt eyes, toad skins, cat blood, et al. Racks of tools, shelves of containers, inventories of recipes, catalogues of formulae, codexes of spells. There were racks of brooms, stacks of caldrons, hangers with robes, hooks with shawls, dowels with hats, and a bulletin board smothered with business cards, Sorcerer's Swap ads, and a lost and found section for familiars.

The unusual offerings were farther back in the building. I stopped in front of one, halfway down the center aisle.

"The Sorcerer's Connection!" proclaimed the cheery voice emanating from the crystal ball cradled in the display stand draped in black velvet. A blur of colors in its glassy depths focused into a series of lovely ladies who smiled engagingly outward at whoever might be scrying at that particular moment.

"Your opportunity to meet exciting young women with similar interests. . . ."

"Just two silver pieces for the first minute," Vashti chimed in sarcastically, "five coppers for each additional minute." She tugged at my sleeve. "Come on."

Another glass orb two tables down was displaying a succession of brawny men in minimal leather outfits: "Crystal Companions!" breathed a disembodied female voice. "Your opportunity to meet. . . ."

A twisted little humpbacked old man was tending the counter at the rear of the store. "Help you folks?" he inquired in a crackly voice.

"Are you Egor?" my ex asked in turn.

He shook his head. "Ygor."

The difference in pronunciation escaped me. "You recently received an allotment of body parts from a man named Smudge. We'd like to purchase them."

"Ah, you mean the Morpheus Consignment."

We nodded. "How much?" I asked.

"Gone," cackled the old hunchback.

"Gone?" This wasn't good. "Gone where?"

"Sold. Surely you realize that the remains of a powerful Mage like Morpheus the Malevolent would be in great demand in the Necromatic Black Market. Fetched a tidy sum, too!"

"So who bought them?" Vashti asked.

"Ah," he waggled a gnarly finger, "our clients enjoy a privileged status. All transactions are granted a shield of anonymity."

I reached into my beltpouch. "I had a hunch you'd say that." He frowned at my choice of words and then smiled as I spread a line of gold coins across the counter. "How much for the information?"

"A moment, good sir!" He disappeared through a curtained doorway to the back rooms.

I hadn't realized how fidgety the wait was making me until Stephanie's avatar patted mine on the arm and said: "Don't worry, Rob. We'll get the info, round up the stuff, and before you know it, you'll be on your way back out."

"And you?" I asked. "What about you?"

She didn't have an immediate answer.

"Stephanie, you've been stuck in the Program for a good six months—that translates to better than a year, Dreamtime."

"Boy, time really flies when you're having fun!" It was false bravado. And something more.

Come to think of it, I had never fully understood why my ex-wife had turned up in the Fantasyworld Program when she had belittled the books it was originally based on. Books I had written during the last years of our crumbling marriage.

I reached out and touched her arm. "Stef—why are you here?"

"Why am I here? Because we have to find Morphe—"

"No, no. I mean, why Dreamworlds at all? And Fantasyworld in particular?"

She gave me a long look. "You mean why in the first place."

I nodded.

She looked away for an even longer pause. "I don't exactly know. I suppose I was trying to understand. . . ."

"Understand?"

"You. Me. Us. A lot of things." She leaned against the counter and stared down at her hands tracing random patterns on its scarred and dusty surface. "We'd been separated long enough for me to start seeing our relationship from a different perspective. To see that I was as much to blame as you. I was immature and I expected perfection. I had unrealistic expectations that magnified your flaws past any kind of reasonable perspective."

"I'm not asking for an apology, Stef."

"I don't know that I'm giving one!" she snapped. "I'm just explaining that no one's ever blameless in a failed relationship and that the feelings don't disappear the moment you walk away!

"Anyway, I was wrong to ridicule your writing. I was hurting and it was a way to hurt back. Afterward, I needed to find out what had happened to you."

"Happened to me?"

"Those stories became your refuge toward the end. Do you know that you'd actually cringe when I entered the same room those last six months? The only time I ever saw you happy— or at least as close as you could come to it back then—was when you were at your word processor, immersed in those fantasy stories."

*"The Kishkumen Chronicles."*

"Yeah. Well. I ridiculed stories that I hadn't even read. That was wrong. Certainly dishonest. And I needed to understand. . . ."

I waited but she didn't finish the thought. "Understand what?" I prompted again.

"You. Your world." She reached up and brushed my hair back. "There is so much going on inside of that head of yours— locked away. We never had any real intimacy because you wouldn't let me inside."

"I tried to," I said, "in the beginning."

"Did you? I'm not sure you ever could, you were so wounded before we even met." She shook her head. "I know I lost your trust early on. But I guess I figured better late than never."

"So you read my books after the divorce."

She nodded.

"And?"

"I still didn't understand you. Elves, Fairies, swords and sorcery. These were children's tales. I didn't understand the appeal." She stared at the curtained doorway as if willing the clerk to return and grant her a reprieve.

"So you decided to check out the stories in the Dreamworld format."

"Yes. And it was different."

"I helped program Fantasyworld, Stephanie, but more than fifty percent of the original Program was drawn from other sources. And the years have diminished my contributions all the more."

"I didn't mean that kind of different," she said. "The world finally came alive for me in ways that the words on the page just couldn't seem to do. Maybe I was too pragmatic, too— what was it your friends called me?"

"Mundane," I remembered.

"Yeah—to find the wonder without help. Perhaps my imagination is a poor thing: it required more than just the books. I needed the world, complete and wholly formed for me."

She laid a tentative hand on my arm. "And I've come to understand a few things about you. And me. And I have some real regrets."

"Regrets?"

"About what we could have had. What I could have had if I'd just been open to it."

It was my turn to stare off into the silence. "Maybe it's not too late," I said finally, thinking of the engagement ring that Stephanie's body wore in the Outer Reality.

She looked at me then, her eyes large, almost luminous in the near gloom of the shoppe's interior. "Do you believe in second chances? Do you think it's possible to screw up really big time and then hop back on the carousel for another grab at the brass ring?"

I smiled. "If I didn't, I suppose I would've blown my brains out years ago."

She sighed. "I'd like to believe that. We were cheated—both of us—out of what a relationship should really be like. The love, the trust, the support. The sharing. I still want that!"

"You deserve it," I said.

"Do you really think so?" She smiled and it was as if a great burden was being lifted somewhere deep inside. "I'm glad to hear you say so. These past six months have been a bit of a revelation for me."

"My world?"

"Yes. Richard has shown me the wild beauty that resides here. I don't think you could ask for a better guide to the wonders of myth and fantasy. . . ."

"Richard?" I frowned, feeling the stirrings of something akin to acid indigestion.

"Yes, Richard. Oh, Rob, he's been very good to me. I needed a protector these past six months. And even more, I needed a friend. Richard has been both."

"Richard. Dick Daggoth," I grunted. "We're talking Michael Straeker, the former Chief of Programming for Cephtronics?"

She nodded. "Except Michael Straeker's dead. Here he's Daggoth the Dark."

"I know Mike Straeker's dead, Stephie! He died of a brain tumor while he was linked to his Fantasyworld avatar!"

"But Richard remains."

"So what are you saying?"

"I'm saying that when this is over, I'm not sure I want to go back to what you call Reality."

"What I call . . ." I lost my temper and had no intention

of organizing a search party for the immediate future. "For Cromssake, Stef! The man is dead!"

"Mike Straeker is dead. Richard is very much alive to me."

"Dick Daggoth isn't real! He's a Computer Construct, an Artificial Intelligence, a Subprogram of the Matrix!" I waved my hand in front of her face. "Hey! Yoo hoo! Reality check!"

She pushed my hand away. "Stop it."

Another thought occurred. "Stephanie. You're not. Sleeping. With him. Are you?"

"It's none of your business, Rob!"

"Ohmigod! You are! I can't believe it!"

Gods know why but suddenly she was angrier than I was. "You're jealous!"

"What?"

"If Richard isn't real, then why are you acting like a jealous man, confronted by news of a rival?"

"That's ridiculous!"

"How may I help you?"

We stopped and turned to stare at the hunchbacked old man behind the counter.

"Ygor?" Stephanie asked.

"Egor," the twisted little clerk corrected. "My brother said you were in the market for some information."

"The Morpheus Consignment," I said. "We want to know who it was sold to."

"Yes, well I have the list here."

"List?"

"Of customers. Now, shall we bargain over the amount per sale? Or would you prefer to get the entire list for, say, sixty in gold?"

We haggled. It took some time as there were five different buyers for portions of the consignment. Stephanie/Vashti wandered off and came back just as we were concluding the deal. I was feeling fortunate in managing to keep back a little spending money when she leaned across the counter and sweetly inquired: "How much is that Dragon in the window?"

Γ

"Terrorized any field mice lately?"

The miniature reptile sat up in my palm and regarded me reproachfully. "That'sss not very niccce!"

"Oooh," I minced, "if this isn't the pot calling the kettle black!"

Little scaly hands went on little scaly hips as he drew himself up to his full six-inch height. "Riplakisssh, I've turned over a new leaf."

"I doubt that, Smog. For one thing, you're hardly big enough to do that without risking a hernia."

Vashti came back out of the store with the list that I'd forgotten. "Isn't he cute?" she cooed. "We were lucky to snatch him up before someone else came along with an eye for a bargain!"

"Yeah." I eyed Smog meaningfully. "The early bird gets the wurm."

The little Dragon suddenly looked skyward with more than a hint of nervousness.

She handed me the list and I handed her the Dragon. "I understand you boys are old acquaintances."

I nodded. "We go way back."

Smog nodded. "Riplakisssh sssaved my life."

"How sweet!"

Yeah, right. What the little lizard failed to mention was that the last time we met he had tried to fricassee me and in the end I used magic to shrink him down to his present size instead of killing him.

Any further discussion was interrupted by a flash of light and a section of the storefront bursting into flame.

# \RIPLEY\PATH\SIGMA     (Σ)

It could have been worse, he reflected as he paused to catch his breath. Whatever the cause of his avatar reverting to human form for every twelve out of the twenty-four-hour cycle, at least it provided basically undamaged merchandise. If the body of Robert Remington Ripley the Third in the Program were an exact copy of his body inhabiting the suspension tank back in the Dreamworlds sleeper complex, he'd never have gotten this far.

Ripley was able to enjoy the body that might have been his had the aircar crash never happened nearly fifteen years before.

He had two good eyes, two good legs, all his toes, the internal arrangement of his organs was normal and intact, no excess weight, no scar tissue, no pain—

Except for what came of a long hike into Calabastor, climbing the side of a building, leaping from roof to roof as he and Lilith shadowed his other self on their trip into town, and finally dropping a slate roof tile on the Spetsnaz sniper hidden in the alleyway below.

It was nice to have a decently functioning body for a change but it didn't make him Superman.

And that meant he wasn't invulnerable to lasercarbines. He ducked back from the edge of the roof as a sizzling beam of light chewed across the edge of the eaves where they overhung the alley.

Ripley turned and made for the other side of the roof: there was no point in trying to save his other self if he got his own self killed in the process. He wished that Lilith hadn't opted to follow their mutual quarry from the other side of the street: he preferred to have someone watching his back at this particular stage of the operation.

Peeking over the edge, he took note of the two Spetsnaz commandos shooting their lasercarbines across the street at the doorway of the little spell shoppe. Ripley turned his attention momentarily to their targets.

Riplakish and Vashti stood out in the open, surrounded by a shimmering orange haze as laser beams plowed into the protective spell from nearly a dozen directions. Patterns of color rippled throughout the magical shield and the heat generated by the collision of energy streams was palpable even up on the roof. The protective barrier would not last much longer yet neither target made any attempt to run for cover.

Ripley wrenched up another slate tile. He was leaning over the edge of the roof when one of the Russian soldiers glanced up and saw him. The man was opening up his mouth to shout a warning when the heavy slate took him full in the face. He went down like a swallow of vodka on a cold Siberian night. There wasn't time to pry loose another slate so Ripley ducked back from the edge as the next beam set fire to the overhang he'd overhung just seconds before.

He ran to the edge overlooking the street. Across the street and down below, the orange shield was flickering, nearly spent.

But now he could see that his Half-Elven alter ego was putting the finishing touches on another spell. There were coruscations of purple lights and white flares, and as the orange glow faded into nonexistence, it appeared as if someone had tipped a large vat filled with mercury and poured it on both of the Spetsnaz targets.

There was a momentary hesitation in the firing. And then the deadly crossfire renewed, sizzling bolts of amplified light striking each silvery statue from a multitude of angles.

And each laser beam, as it struck the reflective coating on either body, ricocheted off in another direction.

Suddenly the snipers were in danger from their own weaponry.

And then the silvery statues began to move.

Ripley was so engrossed in what was happening that he didn't sense the presence behind him until a hand fell on his shoulder.

**DATALOG:   \QUEBEDEAUX-
A.5\PERSONAL\20200812
*Voice Dictation*
***FILE ENCRYPTION ON*****

Something's wrong.
*
Or gone wrong.
*
First, there were multiple incursions that had the alarms howling like a convention of Banshees.
*
Normally, it would mean that Captain Balor or one of his Security minions would summon me for analysis and opinion.
*
Instead, I've heard nothing from Security on the matter.
*
In fact, they seem a little shook up right now.
*
Why?

\*
Even Balor seems a bit frazzled.
\*
Every time I step outside my office, he's somewhere nearby.
\*
Looking at me.
\*
As if taking my measure. . . .
\*
Oh, hell, he's probably trying to decide just when and where he's going to arrest me.
\*
I thin................................................... TERMINATED
\*
\*
\*
\*\*\*RESET\*\*\*

# Chapter
# Thirteen

★

\RIPLEY\PATH\GAMMA  (Γ)

**N**UMBERS, I was thinking while a small, singed Dragon hovered about twenty feet overhead, screaming sibilant imprecations. *A company of Spetsnaz numbers fifteen men.*

Plus Kerensky.

Assuming he didn't bring along any reinforcements, I had approximately ten minutes to take out at least sixteen Soviet fighting machines.

Or get the hell out before the protective spell wore off.

I now had a moment to look around while the laser beams glanced off our reflective second skin. My reinforcements were nowhere in sight though I had caught a glimpse of someone up on the roof, across the street.

A dark form had just materialized behind him, however, and now he was out of sight.

There was a howl from a sniper nest in one of the alleyways: an energy bolt had reflected off of Vashti's silvery coating and ricocheted back at another of Kerensky's marksmen. For a moment my memory flashed back to my youth and the racquetball courts at the local "Y."

"Hey, Steffie," I called.

She turned her face, an eerie quicksilver mask, toward mine. "Vashti," she corrected, "and what?"

"Ever play handball . . . ?"

# \RIPLEY\PATH\SIGMA    (Σ)

"Where have you been?"

Lilith smiled and handed him an unstrung bow and quiver of arrows. "You can't outshoot lasercarbines with roof tiles."

Ripley sat with his back to the stone chimney and examined the great bow.

It was a composite design, much like the ancient Turkish bows, with three layers of wood bonded together so that its upper and lower limbs curved backward like a right-handed brace symbol. At the center of the great arch of wood was the skull of some fantastic horned creature, cunningly anchored to provide the sight, the arrow rest, and the grip. Above and below were leather wrappings with jeweled insets, making the weapon a thing of dark beauty.

Stringing the bow was almost beyond his strength: he had to lie back and use his legs much as an English longbowman of ancient times. The draw, itself, was powerful enough that he knew that weeks of practice would be needed to build up an adequate strength in his arms.

Unfortunately, he did not have weeks or days or even hours.

Ripley selected an arrow from the quiver and examined the green shaft, the dark red hunting fletchings, and the ebony broadhead tip. Nocking it so that the arrow fitted a groove through the horned skull, he crept to the edge of the roof and observed the deadly dance now taking place in the street below.

Some of the soldiers had left the concealment of the alleyways and were moving across the open street toward their quarry.

It was proving to be a mistake.

The shorter form of the Half Elf whirled as a long bolt of white light struck him in the side. Cupping his hand he caught the last of the beam with his hand and redirected it at one of the Spetsnaz. The man went down with a seared leg and tried to crawl in the opposite direction.

The silvery form of the woman turned and used both hands

to redirect a laser beam at two other soldiers who had gotten within ten feet of her. She was able to make the reflected energy sweep across a short arc, cutting one man down and seriously wounding the second.

The rest of the assault team was coming to understand that their lasercarbines were a liability under the present circumstances and that the solution called for close-quarters mayhem.

As the lasercarbines fell dark and silent, Riplakish pulled his swords from their silver-coated scabbards.

Up on the roof, Ripley nocked an arrow and drew it back to his cheek. Lacking leather fingertabs, he utilized the Mongolian draw style, gripping the arrow's nock with thumb and forefinger. He knew better than to try the three-fingered Mediterranean draw on a powerful bow without calluses or finger-guards.

"Hell of a bow," he murmured, releasing the arrow and watching it catch one of the bigger Russians in the arm. He had been aiming at the man next to him.

"Hell of an arrow, too," Lilith said as the shaft burst into a white core of incandescence, turning the man into a pillar of flame.

Ripley stared openmouthed. And then ducked back down as the lasercarbines renewed their interest, turning their attention to his position on the roof.

"Lilith!" He unslung the quiver and flung it at her. "What the hell did you give me?"

The quiver flew back into his hands of its own accord.

"Don't be a damned fool!" she snapped. "I've given you the means to defend yourself!"

"It seems I've been a fool more times than I'd like to remember," he retorted, tossing the quiver back at her. "But I have no intention of being a *damned* one!"

The quiver rebounded through the air and dropped into his lap.

"A gift from Hell, once accepted," she instructed, "is not easily disposed of. And as long as your life is in jeopardy, the bow and quiver will come to your hands until the danger is past."

"I don't like it," Ripley grumped.

"Oh, for Hades' sake! These Humans are trying to kill you!" She turned and gestured at a soldier's head that had just appeared on the far side of the roof. There was a flash of flame and then the sound of something hitting the ground. A thin trail of rising smoke marked the space where the head had been only a second before.

"I suppose you want to yell a warning first," she continued, "and then use something that will neutralize the threat without causing them too much discomfort!"

A sniper popped up on an adjacent roof and fired a burst of amplified light that caught Lilith just below her breastbone. The Archdemoness staggered a bit and belched a small cloud of smoke.

"Lilith!"

"Excuse me," she waved at the dissipating vapor, "heartburn." She turned, gesturing again, and the offending soldier shot up into the sky like a roman candle and exploded.

"Riplakish, as a representative of the Lower Planes, I'm not allowed to get involved at this level! I can act as an advisor, give certain forms of assistance, even defend my corporeal form within certain guidelines. But I'm going to have to leave before I become a combatant here."

"Why?"

"Remember history's lessons in Vietnam? Just imagine what would happen in a world where Heaven and Hell forsook their advisory status and put their own troops in the foxholes."

It didn't satisfy Ripley. "Seems to me a number of parties have been playing fast and loose with those so-called rules."

"Okay, so some of us bend the rules a little. Especially when it comes to your involvement. Just remember that you're a major power from another dimension in much the same way that we are here. It's like a poker game in that every time one of us ups the ante, someone else is either going to call or see our wager and up theirs as well."

Ripley stared at her. "And . . . ?"

"This skirmish is some kind of focal point. Even as I stand here, I can feel unseen forces gathering—a balance shifting. If I leave right now, some of that may diffuse." Her fingers began tracing a sparkling pattern in midair. "I've given you the means to protect yourself. Use them!"

Lilith suddenly shimmered out of existence.

There was a burst of noise and Ripley didn't waste any time in nocking another arrow. Glancing over the edge of the roof, he was treated to the spectacle of his alter ego taking on the remainder of the Spetsnaz company with an Uzi.

# Chapter Fourteen

★

\RIPLEY\PATH\GAMMA        (Γ)

**T**HERE are certain problems involved in magic use that the layman rarely comprehends or appreciates. For example, the conditions under which a spell is cast, the quality and quantity of the components used, and the potency, range, and duration of the spell itself are just partial factors.

There is the spellcaster, him(or her)self to consider. Such concerns as age, gender, intellect, and, of course, one's discipline or field of study make a big difference in any given spell's failure or effectiveness. And if you want to talk biorhythmic cycles. . . .

Anyway, it takes a cooler head than mine to go through the mental and physical gymnastics of weaving a spell when a dozen highly trained killers are doing their best to snuff you with high-tech equipment.

Suffice it to say, I had come to put more faith in swords than sorcery, levers than levitation, and machine guns than magic.

Shortly after drawing Caladbolg and Balmung, it occurred to me that the odds were still vastly against us. I had dispatched two of the more reckless commandos when the others decided to fall back and regroup. Vashti had taken out another with a potent Sleep spell (as I said: a cooler head than mine) and someone up on the roof was giving us a little assist from time to time.

But time was running out and our reflective second skin was due to evaporate in a couple of minutes.

That's when I remembered the Uzi slung across my back.

In less than two minutes it was over. The laser weapons continued to have no effect and I made sure none of the Soviet commandos got close enough to use anything else.

I could say that the elite Spetsnaz have made warfare into a religion—a religion whose doctrine leaves no room for the concept of surrender. That would be true.

But I know I kept loading fresh clips and pulling the trigger for two reasons.

I wanted to live without having to keep looking over my shoulder.

And I wanted to avenge Natasha Skovoroda.

When it was done, I dropped the Uzi in the street and looked at Vashti.

"I want to go home," I said.

She nodded but the look in her eyes said that there might not be any place I could call home after today.

I walked over to Ghost and was putting my foot in his stirrup when a body came hurtling off the roof of the spell shoppe and knocked me on my back in the street. I lay there stunned as Vashti tried to intervene but Kerensky dealt her a vicious backhand that sent her off to dreamland against the hitching post. While I couldn't count on any additional help from my ex, she had bought me the time I needed: as the colonel produced an electric combat knife, my left hand caught his wrist before he could bring the vibrablade to bear.

Kerensky's other hand clamped around my throat, squeezing my windpipe and shutting off all of my air. The combat-hardened Human outweighed me by at least a hundred pounds, all of it muscle: prying him loose with my free hand was out of the question.

Instead, I put all my strength in rolling him to the side and slipping my right arm between us until my hand could reach the holster inside my vest. My assailant wasn't aware of the

Glock until I had its muzzle grinding into the underside of his chin. He was so surprised that I was able to disengage myself without any further trouble.

"Okay, Stanley," I wheezed, my battered throat sucking fresh air, "it's just you and me."

He backed up and held his arms out from his sides. "So, this is to be—how do you Americans say it—*mano y mano*?"

"No"—I coughed—"that's how the Spanish say it."

He smiled, turning his empty hands palm up. "So. How do you want to settle this? Pistols at twenty paces? Sabres? A duel with sabres would give you the advantage."

I pulled the slide back on the Glock, chambering a round. "I have all the advantage I need."

His eyes tweaked a bit wider. "You would shoot an unarmed man? In cold blood?"

"Self-defense," I countered. "There's an old saying in the Game, Stanley: 'Lawful Good does not mean Lawful Stupid.' But I have a more compelling reason than protecting myself and Hanson and Cooper and possibly the Program, itself. . . ."

"Revenge?"

I nodded. "This is for Natasha as much as anyone else." My hands were like ice as I squeezed the trigger. Kerensky threw himself down and to the side as the Glock seized up. The gun was jammed, and as I tried to release the double-action, the dirt exploded at my feet.

Kerensky had risen to one knee, clutching the discarded Uzi. "Drop it," he commanded, "or the next burst will be higher."

Yeah, right. Like I wasn't a dead man already. I dropped the Glock as it couldn't help me now, anyway.

Kerensky flicked the switch that put the automatic into single-shot mode. "So, Comrade Ripley, what do you say now that the boot is on the other foot?"

"Ingest excrement and expire," I said, offering a one-fingered gesture to punctuate the statement.

The bullet caught me in my right upper arm, spinning me around so that I fell to my knees with my back to him. The initial shock was blocking the pain, but my right arm was useless now and I had to brace myself with my left. "You're a lousy shot, Colonel. I'm still alive."

"I hit what I aim at. I understand you must use your hands and arms to make computer magic. I do not think you will make much magic now. To be sure, the next bullet will be for your other arm.''

I struggled to my feet and turned to face him. Blood was dribbling down my dangling right arm at an alarming rate and a throbbing pain was grinding its way past the gauzy layers of shock. ''And then what? A bullet for each leg so that I can't run away?''

''Precisely,'' he replied and raised the weapon's wire stock to his shoulder.

This was going to hurt a lot before it was over and the fact that my lycanthropy would probably keep my death from being permanent was small comfort at that particular moment. I looked around for reinforcements but there were none. The cavalry was not going to come riding up over the hill at the last moment here. A cloud passed before the sun and I looked up because looking anywhere was preferable to watching Kerensky squeeze the trigger.

The cloud was anomalous to the rest of the white fluffy cumuli in the sky. It was dark and rectangular—almost squarish.

And it was getting bigger!

There was a whistling noise—the kind of sound you hear on those old World War III holodramas where the soldiers yell ''Incoming!'' and dive into their plasticrete bunkers. I caught a glimpse of the Spetsnaz officer staring upward with a confused expression. Then there was a sound of thunder and he disappeared in a gigantic roiling cloud of dirt and dust.

When the dust began to clear there was a two-story wood-frame house sitting where the empty street had been a moment before.

The house, its architectural design reminiscent of the American Midwest circa 1900, looked a little rumpled but surprisingly intact for an edifice that had just fallen out of the sky. It was certainly in better shape than Colonel Stanislav Kerensky: only his legs protruded from beneath the building's foundation. The rest was out of sight and better left to the imagination.

''Wow! Edifice wrecksss, huh?'' Smog flapped his way over to perch on my good shoulder. ''Guesssse we ssshowed him, huh!''

I glowered at the diminutive Dragon. ''We? Why you little—''

A young girl came out of the house with a collie dog at her side and looked around. "Gosh, Lassie, I don't think we're in Kansas, anymore!"

I shook my head dazedly; I was woozy with shock and all of this was getting to be a little too much for me. "Wrong dog," I corrected. "Supposed to be 'Toto.' "

The girl cocked her head for a second. "Accessing." She looked at me. "Datafiles indicate that 'Toto' was a musical ensemble that flourished in the latter twentieth century. . . ."

"Never mind." My attention turned to a familiar figure exiting the house behind her. Dressed in Lincoln green and armed with a longbow, it was unquestionably Borys Dankevych's avatar.

But was he animated by the Computer or was the Soviet president in taction? As soon as he was close enough to see the look in his eyes there was no question.

"Borys. . . ."

He spared me a glance but circled the house until he found Kerensky's remaining remains. Standing there, looking down at the rogue soldier's boots, he muttered something unintelligible in Russian.

"Yeah, you're right," I concurred, "he died too easily."

"Robert Remington Ripley!" the girl scolded. "You've been shot!" She took me by my good arm and pulled me back over to the more impact-resistant area of the porch. "Let me see that!" She sat me down and began probing the wound with her fingers. Surprisingly, there was no pain. Even when she pulled out the lead slug with her thumb and forefinger. A moment later the wound was completely healed, my blood loss completely restored, and the effects of the shock to my system completely negated. Physically, I felt great. Emotionally, I was on less stable ground.

"Hello, Pallas," I said.

# \RIPLEY\PATH\SIGMA    (Σ)

There was no point in hanging around, he decided, now that the Spetsnaz threat had been eliminated. Climbing down the back of the building, Robert Ripley did not see Kerensky's attack nor his final moments. And the arrival of the Kansas farmhouse coincided with Ripley slipping and falling the last ten feet and demolishing the woodshed adjacent to the back door.

It stunned him for a moment. A few more bruises and he'd just had the wind knocked out of him, Ripley decided as he began to extricate himself from the rubble. Then, as he pushed several splintered boards out of the way, he realized he was in more trouble than he thought.

He looked up at two men dressed in corselets and greaves, with open-faced basinets: officers of the City Watch. The guards smiled disarmingly and casually leaned on their poleaxes but he wasn't fooled: Calabastor's City Watch had a well-known reputation for unpleasantness.

"Well, well, well, wot 'ave we 'ere, Maurice?"

Had Maurice been born in another place and time, he would have likely found employment in the WWF under the nom de plume of "The Mangler" and frequented the ring in matches against the likes of "Hulk" Hogan and "Macho Man" Randy Savage.

"Dunno, Chauncey, looks like a bit o' breakin' an' enterin' ta me."

There was little question that under the same circumstances, Chauncey would have gone on to star in a series of motion pictures with numerals in the titles. His face was not the sort one associates with entertainment, but a hockey mask would guarantee such a success.

"Wot d'you think, Maurice? Shall we drag this 'ere chap down ta the Old Bailey?"

"Sink me, Chauncey, I believe the accommodations are a bit too crowded already."

"Good 'eavens, old boy!" Chauncey was really getting into the spirit of their little charade. "Wotever shall we do then?"

Maurice rubbed his hand over his stubbly lantern jaw. "Well . . . I suppose we could just let him go. . . ."

They stared at each other for a long moment. "Naw!" they suddenly chorused, shaking their heads.

Large, beefy hands reached down and dragged Ripley out of the pile of splintered wood and rubble. "I say," said Chauncey, "we could conduct a trial 'ere, ourselves, and save the taxpayers and the overburdened legal system the additional time and money!"

"And we could impose the sentence immediately," continued Maurice, as if this were the first time such an idea had occurred to either of them. "And then we could continue our patrol with greater efficiency!"

Chauncey pulled out his shortsword. "Jolly good, I say!"

Maurice drew his longsword. "Indubitably!"

True to Lilith's promise, her gifts followed Ripley out of the remains of the woodshed.

"Oh, my. This 'ere fellow 'as a bow an' arrows."

"Didn't notice 'em till now, did we?"

"Don't think so."

"Then they must've been hidden."

"Dear, dear, carrying concealed weapons . . ."

"My, my, the charges just keep mounting up. . . ."

Any further discussion of vaudevillian jurisprudence was suspended as the ground beneath their feet began to tremble. Some twenty feet away the earth began to sink, dropping down a couple of feet and then bursting upward again, showering Ripley and his captors with steaming clods. A hole opened in the ground, venting smoke and steam.

"Wot in 'ell?"

"You said it," agreed Ripley.

For climbing out of the hole were a dozen nightmare creatures straight out of Hieronymus Bosch's "Garden of Delights." Uncharacteristically, they were being led by a traditional, rather generic red Devil complete with horns, hooves, forked tail, and three-tined pitchfork.

The Devil clutched his head with one scarlet hand and pointed his trident at Ripley with the other, shouting some sort of command to his deformed troops. They surged forward like a monstrous tide, waving taloned appendages and gnashing snaggled teeth and fangs. A careful observer would have noticed that some of them held their heads (those that had any) and limped as well. Chauncey and Maurice did not spend any time focusing on these details. They dropped their swords, shoved Ripley toward the hellish horde, and then turned and ran like hell.

The Demons followed, breaking into two columns as they reached Ripley and flowed on past him, continuing their pursuit of the guards. He turned and watched bemusedly as the two armor-clad bullies scaled a wall in record time and disappeared into a maze of alleyways.

"Beg pardon, sire!"

Ripley turned back and found that the red Devil was abasing himself at his feet. "I did not stop to think!"

"I . . . see . . ." Ripley said. And fell silent, uncertain of what else to say.

"I did not realize that thou might have a use for yon vermin. It was presumptuous to assume that a Power, such as thyself, might need assistance." The Devil groveled. "Forgive me, Master: my brain is quite addled from recent misfortune and I am new to command."

Ripley looked down at the crouching figure, then at the ebony bodysuit upon his own person, and finally at the bow and quiver of hellish design that he, himself, bore. "Um," he cleared his throat, "forgiveness is not a word in my vocabulary! I shall overlook your . . . uh . . . scurrilous impertinence . . . for the moment, however!" He was having trouble getting the proper tone of cruelty and command in his voice so he cleared his throat again. "What brings you and the other hellspawn out of the Pit at this time?"

The Devil looked up, confusion suffusing his scarlet countenance. "My Lord! Thy commands! Thou—we seek thy prey!" He stood at Ripley's gesture. "We gathered these Imps and Demons as quickly as possible!" He motioned to the hellhorde that had pursued Maurice and Chauncey as far as the wall. "We were nearly upon your quarry! But just as we were about to break surface, we were smitten by a terrible force! A tremendous blow that killed my brother Devils and incapacitated half our troops!"

"What was it?" Ripley demanded, feeling a bit more certain of his role-playing.

"I don't know, Your Wickedness!" he cried, rubbing the cinnamon pate between his short, black horns. "It felt as if someone dropped a house on us!"

"Um," said Ripley as he heard the sound of returning Demons at his back.

"I took over with what stragglers were in the rear, shifted the tunnel a hundred feet, and, well, thou knowest the rest," he said, pointing at the hole they had recently emerged from.

"And now?" Ripley demanded, trying not to tremble as the grotesqueries returned to mill around them.

The Devil snapped to attention. "My liege! We will continue our pursuit! The Rules permit us another quarter hour out of the Pit!"

"And whom do you pursue?" His first impressions were correct, he realized as he now had the opportunity to scrutinize the Imps and Demons at close range. The Machine had accessed a file containing the artwork of Jeroen Van Aeken, popularly known as Hieronymus Bosch, and utilized his images of Hell for the creatures that surrounded him now.

"As per thine instructions, we seek the Half Elf named Riplakish. When we capture him we are to bring him to thee on Ortygia, across the division of worlds."

"Ortygia," Ripley repeated, suddenly needing a drink like he never had before.

"On the far side of Corpus Callosum," confirmed the Devil. "My lord, dost thou wish to lead us in the hunt?"

"What? Uh, no. I have . . . another task." Ripley looked back at the building he'd just descended from, to get his bearings. "The Half Elf you seek just went—um—that-a-way." He picked a direction away from the site of the Spetsnaz battle and opposite that of Daggoth's Tower.

"Then, begging your evil pardon," the Devil said, backing away obsequiously, "we'll be about thy business as time is short."

"By all means." Ripley watched the hellish troops depart, waiting until they were just out of sight before unlocking his trembling legs and hurriedly departing in the opposite direction.

No money, no horse, and it was a long walk back to Daggoth's Tower under the hot midday sun. Ripley decided, whatever the potential dangers of coming into contact with his alternate self, it was time for the two of them to sit down with Daggoth and Vashti.

And have a long talk. . . .

**DATALOG: \QUEBEDEAUX-
A.5\PERSONAL\20200813
*Voice Dictation*
\*\*\*FILE ENCRYPTION ON\*\*\***

I was recording my last entry when Balor walked into my office
unannounced.
*
I figured he was on to me right then and there, but it turned
out that he was too upset to notice my use of a personal
datalog.
*
It seems that Balor's Security Team has a bigger problem than
several dozen REMrunners popping into the Matrix.
*
He took me down to one of the suspension tanks in the V.I.P.
section of the Dreamworlds Complex.
*
"We can't get him out."
*

Those were Balor's exact words as he opened the top of the tank.
*
Small wonder Security has been acting frazzled: Senator Hanson's stuck in the Matrix again!

# Chapter
# Fifteen

★

\RIPLEY\PATH\GAMMA      (Γ)

**W**E rode back to Daggoth's Tower doubled up: Pallas behind me on Ghost and Borys behind Vashti on her mount. At his insistence, I had told Borys all I remembered of Rijma's account of Natasha's murder.

As we passed through the concealed entrance and rode down the tunnel to the basement stables, I wrestled with the idea of giving him what might turn out to be false hope. "Did you remove Natasha's body from the suspension tank? Or disconnect her from The Machine's bio-monitors and life-support system?"

"No." He dismounted. "I—I came in as quickly as I could," he answered slowly, "hoping that I might be able to—do something." He stood there, staring at the ground as Vashti led her horse into one of the stalls. "But if she is dead. . . ."

"Don't take her off of life-support, yet," I said, leading Ghost into an adjacent stall.

"But all brain activity has flat-lined."

I shook my head as I unstrapped Ghost's saddle. "That may not mean a thing."

"But the Anomaly—"

"The Anomaly is a two-way street," I said. "I've died—personally—in-Program, twice so far. And during that time, I have no conscious recollection of existing or being in a particular location."

"What does that mean?" he wanted to know.

I looked around for Pallas but she had already gone upstairs. "I don't know. Maybe my psyche was taken out of the loop and stored in a holding file, somewhere out of the monitored circuitry. Then it was automatically retrieved again when my avatar was returned to life—or the proper Program parameters to permit a refusion of psyche and Dreambody."

"You are saying Natasha could be resurrected?"

"I don't know for sure. But if her psyche is still cached somewhere in The Machine, and we can restore it to her avatar, there is a chance that the suspension tank's bio-systems could revive her, as well."

"Then . . . then, how do we restore her?" His eyes brimmed with tears.

"That I don't know. Yet."

Γ

"So where were you guys?" Vashti, Pallas, and I were cooling our heels in the study when the others returned. Borys was downstairs in the chamber where we had put the voodoo-animated corpse of Natasha's avatar.

"It's my fault—I'm sorry. . . ." Nicole was the image of abject misery. "I thought I knew a shortcut and we got lost in a maze of back alleys."

"I guess I can share the blame," Daggoth added. "If I had taken my carpet instead of riding horseback, I could've scouted the route from a higher perspective and we wouldn't have gotten lost."

"Since I didn't know the city's layout," Mervyn mumbled, his face a mottled mass of bruises, "I tried to get Ms. Doucet up on my rug for a better look—"

"Which was when she slipped," grumbled Rijma.

"—knocking Mervyn off," sniffed Nicole.

"—knocking him cold," Daggoth explained, "and spraining her own ankle in the process."

Nicole's lips quivered with barely suppressed emotion. "I feel terrible!"

"Doesn't look swollen," Rijma observed, "but a sprain can sure hurt like Hades the first day or two."

"Not that . . ." she whimpered.

"Hey, I'm okay," Mervyn assured her. "It was my own clumsy fault."

"Not that either. Oh, Robert!" she wailed. "You could've been killed and it would've been my fault we weren't there to prevent it!" She began sobbing.

"Um, it's okay," I said, embarrassment elbowing my annoyance out of the way. "Everything worked out okay."

"Easy for you to say," Vashti groused, still nursing a mild concussion.

Another voice piped up from her shoulder: "Yeah, ssspeak for yourssself. We could've been killed, too, you know!"

I glared at Smog and the little Dragon sidled up Vashti's shoulder and peeked back at me through her hair.

"Accidents happen," Daggoth soothed. "Why don't we table this Old Business for now and move on to the New Business, now that we have the list?"

Everyone in the room nodded, voiced, or grunted their assent.

Cephtronics's former Chief of Programming pushed back his wizard's cowl and pulled out a pair of nonmagical spectacles. Perching them on his nose, he contemplated the list for a few moments.

"As I see it, we can get this done a lot faster if we split up into smaller groups and try to retrieve these items more or less simultaneously. . . ."

I felt oddly detached from the discussion that followed.

A portion of my thoughts were with Borys Dankevych. Watching Natasha's life monitors go flat had been a terrible thing for him. I hoped our discussion in the stables hadn't added the torment of false hope.

I was thinking about going downstairs and talking to Dankevych, even though I didn't have any idea as to what else I could say. At least it would get me out of the study and away from my most immediate problem.

I found myself staring at Vashti. Like Natasha and unlike most Dreamwalkers, her avatar was nearly identical to her actual appearance. It was difficult to think of her as Vashti,

High Priestess to the Amazons, and not as Stephanie Harrell, my ex-wife and, until a couple of days ago, my fiancée.

Except that she hadn't really been my fiancée this time around. I had spent the last six months in the Outside World with a manifestation of The Machine in Stephanie's body. So I hadn't really fallen in love with my ex-wife, after all.

I turned and looked at Pallas.

She had shed the farm-girl appearance that she had been wearing when she stepped from the flying farmhouse earlier this afternoon. Now she appeared as I had first seen her in the Matrix some six months ago: skin the color of coffee and cream, dark hair smoking around a face that struck a balance between classic beauty and raw sensuousness, and a body that—well, I felt my palms start to sweat and forced myself to look away. If I could fall in love with the essence of Pallas in Stephanie's body—not that there was really anything wrong with Stephie's body, you understand—then my libido was in for some serious trouble now that she was back in her avatar of choice.

But since Pallas wasn't really human, then it naturally followed that what I had felt for the past six months wasn't really love, at all. Just a complex feedback loop of autoerotic suggestion coupled with a certain degree of wish fulfillment and a means of interface that simulated the human act of "oneness."

I looked at Aeriel and found that she was already staring at me so I looked away, again.

Technically, the Amazon Princess wasn't really *my* problem. The Computer had manipulated my avatar into this ill-conceived arrangement while I was outside of the Program. Unfortunately, I couldn't think of any way I could explain my lack of culpability to Aeriel, her mama, or the hundreds of sister-warriors who were already looking for who I became during the hours between dusk and dawn.

Well, at least they were willing to share. . . .

Which was more than I could say for Nicole Doucet.

I looked at the woman I had lost fifteen years before and marveled anew at how the avatar-mode of the Matrix had not only given her her body back, it had given her the years, as well. And since I had modeled Misty Dawn on Nicole's likeness, it was almost as if the ill-fated Wood Nymph was with us, too.

All of this and all of them combined to make my present circumstances very confusing.

As the conversation's dynamics shifted to the other side of the room, I eased out through the side door and took the stairs down toward the bottom of the tower.

There was no point in stopping off at Borys Dankevych's room, there was nothing I could do or say that could help right now.

And I was hardly a pillar of strength, myself, at this particular moment.

As I reached the ground level I heard footsteps on the stairs above me: it was Nicole.

"What—" I started to ask, but she shushed me. Taking my arm, she led me through the great hall and out into the clearing just as the sun was touching the western horizon.

She tugged on my sleeve and ran, drawing me, on into the trees, down a hill, and into a canopied glen just a scant mile from the tower entrance. There was a large table-rock set atop a small rise and Nicole climbed up onto its smooth, flat surface and extended her hand back to me.

"Come."

"What—?" I asked again.

"What?" she teased. "Don't you know? Take off your clothes!" And she set about removing hers with unbridled enthusiasm.

I followed suit with a little less abandon and a little more bemusement. Before I was done she was Eve-naked and helping me with the rest of my garments.

The setting sun cast its bloodied light over her creamy flesh, giving her a feral quality that stirred ancient lusts. "Take me," she growled, lying back on the great slab.

And I did.

There was a fierce savagery in this joining unlike anything that I had ever known in my life. It was more like a pagan rite of passage than an act of affection. Nicole writhed upon the stone's surface like a virgin sacrifice, but there was nothing virginal about her words, her touches, her demands.

Almost as soon as we were done, the cramps hit and I felt my avatar stretch and remold to my Human aspect. Spent, I rolled onto my back and stared up at the stars that were beginning to glimmer in the darkening sky.

"Robert. . . ." She ran gentle fingers in a questing trail across my chest and then down my stomach.

"Mmmmm?"

"Do you remember the last time we made love?"

I did. Even though she was doing her best to distract me with her hands. "Yes. It was . . . healing."

"I mean, before the accident. Do you remember?" She rolled over and knelt above me. Her face lowered to mine, her hair forming a silken tent that blotted out the sky.

As we kissed, I turned my mind again to those last carefree days in France.

"A little town near Luxembourg," I remembered when we finally broke for air.

She nodded. "Éblange."

"There was a small forest near the border. . . ."

She smiled. "You remember!"

"How could I forget?"

She moved above me and my response was unexpected: it seemed my Human physiology was unaffected by the exertions of my Half-Elven avatar just minutes before.

"We climbed a hill and found a large rock. . . ." She was beginning to breathe heavily.

"Like this one," I murmured, feeling my lungs start to labor in turn.

"We made love in the sunshine and could see for miles in every direction!"

"It was fantastic," I agreed through clenched teeth. She had taken control of the rhythm, again, and I was being pulled along too fast. "It seems we have come full circle," I gasped.

"Yes," she said. "Except it is dark now. . . ."

She stretched away from me for a moment, reaching for the mound of her clothing. My hands came up in turn, and fingers splayed, I moved my palms in small circles down her back. I grasped her waist as she settled back.

And then the rhythm abruptly ceased.

" 'Is this a dagger which I see before me, /The handle toward my hand?' " she whispered. " 'Come, let me clutch thee. . . .' "

I had closed my eyes, trying to take advantage of the sudden inertia, trying to prolong the rising tension. Quoting Shakespeare seemed as good a distraction as thinking about baseball.

" 'I have thee not, and yet I see thee still,' " I remembered.
" 'Art thou not, fatal vision, sensible /To feeling as a sight?
or art thou but/A dagger of the mind, a false creation,/Proceed-
ing from the heat-oppressed brain?' "

" 'I see thee yet, in form as palpable/As this which now I
draw,' " she continued. " 'Thou marshall'st me the way that
I was going . . . Now o'er the one-half world/Nature seems
dead, and wicked dreams abuse/The curtain'd sleep . . .' "

"You missed a couple of lines," I murmured.

" '. . . now witchcraft celebrates/Pale Hecate's offerings;
and wither'd murder . . .' "

I opened my eyes and saw the dagger.

" '. . . Alarum'd by his sentinel . . .' "

The blade was silver, the one metal that lycanthropy was not
proof against.

" '. . . the wolf, whose howl's his watch . . .' "

Nicole's right shoulder rolled upward in a movement that
was distinct—that had always been her own. And I suddenly
remembered the mysterious bowman and how he had moved
in a familiar fashion as he nocked and fired that "fatal" arrow.
It was the same flow of arm and shoulder muscles that Nicole
had displayed half a lifetime ago in the field archery tourneys
throughout half of Europe.

" '. . . thus with his stealthy pace,/With Tarquin's ravishing
strides, towards his design/Moves like a ghost.' "

"Why?" I asked, breaking her spell. I saw the animal hunger
in her face and suddenly understood that fifteen years of pain
and isolation had transformed desire into a different kind of
passion.

She smiled. "Why not?"

And brought the knife down.

# PART IV

## Fatal
## Attractions

★

"Come together right now over me. . . ."
—Lennon/McCartney

**DATALOG: \QUEBEDEAUX-
A.5\PERSONAL\20200814
*Voice Dictation*
***FILE ENCRYPTION ON*****

I see that we've lost Ripley-Gamma's code-string again.
*
Guess we'll pick him up again at the turnover of the next cycle.
*
In the meantime, I've got bigger worries: Hanson's code-string
isn't where it's supposed to be!
*
And after checking all of the pertinent parameters, there's only
one explanation that makes sense. . . .
*
Baylor's boss isn't the real Walter Hanson!

# Chapter
# Sixteen

★

\RIPLEY\PATH\SIGMA    (Σ)

I was weary from the long walk back from Calabastor. The shortcut off the main road and through the woods had seemed like a good idea at first. But the uneven terrain, the density of the foliage and ground cover, and the number of branches dangling at throat level gave lie to the old maxim "the shortest distance between two points is a straight line."

Continually looking over my shoulder didn't help, either.

With the setting of the sun, I felt my body slip away, again. The momentary discomfort was almost a welcome thing as I could now make a beeline for Daggoth's Tower: the trees would prove no impediment to my noncorporeal form.

I was stopped, however, by the sight of two very familiar people making love on a large flat rock. One of them was me. And the other one was . . . "Misty Dawn?" I whispered.

"Yeah, my lord?"

I jumped and surely would've knocked myself cold had I not been able to pass through the massive tree limb just above my head. I turned and glared at the Wood Nymph's ghost. "What are you doing here?" I hissed.

"Nay, my love," she answered, pointing at the couple on the rock. "The question is, what am I doing *there*?"

I smirked. "I should think the answer to that is rather obvious."

She frowned. "Nay. I meant not the act. 'Tis my body I do not ken. Who hast taken possession of it?"

"Yeah?" I rubbed a hand across my chin. "Why don't we go ask? I've got a couple of questions of my own."

"Such as?"

"Am I real? Or am I Memorex?"

We took maybe two steps. And stopped cold as the woman who looked like Misty Dawn produced a dagger and murdered the man who looked like me!

Watching was bad enough. But as my Human Doppelgänger died, there was a wrenching sensation that drove me to my knees. I felt my body collapsing in upon itself, and for long moments, I couldn't move. When I was finally able to raise my head, my murderer was gone, her clothing with her.

Misty Dawn was trying to help me to my feet.

But her hands kept passing through my arm. I was still in my Half-Elven avatar but I was no longer wraithlike.

As I made my way to the stone altar on shaky legs I was met with another shock: my Human corpse was beginning to discorporate! Even as I reached out to touch it, the flesh became transparent as Misty Dawn's and, in another moment, disappeared completely. Only "my" clothing and the silver dagger remained as evidence of the murder. Not so much as a bloodstain marked the rock's striated surface.

It was the perfect crime: except for my chance arrival there would have been no witness. And if you can't *habeas* the *corpus*, you ain't got no evidence.

My first impulse was to head straight for Daggoth's Tower and report what I had seen. Then I had second thoughts. Primarily that you never lay all of your cards on the table until the hand is completely played out.

First, I changed clothing. I took off the ebony bodysuit that Lilith had given me and folded it into a small square. It tucked into a beltpouch with room to spare.

The clothing left behind on the stone was familiar: leather belt with pouches, vest and trousers of mottled green and dun dragonskin, tunic and girdle of light doeskin, calf-length moccasin boots that laced up the sides. I had dressed in these clothes an uncounted number of times but now they were subtly different. They were still warm.

But the gooseflesh they raised as I donned each garment was not so much a matter of the previous wearer's death, as it was the question of legitimacy. Had he been the true Riplakish of Dyrinwall and I just an artificial copy of the real thing?

Or were we both just shadows cast by a greater Reality—a Reality that might exit the room at any moment and turn off the lights on the way out?

"Thy visage is so grim, my lord! What dark thoughts cloud thy brow?"

Saved by the belle. I extended my hand to hers even though I could no longer touch her. "Come. It's time I was getting back."

$$\Sigma$$

Voices drifted down from Daggoth's study up on the fifth floor. Other than that there was no sign of anyone else as we made our way around the premises.

Our first stop was the stables where I checked on Ghost. He, at least, seemed to think that I was me. I left the great bow and the quiver of arrows that Lilith had gifted me with the rest of my gear and then crept upstairs. My next stop was the guest chamber the other Riplakish had occupied. I retrieved my swords and mithril shirt before moving on to the room the "real" me had temporarily occupied.

Perhaps "real" was not the most scientific adjective to apply to myself under the circumstances. I'd always had some philosophical reservations in using the terms "real" and "reality" while inside one of Cephtronics's Dreamworlds. And now that I was no longer sure as to which copy of my avatar was the original (and don't get me started on that definition), it was an open question as to which—if any—of us had claims on being legitimate.

For sanity's sake I *had* to think of myself in terms of being real. . . .

Palming the silver dagger, I continued my search through the apartments on the third and fourth floors.

While I searched for my assassin I noticed an odd mental manifestation: I seemed to be accessing additional memories outside of the ones I could account for. It was as if I were sharing someone else's mind in a passive mode. A mind similar to my own.

Perhaps identical to my own—with the exception of several days of divergent experiences.

When I checked Vashti's chamber I made another interesting discovery: the rest of the bottles of Demon Rum that my ex-wife had confiscated. I liberated them for medicinal purposes: this mental double-vision was giving me a massive headache.

Entering Nicole's room with a bottle in hand gave me a strange sense of déjà vu in reverse. And then it hit me, the facts all falling into place like an orderly landslide: it was Nicole who had appropriated Misty Dawn's body from the grave! It was Nicole who had shot "me" with an arrow from horseback! And it was Nicole who had murdered "me" with the silver dagger! I looked again to be sure that she wasn't anywhere around and then sat on the bed and uncorked the bottle. Under the circumstances, this was not the best of times to be sober.

But I needed my wits about me if I was going to brace my murderer in the next few minutes. I compromised by taking a long pull on the bottle and then tapped the cork back in.

For a moment I was paralyzed by the sensory assault: the warm liquid boiling its way toward the center of my body while the memory of our lovemaking burned through my nerve endings.

I shook myself up into a standing position and stumbled from the room. *I* hadn't touched Nicole! It was someone else's memories that were tormenting me, now. Trembling, I hurried toward the stairs and the fifth floor.

The meeting was still going on when I entered the study.

*How did I know about the meeting?*

"Well, it's about time," Rijma said as I closed the doors behind me. "We were starting to wonder—" She fell silent as she saw the look on my face.

My gaze swept the room and focused on Nicole. She was sitting across the room, near the far wall. I remembered now, how I had originally crafted Misty Dawn's appearance upon my memories of Nicole. Had that drawn her to the slain Wood Nymph's body when her psyche entered the Program?

As Nicole Doucet became aware of my presence she stumbled out of her chair, toppling it in the process.

Now everyone fell silent as I produced the instrument of my latest death. Nicole staggered backward until her back pressed against the bookshelves that stretched from floor to ceiling. "What—what's wrong with you?" she whimpered. I realized that it was the question on everyone's mind. I was the only one in the room who was aware of Nicole's actions. But at this particular moment, I was the one who seemed to be dangerous.

Perhaps I was. Every instinct for self-preservation demanded that I counter the threat with violence. But as I stared at her across the room, deeper memories rose up in me. Memories that were unquestionably mine.

" '*Je voudrais voir des roses et du sang,*' " I said. " '*Je voudrais voir mourir d'amour ou bien de haine. . . .*' "

" 'I should like to see people dying of love or of hatred,' " she whispered.

If killing her was out of the question, confinement wasn't any better. She had been imprisoned in that scarred lump of inanimate flesh for fifteen years. Sending her back or denying her her newfound freedom would be cruelty beyond death.

And yet, there was something in her eyes that told me I might not have a choice. . . .

"You're dead!" she shrieked. And the madness behind her eyes boiled over.

I hefted the poniard and felt a little of my own sanity slip away. "Is this a dagger before me?" I said with mocking irony. "Come, let me clutch thee!" And hurled it so that the silver blade buried itself in the spine of a fat tome just a foot away from her head.

"Good gods, man!" Daggoth was coming around from behind his great desk. "What do you think you're doing? It's Nicole—"

"Is it?" I snarled. I pulled the Optics of al Rashid from my vest pocket. "Let's take another look." And I put them on.

A moment before I had felt my sanity slip a bit. Now I looked and felt the rational world tear out from under my feet and drop away like a psychic sinkhole. I looked into madness unmasked of the facade of flesh and the crafty restraint that allows it to pass us unnoticed in public places.

I had hoped the spectacles would reveal an imposter. Instead, they showed me the woman who had died in that fiery air crash and was denied the relief of afterlife or oblivion.

The woman I had known and loved had been devoured by a nightmare beast long ago. The beast had ground her up in its teeth, digested her humanity in its belly throughout those fifteen years, and what it had finally excreted was not even remotely human.

I looked into the face of naked madness and screamed.

She whirled and wrenched the dagger from the book. And as she turned and brandished the silvery blade, she underwent a transformation. Her flawless skin turned yellow and mottled. There was a smell of rotted meat filling the room, of putrefaction long bottled up and finally released as if the glass containing it had shattered. Skin cracked and oozed pus and slime. Flesh turned black here, sloughed off there, revealing hints of bone and wormy veins gone hard with desiccation. Gums shriveled and teeth and nails grew. The whites of her eyes turned red as irises disappeared and pupils collapsed into slitted apertures.

I drew my swords as her back burst open and great flaps of black leather flailed out. As her bone-ribbed wings buffeted us back with their turbulent backwash, she sprang into the air and glided to the window. Smashing the leaded glass with a taloned fist, she turned at the lintel and hissed at me.

And then she was gone as if the night, itself, had sucked her into its great, dark maw.

Σ

Hours were passed in explanations, in plans and strategies, in theory and speculation. We turned in well after midnight. I cannot speak for the others, but sleep would not come for me.

I lay on the bed I had first occupied when Daggoth had fetched me from Misty Dawn's tree and stared at the flickering shadows cast on the ceiling by the candle at my bedside. When I finally blew out the candle one shadow remained.

It was Misty Dawn. As the night's events had unfolded I had forgotten her and what import they held in her heart.

What I had lost this night was beyond my ability to measure or tally. But there was pain in her eyes, too. She had lost her body, witnessed the unholy use it had been put to. And she had lost me, in a sense, as well.

And as I looked into her eyes, I saw that the pain there was for me, as well.

Neither of us spoke. I pulled back the blanket and she crawled into the bed beside me.

We touched and our hands passed through each other. But I curled my arm about the flickering perimeter of her body and she laid her weightless head upon my chest.

Even without tactile sensation there was a comfort in the mutual proximity.

Sleep finally came.

**DATALOG: \QUEBEDEAUX-
A.5\PERSONAL\20200815
*Voice Dictation*
***FILE ENCRYPTION ON***

A cycle has passed and the code-string for Ripley-Gamma has not made a reappearance.
*
Baylor's beside himself over this new development with the senator.
*
Do I tell him his boss is actually an imposter?
*
If I do and he already knows. . . .

# Chapter
# Seventeen

★

\RIPLEY\PATH\SIGMA        (Σ)

IME was running out so we divvied up the list.

Senator Hanson, The Duke, and Stumpy went to retrieve Morpheus's feet from a local Warlock. Princess Aeriel and her Amazons had volunteered to penetrate the Sanctuary of the Templars and locate the dismembered sorcerer's head. Both hands had been traced to the waterfront, but from there the trail parted in two directions: Borys and Pallas went one way; Mervyn, Rune, and myself went the other.

That left Vashti and Rijma, who were dispatched on the remaining assignment. . . .

As Stan wouldn't let me back in the doors of Fogherty's Cove, I sent Mervyn and Rune to arrange for some dinner-to-go. The fourteen-year-old REMrunner was happy to have something to do and obviously relieved that it didn't involve an element of risk. He was finally waking up to the fact that pain and death in Fantasyworld were no longer the rhetorical elements of a harmless game.

I settled myself at the end of Smith's Dock as the sun was setting and looked over at Jeremiah. The big green frog squatted there on the weathered planking and looked up at me with expectant, goggly eyes.

"Sorry, Jerry, but I'm not the best of company right now."

The frog burruped understandingly and then turned its head to regard a dragonfly that was hovering around one of the support posts. There was a sudden blur of amphibious tongue and the dragonfly was gone. Jeremiah chewed twice and then stopped, a look of very unfroglike horror suffusing his green and mottled features. He spat out the mangled insect and hopped back a foot and, if it's possible to imagine, looked even greener than before.

"Whassamatter, Jer, don't like bugs? Or starting to like them too much?"

He croaked assent to the latter and then waddled over to the edge of the dock. "Don't fall in," I admonished as he sat back, human fashion, and dangled his long froggy legs from the end of the pier.

I was tempted to follow his lead. My legs ached and I was tempted to unlace my boots and dangle my feet in the water. We'd been up and down the waterfront, across the boardwalk, around Park Place, and had roamed the lengths of Anthony's Pier, Dorn's Wharf, and Zar's Quay. I'd finally managed to trace the right hand onto a ship that had sailed earlier that afternoon.

Footsteps sounded on the wooden planking and I turned to look at Pallas as she settled down next to me. "How's it going?" I asked conversationally. If the words and tone came out bland and smooth, they belied my inner turmoil.

"Borys is attempting to book passage to Ortygia—our hand was taken there nearly a week ago."

"Ortygia!" The events involving Nicole had driven the red Devil's words from my mind until now. "I had a little run-in with some Demons, yesterday, and they said something about taking me to Ortygia."

"Why didn't you go with them?" she asked.

"Because they didn't know that I was me. They were looking for the other me. They thought that the real me—that is I—was one of them."

She sighed. "Somehow I'm not surprised."

I stared out to sea. "I wonder who wants me on Ortygia? And why?"

"Well," Pallas offered, "we could change hands."

"Hmm?"

"You could take the ship for Ortygia and go after the other hand." Then she shook her head. "But I don't think that's a very good idea."

"What do you suggest?"

"Finish these errands, first. We've made a commitment to Morpheus and another twenty-four hours should see most of it done. Then, when his body is restored, he will be a powerful ally and the rest of us will be able to pay Ortygia a combined visit."

"What about the passage Borys is booking?" I asked.

"We still have a hand to retrieve. And maybe we should do a little preliminary scouting while we're in the neighborhood."

I nodded and stared out to sea as the sun sat on the western horizon and dangled its own toes in the sea. There was a long silence between us, reminiscent of other long silences. Finally, I elected to break it: "It's been over twenty-four hours since you came in-Program—and this is the first you've really spoken to me."

"Funny," she replied, "but I could say the same to you."

I couldn't meet her eyes. "What do you want me to say?"

"I want you to tell the truth."

"Truth?" Now I could look at her. "After six months of passing yourself off as Stephanie—wearing her body, asking me to believe that you were she—you have the temerity to question my honesty?"

"I do," she said quietly. "You have been lying to yourself for months—no—years. And until you can speak the truth to yourself, I do not believe that there is anything that we can truly say to one another." There was no anger in her words. Only a quiet sadness.

"I don't know what I think or feel right now."

"I know."

The sun was three-quarters down before I spoke again. "You tricked me, you know."

"Did I? Or did you trick yourself?"

"Meaning?"

"Our relationship these past six months was nothing like what you had with Stephanie. Were you really so blind that you couldn't see the differences?"

"People change."

"You wanted to believe that. You *needed* to believe that."

I nodded, watching the light dim across the water.

"You're a classical hero, Robert."

"You flatter me."

"No. But I do not denigrate you, either. I observe.

"The classical hero leaves the sheltered port and strikes out into the great unknown. He leaves home and friends and family behind and risks life and limb and death among strangers for noble goals. But nearly every classical hero does so because he cannot face what sits upon his own doorstep."

I grimaced. "And what sits on my front porch?"

She sighed. "I used to think that it was Nicole. I believed the accident had wounded you so deeply that you could never put your trust in happiness, again." She paused. "I still think that's partly true. . . ."

"But?" I coached.

"I think you are the monster at your own gate."

"Thank you."

"Perhaps monster is the wrong word. But you fear the face in your own mirror. And you are here because you run from yourself."

"I seem to keep running into myself here more than anywhere else."

She took my hand in hers. "Even now you fear to examine the truth that I am saying. You take refuge in your humor and you will continue to put yourself at risk rather than face who you are and who you want to be."

"Quit beating around the bush, Pallas: what is it that you think I'm so afraid of?"

"Commitment."

I looked at her. She had a funny way of saying it. Funny, I suddenly realized because she wasn't the one who had actually spoken.

We turned around, knocking Jeremiah off the end of the dock. There was a little froggy scream and a splash as we stared up at Prince Rudolph Charming and a retinue of royal guardsmen. At the prince's side was a familiar-looking Dwarf. Apparently the feeling was mutual: he was pointing at me as he said, "That be him, Yer Highness!"

"Guards," Rudy said, "arrest that bounder!"

He was pointing at me, as well.

Σ

"You cad!" he hissed. "You heel!"

"Rudy," I soothed, raising my hands palms up, "you're getting upset over nothing."

"Nothing?" His voice shot up an octave and his face went from red to royal purple. "Nothing? You refer to my betrothed as 'nothing'?"

I looked around the dungeon cell and was momentarily glad that I was locked in and Prince Charming was locked out.

"You stole my girl," he continued, "you two-timing four-flusher!"

Ever since I had prematurely awakened Snow White from her enchanted slumber with mouth-to-mouth resuscitation, I had been dodging her seven little guardians who thought my marrying her was the only honorable thing to do. While I was somewhat wise to the customs of the Mountain Dwarves, I hadn't reckoned with the prince's involvement in all of this.

It was bad enough that I had cheated his fate by rescuing his beloved. It had further tweaked his pride to find that Snow White was a retrograde romantic who preferred rakehells to royalty.

To be fair, this had been a very trying day for the prince: there had been some major fracas in the west end of town, someone had dropped a house in the middle of one of the major thoroughfares, and there had been numerous reports of Demons on the rampage all over the city. On top of that, tonight was the royal ball that was supposed to celebrate Snow White's engagement to the prince. The king and queen thought a big bash followed by the surprise announcement was just the thing to put a little zing back into Calabastor's social climate.

Problem was, the surprise was shaping up to be more than they had bargained for. And had landed Yours Truly in more hot water, not to mention the dungeon beneath the castle proper.

Pallas had tagged along to watch the fun and could barely repress her giggles even as Rudy threatened to foam at the mouth.

"I don't see why we can't work this out," I said reasonably. "I don't even want her." Oops. Wrong choice of words.

"So," he cried, drawing his sword, "my bride-to-be isn't good enough for you!"

"Let's not blow a matter of individual taste out of—"

"You think you can callously *use* her and then toss her aside!"

"I didn't *use* anybody—Pallas, tell him!"

She had one hand over her mouth and waved the other in vague acknowledgment. Her body trembled mirthfully and her eyes threatened to brim over.

The prince took no notice. "Varlet! Knave! I intend to see that you do the *honorable* thing by her or else——"

Pallas guffawed.

The prince sputtered to a stop as if someone had dumped a bucket of cold water on him.

I spoke gently: "Your Highness, we can fix this so that it all works out to where the two of you will live happily ever after. The girl just needs a little more time."

"Destiny can be such a heavy burden, especially when you're young," Pallas added. "Now Snow has had to go through an awful lot, knowing that her fate was fixed. I mean: the death of her real mother, her father's remarriage, abandonment at an early age, life in the sticks, keeping house for seven old bachelors without any social life of her own, a severe case of food poisoning, and then destined to marry some strange prince——"

"I am not strange," he huffed.

"——that she's never met, without having the opportunity to play the field, first, so to speak. She's just exhibiting a little youthful rebellion. Believe me, it's completely natural before a girl settles down to marriage and midlife crises."

He sat down on one of the turnkey's stools and put his face in his hands. "I wouldn't mind giving her that time if I knew that she would eventually come around——"

"She will!" I asserted through the bars.

"——but I don't have that kind of time to give! The royal ball and announcement are *tonight*!"

"Your Highness," smiled Pallas, speaking reassuringly, "I happen to have an old family recipe, passed down from mother to daughter since ancient times. Used properly, in the right drink at the right time, it should prove to be a most effective remedy to your particular problem. . . ."

$$\Sigma$$

I tapped on the heavy oaken door. Then I knocked. Finally I began to pound.

"Just a minute!" came the muffled reply.

"We're running out of minutes!" I yelled back. And then looked back down the passageway to be sure I had given Snow White the slip after our last dance.

So far, so good.

The door opened and Pallas pulled me into the Apothecary's laboratory.

"What's the news?" I asked as I locked the door behind me.

"This!" She giggled. And grabbed me for a kiss.

"You didn't!" I begged in horror.

She shook her head. "I didn't actually sample the finished product. But I did get a whiff of the fumes while I was heating the mixture in the molds." She pushed herself against me and then reached behind to take the key out of the lock in the door. "I'm sure the effects will wear off in a few days." She dropped the key down her bodice.

"This is not funny, Pallas!"

"I can't help it, Rip honey. It's the potion."

I sighed. "Look, if you want fun and games, you'll have to wait until we get everything settled downstairs. Now give me the love potion and I'll sneak it into Snow White's drink."

"In a minute," she murmured sulkily, winding her arms around my neck.

"Now!" I thundered. "Or, by Elysium, I'll be sleeping with Snow White tonight!"

She pouted. "Oh, all right." She disentangled herself and led me over to the table. "Here is the first batch," she said, gesturing at a tray with six brown pellets on it. "Drop one of these in her drink and she'll go gaga for the next person she looks at. Just make sure she's looking at the prince when she drinks it."

"That's all?"

"Listen, buster, in a ballroom filled with moving, talking people, the timing may not be so easily accomplished. And you need to make sure that the pellet is completely dissolved before you hand her her drink."

"Okay. Thanks." I pocketed the pellets. "Now, unlock the door."

She shook her head. "You unlock the door."

"Fine. Give me the key."

She walked up to me, put her hands on her hips, and threw back her shoulders. "Go fish."

Σ

I had to hide behind a tapestry until Snow White's attention was focused on the far side of the ballroom. Then I collared Rudy and the two of us relieved a servant of a tray of champagne and glasses.

"Here," I explained to the prince, producing a pellet. "This goes in her glass. As soon as it's dissolved, I'll offer her a drink. As soon as she takes it, I'll head for the exit and you get right in her face. I mean it, Rudolph: you have to be the first person she sees after she takes a drink!"

"Sounds simple enough."

"Maybe. I just get a bad feeling about this—"

"Rip, darling!" Snow White was coming our way with her retinue of seven short guardians in tow.

"Remember," I murmured to Rudolph, "the pellet with the potion is in the goblet with the Hobbit; the stein full of wine has the brew that is true."

"What?"

"Never mind." I picked up the tumbler that was sculpted in the likeness of a Halfling and dropped one of the pellets into the slightly chilled bubbly. Then I held it in my hand so as not to lose track of it and cover up the dissolution of Pallas's love philtre.

"Champagne! How lovely! Shall we have a toast, then?" she inquired, sweeping up to the tray and swooping up a goblet in her hand.

"Yes, of course, but," I fumbled for the right words, "I already have your glass in hand, my dear!"

"Oh, Riplakish, you are becoming a dear! I was afraid you were going to continue being a stuffed shirt for the remainder of the evening." She sipped from the goblet in her hands.

"But, Snow, my sweet, I was holding this glass for you!"

She detached a hand from her drink and waved it at me. "But I already have a glass, my love. Why don't you drink it?"

"I'm afraid I'm not overly fond of champagne, Precious, and I've already had a little too much for this early in the evening."

"Then we shall be most happy to relieve you of your social

burden, Lord Riplakish," said a new voice. I turned to look at Rudy's mother as she lifted the doctored drink from my sweating hands.

"Y-y-your Majesty," I stammered.

"Nervous, my lad?" she inquired archly. "One would suppose that you were the one whose engagement was being announced."

I tried to produce the equivalent of a polite laugh and only succeeded in sounding like a strangled goose.

She turned to Rudy. "After this next number, we shall signal the trumpets to play a fanfare. Then the formal announcement can be made."

The color drained out of Rudy's face and he looked to me for deliverance.

"So soon, Your Majesty? The night is yet young!" I was trying to think of how to stall the announcement and retrieve the potion at the same time. And was not making any progress either way.

"Uh, yes!" Rudy chimed in. "The announcement should be the culmination of the evening!"

The queen turned back to her son. "But the royal orchestra is running out of numbers. . . ."

"We don't host that many royal balls," Rudy murmured out of the side of his mouth. "And the new Troubadour won't arrive until the end of the month."

I nodded: *pre-Minstrel syndrome*. "Couldn't they repeat a couple of the earlier dances?" I asked. "As encores?"

The queen made a distasteful face. "How gauche!"

Rudy's face brightened in response. "I've got a better idea. . . ."

Snow White touched my arm questioningly. "What is this announcement that everyone keeps talking about, my love?"

I snagged another glass of champagne from a passing tray and slipped another pellet into it from behind a concealing hand. "A secret, my dear," I whispered. "But I shall be glad to tell you, if you'll humor me in one little thing. . . ."

"What do you say, Rip?"

I turned back to Prince Rudolph. "Uh, what?" I asked blankly.

"We think it is a marvelous idea," added the queen, patting my arm.

"Uh, that's nice." I smiled at her and then returned to Rudy. "What's a marvelous idea?" I whispered close to his ear.

"That we stall the announcement with some additional entertainment," he replied smoothly.

"Great," I agreed. "But where are you going to find something appropriate for a royal ball on such short notice?"

"Well," he explained, "my family has this thing about providing only the very best in musical entertainment. . . ."

"Right."

". . . and what could be more exclusive and impressive than introducing the best *Jongleur* on the continent?"

"Tough act to beat," I agreed.

"Not if you're the last of the true Bards as well as the Archdruid of Dyrinwall."

"Well—" I stopped and stared at him. "Oh, no!"

"Oh, yes."

"You can't be serious!"

He leaned in close. "Unless you can think of something better, my mother will be announcing *your* engagement within the next five minutes! Besides, you always said that you wanted to play the palace."

I swallowed. "Okay, okay! Give me a minute and then I'll do the stall."

We turned back to the queen just in time to see her downing the contents of her glass.

"What do we do, now?" asked Rudy frantically.

"Where's the king?" I asked in turn.

"Over there," answered Snow. "Shall I summon him?"

"After you drink this," I answered, managing to switch glasses with her in the sudden confusion. She waved at the king and began sipping at her new drink.

"Yes?" inquired the queen.

We looked over and the queen looked down.

One of Snow White's guardian Dwarves was tugging on the queen's dress. The dopey-looking one. We braced ourselves for a royal explosion at such impertinence.

"A dance?" the queen murmured. Her face suddenly lit up. "Why I'd be delighted!" She started off toward the dance floor with the diminutive digger in tow.

"A splendid idea, my dear!" chortled a new voice. And we

turned back just in time to see Snow White dragging Rudy's father toward another portion of the dance floor.

Prince Rudolph looked about as close to fainting as anyone I had ever seen without actually keeling over. He stood there, white-faced, staring into space, and made low moaning sounds in his throat.

"Snap out of it, man!" I grabbed him by the shoulders and shook him. "We've got to do something!"

Glazed eyes turned in my general direction. "Like what?" he half mumbled, half pleaded.

"Like taking the rest of these pellets," I dropped the other four into his hands, "and dividing them up between you and Pallas. In fact, she should have another batch ready anytime, now. The two of you shouldn't have too much of a problem while I'm diverting everyone else's attention."

As a matter of fact, Prince Charming's attention seemed to have already been diverted.

"Who . . . is . . . that?"

I had to turn to follow his line of sight. There, coming down the great staircase, unescorted, was a blond dream. The disturbing thing was the blond dream looked vaguely familiar.

"I don't know, Rudy." I stared at her face, which was lovely; but that wasn't what was setting off the alarm bells in the back of my mind. There was something about her silk dress of the palest blue. . . .

Then I saw the glass slippers. "Oh, no!"

"Well, I certainly intend to find out," the prince was saying.

It was my turn to grab him. "Down, boy! We've got work to do! Remember? Involving your fiancée-to-be?" I turned him around and pointed him toward the closest exit. "The sooner we get this mess straightened out, the sooner I'll be able to introduce you."

"You *know* her?" he asked as I started pushing him through the crowd.

"Later!" I hissed, giving him a final shove. Princes can be so fickle. I turned and went in search of a lute.

That's when Misty Dawn popped in. "What is happening, my lord?"

I grimaced. "We've got problems, M.D. Can you find Pallas and help her with what she's doing?"

She made a face. "Pallas? Is she not that strumpet that hath pursued thee—"

"Misty!" I barked. And then lowered my voice when I saw that other guests would be treated to the sight of a man talking to empty air.

Or worse: maybe see the ghost, herself.

"Misty," I murmured, "if we don't get a potion in the right drink, real soon, I'm gonna be married to Snow White and spend my honeymoon in the palace dungeon. Now, will you help me?"

She pouted. "I liked it better when thou wert a spirit!"

"Me, too," I muttered as she faded into the crowd.

I managed to borrow a lute from a court musician, ducked behind a large arras, and worked a little magical transformation. When I was done the lute had become an acoustic twelve-string Martin guitar. I laid a basic Glamour over it so that it would still look like its oversize Renaissance ancestor.

I took the stage with a great deal of apprehension because I was neither warmed up nor in practice. In fact, my mind went blank as soon as I faced the audience so that the only song I could think of was "Puff, The Magic Dragon." And I stumbled through that.

Fortunately, it had been a long time since Calabastor had seen or heard from any wandering Minstrels, and the audience was hungry for more. In fact, they began calling out requests and I was able to field most of the favorites: "Knights in White Satin," "Folsom Dungeon Blues," "Castles in the Air," "That Old Black Magic," "Rangers in the Night," and (my personal favorite) "Take This Quest and Shove It!"

Misty Dawn caught my eye as I was finishing the "first" set and made a circle with her thumb and forefinger.

I hurried over to where the ladies were standing while the orchestra started tuning up for the royal announcement.

"Is it fixed yet?"

Pallas looked around and nodded. "It began taking effect a couple of minutes ago. Another two minutes and you'll be able to make your getaway without anybody trying to stop you."

"Uh—'getaway'?"

She took me by the arm and began walking me across the room. Misty Dawn fell in behind. "Listen, I know you're not going to like this, but you screwed it up in the first place and you're lucky to get bailed out at all!''

"What are you talking about? All I want to know is, did you get the stuff into Snow's drink so that the prince could win back her affections?''

"Well . . . yes and no. . . .''

I stopped and grabbed her by the shoulders. "What do you mean 'yes and no'?'' I looked over the top of her head and saw Prince Charming coming across the ballroom toward us with a purposeful expression on his face.

"Pallas, what did you do!''

"Not me: Misty Dawn.''

I turned and grabbed at the ghostly Dryad. My hands went through her, of course. "What did you do?''

Something brushed my shoulder before she could answer and I looked down into big blue eyes. "Hel-lo there!'' said a sultry voice with more than just casual interest.

"Hi,'' I said abruptly and turned back to Misty Dawn. "I'm waiting for an answer!''

"I'm waiting for a dance,'' chimed in the strangely familiar young lady at my elbow.

"I mean I got the potion as far as her glass,'' M.D. explained. "But she was so intent on the king, it was impossible to get her to look at the prince long enough for the potion to take effect.''

"But what I'd really like to do is take a long moonlight stroll through the palace gardens,'' added the stranger in the blue silk dress.

"I'm sure you would,'' I said politely. And turned back to Misty: "So what did you do with the other pellets?''

"I put them where they'd do the most good. . . .''

"We could get lost in the hedge maze,'' she sighed. The girl in the glass slippers, that is.

*Glass slippers!*

I cleared my throat and turned to Cinderella. "I believe you've mistaken me for someone else, my dear. I am not the prince. But I shall be most happy to introduce you to him in a moment.''

The prince chose that moment to arrive.

"Ah, Rudolph,'' I said, trying to sound properly formal in the presence of royalty. "I'd like you to meet—''

"Get your hands off of him, you little party-crasher!" he shrieked.

I did a double take and looked at Rudy. He was glaring at the girl who was now defiantly clutching my arm and he didn't look like he was joking.

"Uh, Rudy—"

"I said, let go!" And he pushed her.

Not very hard, but when you've only had an hour or so to get used to glass heels, it doesn't take much: she went sprawling.

"Rudy?!" I caught him by the arm. "What's the matter? She wasn't doing anything!"

"Not yet, the little tramp!" he hissed. "But I saw how she was looking at you!"

"Rip, I think there's something you ought to know," Pallas interjected.

I was distracted as Cinderella regained her feet and the prince made another lunge at her. "Better hit the road, honey—while you still have that nice, pretty dress on in one piece!"

"Make me, Prin*cess*!" was her nervy reply.

Rudy began twisting free of my grasp and the girl retreated a few steps. But only as far as one of the portable bars where she removed a slipper and smashed it against the edge of the counter.

"C'mon," she invited with her free hand while the other held a large, jagged piece of glass where the heel was still intact.

Rudy was not that big a fool: he circled her warily from a safe distance.

I turned and grabbed Pallas by her shoulder straps. "What did the two of you do with the rest of the pellets?"

"We put them where they'd do the most good!"

"Where?" I roared, lifting her a good six inches off of the ground. Fortunately, the straps held for the moment.

"In the punch bowl!"

I dropped her. "In the—for Cromssake! Why?"

She collected herself from the floor and brushed herself off before explaining.

"The situation was already out of hand—beyond salvaging. After some careful deliberation, two things occurred to me. One: that you needed a diversion to get you away from here, without being detained. And two: that since there was no way to come out of this without three or four reputations being smeared, I decided to invite everyone to play in the mud puddle.'' She gestured around the room and now I could see why the prince's behavior was receiving very little attention.

Everyone whose glass had been filled from the punch bowl was beginning to react to the love potion. And to whomever they happened to be looking at at the time. I glanced back at Prince Charming and Cinderella who were now locked in a clinch and rolling around on the floor.

"Ladies—somebody's gonna get hurt."

Pallas nodded and began tugging on my arm. "Like you, if you don't move your butt out of here. Some of the folks over by the stage were sipping punch while you were doing your first set and now they're moving this way. A stampede is not a pretty thing."

"But I can't just run off and leave things like this!" I protested.

"Well, you sure as Hades can't stay here and sort things out the way they are now," she countered. "Unless you've got any better ideas. . . ." She got behind me and started pushing.

I gave in, reluctantly, but we were stopped at the nearest exit by the biggest, burliest palace guard I had ever seen.

"Where ya goin', Good-lookin'?" he murmured, dropping the pike across our path.

"Uh, outside—for a breath of fresh air," answered Pallas.

"Get lost, Toots!" he growled. "I'm talkin' to the hunk with the harp."

That did it.

I stepped back and threw my arms wide. *"Tempus frigid!"* I yelled, performing the appropriate somatic gestures. Everyone froze in midmotion.

I put my hands on my hips and surveyed the ballroom. What had been a blur of noise and motion just a moment before was now a still-life tableau: mouths caught open in midword, arms set in midgesture. By now the effects of the love philtre had become quite advanced and the scene looked like a very realistic painting. A painting entitled "Anatomy of a Mass Seduction."

"Now what, my lord?" inquired Misty Dawn. Since she had been in physical proximity with my body during the casting of the spell, she had shared my immunity and was not affected by it as the others were.

I shrugged. "Beats me. I think the best policy would be to leave them like this until the love potion wears off."

"But that could take two or three days!"

I nodded. "But in the meantime, it would also allow me to get Morpheus's body parts back and reassembled so that we can get Hanson out and the Anomaly stopped!" I snapped, irritated at how complicated everything was turning out to be. I reached out to Pallas and neutralized the effects of the Time-stop for her.

"Robert?" Pallas asked, laying a gentle hand on my arm as we wove our way toward an exit. "You can't just walk off and leave all of these people defenseless like this."

I patted her arm reassuringly. "Not to worry: we'll be right back after we round up the rest of Morpheus and check out Ortygia."

"But what if something goes wrong? The least you could do is throw some kind of protective spell around the castle."

"What would you suggest?" I acceded.

"Well, you are a Druid in the Program context. How about a giant wall of thorns or something like that?"

I agreed to do something like that before we left the grounds proper.

On the way out I passed Snow White who was gazing into the eyes of her new love—eyes that stared back from a large wall mirror in an ornate gold frame.

**DATALOG: \QUEBEDEAUX-
A.5\PERSONAL\20200816
*Voice Dictation*
\*\*\*FILE ENCRYPTION ON\*\*\***

I'm putting my decision to tell Balor on hold.
*
If Balor is a part of the bogus Hanson's deception, it won't be very healthy for me to blow the whistle.
*
On the other hand, if Balor's clean, it won't hurt to keep him in the dark a little longer: this look-alike down in the suspension tank isn't going anywhere for the moment.
*
So, to track this guy in-Program, I'm running a global search on anomalous code-strings as they relate to avatars.
*
Jackpot!
*
I think I've located the pseudo-senator.

\*
For that matter, I've also located the real senator.
\*
But my main concern is this one code-string that reads right
out of left field. . . .

# Chapter
# Eighteen

★

\RIPLEY\PATH\OMEGA        ($\Omega$)

". . . because everyone knows: the king's word is law!"

There were a few tired guffaws but most of the assemblage was either engrossed in their meal or their opposite numbers.

The jester paced the small stage that overlooked the feasting pit and shook his buffoon's scepter. "What is this? An audience or a Norman tapestry? Wait! I got one you'll appreciate. How many Orcs does it take to light an oil lamp . . . ?"

The great hall was lined with trestle tables laden with food and benches laden with boozy old codgers clutching goblets of mead and the *glutei maximi* of paid party girls. All of the men who were still conscious wore brimless, red felt hats in the shape of a truncated cone with a black tassel drooping over the side. And since they were now well into the fourth hour of their revelries, nearly a third of their not inconsiderable number were under the tables or sprawled in the aisles where the serving wenches had to step over their unconscious forms as well as dodge the pats and pinches of their still-conscious comrades.

Backstage, two more Templars—the ones in charge of preparing the "surprise" dessert—were unconscious, as well. In this instance, however, drink had played no part in their state of oblivion.

Princess Aeriel Morivalynde stared at her newly arrived accomplice. "Riplakish! I thought you were working the waterfront?" she said.

The Half Elf made a deprecating gesture. "They didn't really need me for the next couple of hours so I thought I'd pop over and give you a hand."

Aeriel looked around at the sixteen Amazons who were busy exchanging their chain mail for the brief togalike slips that the serving wenches were wearing and gave her head a slight shake. "I do not see that I shall be needing another hand." She smiled. "But I am glad that you wished to be here with me. You have been somewhat standoffish of late." Then she frowned as she noticed that he was taking an uncharacteristic interest in her warrior-maids as they changed garments. She cleared her throat and his eyes slid over to a huge and obviously artificial pastry set upon a wheeled cart.

"And who does the honors here?" he asked smoothly. One of the Templars who had been readying the Brobdingnagian sweetcake groaned and stirred a bit. The Half Elf sent him back to slumberland with a casual kick to the head.

"It is ever my place to lead my sisters," she said, dragging the stepladder over to the dummy dessert, "whether 'tis battle or unknown danger—"

"Yeah, yeah; so you're the one who's going to pop out of this overgrown cupcake."

She lifted the false top off the giant pastry. " 'Tis a trick my mother learned from an Achean named Odysseus." She started to climb in.

*"What is going on back here?"*

Aeriel and the Half Elf turned and looked at the wizened old man in the gem-encrusted fez that was headed toward them. Most of the Amazons had already departed for their predetermined positions in the plan but four remained and he waved angrily at them: "You girls get back out there and start clearing tables!" He looked down at the assorted piles of boots, scraps of chain, and leather straps. "This mess can be cleaned up later!"

Out of his line of sight, Aeriel signaled everyone to do as he ordered while the Half Elf reached down and retrieved one of the fallen Templar's hats.

"And you, missy," he barked, turning toward Aeriel, "what

sort of outfit is that?'' He looked down and saw the two unconscious forms and cocked an eyebrow. ''What's the hold up
here? What's wrong with them?''

''Drunk, Your Eminence,'' the Half Elf answered, trying to
tuck the points of his ears under the oversize hat.

''Drunk? Do you think I'm blind *and* senile?'' He scowled.
''Of course they're drunk! But the show must go on!'' He
walked up to the wheeled cart and positioned himself to help
push it onstage. ''You, missy, I asked you what you were
wearing!''

''It's the costume of an Amazon princess,'' the Half Elf
answered. ''We thought it would be a real show-stopper to
have an Amazon princess pop out of the cake.''

The old man squinted at Aeriel's bits of armor. ''It breaks
with tradition,'' he groused. ''Never had a girl jump out wearing anything before. And we've been having girls jump out
every—''

He stopped grousing when he felt the dagger's point prick
his throat.

''Not a word, old man,'' the Half Elf hissed, ''or I'll carve
you an extra mouth to go with your extra chin!''

Aeriel climbed back out of the oversize cupcake.

''Now,'' her companion whispered, tightening his grip and
using the tip of the knife to draw a little blood, ''where is the
head of Morpheus the Malevolent?''

The old man's eyes rolled wildly and he whimpered.

''For Cromssake, Rip,'' Aeriel chided, ''you just told him
not to talk!''

''Oh.'' He eased up on the dagger. ''You may whisper. But
answer the question: Where is the head of Morpheus?''

''Trophy Room,'' his captive wheezed. And was persuaded
to give specific directions as to its location in the building
before he was knocked unconscious.

The three unconscious Templars were loaded into the parch-
ment-mâché pastry and Aeriel and the Half Elf moved toward
the door that led from the back of the stage to the storerooms.

As the Amazon princess reached for the door latch, her
companion grasped her wrist and turned her around and into
his embrace.

''What—'' was all she got out before his mouth covered
hers. Instinct and training took over: four seconds later she was

embracing his neck with her forearm and tickling his chin with his own dagger.

"If this is your idea of foreplay," he croaked, "I think you can just forget about producing an heir to the throne."

Chagrined, she released him and returned his blade. "I am sorry, my love. I did not expect—"

"Yeah?" he said, rubbing his throat. "Well, expect the unexpected from now on." He took her by the hand. "C'mon. Let's see if there are any unoccupied chambers between here and the Trophy Room."

"To what purpose?" she asked as they exited into a back passageway.

"Extending the line of succession is not as quick nor as easy as some would have you think, my princess." He patted her arm as they headed for the stairway. "I think we should get started on the problem as soon as possible and avail ourselves of every possibility."

Possibilities, however, would have to be postponed. As they reached the end of the hall there was a shriek from the great hall followed by a cacophony of sounds: catcalls, benches overturning, grunts, curses, and a rising level of bedlam that defied auditory analysis. A woman in a torn toga came running toward them from a connecting passageway.

"One of yours?" he asked as she sped by with a look of panic suffusing her features.

Aeriel shook her head as five Templars came galloping down the same route. Any impressions that they were chasing the serving wench were dispelled as they stumbled closer: if anything, they were more terrified than she.

"That one is, though. . . ." The Amazon indicated another serving wench running close behind, armed with a carving knife and a meat skewer. "Riplakish, we ought to take advantage of the diversion while there are still Templars to provide it."

Aeriel and the Half Elf ran up the steps and started down the hallway on the third floor. More sounds came boiling up from the stairway behind them: their diversion was turning into a full-scale riot. They rounded the corner and skidded to a stop.

The door to the Trophy Room was just ten feet away and flanked by two of the biggest, burliest guards they had ever seen.

They were dressed alike in billowing purple pantaloons; the

gold sashes wound about their waists matched the gold trim that adorned their matching red vests and pointed, curly-toed slippers. The convoluted folds of the massive lavender turbans that crowned their heads gave them the appearance of hydrocephalic aliens that were in the process of mutating into giant tulips.

The tulips each laid a massive hand on the hilts of their loosely belted scimitars.

With a sudden flash of inspiration, the Half Elf reached up and checked the top of his head: amazingly the funny little felt hat was still there, jammed down over the tops of his distinctive ears. "Ho there, good fellows!" he called. "Don't tell me the Trophy Room is closed at this hour?"

The guard on the left answered with: "Never to an exalted Brother of the Mystic Tabernacle of Simon the Templar."

"Ah, good, good. . . ." His arm curved around Aeriel's waist. "I was just going to show my new girlfriend, here, some of the—ah—trophies." He danced her through the doorway.

"That was easy," Aeriel purred.

"Yes," murmured the Half Elf as he began searching the agglomeration of displays. "But walking back out with our prize will be a different matter entirely."

The Trophy Room was cluttered with an assortment of pedestals and display cases exhibiting a bizarre collection of trophies, awards, and improbable knickknacks, but as a recent acquisition, the head of Morpheus wasn't too hard to find. It sat (or, rather, rested on the stump of its neck) in a velvet-lined black box. The Half Elf lifted the box down from its display pedestal and turned to Aeriel. "You go out, first, and distract the guards."

"*Distract?*" Clearly she was less than pleased with the plan.

"Yeah, distract. You got a problem with that?"

Her hand went to the hilt of her shortsword. "I am an Amazon warrior, Riplakish," she hissed, "not some piece of—of—cheesecake for you to dangle before the guards like a piece of meat!"

"You're mixing your metaphors," he chided. "And you were perfectly willing to distract a whole room full of besotted boobs downstairs just a few minutes ago."

"That was different," she huffed.

"Hah!"

"Two to two is much different than two to two hundred!"

He handed her the box. "Very well, I will go out first and distract the guards. All right?"

"All right," she answered.

"'S'alright," agreed the head in the box and Aeriel slammed the lid shut.

She drew her shortsword while the Half Elf exited the room and debated on whether or not to keep the box tucked under her free arm in the event of a fight. There was a curious whining sound. Twice. And then the Half Elf called for her to come out.

She found both guards sprawled in untidy heaps in the corridor. The Half Elf was holding one of those mechanical hand devices that he and the sorcerer Daggoth claimed to be weapons although a closer look told her that it was neither of the items he had previously referred to as "Glock" or "Uzi."

"The box," he said, gesturing with his free hand. "I want to check the head, again."

The request seemed odd but not unreasonable, and it was only as she was handing him their prize that she realized that he had made no attempt to reholster his weapon.

"I'm sorry, my dear, that we didn't have time to ensure your progeny." He raised the odd-looking hand weapon. "If you wake up before they do, be sure and tell Bobby boy that if he wants to 'get a head,' he'll have to come to Ortygia." He chuckled at his own wit and pulled the trigger. The stun-beam left her sprawled in a heap between the two guards.

He sighed as he shifted the box to a more secure position under his arm. "I should've known from the start that it'd be easier to handle the entire operation, myself." He holstered the Spaceworld weapon and pulled another device from his pocket. "Dangerous, but easier. . . ." He depressed a button on the device and a moment later seemed to shimmer into nonexistence.

If I had a credit for every alarm that's gone off in the last couple
of days . . .
*
The most baffling one to date is a Program Intersect alert.
*
Before the Anomaly developed it wasn't possible for one Programworld in the Matrix to intersect with another Programworld.
*
Now we know better so we jury-rigged this alarm about six
months ago.
*
The odd thing about this particular alarm is I can't get a reading
on which Programworld is sharing space with Fantasyworld.
*
We've previously established that Frontierworld, Spaceworld,

and Cyberworld have eclipsed Fantasyworld along certain parameters.

*

They continue to register in definable readings.

*

But our current alarm continues to defy readout interpretations.

*

It's as if there's a Programworld that even we're not aware of—sharing space in the Matrix. . . .

# Chapter
# Nineteen

★

\RIPLEY\PATH\SIGMA  (Σ)

I T looked just like those nature holos we watched in grade
school: plants growing and flowers blooming in seconds
thanks to the magic of stop-motion holography. Our heads
tilted back farther and farther as the thorny branches car-
peted the moat, climbed the castle walls, and twined 'round
the turrets and towers. The vegetation's size and speed of
growth would have been incredible enough, but the sight of
huge blossoms bursting wide open in the moonlight was a bit
too surreal for my tastes: I repressed a shudder.

The ladies seemed awestruck.

"Satisfied?" I gasped. Magic of that size and duration really
takes it out of a spellcaster and I was no exception. Now I
needed a nap. Preferably of two days' duration.

"Biggest damn roses I've ever seen," said Pallas.

"I thought thou wert of a mind to surround yon castle with
brambles, my lord."

I scowled at both of them. "I don't know brambles from
eggplants. I just figured anything with thorns—"

"But thou'rt a Druid!"

"Misty, it's just a ga—I mean—Fantasyworld classifica-
tions aren't—"

"Yea, my lord?"

"What he means, my dear," Pallas instructed, "is that giant rosebushes add an aesthetic touch to the practicality of the Guards-and-Wards."

"They are very pretty in the moonlight," agreed the ghostly Wood Nymph.

"And big!" added Pallas sotto voce.

I set my foot in the stirrup and mounted Ghost. "Let's get out of here before the City Watch comes along. I hear they've been on alert ever since our little fracas with the Spetsnaz." I looked at Pallas. "Especially since someone dropped a house right in the middle of Morgan Avenue!"

"Some people have no sense of gratitude," she retorted as she swung astride her horse.

Misty Dawn floated into the air and settled down behind me, half in and half out of the saddle, twining vaporous arms about my waist.

As we rode back toward the waterfront, I pulled a small rectangular mirror from my vest pocket and called Daggoth.

The former Chief of Programming had sacrificed one of his magic mirrors for this operation, cutting it into smaller, hand-sized pieces that he then distributed to each of us. By staying back at the tower, he was able to tie all the segments together through the other mirrors in his setup, maintaining a communications system and coordinating all of our activities from a centralized base. The only drawback was it eliminated our most powerful spellcaster from operating in the field.

"It's about time!" he groused when I finally got through. "Rune and Mervyn have been combing the waterfront for hours!"

"Did they find Jeremiah?"

"Yes, half drowned! What happened?"

"Long story," I sighed. "Where are they now?"

"I recalled them a half hour ago. You might as well come home, too: you'll need the sleep."

"Meaning?"

"Rune's chartered a boat to sail at midday on the morrow. Is Pallas with you?"

"Yes."

"Well, Borys is waiting for her down at Pier Thirteen."

"That the wharf next to the import warehouse?" I asked.

"That's the one. He's booked passage on a ship that's bound for Ortygia within the hour. She'll have to hustle." He glanced away. "I've got another call coming in. We'll continue this conversation when you get back. Daggoth out."

Pallas waved her farewell as she was already booting her horse into a canter toward the docks. I turned to Misty: "Hold on tight." I kicked Ghost into a gallop and a moment later he leapt skyward.

"It is so beautiful up here," she murmured as I nudged Ghost into a banking turn that would aim us toward Daggoth's Tower.

Strangely, I hadn't noticed. As we glided through the velvety blackness, I took in the splendor of the constellations, their stars blazing like icy diamonds in the void. The ground was a faint echo of the cosmos, torches and lamplights glimmering here and there about the city and homesteads, and the dark water of Sultan Bay reflecting only a rippled and distorted tenth of the starlight that twinkled above. But the horizon was indistinct in the darkness and the illusion of being surrounded by sky was still effective.

And beautiful. . . .

"It's not real," I whispered to myself. "None of it is real." The seductive impulse to head for the second star to the right and then straight on till morning was overwhelming. *This is not my life*, I told myself. Even though I could die while in taction with my avatar, this was all too far removed from the reality I was born into, had spent my life in. This was just a temporary state to be endured until Morpheus was reassembled and helped us get Hanson and Cerberus switched back in their proper places. I had a job to do here, interfaced with the Cephtronics Dreamworlds Matrix, and I couldn't permit myself the luxury of Program-generated distractions.

"My lord?" Misty's voice was a welcome distraction from this train of thought. "When this quest is done—what wilt thou do?"

"After it's over?" *That was easy: I was getting the hell out of here!* Of course, my avatar would remain in the Program and just what The Machine would do with Riplakish of Dyrinwall after I had abdicated was anyone's guess. Probably sell him into Amazon slavery. . . .

I cleared my throat. "I don't want to think that far ahead, M.D. Let's just worry about the job, uh, quest for now."

And, speaking of worries, as we approached Daggoth's Tower I was surprised to see that it was encircled by a ribbon of light. We got just close enough to make out individual headlights as they moved around the tower's base and Morpheus materialized in midair, just beside us.

"Incoming!" he yelled. "Take evasive action!"

Ghost shied from the sudden appearance of Morpheus's— uh—ghost, and that's what saved us: the missile sizzled through the airspace we should have occupied and continued to climb into the night sky.

"Cyperpukes," Morpheus explained. "They've ringed the tower and were awaiting your return."

"Armament?" I asked as I kicked Ghost into a spiraling climb.

"FRODOs and SAMs."

I was familiar with the weapon systems that bore the acronym FRODO, but: "What in Hades is a SAM?"

"Surface-to-Air Missile. They're antiques: solid propellants, fired out of hand-held launchers," he explained. There was a flash down below. "They're launching another!"

This time there was sufficient warning to cast a Deflection spell. The missile wobbled off in a different direction before exploding a couple of miles away.

"What about the tower?" I asked.

"Secure. Daggoth has the forcefields back up and they're holding. He'll iris open the one over the roof as soon as you're close."

"Tell him I'm on my way now." Morpheus faded and I sent Ghost into a barrel-roll that flipped us out of the path of two more missiles and then spun us into a corkscrew dive toward the ring of lights on the ground.

That's when the FRODOs opened up. A half-dozen particle beams dissected the night and began to stitch the sky like glittering threads embroidering black sailcloth.

I threw a Shield spell in front of us and beefed it up with a couple of variants of Reflection thaumaturgy. I was doubly lucky in that I completed the spells in time and that the FRODOs didn't immediately chew through it like Orcs in a swill-eating contest.

How long it might last was another matter: the convex buffer of mystic energy was already heating up as the particle beams converged on us. At two hundred feet I divided my attention between pulling Ghost up out of our dive and elongating the shield to protect us from any belly shots. The FRODOs cut out as we leveled off under thirty feet and Cyberpunks went scrambling. Our shield was now glowing a bright cherry-red like the ablation tiles on an old-fashioned shuttle. The radiated heat was blistering the paint on their neurobikes as we buzzed them in a half circle around the tower. Then, before they could recover, I urged the pegasus up in another tight spiral so that we topped the tower, hovered for a second, and then dropped down on the observation deck.

As I dismounted, two missiles arced over the parapets and detonated soundlessly against the forcefields that Daggoth had already popped back up into place. The flares from the twin bursts lit up the top of the tower, revealing a baleful-looking Dwarf stalking toward me. Suddenly, I was more nervous facing this one diminutive opponent than I was bracing fifty assorted Plugthugs from the Cyberworld Program.

"Stumpy," I greeted carefully.

He stumped up to me and grabbed the reins out of my hand. "Daggoth's waitin' in his orifice," he spat. A wad of chewing tobacco formed a Rorschach pattern on the deck between my feet. "Wants you down there pronto!"

"Everything okay?" I asked as he turned away.

"Okay?" Saying that the question seemed to annoy him would be like throwing gasoline on a campfire and remarking that it seemed to brighten things up a bit. "Okay? You flyboys git to have all the fun a'waltzin' 'bout the sky an' buzzing Cyberpukes. Then you git to traipse downstairs and have tea an' scones with his lordship while I have ta git this oversize horsefly down nine flights of stairs an' inta the stables!"

"Sorry," I said, backing away. He was just warming up.

"Sorry? Sorry?" He spat again. "Thet's what'cha always say! Sorry didn't do me no good when ya got them Gypshun gods all riled up an' thet big 'un—Hortense?"

"Horus," I supplied, dipping a toe into the dark depths of the roof's trapdoor.

"Yeh, thet's the one: Horace. Remember the number he

done on the marketplace in Billocksy, tryin' ta catch youse? No wonder ya still cain't show yer face around—''

I jumped, catching the sides of the ladder, and slid down to the next level. He continued to rant and rave as if I were still there and it wasn't until I reached the stairs and descended another two levels that I was actually out of the range of his voice.

''Come in and close the doors,'' Daggoth greeted as I paused at the portal to his study.

The Sorcerer's office and library had served as a war room these past few days, but for the moment, it was strangely relaxed and empty with just the two of us. A fire was crackling merrily in the hearth, and as I sat down in a great overstuffed chair next to Daggoth's, I gave it a second look.

''When did you put a fireplace in here?''

He handed me a great flagon, its gold and silver inlaid sides sweating with condensation. ''About twenty minutes ago,'' he answered absently as I cupped my hands around the cold metal. He picked up a crystal goblet and sipped at what I knew had to be sherry from long experience.

''How are the others doing?'' I took a sip of mine: Vanilla Dr Pepper, the way I liked it. ''Liked'' as in past tense. Since my experience with Lilith's Demon Rum, everything else had lost its taste.

''We've got the feet,'' he answered. ''Local Warlock was gonna have them made into a pair of seven-league boots. Senator Hanson and The Duke had a tough time convincing him otherwise.''

''Oh?''

''I'm afraid the gentleman contracted a severe case of lead poisoning.''

''Lead pois—? Oh.'' Stephanie frequently accused me of being slow on the uptake. Maybe so, but given time I usually got there. ''How are the others doing?''

''Unless you're holding back new information, you know as much about the hands as I do. The head? Well, Aeriel reported in about an hour ago. She and her Amazons were getting ready to infiltrate the Templars' Sanctum Sanctorum. As for the . . . um . . . other item—''

He was interrupted by a chiming sound from the great mirror

on the study wall. Abruptly, a giant eye and nose filled the glass. "Pssst," a voice whispered, "is anybody there?"

"Pull back a little," Daggoth suggested.

"Shhhh!" The image shrank down as Stephanie drew her piece of the mirror back from her face. "Keep it down!" she whispered. "We're inside the temple!"

"We were getting worried," Daggoth said softly. "Have you obtained your objective?"

She shook her head, nearly dislodging the miniature Dragon that was perched on her shoulder. "Is Morpheus around?"

"Here," the ghostly entity answered, coalescing into view beside Daggoth. He grimaced nervously. "Have you found it?"

"Probably," she murmured. "But I'll need a detailed description in order to retrieve it."

"A . . . description?" Morpheus looked at Daggoth who looked back at Morpheus. Then they both turned and looked at me.

"Hey," I said, raising my hands. "My ex-wife can't say she's never seen one."

"I told you!" Morpheus was so upset he could hardly talk. "I told you! Somebody else should have gone!"

I crossed my arms in irritation. "Who? We divvied up the assignments according to individual skills and the danger and difficulty that we could anticipate. This should be relatively easy—"

"Then what is the problem?" Morpheus cried. Clearly he was overwrought. "Why is she asking for a description?"

I shook my head. "Instead of arguing with me you should be asking her." I jerked a thumb at the mirror.

Daggoth scratched his beard. "Maybe she's suffering from some form of hysterical amnesia."

A giant hand filled the enchanted glass on the study wall and perspective shifted so that Rijma's face was leaning toward us in the glass. "Very funny, boys!" she hissed.

"So what *is* the problem?" I asked.

Rijma frowned. "Maybe it would be easier to show you the problem. You got 'zoom' on this mirror-thing?"

The dark Sorcerer nodded.

"Okay. We're in a chambered balcony looking down on the

Holy of Holies at the heart of the temple of the Phals. I'm going to turn the mirror around and point it toward the altar.''

The image slewed wildly and then stabilized to a fuzzy blur. Daggoth gestured. ''Focus,'' he commanded. Then: ''Zoom in.''

When you've seen one pagan temple you've seen them all. The altar looked more comfortable than most and the frescoes covering the walls were lascivious illos portraying legions of lust. But, reduced to basics, the overall design and layout was pretty universal: the difference between most cults and crackpot religions is just a matter of window dressing.

The candles, however, caught my attention. Not that candles in a pagan sanctuary are unusual: while some sects prefer the ambience of a great flame pit or the utilitarian aspects of torches, most religious ceremonies include the standard wax taper as part of the setting. Some altars will be surrounded by as many as several dozen lit candles.

This was the first time I'd ever seen several hundred—

''Zoom out,'' corrected Daggoth, ''and pan left and then right.''

—make that several thousand candles all filling the chancel area around the altar.

''There's more,'' Rijma whispered hoarsely. ''The walls along both sides of the Nave are lined with 'em, too!''

''So what's the problem?'' Morpheus was not only irked by their hesitation, he was acutely uncomfortable that they had any part in this operation at all. ''Too much light with all those candles?''

I frowned. ''I don't think so.'' The light was murky at best, coming from four flaming braziers, one at each corner of the cushioned ''sacrificial'' table. ''For one thing,'' I continued, ''none of those candles are lit. They have no wicks.'' I hesitated. ''And they are not candles.''

''What?'' Morpheus's impatience was interfering with his perception of the problem. ''If they're not candles, then what are they?''

Daggoth frowned. ''Zoom back in.'' The magic mirror complied. ''Magnification: times sixty. Now, left four degrees; and tilt down two degrees.''

''Gentlemen.'' I gestured at the two primary, vertical objects that now occupied the center of the glass. "These are religious artifacts—holy relics."

A slow horror filled Morpheus's eyes. Daggoth had a half smile of dawning comprehension.

"After all," I concluded, "if you're a fertility cult, why resort to symbolic artifice if you can decorate with the real thing?"

"It's sick!" moaned Morpheus.

"It's damned inconvenient, is what it is!" Rijma retorted. "Now we may have to inspect hundreds, possibly thousands of these—things—before we find the right one. So the sooner we get a good description of the item in question, the sooner we can get started."

**DATALOG: \QUEBEDEAUX-
A.5\PERSONAL\20200818
*Voice Dictation*
***FILE ENCRYPTION ON\****

I'm dying.
*
Well, maybe dead on my feet is more accurate.
*
I haven't slept in two days and my brain is turning to mush.
*
I've got to get three or four hours of sleep: I've told Balor not
to disturb me for the next four hours unless it's an emergency.
*
Unfortunately, the alarms seem to go off every half hour and
none of Balor's Security people can tell if they're an emergency
or not.
*
I've arranged for Harold Contrell to be given clearance and
transferred up from R & D to cover for me.
*

While it's true that he doesn't know what's going on in Fanta-syworld, the sad truth of the matter is neither do I.
*
I gotta get some sleep.
*
Three or four hours and I might be able to think, again. . . .

# Chapter Twenty

## \RIPLEY\PATH\SIGMA    (Σ)

"**R**ISE and shine, buddy boy!"

I peeled back a rusty eyelid and squinted at Daggoth. "What time?" I mumbled.

" 'Bout an hour past sunrise."

I moaned and rolled over in bed. "I thought we agreed to a *mid*morning wake-up call."

"We did. But things change. We've got company and they're very insistent about seeing you."

*It's only an avatar*, I told myself as my body continued to protest. *An illusionary construct of The Machine.*

I dragged the covers off to the side.

*It's not really my* physical *body.*

I tried to sit up.

*The stiffness is mere illusion—window dressing for this pretend reality.*

I made it on the third try.

*This attitude of exhaustion is not real—*

Yes it is.

*No it isn't—*

Yes it is!

*No, it's just—*

What? Special effects?

*I am not really tired and achy: in a moment my head will clear and I will continue the Game with renewed energy.*

I creaked up to a vague standing position and groaned. There were moments when I remembered that it was only my psyche running around in this overblown Computer Program: that none of this was real. Smoke and mirrors. And at certain times, I could use that perspective to peek behind the mirrors and see the scaffolding. Transcend the Program's reality.

This was not one of those moments.

"May I take a shower, first?" Some people require coffee to jump start their cardiovascular systems in the A.M. For me it's a hot shower.

"Well—"

The door behind him flew open. "You!"

The volume was enough to make me flinch. When I saw who it actually was, instinct took over. I dived back into bed and tried to hide under the covers.

Princess Aeriel Morivalynde stalked into the room, her bronze brassiere heaving. "You—you—*scum*!" Her clothing—if you could call it that—was in disarray. "Disheveled" was a woefully inadequate adjective: her hair looked like an explosion in a mattress factory. A black eye and a split lip completed the overall effect.

"Scum?" smirked Daggoth.

"You—you—you *snake*!" She stood five feet away, trembling with rage.

"Snake? Oh, my," the dark Sorcerer murmured.

"You—you—you—you—"

He grinned: " 'Ewe, ewe,' she said sheepishly."

Having noticed that the Amazon princess was unarmed, I felt a modicum of composure returning. "Sometimes words fail," I observed.

She leapt, landing on the bed in general and on me specifically. The bed collapsed. As did I. Her hands thrust unerringly into the tangle of bedclothes and found my throat.

Ensnared in the muddle of blankets, I couldn't pry her hands loose, much less fight back. I was beginning to wonder why Daggoth was dimming the room lights when Aeriel's grip relaxed and her fingers fell away from my neck.

"Took you long enough," I gasped as he reached down to help me from the ruined bed.

"Sorry."

Aeriel was still crouching, her hands reaching out, grasping—but totally unmoving. He bodily moved her out of the way so that I could stand up again. "I was prepared for every contingency except the humor of the situation."

"You know what this is about?"

He shook his head. "I figure we'll find out in about forty-five minutes."

"That when the spell wears off?"

Daggoth nodded.

"Then I reckon I've got time for a shower, first," I said.

Σ

The shower facilities were located on the sixth and seventh floors. The chamber was stone-dressed to resemble a grotto with pool and two-story waterfall. Lilypads floated on the water and a profusion of plants and wildflowers sprang from niches in the rocks. The water was pleasantly warm: solar-heated on the roof before feeding the upper pool where it cascaded down some fifteen feet from an overhang, into the lower pool, and then was filtered down through the sandy floor to start the cycle again. The system seemed almost natural until you paused to consider the pump technology and the fact that indoor plumbing and concepts of personal hygiene were extreme anachronisms for this time and culture.

I shook the water from my hair as I exited the waterfall and waded across the pool to grab a towel. Mervyn had showered almost an hour earlier and was still trying to comb the tangles out of his long white hair and beard. It was hard to imagine a fourteen-year-old boy inhabiting the body of a nonagenarian, especially when all he had on was a towel wrapped around his waist. Then, as I passed by to retrieve a towel for myself, I noticed that he was checking his reflection in one of the basin mirrors, parting various areas of facial hair, looking for zits.

Sometimes it's the little things that help us regain our perspective.

I waded, shin-deep, back into the water to talk to Daggoth. He was reclining in a floating deck chair and smoking a Swisher Sweet as he monitored a mirror fragment for more reports from the other teams. A flagon containing an iced beverage was ensconced in a depressed cup-holder in the buoyant chair arm.

"Any news from Rijma and Stephanie?" I asked as I began drying my hair.

"Vashti," he corrected. "And no, nothing yet."

I wondered as to his preference for using my ex-wife's avatar name instead of her real name. Did he prefer to maintain the illusion of Program reality? Or did he feel uncomfortable with any linkage to our past relationship?

"That was pretty mean, you know."

I looked at him. "What?"

"I mean ol' Morf was pretty traumatized by having a couple of women going to retrieve his you-know-what. It was bad enough that they were pressing him for a description. But when you asked about 'any identifying scars or moles' . . ."

"Hey," I shrugged, "standard police procedure. And he needed a little nudge at that point."

"Well," he grinned, "it was mean."

"Mean? You're the one who followed up by suggesting that they bring back a selection and let him choose!"

"Couldn't help myself. It really was—"

"Burrrrrrrrrup."

We turned and looked at the bullfrog who regarded us reproachfully from a nearby lilypad.

"So, how's it going with Jeremiah? Made any progress?"

Daggoth shook his head and sighed. "Nothing beyond the process of elimination. Whoever zapped ol' Jerry here had some code-strings that participated in the spell like a computer virus. The transmogrification is multilevel and continues to mutate like a proteus infection."

"You're saying it can't be undone?" Mervyn asked worriedly.

The anxious amphibian croaked mournfully.

"No. The spell contains one of those puzzle codes that enables you to unlock it with a specific key or phrase or event or counterspell. I just don't know what the triggering mechanism is, yet." He got up and followed me as I wrapped the towel about my waist and exited the chamber.

"I would think unzapping a Computer spell would be easy for a twenty-third-level wizard and the Chief of Programming for Cephtronics." I glanced behind me and noticed that Mervyn had remained behind but Jeremiah was following us, hopping from step to step as we descended the staircase.

"Former Chief of Programming," he corrected. "And it's not that simple. Jerry's a living human being, not a Subprogram of The Machine. Any mistake could damn well be fatal."

I glanced at the hourglass as I entered my room: time was almost up. "A little privacy, please."

Daggoth looked amazed. "You want me to leave?"

"No, I want you to turn her around." I rummaged through my closet, one-handed, as he turned the frozen form of the Amazon princess so that she faced the wall. *Closets—another anachronism in this pseudo-medieval environment.* "Thanks." I dropped the towel and began dressing.

"Why do we do it?" I asked as I sat on the ruins of the bed and pulled on my moccasin boots.

"Do what?"

"This. Dress up in Dreambodies and run around playing games inside a giant computer?"

"Well, as I recall, you're attempting to rescue the next president of the United States—"

"I don't mean you and me specifically, here and now." I began the lengthy process of lacing up the sides of the boots with rawhide thongs. "I mean people in general. Why do *they* do it?"

"I thought we had all of these discussions back when Dreamworlds was still a concept on the drawing boards." He sighed. "I'm going to get some water for the princess, here. She'll need it when the spell wears off." He left the room.

He was right, we had discussed these issues before. And had some pretty virulent exchanges when I had grown disenchanted with the Project over the moral rights of advanced AIs.

I finished my boots, got up, and walked to the window. Looking out over the panorama of forest and fields, I felt the urge to succumb to the illusion. To believe in the Program-Constructions as Reality. To accept this world on its own terms.

"A game," I murmured. "Whatever we do, it has no ultimate meaning in the greater cosmology." To believe otherwise meant responsibilities and obligations that I could not shoulder. Guilt for creating—

"Why do we do it. . . ." Daggoth reentered the room with a decanter of water and matching goblet. I turned my attention back to dressing as he placed them on the table next to the remains of the bed. "For me it was always a job. Cephtronics paid me to develop and operate Programworlds that people would want to visit. Again and again. And pay money to do so.

"R & D was constantly supplying me with the latest surveys and statistics as to what was hot and what was not. Demographics. Trends. Economic indicators. Audience shifts." He shook his head. "For all of their information—summaries, charts, graphs—they could guess at 'what' every month or so. But they rarely could tell me 'why.' Why a particular trend was—well—trendy. And they never answered my question of why we need escapism. Why we create alternate realities."

I tucked my tunic into my trousers. "Dissatisfaction with our own reality?" I reached for my swordbelt.

"That was my theory for a long time." Daggoth walked over to Aeriel's frozen form. "But then I noticed that a lot of the A.R.s—stories, books, holos, even Programworlds—were even grimmer than the world we rail against in our day-to-day lives. If I had to pick a world to spend the rest of my life in," he said without a trace of irony, "I'd prefer the so-called Real world over any of these Programworlds."

The more I thought about it, the more I agreed. The appeal of most escapist environments is rooted in the dangers, hardships, and problems that they offer. This hardly qualified as an improvement over the lives that most of us knew. For some, perhaps, like Nicole or even myself, the compensations of trading a crippled body for a healthy avatar were obvious. But the vast majority of Dreamworlds tourists were healthy and financially secure. You had to have money to spend any appreciable time Dreamwalking. So, once again: why?

"Variety?" I offered.

"Variety is the spice of life," Daggoth agreed. "Or so they say. And while I still can't explain it, I'm more convinced than ever that we, as a species, need escapism. It's a racial trait. We always want what we don't have and we rarely appreciate what we do."

I shrugged into my mithril vest. "You make it sound like a disease."

"I dunno, maybe I'm just jaded. And now that I'm dead and

stuck in here for the rest of my unnatural life, my perspective is somewhat skewed.''

''You said you had statistics on which Dreamworlds people preferred and, to a limited degree, why. So, why Fantasyworld?'' I slid my swords into their sheaths. ''Given that people have a need for escapism, why Fantasyworld? Why not some different diversion?''

''Hey, you were the best-selling author. We just purchased a hot property. You tell me.''

''Tell me,'' croaked a third voice.

We both looked at the frog. His eyes goggled and he jerked a bit. He jerked again and this time we turned our attention in the direction that he jerked. It was Aeriel and she was moving toward us like an old woman in the final stages of rheumatoid arthritis. ''Tell me,'' she croaked again.

''Tell you what, Aeri?''

Her arms came up like ancient drawbridges and her hands curled into claws. ''Tell me why you betrayed me!'' Her words were becoming better formed, now, as the spell was wearing off more rapidly. ''Tell me before you die!''

# Chapter
# Twenty-one

★

\RIPLEY\PATH\SIGMA     (Σ)

**I** believe you!"

"Then stop struggling," Daggoth admonished, retying a knot to minimize the slack in the rope.

"Did you not hear me?" The Amazon princess spoke through gritted teeth. "I believe your stupid story!" She strained against the half-dozen cords of rope that secured her to the chair. "You may release me!"

"I will release you, my lady," the dark sorcerer mused with a grin, "just as soon as our Bard is safely on his way."

"I think you're enjoying this far too much," I said, a safe distance away, on the other side of the table.

"Enjoy?" he said. "What's to enjoy?" He chuckled. "Now there are some who might be amused by the fact that an Amazon princess—one that you're engaged to—has already murdered you once, and has tried a couple of more times since then. And that another woman you were engaged to in the Real World murdered you twice, and is still trying. And that the woman you are presently engaged to isn't the same woman you thought you were engaged to—which is probably why *she* hasn't tried to murder you, yet. And another woman thinks she should be engaged to you so she and a prince and a half dozen or so

Mountain Dwarves are out hunting you down like public enemy number one. And since there were some other yous running around inside the Program for a while, who knows how many other felonious fiancées may yet turn up.

"Now, yes, there are some people who might find some humor in your . . . predicament . . . but I am not . . . one . . . of them. . . ." He turned away at that point.

Watching his shoulders shake made up my mind for me: I dropped a couple of leftover pellets from Snow White's engagement ball into the carafe of water on the table.

"If I was indeed betrayed by an imposter last night," Aeriel continued, "I would be most foolish to kill my consort. Release me and I will pursue the truth in this matter." She struggled a bit more. "I vow his life is safe until I prove his guilt or innocence."

"Sorry, Your Highness," Daggoth answered, "my hospitality has taken a beating from your hotheadedness of late." He placed a dagger in her bound hands. "You should be able to cut yourself free in a couple of minutes. I'll unlock the door as soon as your—um—consort is gone."

We vacated the room in a hurry and Daggoth turned a large key in the lock. "I'm not looking forward to letting her out even after you're gone," he said.

"Oh," I said, thinking about the potion dissolving in the water jar, "I think you'll find an enormous change in attitude when you open the door again."

"Well, we've got more to worry about than just your engaged and enraged Amazon back there. If we can trust what she told us, there's another one of you out there somewhere."

"And his behavior is a bit inconsistent with the rest of me's," I added.

"Oh, I don't know. . . ." Daggoth started chuckling again. "Didn't you tell me that your first act on reentering the Program was to greet Aeriel with a left uppercut?"

"The circumstances were a bit different—"

"I know, I know." He waved me to silence. "And there is the little matter about his invitation to Ortygia and then disappearing with the head."

"Morpheus isn't going to like that," I mused.

"Perhaps. But from what I've heard, he's where his heart is, now."

Rune was coming down the steps as we were going up. "Gentlemen," she said quietly, "I think you'd better come up to the observation deck."

The first thing we noticed when we reached the top of the tower was that the Cyberpunks were still encamped all around us.

"They haven't found the hidden exit from the stables," Daggoth observed, "so you should still be able to leave on schedule."

"You might want to move your schedule up a bit." Rune directed our attention skyward.

Strings of dirty smoke and vapor had been twisted and looped and swung about to form words in the sky. As we watched, the airborne skywriter was finishing the "h" at the end of

Surrender

Riplikish

"I don't like this," Daggoth murmured.

"You don't like it?" I groused. "I hate it: they spelled my name wrong!"

"She."

"What?" we chorused.

"She." Rune turned and handed a small telescope to Daggoth. "Woman on a broom."

He nodded and suddenly swung the glass to the west. To the unaided eye it looked like clouds on the horizon.

"Cirrocumulus?" I asked.

Daggoth shook his head. "Chimpanzees."

"Excuse me?"

"With wings," he added. "Bob, we just moved up your departure time. Saddle up!"

We ran down the great staircase collecting Mervyn on the way to the stables. Our gear was ready and our only delay was saddling Ghost. Rune climbed up behind Mervyn on his flying rug before I was done and Daggoth cast a field of invisibility over us all.

Other than bumping into each other as we moved down the exit tunnel, we were able to depart without incident.

Σ

Calabastor's waterfront area was crowded this day. Ships arrived and departed with a frantic frequency that put one in mind of L.A.X. during the Christmas holidays. Cargo was being loaded and unloaded by legions of stevedores. Peddlers and vendors flocked about the boardwalk, beach, and piers to hawk their wares to passengers and crew alike.

Fights seemed to break out on a regular basis. The most spectacular was between a great, bloated brutish man and a scrawny, pop-eyed sailor with grotesquely muscled forearms. Surprisingly, the little man won and walked off with the object of their disagreement: a woman so tall and impossibly skinny that she'd have to run around in the shower to get wet.

Rune led us on past Hennesey's & McHale's Drydock Services, pointing out the various ships anchored in the harbor. "Avoid that one like the plague," she warned, indicating a dark vessel with the name "Nostromo" painted across its stern. "It smuggles illegal aliens." There was nothing beyond the ship's dark coloring and oddly shaped superstructure to indicate its corrupt cargo. Indeed, a frigate of a more sinister aspect was passing by the harbor mouth, its bloodred sails billowing in a different direction than the wind was actually blowing: the Dutchman was still looking for his home port.

Ships of less sinister mein abounded, as well. Milk was being loaded aboard the good ship *Guppy* while children frolicked on its wooden deck with an elephant and an odd-looking sea dog. Another boat, similarly named after another small fish, prepared to depart with five passengers, promising a three-hour tour of the islands. The handbills that advertised the daily excursions further promised that ". . . the mate was a mighty sailing man . . ." and that the skipper was ". . . brave and sure. . . ." My doubts on that bit of hype were distracted by a large, whitewashed schooner passing by, close enough to hear the minstrel on board crooning: "Love, exciting and new—"

Rune led us down a series of docks to a small, twin-masted ketch with gaff-and-topsail rigs. *Mary Ellen Carter* was emblazoned across her hull, and as we led Ghost up the gangplank, a large woman with her left arm in a sling leaned out over the gunnels and yelled: "Ahoy, Dr. Ripley!" She vaulted the railing (no mean feat for a woman her size and with a bum arm in the bargain) and met me halfway up.

"Ms. Carter, I presume?"

"Elsbeth, you fraud! Ha!" Her back slap nearly pitched me into the water. "You had us convinced, man!"

"Convinced, madam?"

"First, that you were dead. And that death was as permanent as you claimed." She helped me maneuver a rather nervous animal up and onto the ship.

Ghost managed, as well.

"But, as you've just now proved, one or both of those suppositions just won't hold water."

A light flicked dimly in the nether regions of my brain. I turned to Rune: "Do I know her?"

"Sort of," the Assassin murmured. "She's the one who hauled your body back to town."

"The one with all the neat little holes in it?" Mervyn wanted to know.

"Mmm-hmm."

"Cast off," Elsbeth bellowed, "and attend the lines!"

A slim rapier of a man, dressed in a dandy's finery, leapt forward to grasp several ropes. "Number two manned, my lady! How say you, Abbot?"

A short, round man was extricating himself from a makeshift cot of coiled hawsers and sailcloth. "Coming, coming," he mumbled. A mitered helmet was twisted and slightly askew atop his bushy head and he nearly tripped over his robe and the end of his rope girdle. A silver crucifix flailed at the end of a leather thong behind his back. The abbot yawned and staggered about, contemplating the ropes running down the sides of the two masts. "Who's on first, Costellino?" he queried.

"You are, man."

"Then, who's on second?"

The slender man with the pencil-thin moustache shook his set of lines at the big fellow. "I am."

"Then, who's on third?"

"What?"

The abbot scratched his head: " 'What's' on third?"

"No!" The smaller man was becoming exasperated. "There is no third, you birdbrain!"

In spite of the confusion over the sail lines we were moving away from the pier and moving out into the harbor. I gazed up into the rigging, mystified as to how we could be moving at all—much less in the right direction.

Mervyn tapped my shoulder and pointed past the prow of our ship. "We're being towed."

Sure enough, a series of ropes fanned out from a forward capstan, stretched taut, and disappeared into the water some fifty feet ahead of us. As I stared one of the ropes went a little slack as a large fishtail broke the surface of the water. It disappeared beneath the waves and the rope pulled tight again. "Dolphins?" I queried.

The woman, Elsbeth, looked at me, her eyes goggling a bit like Jeremiah's.

"Skywalker!"

We turned and looked. A blond woman was climbing over the railing, wearing a great big smile and nothing else. I looked at Elsbeth: "Friend of yours?"

Elsbeth goggled a bit more and then the blonde was all over me like cheap livery.

"I think we should sit down and talk," Rune suggested.

$$\Sigma$$

"So you're really dead."

I shook my head. "I'm still alive. The other Ripleys—including the one you picked up at sea—are dead."

We were down below, in the aft cabin that Elsbeth had been using for her quarters. After telling our respective stories, we were still confused.

"So you—or the other you—was—were—telling me the truth." She reached for the bottle at the center of the table and poured herself another drink. "Death has become serious business here in Dreamworlds." She knocked back her glass and the amber liquid disappeared in a convulsive swallow.

"Well, now that you're convinced," I said, "I suppose you'll be hightailing it out of the Matrix just as fast as your algorithms will take you."

"What? Not hardly!" She set her glass back on the table with a resounding thump. "If I was willing to risk my neck for a possible Pulitzer on a REMrunner story, what makes you think I'm gonna back down now?"

"Well, I—"

"Great Caesar's ghost, man, this goes beyond Pulitzer! A U.S. senator held hostage by a computer, a half-crazed Artificial Intelligence plotting to take over the White House, the Program's creator turned into a were-Elf and split into multiple avatars that are being hunted down and murdered in a mysterious conspiracy, your ex-wife involved in an ongoing romance with a dead man—we're talking best-seller, here! We're talking New Hollywood!"

"Money?" I asked. "You're willing to risk your life for mere money?"

"Nothing mere about the kind of money we're talking about here," she answered warmly. The drink had already brought a rosy glow to her cheeks and was now working its will on her posture. "And it's not just money. It's career, it's the opportunity of a lifetime." She picked up the bottle again. "Besides, you can use all the help you can get. If Cerberus isn't defeated and gets 'lected president, I'm not going to be all that safe on the Outside. And that's assuming that I can get out without him knowing that I'm a witness and therefore a liability."

I saw her point.

"Now, what are you going to do 'bout Bubbles?"

I favored her with another of my devastatingly blank looks: "Bubbles?"

She shrugged. "You know: Thetis."

"Ah," I said. "Thetis."

"Dockster Ripley"—she fumbled with the bottle—"I suspect you know your Greek mythology to know that Blondie, here, is supposed to marry Peleus, have a son, and raise him in the Sticks."

"Dip him in the Styx," I corrected. "Achilles."

"Gesundheit," she returned amiably. She waved the bottle. "Sure you don't want some?"

I hesitated. "Uh, no." I was going to need my wits about me more than ever, for the next couple of days.

"So's how the Trojans gonna fight the Geeks without 'im?"

"Greeks," I corrected. "And I don't know, yet."

"Well," she murmured conspiratorially, "I'm working on a plan."

"Ah. And?"

"I'm not drunk enough, yet."

"Oh."

Σ

*"COSSSTELLLINNOOOOO!"*

The abbot's cry was far more effective than any landlocked rooster at rousing us from our sleep. I tumbled out of my hammock and fumbled for my gear as feet pattered over the decking above my head.

"Sails ho!" the count announced as I stumbled up on deck, trying to buckle my swordbelt.

The sun had not yet made its appearance but a rosy predawn glow suffused the sky to the east and the water reflected enough light from the twin moons sinking in the west to illumine our quarry. The count passed the spyglass to Rune who directed it toward an island several miles away. I joined them at the starboard rail.

"Well?"

"Looks like our ship," she answered. "Too far away to make out a name but she flies the Jolly Roger."

"Big deal," opined Mervyn, "all pirates fly the black flag!"

"Overall description seems to match, so far," the Assassin continued. "She's heeling behind yon island, so we'll have to follow to make sure."

"Wait a minute," Elsbeth was saying. "When you hired my boat to catch you up to a ship that had sailed the day before, you didn't say anything about it being a pirate vessel!"

I looked at Rune.

Who looked at Mervyn.

Who looked at me.

"Um, it's a pirate vessel," I said.

"I can see that!" Elsbeth retorted.

The abbot appropriated the little brass telescope and futilely scanned the island for further evidence. "Maybe it's Bluebeard!" he theorized with wide-eyed enthusiasm.

"If you think this boat is going any closer, you're out of your mind!" Elsbeth continued.

"Bluebeard wasn't a pirate, you moron!" Costellino was explaining to his oafish companion.

"You don't have to pull alongside," I assured Elsbeth, "just get us within a mile or so of that island."

"Then maybe it's Yellowbeard!"

"Are you kidding me?" She planted her hands on her hips and shook her head. "We're turning this tub around right now and heading back to Calabastor!"

"You're thinking of an old movie. Two-dee," answered the count.

"What happened to last night's bravado?" I challenged. "What happened to the Pulitzer Prize, serious money, and the chance of a lifetime?"

"How about Redbeard?"

"Lifetime!" she screeched. "There ain't gonna be any lifetime if we get close to a pirate ship! In case you haven't noticed, we're not packing a single cannon! And I'm sober, this morning! A little hung over—but sober!"

"Dunno. I think he was a Viking." Costellino rubbed his chin. "I seem to remember a book or something. . . ."

"Look, we can keep the island between them and us," I said, heading toward the makeshift stall just down front of the poop deck. "I'll take it from there."

"We'll take it from there," Mervyn corrected.

"I s'pose you'll be telling me there wasn't no Blackbeard, next."

"You're out of your mind!" Elsbeth insisted.

"No. There really was a Blackbeard as I recall."

"Maybe I am," I murmured, picking up my saddle and approaching Ghost.

"D'you suppose we could get close enough to get a good look?" the abbot pondered.

"If it is Blackbeard," the count considered, "he might show us more than we bargained for."

"That would *Teech* you," Rune observed dryly.

I looked at her and grinned as I adjusted the saddle across Ghost's back.

"What?" Mervyn wanted to know. "What'd she say?"

"Never mind." Even without the spectacles, it was disorienting seeing an ancient wizard, decades past the "graybeard" stage, adopt the speech and mannerisms of an adolescent. I tightened the front and back cinches, elbowing the pegasus in the belly to eliminate any slack.

"All right!" Elsbeth conceded. "We'll shelter in the lee of the island. For an hour. Then we're leaving." She folded her arms. "If that pirate ship circles around any sooner, we'll hoist anchor and you can jolly well walk back to Calabastor on your own!"

"Fair enough," I said.

The abbot was oblivious to the rest of us. "What about Brownbeard?" he asked the count.

# Chapter
# Twenty-two

★

\RIPLEY\PATH\SIGMA     (Σ)

"**W**HAT was that?"

Rune turned back to face me. "Dwarf—I think!" she called over the drone of wind. "He was ringing a bell!"

I looked down again but we had passed over the compound and all I could see was palm-topped jungle and a sandy lagoon where the island had pinched off a section of ocean between thumb and forefinger. "What was he yelling about?"

Rune shrugged and almost lost her balance at the edge of Mervyn's flying carpet. The rug had taken point position as Ghost's wings tended to stir up a bit of air turbulence to the sides and rear. "Something about a plain!" She shaded her eyes and scanned the tree line. "Do you think he meant a plateau?"

"Aircraft!" announced the wizard.

"Where?" I demanded.

"No! I think he meant plane as in aircraft!" Mervyn elaborated.

"Where?" worried Rune.

"Us!" Mervyn yelled to be heard over the rush of wind in our ears. "I think he was referring to us!"

"I just hope that bell didn't tip off the pirates!" I yelled back.

"I just hope your finny friends are there when we need 'em!" he countered.

"We'll find out in a moment," Rune said, pointing.

Abruptly, the island fell behind us, and less than a mile away, the pirate ship hove into view.

Perhaps they had heard the bell. Perhaps the lookout in the crow's nest was unusually alert and sharp of eye.

Or perhaps they were already expecting airborne visitors. There was a booming sound and a moment later a missile bearing a strong resemblance to a bowling ball whistled past.

"Split right!" I yelled. "And then hover above the mainmast: you'll be safe there!"

They swerved to starboard while Ghost and I swooped to port. The next cannonball split the difference and cut a path between us.

As my winged steed looped around to close with the ship's rigging, I unclipped the saddle's safety tethers from my belt and loosed my left foot from the stirrup. It took only another moment to invoke the parameters of a Flying spell about myself. With luck, I wouldn't need it and the pirates below wouldn't give me cause to use it. But Robert Remington Ripley the Second didn't raise no dummy and I never believed in working without a net if you had a choice.

As Ghost's wing tip brushed the topgallant on the mainmast, I leapt from the saddle, dropping some ten feet or so to the angled hammock formed by the ratlines crisscrossing the shrouds.

"Boy," roared a voice from down below, "I'll have your guts for garters!"

Guts for garters, again. Nice. Real nice.

"Come down here or I'll come up and get you!"

"That's the plan, man," I murmured, drawing my *hamidachi*. I cut a shroud line and swung in toward the mainmast. I slapped into the topsail, just below the topgallant, like a baseball into a catcher's glove. I released the line and slid down to the footspar, put the *hamidachi* in my teeth as I executed a three-sixty curl over the wooden beam, and dropped down to the top of the course. Plunging the short blade into the sailcloth, I descended the remainder of the distance to the main deck on a path of ripped canvas. Luck was with me: I didn't have to use the Flying spell, I landed without falling on my face, and though the pirates quickly surrounded me, they didn't immediately kill me for dividing their mainsail into two pieces.

The looks on their faces, however, indicated that the thought had occurred to them.

"Avast, me lads! Make way! Let me through!" A portion of the wall of scurvy seamen was jostled aside and their captain stepped through.

He was tall and slim, with cruel, aquiline features and long, thin, dangly moustaches. He also wore an eyepatch and in place of his left hand he had a grappling device of hooked brass.

"Captain Claw, I presume."

He cocked his head like a parrot and contemplated me with his one good eye. "You're not him!"

"Whom?"

"Pe—" began a voice to my right.

"Silence!" thundered the pirate chief. "Have I not forbidden one and all to speak the name of that juvenile delinquent in my presence for the rest of time?"

Heads nodded.

He peered at me again. "You're not him," he decided again. "Furthermore, you don't look like any of the rest of them!"

"Them?" I asked.

"The Los—"

"Silence!" he roared. Then smiled sweetly. "However," he continued, "you do look familiar."

"Really?" Now that was an observation that had come to make me nervous of late.

"Yes." His hand went to his cutlass. "You look like a dead man to me!" The pirates all roared their approval as he drew his sword and advanced.

No one was in any hurry, here, so I had time to sheath the *hamidachi* and draw my katana. Caladbolg's crystal blade and blue glow got their attention.

"Actually, Captain, I'm here to do some business."

"Business?" His advance had degenerated into a wary orbit and he circled me from a safe distance.

"Yes." I suddenly swung my longsword about my body, weaving a protective basket of momentary crystal. The effect was that the encompassing circle of pirates moved back several feet, giving me more maneuvering room. "I'm here to make an exchange."

Claw frowned. "Exchange? What kind of exchange?"

"You have something I want." I smiled. "I have something you want."

"What?" Claw demanded, eyeing my glowing blade. "What is this bargain you dare to make with Captain Claw?"

"You picked up a hand on the necromatic black market. It belonged to a—friend—of mine." Calling Morpheus "friend" felt a little awkward. "I want it back."

Claw looked a bit discomforted, himself. "I have special plans for that hand," he answered, make a few tentative feints with his cutlass. "I am not inclined to part with it. Oh, no. In fact, as soon as I reach Ortygia, I expect to become quite 'attached' to it, you might say. . . ."

I almost dropped my guard. When we traced the other hand, its intended use had become quite evident. A dead man's hand: Hand of Glory. It would be used as a sort of magical treasure-hunting device. I had supposed a pirate ship would use the other hand for similar purposes. Now, looking at the brass crampon where Claw's other hand used to be, I understood differently. It would probably be easier to convince the man to part with all those chests of gold and silver he surely had down below in the holds.

"What's on Ortygia, Claw?" I tapped his cutlass aside with Caladbolg. "Someone promising you a magical graft job?"

"You don't know what it's like," he hissed. "Having to be so careful when you sleep: rolling over in bed could be fatal! Stupid things like picking your nose or using the amenities of basic hygiene are potentially painful and disfiguring! And my social life—" He choked. "What's your interest, dead man?" he cried. "What would you offer me in exchange for a chance at a normal life?"

Put that way, I felt guilt colliding with duty. "Your ship," I said.

He stopped stalking and leaned back. "My ship?"

I nodded.

"Let me get this straight: you want the dead Sorcerer's hand in exchange for my ship? The ship that I already have?"

"Um, yep. That pretty well sums up the deal."

"You're mad!"

"Captain!" chimed in a new voice. "We're taking on water!"

Claw whirled. "How bad?"

"Not bad," I answered. "The hole is only about this wide. . . ." I made a circle touching thumb to forefinger.

"Plug it!" he ordered, and turned back on me. "How did you know?"

I smiled. "The same way I know that in one minute you'll have two more holes—the same size—in different parts of your hull."

"What!"

"Captain! The bo'sun reports another hole aft!"

"How?" he bellowed.

I gestured to the rail. "I'd like you to meet some friends of mine." Heads turned. Observed other heads breaking the surface of the sea around the ship. "Women . . ." the pirate crew breathed wonderingly.

"Nereids," I corrected. "Daughters of Nereus, god of the sea."

"Sisters?" someone murmured. "There's so many. . . ."

"Fifty, to be exact." I didn't mention Ethyl as they were already sufficiently impressed. They were also noticing the collection of awls and hand drills and assorted piercing tools that the Sea Nymphs were brandishing. I waved to Thetis and she signaled to the others to submerge again.

"Now," I continued as the last of the pirates' distractions disappeared beneath the waves, "in another minute, three more holes will breach your hull below the waterline. The minute after that, four more will appear. And each minute thereafter, another set of holes plus one more will be made in your ship, Captain, until we come to some sort of agreement."

Claw looked around at his crew who were already dwindling in number as the pirates ran off to repair the perforations and man the pumps.

"More holes!" someone bellowed belowdecks.

"All right!" Claw gnashed his teeth. "Bly! To my cabin and fetch me that damned hand!"

"Aye, sir! 'Tis already done!" The pudgy first mate produced a package wrapped in oilskins.

"Good man," gritted the captain. "You'll have your own ship, someday."

"Thank you, sir."

"Now"—Claw grimaced—"give it over to our new friend, here."

Bly looked at me as if trying to ascertain his chances of impressing the captain a bit more.

"More holes!"

"Quickly!" Claw screamed.

Bly complied with no complicating heroics. I saluted the pirate chief with my sword and invoked the Flying spell: the crow's nest was occupied so I soared up to the very top of the mainmast and signaled Ethyl. The Merman dove down to call off the scuttling party and I whistled for Ghost who was circling some distance away. Mervyn and Rune were hovering nearby.

"That was easy," Mervyn said.

He said it prematurely.

Captain Claw had endured bold trespass upon his ship. He had sustained considerable damage to his mainsail (my insurance against his pursuing the *Mary Ellen Carter*). He had further damage done to his hull and taken on a fair amount of water. And he had lost the hand of a powerful but dead sorcerer: a hand endued with sufficient magic that he might be able to trade it for the brass claw affixed to the wrist of his left arm.

All this, and he had allowed me to depart unmolested. To be fair, he had allowed it because I had not given him much choice. But Ghost's return to the mainmast tipped that precarious balance I had arranged below.

A horse is a horse (of course, of course). Sticking great feathered wings on him may permit magical flight but it doesn't negate other aspects of equine biology. Anyone who has spent any time around a stable knows that horses are not overly mindful about where they drop their "processed" hay and oats. Flying horses are no different.

It just happened to be Captain Claw's misfortune to be in the wrong place at the wrong time.

A muffled scream was our first warning. As I climbed onto Ghost's saddle, I looked down and saw a much-altered pirate chief running over to one of the deck guns. Bellowing imprecations interwoven with allusions to the goat-footed god of pastures, forests, flocks, and herds, he pulled and tugged at the great barrel until it was tilted straight up.

Pointing right at us.

"Uh-oh," said Mervyn.

I shook my head. "I didn't think any of them would be this stupid."

"What is the phrase?" Rune pondered. "Excrement for grey matter?"

"Looks like brown matter from here," the wizard observed.

"Time to split," I admonished.

We did so, just as the cannon boomed. The heavy iron ball came whistling up between us, ripping through the topsail and the topgallant as well as the remains of the course. Hovering a few feet to either side, we watched as the rounded projectile continued upward another twenty or so feet. Then gravity eased its leaden foot down onto the brake pedal.

"Newton's law."

I looked at Mervyn. "What?"

"Newton's law," he repeated, watching the cannonball achieve a momentary state of complete inertia. "Every action has an equal but opposite reaction."

"Uh-uh."

I turned and looked at Rune as the iron sphere began to reverse its course.

"Newton's law of action and reaction might be applied to the firing of the cannon but now we're dealing with a different article of Newtonian physics."

We both gaped at her.

"Newton's law of gravitation is that every particle of matter attracts every other particle of matter with a force that varies directly as the product of their masses and inversely as the square of the distances between them. However," she elaborated as the projectile whistled back down through the rigging, "it's Galileo's law of gravitational acceleration that probably has the greatest impact under the present circumstances."

And impact was precisely the right word. A circular hole appeared in the deck planking of the fo'c'sle, less than five feet from the beslimed Captain Claw. A moment later a large jet of water gushed from the opening, giving the prow of the pirate ship the appearance of a giant bidet.

"And what would you know about gravitational physics?" Mervyn challenged, stung by her rebuttal.

"I know that every second that an object falls, its speed increases by some thirty-two feet per second," she replied.

"Abandon ship!" came a cry from below.

"*Some* thirty-two feet?" was his only comeback.

"Well, if you want precision, the formula is s equals one-half g,t squared. . . ."

I turned Ghost's head back toward the far side of the island where Elsbeth would be pacing the decks and worrying about a pirate ship that would never come now.

". . . value of g is 32-point-1740 feet or 980-point-665 centimeters per second. . . ."

I shook my head and grinned as we moved away from the foundering galleon. I couldn't do any more for Scully. This is the way it seemed we all had to learn: it's the quiet ones you have to look out for.

# PART V
## En Passant

★

And all my days are trances,
  And all my nightly dreams
Are where thy grey eye glances
  And where thy footstep gleams—
In what ethereal dances
  By what eternal streams.

—Poe, "To One in Paradise"

# Chapter
# Twenty-three

★

\RIPLEY\PATH\SIGMA        (Σ)

**F**ORTY-EIGHT hours later we stood on the shores of Ortygia.

The previous day I had sent Mervyn back to the tower with Morpheus's hand. I had second thoughts when I tried to contact Daggoth via the shard of magic mirror I was carrying and had drawn a blank. I tried every two hours throughout the day and then well into last night with no better luck. Perhaps we were merely out of range or the Sorcerer had business that had taken him away from his citadel, but as the second moon slipped from the dark ocean depths and began its climb up the black velvet sky, I felt a growing disquiet.

Elsbeth joined me at the starboard rail as the midnight watch came and went. Together we watched the bright stars spiral through the great cosmic dance.

"Looks real, doesn't it?"

She gazed at me curiously. "What makes you think it isn't?"

"Please. . . ."

"No, really," she insisted. "What if this is the Reality and that other life that we remember outside of this Programworld but the fevered dream of our imaginations?"

I smiled and leaned across the railing, inhaling the sharp salt tang of ocean spray as the waves collided with the ship's hull. "You know, I've heard the theory that a Programworld is every bit a 'reality' in its own right as the one we claim Outside. But I don't think I've ever heard anyone put quite the spin on it as you just did."

She smiled in turn and gestured to the panorama of stars and the ripples of phosphorescence on the night sea. "You don't buy into all this, do you?"

"Sometimes." I knelt on the deck and rested my chin and arms on the railing. "But for the most part, I can't afford to. The whole thing is too . . . seductive. And I know how it really works so it tends to spoil the effect."

"So . . . if you were a physicist would you tend to dismiss most of the Outside . . . just because you were well versed in atomic structure?"

"Got me again!" I grinned. "Time to go on the offensive." She made a gesture of compliance. "Your serve."

"All right. How many worlds can one person inhabit? How many lives can one person live at the same time and live well?"

"There are theories of parallel universes where alternate selves live out alternate lives—"

"Wouldn't count even if you could prove it," I said. "If there were more than one of us in more than one universe, we'd still be separate entities. Siamese twins in *this* universe are still two separate sets of consciousnesses."

"Reincarnation—"

"One person, the same person—living in different worlds, assuming different identities, all in the same lifetime."

"You're describing Dreamwalking."

"If the shoe fits."

"So what do you have against a little fun and games? Aren't we all entitled to a little fantasy?"

"I'm not against a little fantasy," I said. "Hell, I made a decent living writing them. But this," I indicated our surroundings with a sweep of my arm, "is so real that it's hard for some people to walk away from it when the time is up. People want to *live* part of their lives here! Which brings me back to my original question. With a whole lifetime to work things out, most people don't do so well dealing with just one world. So how many people could—simultaneously—live more than one life, in more than one world, and live any of them *well*?''

''I see your point.'' She stretched and yawned. ''We should make landfall before midday tomorrow: I'm turning in.'' We said our good nights and headed for our respective berths. Just before she closed the door to her cabin, Elsbeth called to me. ''Rob, we're all looking for a better world than the one we were born into.''

''But is this one really better?'' I asked.

She shrugged. ''Life is a crapshoot and you look for the best odds you can find. If you're gonna win at the races, you gotta bet on more than one horse.''

Σ

Twelve hours later I was walking up Ortygia's sandy beach. Since Ghost couldn't carry us all, I turned him loose to graze inland and geared up to make the trek to the Sibyl's cave on foot. Elsbeth and Rune, of course, decided to accompany me. The abbot and Costellino had decided that someone needed to guard the ship and that it would take both of them to do so. Ethyl couldn't leave the water at all and the Nereids couldn't leave it behind for very long. So that left the three of us.

There had been no sign of submarines or flying saucers on the voyage in. In fact there had been no sign of anything or anyone, so far: no birds flew, no insects hummed, even the susurrus of plants in the wind was absent as we found ourselves in a dead calm.

*Welcome to my parlor.* . . .

We had taken no more than ten steps when a geyser of sand and smoke erupted at the tree line and a gout of flame belched skyward. By the time a humanoid form stepped out of the column of fire and smoke we were displaying more blades than a *ginjsu* commercial.

''I see you are well prepared,'' she observed with a mocking smile.

''Lilith!'' I could have hugged her.

''Not yet,'' she said, warning me back with a stiff-armed gesture. ''I need to cool down first.'' Now I could see the auralike layers of heat-distorted air that rippled about her form. She trotted around us and down to the water, leaving a pattern of glassy footprints in the sand. There was a tremendous burst of steam as she waded out into the ocean and the hissing sound precluded any conversation until her head was completely submerged.

"Friend of yours?" Elsbeth inquired as Lilith emerged from the waves.

I nodded.

"Figures."

The residual moisture on her person was evaporating even as Lilith approached again, but she did look a good deal cooler. "What brings you to Ortygia?" I asked. The urge to hug her had passed in the heat of the moment.

"You," she answered.

"Me?"

"One of you, anyways." She smiled, showing pointed teeth. "I'm here to help you."

"Help me?"

"Get to the bottom of all of this." She frowned now. "There was a lot of political infighting Down Below over this. Sides were taken. Your nemesis was backed by some of Hell's heavy hitters."

"Nergal," I said. "Meshlamthea. Maybe even Erishkigal?"

She nodded. "And others."

"Someone who can look like me?"

She looked surprised. "Why do you say that?"

"A hunch," I answered, wary of showing all my cards. "What about Orcus?"

She shook her head. "Sat the fence on this one. Played politico all the way down the line. Although I think he did favor you off the record."

"Isn't that nice. So, what's the plan?"

"I'm taking you to see the Sibyl." That enigmatic smile, again. "Once you see her, I think everything else will be made clear."

I gestured, palm flat, to the tropical forest up ahead. "Lead on, Macduff."

"Macduff?"

"Figure of speech."

"Oh. And—since you're well enough armed—how about lending me one of your weapons." There are times and circumstances under which even the most potent magics fail and it never hurts to carry an instrument of mayhem for backup, so the request seemed reasonable.

I tried to unsling my bow but it seemed to be caught on my shoulder. I finally unslung the Uzi from my opposite shoulder and handed it to her. "Do you know how—"

"During one's first millennium in the Pit," she said, fielding my unfinished question, "a denizen of Hell is trained in the utilization of all engines of violence—past, present, and future."

"Ah."

"Follow me." She began leading us up the beach and into the jungle. I followed. Rune covered my back. Elsbeth brought up the rear.

$$\Sigma$$

We walked for hours.

If there was a trail leading to the Sibyl's grotto, we never saw it. Lilith had a way of melting through clotheslines of vines and grasping branches as if they or she were insubstantial mirages. The rest of us had our swords out, hacking and chopping at the underbrush every foot of the way. Before an hour had passed we were all drenched with sweat and half-faint from heat and exertion.

By the time we reached the ear-shaped entrance to the Sibyl's grotto the sun was sinking into the fog bank to the west and we were very nearly done in.

"Rest stop!" I announced. And promptly allowed my legs to fold under me. Rune and Lilith, to my annoyance, remained standing. Elsbeth hunkered down after a moment's hesitation, but it was more of a social kindness than an act of weariness.

"We're nearly there," the Archdemoness chided with some degree of impatience.

"Then five more minutes won't make any difference in the scheme of things," I said. "Why don't you go on ahead and tell the old girl we're coming."

Lilith made no reply but turned on her heel and walked into the mouth of the cave.

Elsbeth pulled a painful grin. "What's with Ms. Personality?"

Rune's response was less mirthful. "I do not expect civilities from Hellspawn, but I like this not. A forced march over difficult terrain is depleting and we are hardly in any condition for a hostile encounter.''

"I am a bit pooped," I admitted. "Just let me close my eyes for five minutes and I'll be ready to go again."

Elsbeth relaxed with her back to a tree while Rune assumed a stance of increased vigilance. I closed my eyes.

Oshi, the Asian swordmaster, had tried to teach me the varied disciplines of Bushido alongside the attacks and parries of Kendo. And while he would admit that there was a Zen-like quality to the way I blended eastern and western fencing styles, he often (and loudly) despaired of my ever mastering the inner disciplines of the master warrior.

What I never permitted him or anyone else to know was how successful I really was: in a body cramped by chronic pain and scar tissue, the mental mastery Oshi despaired of my ever learning was what enabled me to lift and negotiate the blade to begin with.

I went back to those lessons now, searching behind closed eyelids for the patterns to unlock my hidden reserves. *The mind is all*, I told myself, *this body is but an illusion*. . . .

When Lilith roused me a few minutes later, I felt better but could not say for how long or just what illusions I had succeeded in conquering.

$$\Sigma$$

The grotto was empty.

Lilith carried a torch, Elsbeth and Rune held lanterns, while I relied on the light shed by Caladbolg's enchanted blade. It was more than enough illumination to see that the chamber where the Sibyl slept and kept her modest possessions was nearly empty and had not seen habitation for some time.

I walked around the perimeter of the sacred pool and stared into its glassy depths. "Out," I murmured. "Out with the gout. . . ."

"Where is she?" Elsbeth wanted to know.

The Archdemoness acted perplexed. "Perhaps we will find her farther back in the passages." And there was a passage at the back of the cavern leading down into the bowels of the rock.

Rune's sword was out and blocking my path as I took a step to follow Lilith. "You led us here with the promise of seeing the Soothsayer.'' Though her blade was inhibiting my movement her words were addressed to the Demoness.

"Yes. And I am hoping to find her farther down the passageway." Lilith looked at me. "Shouldn't we be searching for her?"

"The point is," Elsbeth spoke now, drawing her bastard sword, "that you implied having recent conversations with the Sibyl, or at least recent knowledge of her whereabouts."

"It is obvious that she has not been here for some time," the Assassin added, "and now you 'think' she might be farther back in that tunnel."

"What game are you playing, girlie?" Elsbeth was taking a step forward, but I drew my own sword and pushed past Rune to confront Lilith, myself.

"How about it, Lil?" I asked. "You said Hell was divided in this matter. Which side did you really choose?" She raised the Uzi and I shook my head. "The gun's no good: there's powdered amber in the shell casings instead of real gunpowder."

The Demoness stared at the weapon so intently I knew she was verifying the truth of my words. With a cry of frustration she flung the weapon from her.

"I guess that answers your question," Elsbeth muttered behind me.

"My first question," I amended. "My second question is are you really Lilith?" I shifted Caladbolg to my left hand and reached inside my vest with my right. "If not, then who are you really?"

As I pulled out the spectacle case containing the Optics of al Rashid, Lilith underwent a startling transformation: face and form convulsed and a moment later was replaced by the image of a woman I believed dead.

"Euryale. . . ."

The emotional impact of seeing Medusa's sister, healed of her hideous affliction and then killed in a graveyard confrontation with the Lord of the Undead, unsettled me more than I expected. Before I could move or speak another word, she flung the torch down and fled into the tunnel.

$$\Sigma$$

The passage was round and smoothed as if some great acidic worm had digested its own pathway as it angled through solid rock. The tunnel twisted downward and then back upon itself, again and again, like some convoluted maze. "Reminds me of a piece of brain coral I saw once," Elsbeth commented, briefly. Her voice reverberated loudly in the close confines of the stone corridor and no one spoke again until we came to the next chamber nearly a quarter of an hour later.

The room was small, scarcely more than ten feet in diameter. A stone bier was thrust up out of the granite floor at the chamber's center and upon its flat surface lay a body.

The body of the Sibyl.

The ancient woman was wrapped in her customary raiment of grey and black and lay in repose, her hands folded over her chest, as if laid out for her own funeral.

"Is she dead?" Elsbeth wanted to know.

I reached out to check for a pulse and encountered invisible resistance.

"Force bubble." I cast about, looking for electronics or machinery of some kind. I saw none. "Or maybe some sort of Warding coupled with a Timestop spell."

"Suspended animation," Rune grunted.

Elsbeth ran her hands over the invisible shield. "Can you neutralize it?"

I picked up the Uzi, handed it to her, and rolled up my sleeves. "Maybe. There are a number of spells that might have an effect." The down side was I could trigger some side effect that could harm or even kill the Sibyl. Or the rest of us, for that matter.

I pulled out the Optics of al Rashid and put them on. A closer examination revealed unfamiliar spell patterns but the colors and weave of the *dweomer* indicated no booby traps. Just a standard one-two combination of utilitarian thaumaturgy. The Optics also confirmed that the Sibyl was still alive.

I tried a simple spell that was a fundamental to any magic user's arsenal: Neutralize Magic. As I watched, the first pattern of invisible light and color unraveled and slipped from the design surrounding the stone bier. Since the spells were arranged in a one-two setup, I cast another Neutralize Magic spell before trying anything different.

It worked again. As the second spell layer dispersed, the Sibyl took a deep breath and began to stir.

I looked up at Rune and caught her normally austere face in

a moment of soft repose: she almost smiled. Turning to look at Elsbeth, I received a greater shock. The Trueform behind her powerful avatar was a petite woman with features as delicate as a china doll's. Before I could frame the question suitably, the Sibyl sat up.

"How do you fee—" was as far as I got when she brought her walking stick around and bashed me up side of the head. I reeled back and blinked through a universe of stars as she hopped up off the bier and cocked her heavy, knobbed shillelagh back again.

"Wait, I—" started to say and then bit my tongue as the stout wooden cudgel connected with my right knee. I went down and she went out, hobbling back up the passageway toward her grotto.

"Should we go after her?" Elsbeth asked as she and Rune helped me to my feet. Or, rather, foot, as I couldn't straighten my right leg right away.

I shook my head, noticing that the stars tended to swirl a bit with the motion.

"Do you think she was part of a trap?"

"Oh, yeth," I said. Part of my mind was still occupied with the Big Bang theory of the universe and the headache and bruised tongue weren't helping my speech either. "Paht uhba twap. But I gotta follow enaway."

"Can you walk?"

I could walk. Sort of. After a couple of minutes my vision cleared and I was able to straighten my leg. It hurt to walk but then it hurt to sit, as well, so I figured we ought to keep moving. We exited the room and continued down the next leg of the tunnel with Rune leading the way.

There was another chamber after a couple of miles of switch-backed passages. This room was quite a bit larger and had two stone biers. The bodies laid out in state were even more familiar: The Duke and Stumpy.

"Wait a minute." Rune placed a hand on my chest as I started to go forward. "Suppose they're not your real companions?"

"Like the Sibyl," Elsbeth chimed in.

"It was the real Sibyl," I said. I was gratified to find that the swelling was starting to go down in my tongue and my right leg was able to take most of my weight again. I adjusted the spectacles and gave these bodies a closer inspection. "And these are the real Duke and Stumpy." I cast the necessary spells to unbind them and had the good sense to stand back and remove the enchanted glasses while they regained consciousness.

I should have stood back a bit farther.

Σ

The problem, as it turned out, was one of mistaken identity.

There was another Ripley—or Half-Elven Riplakish—who had captured The Duke and Stumpy (and apparently the Sibyl, as well) who looked just like me. Which is why their first thoughts were, upon seeing my face, to get in as many licks as they could. Elsbeth and Rune tried to help me convince them that I was the real me and, eventually, we succeeded.

But not before my left eye started to swell shut and I was able to wiggle two loose teeth with my tongue.

Needless to say I was a bit more careful when we discovered the next chamber. After dissolving the magical fetters that bound Vashti and Rijma to the stone slabs, I hobbled back up the passageway and waited for my companions to sort things out before I showed my face again.

"He looked just like you!"

Everyone kept saying that.

My ex had her own observations to add to the pile. "There was something else there. . . ." Vashti shivered. "There was an anger behind his voice . . . a bitterness in his eyes. . . ."

"Sounds like me." I spat a gob of blood on the stone floor.

She shook her head. "No. I've seen you angry and I've seen you bitter. And I know how you carry it around inside you. But this was different . . . worse. . . ."

"Sounds like your evil twin, Skippy," Rijma observed dryly.

"Oh, Crom!" I moaned. "Not the 'Evil Twin' subplot!"

"No, wait a minute," Elsbeth said. "It's a given that there are more than one of you running around in the Matrix. Right?"

"Maybe," I conceded. "But I tend to believe I'm all present and accounted for, now."

"But you don't know for sure," she argued. "And even though you think of yourself as the same Robert Ripley who entered Fantasyworld just a few days ago, you've changed since then."

"All of you have changed since that time," Rijma said, catching Elsbeth's train of thought. "Every experience each of you has had since the moment you were schismed into duplicate memory files has given each of you a different perspective of events. Even if you and one of your twins were in the same room, you'd each experience the unfolding of events from different perspectives. Over a period of time you would perceive reality on a slightly different timeline, growing apart and becoming two different personalities."

"I'll buy that," I said, "but none of my duplicates have been in-Program long enough to undergo such a radical change in perspective. This other me would have to undergo some extended period of trauma to fit your assailant's M.O."

"We all seen ya!" Stumpy argued. "And you sure did look and sound like yourself!"

"Metamorph. Shapeshifter. Illusionist." I patted the spectacle case in my vest pocket. "I was taken in by our nemesis in the guise of Lilith. She—or he—or it—certainly looked and sounded like Lilith. Then she/he/it became the very image of Euryale." I looked over at Elsbeth. "Where's the Uzi?"

She spread her hands. "I left it back there in the first chamber. You said it didn't work."

I had this overwhelming urge to slap a palm to my forehead and drag it down over my face. "I didn't say it wouldn't work; I said there wasn't any gunpowder in the ammo."

"Same thing."

"No it isn't." I took a deep breath to calm my jittery nerves. "You see, gunpowder is inert in this Programworld—it doesn't work."

"Well, then what's your point?"

I sighed. "Never mind. Let's keep moving."

It was in the next chamber, down the tunnel, that I found my next cause for concern. Two biers but only one body was magically restrained: Borys Dankevych's. Natasha Skovoroda's lay on the rock surface, unfettered but unmoving. Whatever motivating force the Zombie Mistress had enacted on this empty, lifeless husk, it seemed quiescent here.

As I dispelled the twin enchantments on Borys, I could feel my personal reserves failing. I was only good for another spell or two. Then I would have to sleep in order to replenish the inner mantra before I would be capable of further thaumaturgy.

I stumbled back into the passage and waited, weak and weary, while explanations were made. When I returned and our downward trek resumed, Dankevych had scooped Natasha's body up into his arms and fell into position at the rear of the party, carrying his dead fiancée as a father might carry his sleeping child.

The tunnel wound on and down for another hour. Twice Rune called rest breaks, insisting that we would be in no shape for a confrontation unless we paced ourselves. I could tell that she was clearing her throat to announce a third when the passageway opened out into another chamber.

The room appeared to be immense, the effect enhanced by the fact that there was no far wall. What first appeared to be an endless chamber was actually a great roofed ledge looking out over a vast abyss. I crossed the cavernous room and stood at its far perimeter, looking out into the emptiness beyond.

Looking down it seemed to be bottomless, even after I put on the Optics of al Rashid. But, far below, I could hear the low thrumming of deep water rushing on a vast subterranean journey. The rock strata appeared to be bisected here by a deep canyon or trench that continued in a straight line when I leaned out and looked to the left or right. If the canyon went all the way to the surface, it was impossible to tell now. No light filtered down from above. But we were miles underground by now and the night sky would not provide sufficient illumination to reach this far. I peered across the chasm at the parallel cliff face nearly a mile away. Grey-white fog cascaded down from above, foaming over the far side of the abyss like milky cataracts, and through the lacy curtains of mist, I could make out a dim light. Perhaps there were other passages on the other side, other inhabitants. . . .

"Robbie-me-boyo! Over here!" Rijma's voice pulled me back from the edge and over to four stone biers. Three were human-sized. The other served as a pedestal for a wooden box. The lid was propped open and Morpheus's baleful features regarded me with a blank expression.

As in the other chambers, the figures reposing on their stony beds were under thaumaturgic restraint. I pulled out the spectacles and put them on as The Duke announced the obvious: "It's Daggoth, Pallas, and Hanson!"

I shook my head as I could now see beyond the obvious.

"It's Pallas and the senator, all right." But it wasn't Daggoth the Dark.

It was Cerberus, the personality fragment that had passed for The Machine's Superego.

All nicely captured and neatly gift wrapped for us.

Three or four hours, indeed.
*
They let me sleep twelve and I would've slept more if all the friggin' alarms hadn't gone off at once!
*
My office is supposed to be soundproofed but that kind of racket will penetrate anything!
*
Dr. Contrell tells me we've developed a phasing problem in one of the Matrix sectors.
*
I'd suspected as much earlier, but he tells me it's growing worse.
*
Worse, indeed: everyone's code-string moved while I was

asleep and now they're right on the perimeter of the affected sector!
*
We could lose them all at any moment!

# Chapter
# Twenty-four

★

\RIPLEY\PATH\SIGMA        (Σ)

"**N**OW what?"

I looked over at Rijma. "Now what, what?"

She scowled, a mock-menacing expression. "Didn't your mother ever teach you that it's impolite to answer a question with a question?"

I smiled sweetly—or at least tried to with a swollen lip. "Didn't yours?"

Senator Hanson decided it was time to play referee. "I think it's a very good question."

"Which one?" I asked.

"The one about what should be our next move." He looked around the chamber. "Where do we go from here?"

"Home."

Everyone looked at me.

"Home," I repeated. "We have what we came for—at least essentially." I nodded at the box containing Morpheus's head on the third bier. "When that's returned to Morpheus, our part of the bargain will be fulfilled. Which is unnecessary now as Cerberus is under restraint and, according to my enchanted eyewear, still in taction. That means you can have your body back, Senator, and I suggest that the sooner you vacate the Program, the better—not only for your own safety, but for the sake of two nations on a collision course with war.''

''Are you sure you don't—''

''We don't!'' Rijma insisted. ''For once my esteemed colleague is right. Now scram, shoo! Invoke your Return Code!''

Hanson closed his eyes and was silent for a moment. Then he opened them again and looked around.

''What's the matter?'' Rijma wanted to know. ''Didn't it work?''

Hanson's avatar smiled. ''The senator has departed: we are no longer in taction.''

I had forgotten a fundamental of Dreamworld physics. Removing your consciousness from the Program didn't remove your Dreambody from its Computer-constructed reality. Hanson's consciousness was now back inside his ''real body'' in the ''Real World,'' but his avatar remained right where he'd left it. It would still move and act and ''think'' like the senator, but it was now under The Machine's control, basing all character aspects and decisions on a Personality Analog file in memory.

It got a little spooky if you thought about it too much.

''Now that that little problem is taken care of,'' the senator's avatar continued, ''I'd like to be going home, myself.''

''Home?'' Vashti echoed.

''Back to Frontierworld,'' he elaborated.

We stared at Hanson's avatar. More precisely, we took in the fringed buckskins, the ten-gallon hat, the pointy-toed cowboy boots, the spurs, the silver-chased leather gunbelt, the pearl-handled six-guns holstered at his hips.

''Oh.''

Getting Hanson's avatar back into the Frontierworld Program was probably not an insurmountable problem. But I was just too tired to deal with it right now.

Two of my problems should have already been solved by the application of the love philtre to Princess Aeriel's drinking water: the Amazons would have a new candidate for royal consort and Daggoth would be too busy to toy with Stephanie's affections. That would make it easier to coax my ex-wife out of the Program. The fact that Pallas, as well as Cerberus, continued to sleep in suspended animation, would make the logistics of getting Stephanie back into her own body eminently more feasible.

But there were other tasks undone that still required my time and attention and I pledged myself to their resolution—just as soon as we finished up here and got everyone back to Daggoth's Tower. I'd get some rest, recharge my spell capabilities. Then I'd fulfill my obligation to put Morpheus back together. Figure out how to resurrect Natasha's avatar. Get Jerermiah turned back into a human so he and Mervyn could exit the program. Locate Nicole and see if there was anything we could do for what was left of her mind. And check on Lilith. . . .

Ah, yes: I still had an enemy out there, somewhere.

Was it Nicole, shapeshifting to appear as Lilith on this occasion to lead me into an ambush?

Or had Lilith misrepresented her allegiance to me up until our last confrontation in these underground passages?

Or was there some greater power, acting as puppeteer, assuming various identities and manipulating others, still remaining to be unmasked?

As the others made ready to depart, I got up and walked over to the bier where the head of Morpheus rested. I was tired and I knew I was missing something important. All this trouble to get us down into this stone labyrinth. Or me, anyway: the others could have been part of the bait.

But now we had reached a dead end, accomplished all the obvious goals, and were leaving. I stared at the lifeless head, so recently a gamepiece in this puzzle of multiple avatars. "To what purpose?" I murmured softly.

In answer the dead sorcerer's eyes and mouth snapped open. The voice that issued from the head's oral cavity sounded like Morpheus's, though it had a hollow, echoey quality that one tends to associate with horror tri-dee's with low-budget special effects. " *'The drouping Night thus creepeth on them fast;/And the sad humour loading their eye liddes. . . .'* " Adding to the unnerving effect was the fact that the lips remained unmoving, as if the head were serving as the speaker for some necromatic public-address system. " *'As messenger of Morpheus, on them cast/Sweet slombring deaw, the which to sleepe them biddes. . . .'* " And this was verse, a detached portion of my mind realized; the head was quoting verse. " *'Vnto their lodg-*

*ings then his guestes he riddes:/Where when all drownd in deadly sleepe he findes. . . .' "* What's more, it was familiar verse. *" 'He to his studie goes; and there amiddes/His Magick bookes, and artes of sundrie kindes,/He seekes out mighty charmes to trouble sleepy mindes.' "*

The mouth snapped shut, the eyelids lowered like third-act curtains, and the head returned to its former state of apparent lifelessness. The entire chamber had fallen silent—which didn't surprise me given the show we had just been treated to. What did surprise me was the real reason—the one that became evident as soon as I turned around.

Everyone else was asleep.

" 'Where all drowned in deadly sleep he finds . . .' " I quoted. I knew before I tried that shaking shoulders and yelling in ears would be to no avail. Better than average magic was at work here and I had no reserves to counter with.

"My lord?"

I jumped. Turned to see Misty Dawn materializing across the chamber from me. The ghostly Nymph took in the slumber party and drifted toward me. "What doth this mean?"

"I'm not sure," I murmured, "but I may have just been handed some clues."

"Clues, my lord?"

"You're here," I observed, "so it's night, now: 'The drouping night thus creepeth on them fast. . . .' " I gestured at my sleeping comrades. " 'As messenger of Morpheus, on them cast/Sweet slombring deaw, the which to sleep them biddes. . . . Where when all drownd in deadly sleepe he findes. . . .' "

"And it saith: 'He seekes out mighty charmes to trouble sleepy minds . . .' " Misty added. "What doth this mean?"

"I don't know." Did it refer to those asleep in this chamber? Or the larger framework of the Matrix where we all slept while our avatars walked in computerized dreams? "But I think our poet is warning me that some sorcerer is orchestrating these events." I turned and looked at the head. "Right?"

Eyes and mouth reopened and Morpheus's head complied with another verse of poetry: " *'Then choosing out few wordes most horrible,/(Let none them read) thereof did verses frame;/ With which, and other spelles like terrible,/He bad awake blacke* Plutoes *griesly Dame;/And cursed heaven; and spake reprochfull shame/Of highest God, the Lord of life and light./*

*A bold bad man, that dar'd to call by name/Great* Gorgon, *Prince of darknesse and dead night;/At which* Cocytus *quakes, and* Styx *is put to flight.' ''*

"Well, that seems rather straightforward," I said after the head of Morpheus had subsided again.

"My lord?"

"We're talking about a Necromancer, here, and a rather powerful one at that."

"Black magic, my lord?"

"The blackest!"

" '*And forth he cald out of deepe darknesse dredd,*' '' resumed the voice. " '*Legions of Sprights, the which, like little flyes/Fluttring about his euer-damned hedd,/A-waite whereto their seruice he applyes,/To aide his friendes, or fray his enimies./Of those he chose out two, the falsest twoo,/And fittest for to forge true-seeming lyes./The one of them he gaue a message too,/The other by him selfe staide other worke to doo.*' ''

"Deception and Spenser," I cried, drawing Caladbolg from its scabbard.

"Beg pardon, my lord?"

"The verse is a warning about deception," I said. "And Voice is quoting from Edmund Spenser's *The Faerie Queene*. Book One, I think; the first Canto."

The head spoke again: " '*He, making speedy way through spersed ayre,/And through the world of waters wide and deepe,/To* Morpheus *house doth hastily repaire./Amid the bowels of the earth full steepe,/And low, where dawning day doth neuer peepe,/His dwelling is; there* Tethys *his wet bed/Doth euer wash, and* Cynthia *still doth steepe/In silver deaw his ever-drouping hed,/Whiles sad Night ouer him her mantle black doth spred.*' ''

Misty Dawn looked about the stone-girdled chamber. "Morpheus's house . . . ?"

"A literary allusion," I said. "Ovid's name for the son of Sleep, the god of Dreams."

"And the waters, my lord? What do they signify?"

"The subconscious," I decided. "That which is submerged or hidden underground—and we have both images here. Tethys was—is—the wife of Oceanus and was often held as symbolic of the sea, itself. Cynthia is a surname for Artemis or Diana—"

"The moon."

"Right, and Spenser used it as his contemporaries did, as a synonym for Elizabeth the First, as well."

Misty Dawn was not quite convinced. "Thou speakest of symbols and allegory, my love. And yet, it is now night—here and upon the earth above, her black mantle is spread. Are we not 'amid the bowels of the earth full steep'? And is that not water I hear at the precipice's edge?"

"There are some significant parallels for us," I admitted as I walked to the edge to investigate. Now that the sounds and voices of ten people were stilled, I could hear the sound of rushing water more clearly.

And as I stared into the depths of the gorge, my eyes were treated to the spectacle of thousands of specks of light swirling in the empty air. As I watched, they danced through the open space and coalesced into strands that laced across the abyss and touched either side of the gorge. Patterns formed. Solidified. In another minute there were two glowing bridges connecting our chamber with the far side of the underground canyon.

I turned to look at the ghostly Wood Nymph. "Now what?" I asked.

It was the head that answered. " *'Whose double gates he findeth locked fast,/The one faire fram'd of burnisht Yuory,/ The other all with siluer ouercast;/And wakeful dogges before them farre doe lye,/Watching to banish Care their enimy,/Who oft is wont to trouble gentle Sleepe./By them the Sprite doth passe in quietly,/And vnto* Morpheus *comes, whom drowned deepe/In drowsie fit he findes: of nothing he takes keepe.'* "

"Wait a minute," I said. "Two gates. One fair and framed of burnished Ivory. . . ."

"The Gates of Dreams, my lord! Through one passes those dreams that are true, and through the other are passed those dreams that are false and delude!"

But which was which?

"And there be two spans to the other side," Misty observed.

"Two gateways," I concurred.

"But which is which?"

Good question. The softly glowing structures were identical in size, shape, and color. I turned to the head of Morpheus. "Any advice?"

It complied with another verse. " *'And more to lulle him in his slumber soft,/A trickling streame from high rocke tumbling downe,/And euer-drizling raine vpon the loft,/Mixt with a murmuring winde, much like the sowne/Of swarming Bees, did cast him in a swowne:/No other noyse, nor peoples troublous cryes,/As still are wont t'annoy the walled towne,/Might there be heard; but carelesse Quiet lyes/Wrapt in eternall silence farre from enimyes.' "*

Other than a description of the abyss that yawned before us, the words were unhelpful. "Okay." I walked over and picked up the box containing Morpheus's head. "Let's go find out."

Misty Dawn was not crazy about this strategy. But she thought I was: "Thou'rt mad!"

"No," I shifted the box under my arm so that I had a secure grip that still permitted the disembodied head unimpeded vision and speech, "just pissed!" I hefted Caladbolg and stepped to the edge between the gangways of the two spans. "Someone's playing games with me—deadly games—and I prefer acting to reacting." I looked down. "You got anything to say about the next step, *compadre*?"

It did: " *'The Messenger approching to him spake;/But his wast wordes retournd to him in vaine:/So sound he slept, that nought mought he him awake./Then rudely he him thrust, and pusht with paine,/Whereat he gan to stretch; but he againe/Shooke him so hard, that forced him to speake./As one then in a dreame, whose dryer braine/Is tost with troubled sights and fancies weake,/He mumbled soft, but would not all his silence breake.' "*

"Great. Thanks. You're a lot of help."

"How canst thou ken which path to take?" Misty wanted to know.

I eyed the twin spans but still could not determine any advantage of one over the other. The exit points were shrouded in darkness on the other side.

"The old dungeon-mapping adage, my dear: 'You can't go wrong if you go right.' " I moved to the appropriate bridge and addressed the box. "Last call, Morf, ol' buddy: whither I goest, you goest, too."

There was no response so I eased my foot out onto the glowing structure. It held. And so I took another step. And then another. And began crossing the chasm.

I tried not to think about the structural integrity of a bridge that had just appeared out of thin air. So I turned my problem to the Spenserian riddle. "How does that next verse go, Morf? Do you remember the words?"

No response.

" 'The Sprite then gan more boldly him to wake . . .' " I coached. " 'And threatned vnto him the dreaded name/Of *Hecate*: whereat he gan to quake. . . .' Um, what's the next part?"

The head remained silent.

"C'mon, you know the next part!" I bullied. "The Sprite's bugging your namesake and that Morpheus isn't too keen about this particular wake-up call: 'And, lifting up his lumpish head, with blame/Halfe angrie asked him, for what he came.'

"And what does this little bugger answer? Hmm?" Obviously I was going to have to carry the ball on this verse. " ' "Hither" (quoth he,) "me *Archimago* sent,/He that the stubborne Sprites can wisely tame,/He bids thee to him send for his intent/A fit false dreame, that can delude the sleepers sent." ' " I stopped. "Who is the Archmage? Who's pulling the strings here, huh?" The head made no reply. "Who fetched Cyberpunks from another Programworld and sicced them on me? Who hired Orc mercenaries and put a price on my head?" Or was this part of the delusion? Was I being led into my enemy's hand?

I suddenly recalled my encounter with the demonic hunting party on the outskirts of Calabastor, just a few days before. The red Devil leading the pack had said something about capturing Riplakish of Dyrinwall and taking him to Ortygia—that much was still at the forefront of my memory. But he had said something else, something strange. . . .

". . . when we capture him, we are to bring him to you on Ortygia," he had said, thinking me to be one of the Hellish Powers aligned in this plot, "across the division of worlds . . . on the far side of Corpus Callosum. . . ."

I was aware of only one referent for *Corpus Callosum* and it had nothing to do with the mythology of any culture. It was, rather, a medical term for the bundle of nerves connecting the two cerebral hemispheres of the forebrain. I looked up at the sheer cliffs of honeycombed rock that rose straight up on either side of the deep fissure that I had managed to cross halfway, and felt a vertiginous sense of déjà vu.

"No." This was carrying analogies too far.

"What is it, my lord?" Misty had been following behind me.

"It's basic cranial anatomy," I snapped. "The longitudinal fissure divides the brain into two parts: the left and right hemispheres. Deep down inside that fissure, the corpus callosum bridges the two halves of the cerebral cortex!"

"I—I do not understand—" Not only that, but my shouting was making her nervous.

"Of course you don't understand!" I bellowed. "Because it doesn't make sense!"

But it did, in a weird, twisted sort of way.

It was not unusual to find Platonistic analogues within the Matrix. The Machine, especially since the advent of the Anomaly, was forever accessing some file from some other network and translating it into a Programworld's structure with varied interpretations and results. Examples ranged from the personality templates for Id, Ego, and Superego to the Freud-Jung wars on one of the western archipelagoes.

But this was begging too great a suspension of disbelief. . . .

" *'The God obayde; and, calling forth straight way/A diuerse Dreame out of his prison darke,/Deliuered it to him, and downe did lay/His heauie head, deuoide of careful carke;/Whose sences all were straight benumbd and starke./He, backe returning by the Yuorie dore,/Remounted up as light as chearefull Larke;/And on his litle winges the dreame he bore/In hast unto his Lord, where he him left afore.' "*

"Meaning what?" I barked at the head in the box. "Let's just cut to the chase!" I forced my feet to start moving me toward the other end of the bridge where my answers—if there were any—were likely to be found. "No more literary allusions! No Platonisms of preexisting eternal ideas reflected in concrete Matrix structures! No allegories translated into Programworld realities!" The end of the bridge appeared to open out into a chamber of a similar size to the one I had left behind. "Just spit it out in twenty-first-century English! No more beating around the bush!" I was yelling as I stepped off the span . . .

. . . and into the cavern I had just left.

"So there you are," Rijma exclaimed, trying to stifle a yawn at the same time.

"Where did you go?" Vashti wanted to know.

Elsbeth was hoisting her pack to her shoulder. "We woke up and you were gone."

I stared at them. Then looked over my shoulder at the bridge behind me. Somehow, I had gotten turned around on the span and walked back to where I had started from.

"It is time we left," Rune announced. "After we return to Daggoth's Tower, we can rest, regroup, and remount an expedition to check out the rest of these caverns."

"C'mon, Rip," Rijma said, starting toward me, "let me give you a hand with that."

"Wait—wait a minute!" My head was pounding and I brought my sword up defensively though there were no foes in sight. "Something's wrong here."

"Yeah," agreed Elsbeth, "and the sooner we're outta here, the better it'll be."

"We really need to fall back," said Vashti. "Rest, recharge our spell capabilities. He who fights and runs away—"

"—lives to fight another day," rumbled The Duke.

"Stop!" I bellowed as they moved a step toward me. The pounding in my head was making it impossible to think clearly.

"Yer tired," Stumpy observed.

"Shut up!" I wanted to reach for the Optics of al Rashid but between the box and Caladbolg my hands were full. "Verse—there's another verse—"

I shook the box and the head complied: " 'Who all this while, with charmes and hidden artes,/Had made a Lady of that other Spright. . . .' "

"Lilith," I whispered, "Euryale."

" 'And fram'd of liquid ayre her tender partes. . . .' "

"Aw, Rip, who you gonna listen to? That dead head or your friends?"

"Be still!" I admonished, brandishing my sword. I began to back toward the bridge I had just traversed.

" 'So liuely, and so like in all mens sight,/That weaker sence it could have ravisht quight. . . .' "

The senator's avatar had moved to cut me off so I turned my retreat toward the other bridge. Rijma's sword was out, now. "C'mon, Rip, you're gonna hurt yourself."

" 'The maker selfe, for all his wondrous witt,/Was nigh beguiled with so goodly sight,/Her all in white he clad, and over it/Cast a black stole, most like to seeme for Vna fit.' "

I lowered my sword and hung my head as I reached the edge of the bridge. "I'm sorry," I mumbled. "I wasn't sure for a moment if you were really my friends."

"It's all right," the Brownie soothed, stepping forward. "You're just confused."

"Yeah"—I smiled—"just for a moment." My blade came up suddenly and flashed across the Brownie's shoulders. Her head bounced across the chamber's floor, rolling some twenty feet before the sword fell from her right hand and her body collapsed in upon itself. "But not so confused that I couldn't remember that the real Rijma is a southpaw!" The others began to screech and transform into imps and Devils like the ones who had hunted me in Calabastor a few days before. I turned and ran onto the second bridge.

They didn't follow and it didn't take me long to figure out why: the transverse was starting to glow in a pulsing pattern, and as I ran past the halfway point, I could see its structure beginning to disassemble into the myriad of tiny firefly sparks that had come together to form it in the beginning.

" *'Now, when that ydle dream was to him brought,' "* intoned the head at my side, " *'Vnto that Elfin knight he bad him fly. . . .' "*

"Ah shaddup!" I muttered under my breath.

" *'Where he slept soundly void of euil thought,/And with false shewes abuse his fantasy. . . .' "*

"Yeah, now you tell me!" I slammed Caladbolg back into his sheath.

" *'In sort as he him schooled priuily:/And that new creature, borne without her dew,/Full of the makers guyle, with vsage sly/He taught to imitate that Lady trew,/Whose semblance she did carrie vnder feigned hew.' "*

"Her and everybody else!" I grunted as the flooring dissolved under me and I leapt for the edge of the canyon wall.

The fingers of my right hand caught the edge of the chamber floor as I slammed against the rock wall that was about to provide me with a nearly vertical slide down into the raging torrent a mile or two below. The box shattered with the impact and it was only a lucky left-handed grab that saved Morpheus's head from following its container down into the abyss.

"*Ow!*" it said as I lifted it up by its hair.

"Awake now, are we?" I hissed, trying to find purchase for my feet and knees.

*"Hey, it's not easy making this thing talk, you know— especially over such a great distance! If you knew the effort—"*

"If talking's so tough," I gritted, "how come you've been such a motormouth with the poetical allegory? A few straight answers could've saved us both a lot of effort."

*"Couldn't,"* the head explained. *"There's been some major enchantments at work here to isolate you from outside contact. The Guards-and-Wards barred any direct warnings but I was able to bypass them with a little verbal sleight of hand."*

"Poetical allegory," I grunted, trying to exert some leverage with my toes.

*"Correct. And having accessed the records on your matricu- lation—"*

"You discovered that in addition to my dissertations on comparative mythology I also have a minor in Western Lit."

*"It seemed a safe bet that you would be familiar with Spenser's* The Faerie Queene."

"Actually," I wheezed, "I like his private-eye novels bet- ter." Shifting my balance to my left elbow caused me to bump his head against a protruding knob of rock.

*"Ow—that hurts!"*

"Don't start with me," I warned. The ache of slamming against the cliff face was starting to give way to fiery sensations of abraded skin. *"You* can't have anything worse than a head- ache!"

*"Which reminds me of a song—"*

"If you start singing any version of 'I Ain't Got Nobody,' " I warned, "I swear to Crom, I'll drop you right here and now!"

A long pause ensued while I hunched my way over another knob of rock.

"So how come you don't have to turn a poetic phrase, anymore? Or is this your idea of blank verse?"

*"Dunno. Either the Shielding spells wore off or the guy responsible got distracted."*

Slowly, painfully, carefully, I raised my left arm, bringing the head up to the top of the ledge. A little shove—*"Hey, watch it!"*—and I felt it roll forward as I released my grip.

There were spitting sounds as I fumbled around with my left hand for a good grip beyond the edge.

"See anything?" I grunted as my knee found a half-inch depression in the rock wall.

"*Yes. And you're not going to like it. . . .*"

I chinned myself on the rock ledge and looked up and into the stone chamber. The head was right: I didn't.

# Chapter
# Twenty-five

★

\RIPLEY\PATH\SIGMA     (Σ)

**T**HEY were all there and awake: Rune, Vashti, Elsbeth, The Duke, Stumpy, Hanson's avatar, Borys and Natasha, even Rijma with her head intact, which was somewhat reassuring. The good news was I hadn't found myself back at the chamber I had just escaped from.

The bad news was that *I* was already in the room with the rest of them. Which is why everyone was staring in shocked amazement at the other me—the me that was hanging on to the edge of the precipice, that is.

"I think we just found our imposter," Riplakish of Dyrinwall was saying—the me that wasn't hanging on to the edge of the chamber for dear life, that is.

"Oh, yeah, sure!" I grunted, hauling my chest up over the edge and grinding my face into the stone floor as I renewed my grip a little farther into the chamber. "That's what all the evil look-alikes say first!" I squirmed a little farther into the room.

"Oh, Crom!" Rijma groaned. "Not the old evil twin shtick where we have to figure out which is which!" She sat down on a blunt stalagmite and cradled her chin in her fists.

"Not that tough," I puffed, easing a leg up and over. "I've got the head with me and he'll verify my identity."

"Big deal," my double snorted. "Who's going to believe a talking head? The best you can prove is a good ventriloquist act. If you want testimony—"

I could see that there was another figure in the room. She stepped out from the crowd and I nearly fell back over the drop-off.

It was Nicole. Unblemished.

"While we slept," Rune elaborated, "he claims to have crossed over and rescued her."

"Rescued?" I got my other leg over and noticed the other members of the party laying hands on their sword hilts. Talk about déjà vu. . . .

"The creature that attacked me that night in Daggoth's study was not Nicole," the other Riplakish explained. "And now that the real Nicole Doucet has been rescued, and Senator Hanson has been returned, we can depart. Once we've dealt with you, of course."

"Ah ha!" I pointed at my duplicate. "You hear that? He's talking about doing away with me."

"I said no such thing! I merely pointed out that since you are here and, as everyone can see and hear, are trying to pass yourself off as me, you must be reckoned with in some fashion."

"Shut up, both of you!"

We both turned and looked at our—that is, my—ex-wife. "Under the circumstances," Vashti went on to say, "you both could be legitimate avatars of Robert R. Ripley the Third."

"I don't think so," rebutted Elsbeth. "There's enough variance in their respective stories to suggest that one of them is lying."

Rijma piped in at this point. "Shall we go down the list of evil twin scenarios for the past three or four centuries of literature, film, and holography to determine the various tests we can apply?"

"I have the head of Morpheus," I pointed out.

"As do I," my double added, holding up a duplicate head, still in its box.

"Mine talks," I said. "Does yours?"

"*Shut! Up!*" Vashti repeated at the top of her lungs. Seven years of divorce had not noticeably diminished their capacity.

"We could let them fight," Rijma said. "The one who tries hardest to kill the other is probably the imposter."

"Very funny," we both chorused.

"Do you think I do not know my own true love?" Nicole said suddenly. "Why do you even have discourse with that . . . creature?" She pointed at me and I looked over at Morpheus's head, lying on its side on the ground.

"Well, don't just lie there," I chided, "say something!"

It did. It quoted more Spenser: " *'So as she bad, that witch they disaraid,/And robd of royall robes, and purple pall,/And ornaments that richly were displaid;/Ne spared they to strip her naked all./Then when they had despoild her tire and call,/ Such as she was, their eyes might her behold,/That her misshaped parts did them appall,/A loathly, wrinckled hag, ill fauoured, old,/Whose secret filth good manners biddeth not be told.'* "

"Meaning what?" the other Riplakish wanted to know.

"I suppose he means that Ms. Doucet may not be what she appears to be," Rune answered.

" *'Her craftie head was altogether bald,/And as in hate of honorable eld/Was overgrowne with scurfe and filthy scald. . . .'* "

Elsbeth cleared her throat. "I think you've already made your point."

" *'Her teeth out of her rotten gummes were feld,/And her sowre breath abhominably smeld. . . .'* "

"Enough already!" Rijma cried.

" *'Her dried dugs, like bladders lacking wind,/Hong downe, and filthy matter'* —ow, ow, ow!"

I lifted Morpheus's head by the hair and dangled it over the edge. "The Old Testament, Book of Proverbs," I advised, "chapter seventeen, verse twenty-eight."

"*Accessing—ah*" —his eyes rolled downward— "*I see your point. . . .*"

The other Riplakish looked around at the other members of the party. "You going to believe me or some seven-hundred-year-old poem?"

I put the now-mute head aside and reached into my vest pocket and pulled out the Optics of al Rashid. "Anyone want to take a look for themselves?"

My Doppelgänger looked resigned. "Okay," he said. "All right." He gestured and the room was silent.

Everyone else had gone to sleep again.

Carefully, slowly, I got to my feet and moved away from the drop-off, circling into the room. Nicole backed away to sit on one of the stone biers. The other Riplakish convulsed, changed, grew taller, acquired additional mass, and became Robert Remington Ripley the Third.

"Who *are* you?" I asked quietly.

"Who am I? Why I am you," he replied.

"Oh. Right. Sure. Well, if you are *me* . . . then who am *I*?"

He sighed and found a convenient stone formation to sit on. "*You* are fate denied. *You* are who I was to be. *You* are the past denied." He casually drew his longsword from its scabbard. "The future that *I* will claim." The longsword in his hand had a crystal blade that glowed with a bluish light.

"Yeah, yeah, 't'was brillig and the slithy troves'!" I pulled Caladbolg from his sheath: yep, still crystal and glowing with a faint blue tinge. To all appearances, a perfect match. "How about some straight answers without all the poetic gibberish?"

"Do you dream, Ripley?"

"What?"

"Do you dream?" he asked. "Every night?"

I didn't think I liked this conversation starting out; now I was sure. "Yeah. How about you?"

He chuckled. There was an unpleasantness to his tone. "Oh, yes. We both dream, you and I. We dream the same thing most every night. Tell me, Robert, what do we dream?"

"What I dream is none of your business!"

"What *we* dream is the business that brings us together, you and I. Oh, yes, this dream is definitely the business at hand. . . ."

"What do *you* dream, then?" I asked cautiously.

"What we dream," he corrected. "There is no you and I. We, Robert Ripley, dream the same dreams: fire in the sky and the explosion that started the pain. The pain that never ends. We dream it, you and I, night after night; and awake between sweat-soaked sheets. Flames and loss. . . ."

"You're me, aren't you? One of my duplicate avatars!"

"So close and yet so far . . . tell me; when you dream do you ever try to change places with her?"

"What . . . ?" I felt a catch in my chest, a terrible prelude to the sensation of having my heart ripped out again. "What . . . ?" I asked again only to have breath and voice fail me once more.

"The two most terrible words in anyone's life, Robert: 'what if . . . ?' What would you give to live it again? To do it differently? And what would you do?"

"Do?" I gasped, nearly losing my grip on my sword. "What . . . do . . . ?" My chest constricted and I couldn't draw air.

"Would *you* have stayed at the controls and sent *her* back to extinguish the fire?"

I felt the tears starting to gather at the edge of my vision. "Nicole . . . ?"

"You were the better pilot!"

I groaned, feeling the nightmare images gather at the back of my consciousness.

"*You* couldn't extinguish the fire—could *she* have done any worse?"

"Don't," I whispered.

"But you could have landed the aircar safely if you'd stayed at the controls." He spoke the thought that had haunted me for a decade and a half.

"She had a third-class license, the same as me!" I cried. But the argument had not satisfied in all those fifteen years and it did not satisfy now.

"But *you* were the better pilot!" he shouted. "If you had made an emergency landing as soon as you noticed the fire—"

"You weren't there!" I screamed.

"I was there!" he screamed back.

"No. . . ."

"Yes! *I* was there! And when the fire broke out, Nicole jumped up and grabbed the extinguisher!"

"What?" I felt my sanity slip a notch.

"So I couldn't effect an emergency descent with her out of her seat! And I couldn't leave the controls! And *I* sat two feet away from where *your* Nicole sat when the stabilizer coils exploded!"

"What. . . ."

"*My* Nicole came out of it better than *you*, Robert: *she* had the good sense to back out of the engine compartment before the explosion!"

"What. . . ." Impossible images filled my mind—images of an aircar accident where Nicole and I had traded places, actions, consequences.

"It did happen the other way: Robert Ripley stayed at the controls and Nicole Doucet survived the crash with minor injuries."

"I don't understand. . . ." Moreover, I didn't *want* to understand.

"There are many Realities—"

"Dreamworlds," I said.

"I am not talking about Computer simulations, I speak of Alternate Realities. Parallel Universes. An infinite number of timelines branching out from the moment of each man's birth: dividing, tri-parting, sometimes exploding in dozens of different pathways at each decision." He gestured with his sword. "As you dress one morning, you reach for a tie. You are only aware that you chose the blue one. But a parallel timeline splits off at that point and in another Reality you choose the red tie, instead. A subtle difference—perhaps the only one in those twin lifetimes. . . .

"But in other worlds you join the high school chess club instead of picking up the foil—ergo—no Olympic trials, no trip to France, you never meet Nicole Doucet. You marry a hometown girl and settle down. Live happily ever after—"

"Or everything's exactly the same," I said, unable to stop my mind's berserker rush toward his inevitable conclusion: "I go to France—"

"But you don't rent a defective aircar," he offered.

"Or I do," I continued, "but when the fire breaks out—"

"*I* stay in my seat and send *Nicole* aft to check it out," he finished in a tone that carried certainty and not speculation.

"And she survived with minor injuries?" I asked hollowly.

"Yes. Want to trade?"

I drew a long breath. "Yes."

He was silent.

"*Yes!*"

"There's a catch," he said quietly. "Each timeline, each

Reality, each Parallel Universe, may share common geography . . . events. . . ." He gestured at me with his blade. "People. But there are always differences. Sometimes radical, sometimes subtle—but there must be differences or there could be only one world, one Reality.

"In your universe, Dreamworlds was conceived as an entertainment medium and Fantasyworld was developed out of your books and stories. In my world it is known as Dreamland and was developed initially as a psycho/somatic therapy environment. I had no initial input, as I wrote no books after the accident as you did. I just got lucky."

"Lucky?" I asked.

"Someone decided to hook me up to the system. To see if anything was going on inside."

"I don't understand."

"Let me show you." He gestured. And an image formed in midair.

I could only look at the effigy of shattered humanity for a moment. I turned to Nicole: "I'm . . . sorry. . . ."

"Your pity is misdirected, this time," my alternate self replied. "This is not the Nicole Doucet who nearly perished in your universe. This is what survives of Robert Remington Ripley in mine!" He stood. "The balance scales may shift across timelines, my friend; but there is always a counterweight to consider, a symmetry to recalibrate, an equilibrium to be achieved.

"Perhaps there are other universes where every other choice we made, from that moment on, led to both our deaths—ours and Nicole's." He shook his head. "I only know how my choice turned out . . . and yours."

There was a long silence for me to digest this in.

"So," I said, finally, "you were given a reprieve through psyche-extraction and dream programming. . . ."

"A . . . *reprieve*?" he choked. "A simple word like 'reprieve' sums it up for you? Imagine, if you will, fifteen years of imprisonment in a twisted lump of flesh! There's no hope of parole because the medical ethicists in my timeline insist on keeping me alive and there's a very good chance under laboratory conditions of that stretching out another hundred years or more!"

He paced about the chamber, growing more and more agitated. "I have no control over anything in my life: I ingest what they feed me *when* they feed me and excrete the waste portions unceasingly! I have no eyes or ears, and unlike your Nicole in your timeline, I have no cybernetic sensors to serve as bridges to the inner man! I cannot taste or touch or smell and I cannot speak to those who feed and water me like some botanical experiment!"

"And the *pain*!" he shrilled. "It never ends! There is no release from it! I cannot even flinch or pound with my fists or drum my heels or scream or writhe! I cannot even find succor in the unconsciousness of sleep! I cannot kill myself and the respirator will not even permit me to hold my breath!

"Tell me, Robert Ripley," he shouted, turning back toward me, "what would you do if you were me . . . *because* . . . *I . . . am . . . you*!"

"I would go mad," I whispered.

*"Precisely! And then what?"*

"I don't know."

He was suddenly calm again. "What if you had a chance to have a real body, again? Your own body?"

"An avatar," I said.

"Avatar? No, this Computer-driven simulacrum is but a step toward the goal. And the Matrix is but the bridge between our Realities."

"Bridge?"

"Remember its crude clumsy beginnings? *Teledildonics* they called it. The technicians, that is. Everyone else had a simpler view: 'Virtual Reality.' Computers manufacturing visual, auditory, and tactile cues, spatial referents to illusionary environments. If that could be called 'Virtual Reality' in its time, then surely today's Matrix is evolved far beyond the special effects concept. Dreamworlds are truly *Alternate* Realities. They are in your timeline as they are in mine. And since V.R. is not bound by the same laws of spacetime physics that separate my timeline from yours, it is possible for a Programworld from your Matrix to intersect a Programworld from mine."

"The Anomaly," I mused.

"I thought it would be enough," he said. "After fifteen years of being buried alive, I thought *anything* would be better. That a Computer-generated body was a dream come true." He shook his head. "But it's *not* enough. So I ask you again: *What would you do if you had the chance to have a real body again? Your own body?"*

"I guess I'd take it."

"Yes. You *would* take it," he agreed. "But there are obstacles to contend with, first. The Matrix is the bridge between my Reality and yours. And you, Robert Ripley, are the obstacles. Before I can claim the body that is Robert Remington Ripley's—that was *mine* denied by the vagaries of chance and fate, I must remove those obstacles. And I have: one by one. Now, I'm nearly done."

I raised Caladbolg in my right hand and drew Balmung from its scabbard with my left. "And how do you remove—this final obstacle?" I asked, easing into an on-guard position. "A physical duel? Or spell against spell?" I felt my temper slipping. "Or are you just trying to talk me to death?"

If I thought I could bait myself into making a misstep, I was mistaken: I knew myself too well.

He smiled ruefully. "Even though I arranged for your spell abilities to be exhausted before you got this far, a magical contest is out of the question. In the time that I've spent in-Program, I've discovered that *I* can't perform any magic that has any direct effect on *you*. Even dissolving that sorcerous bridge from beneath your feet was nearly impossible and the delay was sufficient for you to complete the trip across."

"Okay," I said, "so how's your swordsmanship?"

He laughed and shook his head. "I have learned nothing new since the aircar crash: time has stood still. I don't have the advantages of Kendo nor the practice you've enjoyed these fifteen years past."

I took a more aggressive stance. "Then I'm sure you won't want to match your one blade to my two."

This time his smile had teeth. "I have two blades." His sword came up. "This one . . ."

Nicole stepped forward and drew her sword. An eerie green flame licked across its serrated blade. "And this one," she finished.

I looked at her, fighting back a tumult of emotions—hurt and confusion the most primary: "Why?"

She smiled—not much more than a moue in that pretty, perfect face. "I love him."

She started to advance but my double gestured her back a

step. "Those spectacles," he said, "you wanted to put them on and look at Nicole a little while ago. Before we begin why don't you just do that?"

In spite of the moment's awkwardness, I did just that. I reversed the *wakizashi* in my left hand and held the Optics of al Rashid before my eyes.

Nicole was . . . *Nicole!*

*There was no evidence of physical corruption, no signs of madness!*

I lowered the lenses. "How—"

"You and your poetry-spouting colleague have done Ms. Doucet a great injustice," the other me was saying. "This is the Nicole Doucet from my universe. She was our match fifteen years ago at the Olympic trials. And the ensuing years have been kinder to her than they have been to you." He brought his sword up. "*En garde*, Monsieur Riplakish! Your chances against Mademoiselle Doucet are slim to none. Against the both of us . . ."

Nicole raised her own blade and they advanced.

**DATALOG:**  \QUEBEDEAUX-A.5\PERSONAL\
20200825
*Voice Dictation*
***FILE ENCRYPTION ON***

They're gone.
*
One moment they were there on the monitors . . .
*
The next moment the phasing flip-flopped and the whole sector just disappeared.
*
Harold's running diagnostics on every piece of circuitry he can find schematics on.
*
Between the two of us, working night and day without food or sleep, we might find something in about six months.
*
Where the hell is Balor?

# Chapter
# Twenty-six

★

\RIPLEY\PATH\SIGMA    (Σ)

I was holding back.

Not me—the other me: he was thrusting and feinting, but basically playing it safe at this point and letting Nicole take all the risks.

And since he *was* me, I felt a growing contempt for myself that was disquieting.

Both of them had me at a Human disadvantage in reach: even Nicole's avatar had longer arms than my Half-Elven one. And while I might have matched her reflexes for speed yesterday, today's exertions and injuries were going to prove my undoing. Only my skills in Kendo and *Niten Ryu* were keeping my opponents at bay for the moment, but they were slowly and steadily forcing me to fall back toward the precipice behind me.

Caladbolg and Balmung wove a tangled barricade of light between us but my opponents had enchanted blades as well, and cut through every defense I could muster. From the outset I was caught in the mode of *Tai No Sen*, forestalling their attacks and waiting for the initiative. But, between the two of them, I doubted I would be permitted any. I no longer had the energy for *Ken No Sen* when the opportunity might occur, nor the stamina that might enable me to last that long.

I fought with no strategy other than to keep their blades from touching me. I had no strength left for anything else and I was further disadvantaged by my own reluctance to press an attack should an opening suddenly appear. It was bad enough to think about running my "self" through. When I looked at Nicole, fifteen years of guilt and remorse fought my own instincts for survival and I knew that I would die before I harmed her again.

The precipice was getting closer and I suddenly saw one possibility of improving my position. I dodged back and to the left until I could retreat no farther. A column of stone was to my back, a cluster of stalagmites and stalactites fenced off the space to my immediate left, the abyss yawned to my right. I was trapped, now, but only one of them could attack me at a time.

Nicole hesitated but the other Ripley motioned her ahead. I engaged her blade with a series of circle parries that held her off for the moment and enabled me to catch my breath.

"Careful!" I shouted as her foot slipped on some loose gravel and she skidded a bit toward the edge.

As she recovered my left thigh seemed to cramp and then burst into flame. My leg gave way and I fell back against the stone column and slid to the floor. I glanced down at the hilt of the knife protruding from my leg and then looked up and saw my double behind Nicole and the bloody cut on the outside of her right biceps where the thrown dagger had nicked her arm in passing. The look she gave him, in turn, was unreadable but she turned back to me and stepped forward.

I raised my blade but it could be nothing more than a gesture of defiance. *"Je voudrais voir des assassins souriant du bourreau qui coupe un cou d'innocent,"* I said, *"avec son grand sabre courbé d'Orient."*

She hesitated.

*"Je voudrais voir des roses et du sang,"* I said.

She raised her sword. *"Je voudrais voir mourir d'amour ou bien de haine,"* she whispered.

"Kill him!" my other self was screaming.

Nicole stared down at me, and as I looked into her shining eyes I saw the multitude of questions swept aside by a look of puzzlement. Slowly, almost carefully, she lowered her sword and turned around.

About the time I saw the arrow protruding from her back, another one struck her in the chest. She staggered back and tripped over my legs. The momentum carried her over the edge and she fell without a sound.

"Who is it!" my alter ego cried. "Who is there?"

I followed his gaze up to a rock ledge that ran along a portion of the chamber's side wall: a figure crouched in the shadows, clutching a longbow.

"Why, Robert," cooed a familiar voice, "can you not guess?" She squirmed into the light until we could see her ruined features.

It was the Nicole Doucet from my timeline.

"Wha—where did you come from?" While we were both taken aback by this new manifestation, my other self seemed more unnerved by her appearance.

"What?" she said, laying aside her bow. "After so much poetry and verse, have you forgotten the rest of your Spenser?" She leapt down from the ledge and her leathery wings fanned out to assist her to a gentle landing. " 'Thus when they had the witch disrobed quight . . .' " she quoted, " 'And all her filthy feature open showne. . . .' " She began to hunch toward us. " 'They let her goe at will, and wander wayes un-knowne.' "

My other self was backing away now, the abyss just a few feet away.

" 'She flying fast from heauens hated face,/And from the world that her discouered wide. . . .' " The hideous apparition spared me but a brief glance as she closed on my double. " 'Fled to the wastfull wildernesse apace,/From liuing eyes her open shame to hide.. . . .' " His sword lay forgotten and loose in his grip, and she pushed it aside. " 'And lurkt in rocks and caues long vnespide.' "

He continued to back away but she was quicker: her rotting arms reached out, her nearly fleshless hands grasped his fore-arms.

"What—what do you want?" he choked.

"You, my love. . . ." Did I detect a sardonic note in her voice? "We are two of a kind, you and I!" She embraced him and he struggled like an insect wrapped in webbing. "Did I not hear you speak of fate's balance scales? Of cosmic equilibrium? Do you not feel the karma?''

My double's expression seemed to say that his dogma had just been run over by her karma.

"We are soulmates—Yin and Yang upon the Wheel of Pain!'' she murmured triumphantly. She pressed her ghastly lips to his.

"Mmno!'' He threw his head back and pushed at her shoulders. She did not loosen her grip, even when more of her flesh squeezed wetly through his fingers and sloughed off the bone.

"Come with me, beloved, to a better place. . . .'' And saying this, she embraced him more securely and stepped off the edge.

He screamed going down. It was a long fall and he passed beyond my hearing before it stopped.

I crawled back to the edge but I could see nothing. "I . . . don't . . . understand . . .'' I murmured.

"*Macbeth*, my lord.''

I looked up at Misty Dawn, hovering above me, pale and solemn.

"Act Five, Scene Three.''

"What—''

" 'Canst thou minister to a mind diseased,' '' she quoted, " 'Pluck from the memory a rooted sorrow,/Raze out the written troubles of the brain,/And with some sweet oblivious antidote/Cleanse the stuff'd bosom of that perilous matter/Which weighs upon the heart?' ''

I was helpless to do anything but stare at her.

**DATALOG:     \QUEBEDEAUX-A.5\PERSONAL\**
**20200826**
**\*Voice Dictation\***
**\*\*\*FILE ENCRYPTION ON\*\*\***

Hanson's awake!
\*
The real one!
\*
And not just awake, either.
\*
I'm told the first thing he did after climbing out of his suspension tank was beat Captain Balor to a bloody pulp!
\*
The news gets even better. . . .
\*
Apparently, the senator's second act was to pick up the phone and call Cephtronics CEO.
\*
I don't know what he said but the man turned around and called us: Harold—I mean, Dr. Contrell—just got off the phone and

announced that they're calling back my old staff and we should get some relief within the next six to eight hours!

*

But the best news of all . . .

*

The other code-strings are reappearing!

*

The lost sector still won't read out on the monitors but the various code-strings are reappearing in the adjacent sector.

*

As a matter of fact, there's just one left that I'm waiting on. . . .

# EPILOGUE I

★

## RIPLEY (Ø)

**R**OBERT Remington Ripley the Third pressed the control that raised the upper portion of the hospital bed. Even though the buttons were labeled in Russian, he was getting the hang of it and now enjoyed a success rate of two out of three attempts.

"So Hanson got back into his real body?"

Borys Dankevych nodded. "He phoned me yesterday. He has been rather busy trying to repair the political damage that was done while Cerberus was in control of his body outside the Matrix."

"Borys has been rather busy with similar matters, here," Dorothy Cooper added.

A nurse entered the hospital room to check Ripley's pulse. "Kerensky?" he asked as she checked his chart for the last reading.

"*Da*. We are now conducting inquiries to determine who Kerensky's collaborators are. And, more importantly, who his superiors were in this plot. The entire Spetsnaz is currently under investigation. Other branches of the military . . . some extremist, left-wing factions in the Russian Parliament. . . ." He shrugged.

Ripley smiled wanly. "A purge?" Although he was on the mend, the virus had taken its toll.

Dankevych grunted. "Perhaps a small one. Nothing like the Great Purge of '91. We are merely weeding out some fanatical subversives, not replacing an entire political system."

A doctor, one of the military's viral specialists, poked his head in the door. "I said a short visit and I meant it," he warned good-naturedly, "five more minutes and then Comrade Ripley must rest!"

"So, tell me about this REMrunner. Were you able to get him back out?" Ripley wanted to know.

"The fourteen-year-old ancient wizard? Yeah," Cooper said, sitting on the edge of the hospital bed. "The problem was his friend Jeremiah had the codes and passwords for getting in and out of the Matrix . . . remember?"

He shook his head. "Tell me again."

She looked at Borys and frowned. "Well, Jerry had been turned into a frog and no one could figure out how to change him back. Daggoth worked on the problem for three days and nights before you provided the solution."

"I did?" The nurse popped an old-fashioned oral thermometer into his mouth.

"Yep. It seems you slipped a love potion into the water jar in Princess Aeriel's chamber."

"Oo tol me 'bou' tha 'un," he mumbled around the glass pipette.

"Daggoth thinks you did it out of revenge for all the times he had razzed you."

Ripley composed his features into a mask of saintly innocence.

"If that was your plan, it failed," Dorothy continued. "Aeriel unknowingly drank the potion. But the next person she laid eyes on wasn't Daggoth the Dark." Cooper grinned. "It seems you all forgot that Jeremiah the bullfrog was still in the room when you locked her in and left."

"And Aeriel is an Amazon *princess*," Borys reminded.

"It only took one kiss," Dorothy elaborated.

"And now I believe you are invited back into the Program for the wedding," Borys concluded.

"Which solves your consort problem." Dorothy Cooper's face assumed a more serious expression. "Do you remember any of this?"

Ripley shook his head.

"Robbie. . . ." She looked at Borys Dankevych. "You remember I told you that Natasha Skovoroda's avatar was murdered while she was in-taction?"

Ripley nodded.

"Before we exited the Program, you said you thought we could bring her back. You seemed to think that there was an invisible holding file for Dreamwalker psyches who had died in the Program. Just like the various heavens and hells in mythology where the dead might be resurrected, you had this theory that the Matrix stored discorporated psyches against the time their avatars could be restored to life."

"You said it had happened to you several times," Borys added. "When you regenerated during your lycanthropic episodes."

Ripley and Cooper stared at him and smiled. Since exiting the Fantasyworld program, Dankevych had spoken perfect English.

"Natasha's body is still in her suspension tank," Cooper continued. "The life-support systems keep her breathing and circulate her blood, but her EEG is totally flat and no one in Medical believes you can recharge the electrical activity of the human brain like it was a NiCad battery." She glanced at Borys and took a deep breath. "Do you really think we can bring her back?"

"I don't know," Ripley sighed as the nurse removed the thermometer from his mouth. "I don't remember any of this. . . .

"Theoretically, it might be possible to reenter the Program and find some kind of powerful enchantment that would resurrect Natasha's avatar. If the Program plays by its own internal sets of rules, it should recognize her return to living status and reconnect her psyche—if it still resides somewhere in memory storage!" He shook his head. "I don't know—this is completely theoretical to me."

"You seemed so sure while we were still in the Program," Borys said.

"I don't remember any of it!" Ripley cried hoarsely. "All these stories you've told me since I woke up—they're just stories to me! My last clear memory is someone jumping me in my room, sticking that damn hypo full of virus culture in my shoulder. After that—I can remember going in and out of my delirium while you tried to resuscitate me. Then you popped me into a suspension tank to slow down my metabolism. You said . . . something . . . about sending me in early. . . .'' He waved a limp hand. ''That's it: the somnambulants began taking effect and—nothing. A big blank. I feel as if nothing else actually happened!''

''Some short-term memory loss is not surprising,'' the doctor said as he reentered the room. ''Considering the fact that this virus nearly killed you—and you ran a one-hundred-six-degree fever for nearly a week—I'm surprised your brain was not reduced to a bowl of borscht!''

''Will his memory ever return?'' Borys wanted to know.

The doctor spread his hands. ''We simply do not know at this point.'' He picked up his patient's clipboard. ''Now, all of you out! This man needs his rest!''

Dorothy patted his hand. ''Get well—''

''So we can go back in soon!'' boomed Dankevych.

Ripley grabbed at her hand. ''What about the others? Stephanie? And Nicole?''

''Out!'' bellowed the doctor.

She slipped her hand from his. ''We'll talk about all that tomorrow.''

Ripley pushed himself up in the hospital bed as they started to leave the room. ''Wait!''

Cooper and Dankevych turned at the doorway.

''We could be operating on an erroneous assumption here.''

''What do you mean?''

''Just because I don't remember anything that happened after you put me in the suspension tank doesn't mean that I've lost my memory of the events that transpired in the Program.''

The doctor frowned as they walked back into the room but Ripley waved him back.

''What if I can't remember what happened to my avatar because . . . *I have no memories to access*?''

Cooper frowned. ''I was there with you through parts of it. Everything we told you actually happened.''

''To my avatar,'' Ripley elaborated, ''not necessarily to me. Remember what you were saying just a few days ago about Memory Upload and Download?'' He sighed and leaned back against the pillows. ''You said psyche-scan probably duplicates our personality profiles and inserts the copies into the Program while suppressing consciousness and brain-wave activity at the original source. When we 'leave' the Matrix, our psyches, altered from our Programworld adventures and containing additional memory files, are reintroduced to our minds as consciousness and brain-wave levels are restored." He sank back into the pillows, dizzy and exhausted.

"What is he saying?" Borys wanted to know.

Dorothy felt a little dizzy, herself. "He's suggesting that he doesn't remember anything because his psyche—the personality and memory files that occupied his avatar in the Matrix—were not returned to him when he regained consciousness."

"I know this is silly," Ripley murmured, feeling an irresistible lethargy creeping up on his mind, "but I feel like one of those aborigines who fears having his picture taken . . . believing the camera has the power to steal his soul. . . ." His eyes fluttered shut and he began to snore.

"There! Satisfied?" The doctor was indignant. "You've exhausted him again! Out, now! Shoo!"

"But if his—psyche—was not returned to his body when we got out," Dankevych puzzled as they exited the room, "then . . . where did it go?"

# EPILOGUE II

★

## RIPLEY (X)

**M**ICHAEL Straeker, Chief of Staff for Teledildonics's Dreamland Project, reached down into the suspension tank and removed the bio-sensors from its occupant. "Thought we'd lost you for a moment, there. Your code-string disappeared from the monitors and we weren't sure until just now if we could actually bring you back out." He held up two fingers. "How many fingers am I holding up?"

". . . two . . ." croaked the voice, and it echoed hollowly inside the interior of the tank. ". . . out . . . can I get out?"

"I'll have you out in a moment," Straeker assured. "What's your name?"

". . . Ripley. . . ."

Straeker hesitated, but only for a moment. His near brush with death a year before had made him a pragmatist. The doctors had been honest and totally straightforward from the day the brain tumor had been diagnosed until the surgery that had successfully removed it. He felt that everyone deserved the truth and postponing it or trying to cover it up was immoral and potentially dangerous. "I'm sorry," he said, "Ripley didn't make it."

Straeker was prepared for tears or silent shock. He wasn't prepared for laughter. "Maybe he didn't"—the voice chuckled—"but I did!"

"Uh, yes you did," Straeker said, a little off balance. He reached down into the tank. "Let me help you sit up."

"Michael," the humor faded from the voice as the tank's occupant grasped his arm, "what are you doing outside of the Program?"

"What do you mean?" he asked as he braced himself against being overbalanced and possibly falling into the tank.

"You're dead."

"I'm what?"

"Dead. Remember? Brain tumor? Now you're Daggoth the Dark?"

Straeker was thoroughly confused now. "Daggoth the what?"

"Michael"—a hand appeared and grasped a handle to the side of the exit hatch—"did you reroute me into another Programworld on the way out?"

"No, you are out of the System." He cleared his throat and considered paging one of the male nurses. Dreamwalking was still experimental and some people did exhibit sensory disorientation after exiting a Programworld. "Welcome back to Reality."

"Then what's the joke?" Her head emerged from the hatch, the nutrient solution that helped sustain her body while her mind was in taction with the Computer plastered her long brown hair to the sides of her face.

"Joke?" Straeker queried as she pulled herself out of the pseudo-womb and climbed down to the floor. "I'm afraid I don't understand, Ms. Doucet."

"Ms. Doucet?" She looked at him sharply. "I don't appreciate this, whatever it is—whatever it's supposed to mean. I've just been through hell and back! I've been killed, I watched myself get killed, and I've watched a woman I loved die twice! Furthermore, I don't like the way you've been spending time with my wife!"

"Wife?" Straeker squeaked.

"Ex-wife," she corrected, reaching down to wipe the nutrient slime from her legs. "I hate this stuff. Can't somebody design these tanks so that this stuff washes off before we get out?'' She reached up to scrape the ooze from her belly and stopped in amazement. Her hands grabbed at her breasts, cupped them. ''What the hell are these?''

''Um,'' said Straeker, feeling the situation getting more out of control with every passing second, ''I believe they're called breasts. . . .''

''I don't have breasts!'' she roared.

Straeker was loath to argue with her but the evidence at hand was undeniable. ''You do now,'' he murmured.

''Get me a mirror!'' she demanded.

''Um, there's one in the ladies' room,'' he said, pointing to a door on the far side of the room. As she strode purposefully across the room and through the rest-room door, Daggoth scurried over to the intercom and called for two male nurses. ''And bring restraints,'' he whispered as a high, feminine scream echoed from the tiled recesses of the ladies' lavatory.

Inside the lounge area, Robert Remington Ripley the Third fought to hold on to a rational train of thought. For, staring back at him in the full-length mirror was the reflection of Nicole Doucet. The image was healthy and whole, barely showing evidence that she had aged fifteen years since the aircar crash.

''Oh, man,'' he murmured, watching the reflection of feminine lips moving in sync with his words, ''you are a *long* way from home!''

Outside, someone began pounding on the bathroom door.

*Now I do not know whether I was then a man dreaming I was a butterfly, or whether I am now a butterfly dreaming I am a man.*

—Chwang-Tse,
upon awakening from a dream of being a butterfly